Shattered Divinity

Aaron Yoder

AARON YODER

Contents

Chapter One

Leper Xentoth tapped his long fingers rhythmically on the small wooden table, his eyes fixed on Queen Rinawen. She was his only friend, yet today, she felt like a stranger.

"Take the shard of Theora with you," she insisted.

Then she resumed preparing to journey to Ambrosia, the bustling capital of Kalazaar. The bow-shaped shard hung around her neck.

Why would she want to go alone? Especially when she has a very powerful relic dangling around her neck.

She took off the shard as her golden hair fell around her neck and shoulders. "Just hold on to it for a few days. I'll come get it when I return."

"I don't want it," Leper protested, pushing it back towards her, "you need it for your safety. You're a beautiful woman and shouldn't be wandering around all those people defenseless."

"Well, I'd take you with me," she joked, pointing to his horns, "but those might give us away."

Leper knew all too well that he could not walk through any city without being ridiculed or attacked because of his appearance, specifically the horns on his head.

"I wish I could join you in Ambrosia, Rin," he said with a smile, "but you'll have to take that shard and go on your own."

The shard of Theora held divine power from the goddess Theora. It allowed its wielder to move rocks or mountains, reshape the ground and vegetation, and even enhance plant growth and health. For generations, the shard has been in the possession of Kordry, which is known for its abundance of food thanks to the shard's abilities.

His gaze shifted to Rinawen's vibrant green eyes. Her outfit was simple yet eye-catching. The green leather shirt hugged her curves perfectly, and the intricate patterns added a touch of elegance. The leather had delicate leaf and vine patterns etched into it. Her brown pants were well-worn but sturdy, and the boots showed signs of extensive travel. Despite the simplicity of her attire, she carried herself with poise and elegance. The fresh fragrance of lilacs always emanated from her. *She is beautiful.*

Her golden locks cascaded down her back, shimmering like a sunbeam. Carefully arranged, every strand of her golden locks adorned with small braids and delicate flowers that represented her deep connection to nature. She embodied the spirit of her people and their town.

"Lep, I'm not asking you to take it. It's an order. You're taking this shard," she insisted.

Leper shook his head. "Why don't you at least bring your husband? Make him leave the castle for once."

"Larnadix? You know exactly why. Since his kidnapping five years ago and spending that night with his captors, that's why. When the guards found him the next morning, he refused to leave the castle. He's become a scared, reclusive man," she furrowed her brow, "he's not the same man I married."

Leper had struck a nerve, but her words rang true. Larnadix had never been the same after that incident. And what made it worse was that they never found or caught the culprits.

"Why don't you travel with the Or'armwell family?" He urged.

"They've already left. Are you going to be stubborn about this?" Rinawen shrugged her shoulders. "Fine. If you don't take this shard, I'll make sure you have no visitors for two weeks, maybe even a whole month, since I won't have to come back and retrieve it," she threatened.

"You're bluffing. Your daughters will come see me," Leper dismissed her threats with a playful grin.

I spend enough time out here by myself. He became orphaned at a young age and lived in an abandoned hut concealed in the woodlands of Kordry. But he longed to travel and see different places and meet new people.

Rinawen stood up from her chair. "Not if I don't allow them to."

"Uh oh, she's using her serious tone." Leper continued to tease, but when he saw the scowl on her face, he quickly changed his tune. "Fine. I'll take that stupid shard against my better judgment. But I swear, if anything happens to you, Rinawen, I will tear that place to the ground."

"Don't worry. I'll be fine. Just don't lose it, and don't do anything reckless, understand?" She crossed her arms over her chest.

"Yes, my queen," Leper poked back.

Leper trusted her judgment. She had been ruling Kordry since the age of twenty-four. Her parents groomed her for leadership, arranging her marriage to Larnadix when she was fifteen, a wealthy noble from Wen-Tath.

Leper cradled his arms around her and warned her to be careful, especially around Nalecht. He had a gut feeling that he couldn't trust the man, especially after what Rinawen had told him about his past and how he became the Anyth.

"Rules are rules," Rinawen sighed as she headed for the door. "Nalecht may have become the Anyth through a technicality, but that doesn't mean we can ignore any potential risks that come with him being in power."

"I just hope those rumors about him killing his family aren't true," Leper narrowed his gaze on her.

"Eventually, the truth will come out. Whether it was King Brebian's doing or Nalecht's own actions, only two people know for sure. But until then, we need to keep the peace and do our best to maintain order," Rinawen gave a half-smile.

"I know it's the penta-annual meeting, but don't you find it suspicious? Someone is clearly lying to everyone, and neither of them has the courage to face their crimes," Leper pointed out.

Every five years, all the royalty would gather in the capital to discuss important matters like food and material supplies for each kingdom. They collaborated to ensure the prosperity of all kingdoms and maintain peace throughout the world. This system has been working efficiently for centuries.

Leper reached down and grabbed the shard from the table. He felt the power run through his veins as he touched it directly. A constant pulse emanated every five seconds. Carefully, he placed it over his chest.

"Perhaps you're right, Lep. But that incident happened years ago, and we've moved on from it. What puzzles me is how either of them could have defeated Yusef, Nalecht's father. He was a highly skilled and honorable warrior, nothing like..." Rinawen trailed off, her hand resting on the door as she narrowed her eyes at him. "You know what? It's not important. Just be careful with that shard. I'll know if you use it for anything reckless."

Right, be careful with one of the most priceless and powerful relics in this world.

The following morning, Leper took his beloved rocking chair, positioned it near a window, and immersed himself in a magical book Rinawen brought him from the library. The musty, woody smell of old paper wafted up to his nose, mingling with the sharp, tangy scent of the ink and the faint aroma from the leather binding that held the pages together. He searched for more information on this shard Rinawen plopped in his lap. Yet something about it felt comfortable around his neck, almost calming.

His dwelling resembled more of a humble hut, lacking partitions between the kitchen, dining area, and living space. Only a single doorway separated his bedroom from the main living area. Adorning the bare walls were paintings depicting a grand castle, majestic mountains, and a sprawling desert—places he yearned to explore. However, for now, he remained confined to this modest abode tucked away in the woods.

A faint rustling outside the door caught Leper's attention. Reacting swiftly, he reached for one of his chakrams, a pair of circular-bladed discs with a three-quarters crescent shape. Leather enveloped one edge of each disc, providing a secure grip without the risk of injury. Cautiously, he pressed his head against the door frame, carefully peering outside. The sound of giggling confirmed the identity of the visitors, and a smile tugged at Leper's lips.

Silently closing the door, ensuring it did not emit any noise or become latched, Leper tiptoed to his room. He carefully pushed open the window, feeling a cool breeze brush against his face. The soft grass outside beckoned to him, its emerald blades glistening with droplets of dew. The sky was still a hazy gray as the morning clouds slowly drifted away, revealing a brilliant burst of sunlight. As he stepped onto the plush grass, it felt like walking on a freshly made bed, each step sinking slightly into the damp earth beneath. Moving with stealth around the house, he arrived at the corner where the front door awaited. Just as Zanera and Kelindra, the daughters of Queen Rinawen, reached the same spot, Leper took three large strides and, with a playful gesture, captured Kelindra's waist in his grasp.

"Raaaawwwwwwrrrrrr," he hollered.

"Ahhhhhh!" they both screamed. Birds taking flight from their nests, among other rodents, fled back underground.

"You scared me!" Zanera poked him in his muscular chest.

Kelindra, an energetic eight-year-old, playfully tugged at the horns adorning Leper's head. He chuckled, then lifted her and settled her securely on his broad shoulders. Clinging onto his horns, she imagined herself steering a majestic chariot through the skies while Leper played along.

He gently lowered her back onto the ground and ruffled her soft, shoulder-length brown hair. She beamed up at him with her bright brown eyes, dancing with excitement and happiness. Moments like these filled his heart with pure joy.

"What are you two troublemakers up to?" he asked.

"Came to keep you company," Zanera smirked. At fourteen years old, she possessed the grace of her mother, her long blond hair flowing elegantly. Skillfully braided along the side, her hair framed her face, accentuating her features and drawing attention to her elvish ears.

"C'mon, I'll make some tea for us." Leper led them inside. "Has your mom left for Ambrosia, then?"

"Yes, she left yesterday, right after she got back from your place. Said she was going to stay there last night and leave right after their meeting or whatever," Zanera plopped herself in his chair.

Leper rustled through some cupboards, "did you tell your father you were coming here today?"

Zanera huffed. "No. You know our father doesn't trust you."

"But you trust me, right?" he called.

Kelindra's spirited voice rang out. "Of course, Mr. Leper. You're the best uncle we have!"

"Someday, I'll be able to get out of this house and see the world with you guys," he said.

Declaring that there was no tea caused a small uproar as they playfully attacked him for not having any available. After their scuffle, Leper checked his stock of healing and revival vials with Kelindra while Zanera settled in to read his book. It was a small metal enchanted box, magically linked to the pouch on his side, where he kept the vials. As long as there were vials in the box, he could access them through the pouch. Although he rarely used them himself, he often gave them to Rinawen for distribution among her soldiers or anyone else who needed them.

Living alone for twenty-three years because of his people's past mistakes or bad habits had given him plenty of time to make vials, read books, train with his chakrams, and take care of himself through exercise. The mere sight of a Chernzerk could send the public into mass hysteria, making it vital for him to stay hidden from prying eyes. One glimpse of his horned head would incite chaos and fear. He yearned for the day when he could venture out and meet new people, have new experiences, and explore the wondrous cultures and places of the world.

"Well, this is boring. Maybe we should go grab some tea from the castle and come back? Then we could make more vials or play games?" Zanera suggested as she shoved the book into Leper's broad chest.

"Sounds good to me. I'll need to gather some ingredients first, though, so you can go get the tea," Leper replied, taking the book from her hands. "Oh! And if you pass by the bakers, can you grab one of those blueberry tarts for me? They are my favorite."

As they rushed out the door, Leper went to set down the book but noticed that Zanera had flipped it open to a different page. *That's strange...Someone scratched out most of this page. It seems like someone purposely made it unreadable.*

He squinted and strained his eyes, trying to decipher the words, but it was mostly illegible—something about shards, the Chernzerk, and other symbols and glyphs he didn't understand.

Leper gripped the book tightly as if he were trying to unlock its secrets through touch alone. He could feel the rough edges of the scratched-out words under his fingertips, evidence of someone's deliberate attempt to conceal information. His brow furrowed in deep concentration. He looked back and forth between the open page and the door, caught between two worlds. The book itself seemed to radiate a mysterious energy, its scratched-out words taunting him with secrets. He suddenly shook himself out of his trance, realizing that he had been standing there for too long.

Leper placed the book gently on the rocking chair right after he broke his trance, marking the page before stepping outside into the shroud of trees and vegetation. This was his secluded sanctuary, a perfect place for him to gather ingredients for his potent vials while remaining hidden from the public eye—his key priority as the only Chernzerk. A hundred years ago, Pasileveo, Anyth Nalecht's grandfather, had eradicated all other Chernzerks for their destructive tendencies. Leper didn't even know who his parents were or how he came to be born. But with Rinawen's help, he would one day be able to answer that question and walk freely in society without fear or judgment. *Hopefully.*

As he walked through the forest, searching for Veridian root and green tea leaves, among other ingredients, the sun peeked through the trees. Glancing up at the sky, Leper could still see Luna Novara, the moon shining brightly with a deep blue hue. The cool breeze rustled the leaves, and Leper wandered farther than he had intended until he heard the whooshing of ocean waves.

Curious, he followed the sound to find a large cargo ship flying Xaneth Harbor's brown and yellow colors, lowering a canoe into the water. What are they doing here near Kundry on a day when the queen was not present? Leper felt his heart rate increase as he realized he needed to remain unseen at all costs, especially after Rinawen's warning.

He called upon the shard of Theora, summoning a large green leaf from the ground to provide cover as he watched the intruders row towards shore. The leaf touched his lips as it sprouted and put a bitter taste in his mouth, almost like chewing on grass. It made his tongue tingle and caused him to sputter in surprise.

Every instinct told him to run, but his curiosity kept him rooted in place - after all, these were his woods, and he knew them like the back of his hand.

The Veridian root Leper needed for his mixing was just out of reach. He fought the urge to grab it and run, knowing that it would only draw attention to himself. As the canoe made landfall, Leper slowly crept towards the plant and carefully dug it out before placing it in his burlap sack of ingredients. He backed away when two men who appeared to be seasoned fighters, possibly in their late thirties or forties, pulled the canoe onto shore. They weren't dressed as guards in the city's colors or wearing armor. Their attire was a mishmash of leather, cloth, and hide.

Leper watched as the two men bantered and secured their canoe to the shore, his eyes never leaving them. He had barely noticed the leaf he had sprouted for camouflage until he tripped over it, landing with a loud thud and causing his weapons to clang together. *Son of a bitch, you really are an idiot.*

Leper quickly regained his footing, using the leaf as cover once again. The leaf gave off a faint earthy scent, mixing with the musty smell of the forest floor.

The sudden noise caught the attention of the two men, who now stood with their swords at the ready. "Who's there?" they called out into the trees.

His heartbeat became an earthquake, each thump like a boulder crashing against his ribs, threatening to break free from his chest and reveal his secret. His eyes widened, and his palms grew slick with sweat, a cold fear gripping him like icy claws.

He couldn't get caught now, not after living in hiding for twenty-three years, thanks to Rinawen's protection. The intruders slowly approached, scanning their surroundings with sharp eyes. Leper considered using the shard to eliminate them, but he was no murderer, and it would only draw more attention from the ship out in the ocean. Instead, he used Theora again to cause a branch to fall in the distance, diverting their attention.

"Show yourself!" they demanded loudly.

Knowing that carrying the sack of ingredients would slow him down, Leper abandoned it by a tree, planning to retrieve it later. Grabbing his chakrams to prevent any more noise, he bolted towards his house, creating dense brush and thorny vines behind him to slow down his pursuers. He ran as fast as his legs could carry him.

Chapter Two

Leper left the two men behind as he quickly navigated through the thorny patch he created with Theora's shard. An hour later, he circled back to his house. The shard pulsed with power on his chest as he ran through the trees. Instead of heading straight back home, he took a longer route to shake off any potential pursuit. He needed to get rid of these men and protect his island. To get them back on that boat and sailing back to whatever miserable place they came from.

The evening sunlight streamed through the canopy of trees before setting behind the ocean. Leper was grateful for his morning jogs, keeping him in good shape for moments like this. As he slowed down from a sprint to a jog and eventually a quiet walk, he scanned the area and approached his house.

Sweat dripped down his face from both physical exertion and nerves. He entered his house and locked the door securely.

"Excuse me, sir! Where have you been?" called Kelindra's sweet voice.

Leper's heart dropped as he turned to see Kelindra sitting in his chair, holding a bag of tea. He frantically searched for Zanera, but she wasn't in sight. *Where is she? Why can't I see her?*

"Kelindra... where is your sister?" He said frantically.

Her eyes lit up at him. "Nope! Horn shake first!"

Leper let out a quick scoff and bent down to horn shake. "Okay, where is she?"

"Outside! Looking for you, dummy!" she laughed.

Leper quickly lied to her, saying that he had run back and locked the door because of a bear. He wanted to make her understand the danger but not overwhelm her at such a young age. Once he instructed her to lock the door behind him, he grabbed his large hat. The hat was made of dark green velvet and large enough to cover Leper's horns completely. Sparkling gems in various shades of green and red adorned the seams and reflected the light, giving the hat a regal appearance.

With luck, he could reach Zanera before the intruders did and bring her back to safety, at least until he could escort them off the island. He gripped his chakrams tightly in his hands - weapons he practiced with for hours every day, just in case a situation like this arose. After all, there weren't many activities for someone who had to avoid crowds and public places as a way of life.

Pushing through the woods and heading back to the ocean, a small branch smacked against his face, knocking his hat to the side. He grunted in pain but didn't slow down. As he squinted through the trees, he could hear a familiar voice shouting out.

"Get your filthy hands off me!"

Leper recognized Zanera's voice immediately. Turning to his left, he saw two men holding her arms and dragging her towards the ocean.

He adjusted his hat and took a deep breath before tucking Theora's shard under his shirt. He could feel the cold glass touch thrum against his bare skin. Its brown glow had faded to a faint light, showing that he had used most of its magic. He would have to wait for it to recharge in the moonlight before using it again, but he still had some magic left.

Leper approached carefully, making sure not to alert them too soon. When he was about twenty feet away, he shouted, "Let her go!"

The men turned around, surprised by Leper's sudden appearance. "Who are you? And what is that thing on your head?" one of them asked.

"Yeah, and what are you going to do with those silly chakrams?" the other one chuckled.

Ignoring their mocking remarks, Leper held his ground and demanded, "Just let her go."

"Alright, hat man," one of them taunted as he drew his sword. "Do you really think you can take both of us?"

"I don't want a fight." Leper held up his hands. "What do you want? I have gold, food... I can even offer vials that can heal wounds."

The men laughed at his offer. "I have the queen's daughter here," one of them boasted. "She wandered out here alone, and now you think you have enough to trade for her?"

"Kill him. Once we bring her back to Nalecht, he'll have the upper hand to get the shard of Theora from Queen Rinawen. But we need to get moving, or that ship's going to leave without us. Come on." The other bandit instructed.

Leper shifted his stance. "Why does he need another shard? Doesn't he already have one?"

"I don't care what he wants it for. All I'm concerned about is delivering this elf bitch to Ambrosia and getting my reward for helping him retrieve the shard from Rinawen." The bandit advanced towards Leper, "But first, I'll have to eliminate you as a witness."

Leper looked at Zanera. Her face portrayed sadness and disappointment, like she had failed at something. He knew that expression too well. There was no way he was letting them leave this island with Zanera or the shard.

"If you're looking for a fight, I'll give you one. But neither of you are leaving this island with her." Leper tightened his grip on his chakrams.

The bandit lunged at Leper, aiming for his chest with his sword. Leper quickly dodged the attack, narrowly avoiding the thrust. But then the bandit swiftly flicked his sword upwards. Leper had to contort himself backwards to avoid being hit in the face, once again his hat tipping off balance.

The man's eyes widened, "Demon...Cherno!" he cried out.

The man's cry was a piercing shriek that echoed through the forest, bouncing from tree to tree.

Not good. Not good, I'm a dead man. He heard Zanera fighting against the other bandit, who was dragging her towards their ship. He couldn't let them get away. His moment of hesitation gave the bandit an opening, and he struck Leper on the head with the hilt of his sword.

Leper's hand moved instinctively to his head, where the warm wetness of blood greeted his fingertips. He winced at the sting of the wound and growled. Leper used the power of the shard to ensnare the bandit in a tangle of branches. With him temporarily out of the battle, Leper turned his attention to the man dragging Zanera through the woods. He called out to the shard once more, but there was no response. The magic was gone, and he would have to rely on his chakrams to handle this enemy.

Zanera ripped her arm free of the bandit's grasp, and as she moved away, Leper wound up and sent a chakram flying his way. As the man stood, staring at Zanera, Leper's chakram embedded itself into the tree beside him. *Shit.*

He darted for the ocean.

"Shut him up!" Leper pointed back at the restrained bandit as he zoomed by Zanera.

Weaving through the trees, Leper patiently followed him, slowly closing the distance until he was sure he wouldn't miss. With each step closer to the ocean, Leper's nostrils filled with the humid, briny scent of saltwater. The taste of the ocean was almost palpable to Leper as he got closer and closer, like a burst of salty air on his tongue. Steeling his gaze, he wound up and sent his last chakram flying where it connected with him, digging deep into his back. He flopped onto the ground, landing with a thud, and Leper could see the ship beginning to set sail again.

Wanting some answers, he removed his chakram from his back and rolled him over. The man was barely breathing, but he squinted his eyes at Leper. "Xartazza?"

"What did you say to me?" Leper shook him, but it was too late. He already passed out from the fatal throw.

Leighth Or'armwell struggled to contain her astonishment at the Anyth's preposterous demand. They had already come over for the penta-annual meeting at midday today, and now they had to have dinner late at night with Nalecht in his castle. *What in the gods' name could he possibly want with another shard of the divine?*

Anyth, High King, Nalecht H'xeon, occupied the head of the opulent table within his majestic castle of Ambrosia, the capital city. A bounty of food towered on the table, and the sweet scent of honey-soaked ham filled Leighth's senses. Her brothers shoveled their meals without a care, seemingly oblivious to Nalecht's demeanor and unusual request. His attire, a simple cloth outfit, appeared disrespectful in Leighth's eyes. His cascading, snow-white hair flowed to a length just beneath his shoulders, while his nose resembled a slender toothpick, possessing a long and pointed shape. Beady and black, his eyes bore into Leighth's. Elven ears, barely visible, discreetly emerged through his lustrous, lengthy locks. Beside him sat Borlden Gruzca, his shrew, wearing an arrogant grin.

"This is a family heirloom that we have passed down for generations in our house. The person who holds it is the rightful ruler to Kundry. I—" her father Jaynoh's eyes darted back and forth as he sought an exit. "I can't give it up."

"I don't need the bracelet. You can keep the bracelet; I just need that specific trident." Nalecht said, his eyes locked on the bracelet around her dad's wrist.

"What do you need that trident for?" Leighth put her fork down as she swallowed the last bite of ham. The honey-soaked ham melted in Leighth's mouth, the sweetness of the honey balancing perfectly with the savory meat.

"Children don't need to worry about what adults do," said Nalecht.

Her dad glanced at her, narrowing his eyes while pursing his finger against his lips. "Shhhh."

"Well, this is stupid, just like I thought. That's our pendant and family crest. He has no right trying to take it." Leighth scrunched her face, peering back at her dad.

Even her brothers stopped slopping so loudly. Her father clutched the bracelet around his arm. She could see the blood rushing to his face as he closed his eyes. Something didn't feel right about this.

"I'm not sure you're understanding the Anyth," Borlden said, his voice crackling. "We're taking that trident."

Borlden rose from his seat beside the Anyth, his jet-black hair cropped short and slicked back with a greasy sheen. The impression he gave was that he hadn't attended to personal hygiene in months, equivalent to fifty or sixty days, depending on the month. Cloaked in darkness, his attire included a hood pulled back and a flowing, dark overlay matching the shade of his hair. Black-felt gloves covered his hands. His nose appeared flat, lacking a defined tip. Large and brown, his eyes harmonized with his unkept appearance, framed by bushy eyebrows mirroring the disheveled state of the rest of him.

"Will I get it back?" Jaynoh's hands trembled.

"No," Nalecht answered as a grin crept across his face.

"I can't just give it to you," Jaynoh stuttered. "If I return home without this shard, they will remove me from the throne. Like I said before, whoever holds this shard is the rightful ruler of Kundry."

Nalecht erupted in laughter as a wide grin grew on his face.

"Unfortunately, whether or not you agree doesn't matter because I only need one thing. I'm taking that shard. I'm just giving you the opportunity to hand it over," Nalecht commanded.

"I can't. Why would someone need two shards, anyway?" Jaynoh pleaded.

"You let me worry about that," a knowing grin escaped Nalecht's face. "Just hand it over."

Leighth's father bolted toward the door. She tried to jump up after him, but her mother grabbed her arm, holding her in place. Beads of sweat formed on his short, dark hair and tanned skin, an incongruous sight against the backdrop of his yellow silk garb with silver outlining the colors of Kundry, Leighth's homeland. What does he want with another shard? He already has a powerful shard. What in Theora's name could he do with two?

The bulwarks, a faction honed through rigorous combat and earned their distinction by emerging victorious in countless tournaments against formidable adversaries, whether human or beastly. Adorned in immaculate armor and bolstered by an invincible repute, they stand as the ultimate safeguard for royal patrons, drawing their short swords with practiced swiftness as they braced for the impending threat. As Jaynoh grasped his dagger, the shard of Hathor on his wrist emitted a soft, pale blue glow, hinting at its extraordinary power to enhance his combat skills with any weapon he wielded.

Jaynoh displayed prowess in his battle against the bulwark, deftly parrying and searching for weaknesses in the formidable armor. However, his efforts were in vain as he succumbed to the overwhelming force of the three attackers. Pinned to the ground with a knee on his back, he lay defenseless.

"You see, we could have chosen the easier path," Borlden taunted. His high-pitched voice sounded like metal scraping metal.

Guided by the bulwarks, Leighth was led out of the dining hall, arms bound with ropes, hands useless. Leighth jolted and yanked on her captor's grip, trying to get away. A swift backhand across the face with the metal plate armor made her reconsider.

Amidst the splendor of the capital city, Ambrosia's castle unfolded its magnificence before them as they traversed through resplendent hallways. The corridor walls were decorated with portraits of the Anyths that came before, bridging history to the present as they led them to the exterior. Banners and statues immortalizing those depicted in the portraits stood with a proud presence throughout. The external expanse of the castle mirrored its internal grandeur, with buildings gracing the streets of the residential district. Just beyond, a tower rose skyward like an outstretched finger. An unparalleled pinnacle of architecture, its composition boasted the most precious materials: a foundation of diamond, followed by layers of gold and crystal, and crowned with a ruby tip. Leighth identified this awe-inspiring structure as a hub for shrews to gather and learn. Bells rang out in the city. Her mind whirled as her heart pounded relentlessly in her chest.

The dark, heavy clouds obscured the stars and threatened to burst with rain at any moment. The damp and cool air made her mother's dress flutter in the wind as they were pushed onto the stage.

"Citizens of Ambrosia. We have been brought a traitor today!" Nalecht's low voice echoed. The crowd erupted in boos. What started as a small gathering turned into a crowd of thousands.

"I would like to, yet again, demonstrate what happens to the people who would withhold anything from this great city achieving immortality!" Nalecht withdrew his sword from its hilt.

Leighth's eyes darted back and forth. *Immortality? Did that shard provide more than just immediate training with weapons?* Nalecht yanked the shard from her father's wrist and signaled the guards to grab the children and bring them to the front of the stage. The city brightened as poles imbued with light magic started to glow.

"No!!" Jaynoh struggled to throw himself in front of her brother. The bulwarks restrained him. "Do what you want to me... they are just kids!! Cowards!"

While wearing a yellow sundress to compliment her father's attire, Kendra, Leighth's mother, sobbed uncontrollably. Her usually long, dark hair, which typically reached midway down her back, was elegantly styled into a bun. Leighth fashioned her own hair into a bun, though her hair was notably shorter. Leighth didn't care for dresses, opting for brown pants and a yellow shirt. The Kundry elves' hair grew at a snail's pace compared to anyone else. Leighth's hair extended to her shoulders when left down, and she had never cut it in her seventeen years of life.

Her mother's eyes were tightly shut, and she directed her head downwards, unwilling to witness the impending horror. The three children knelt together at the front of the stage, their eyes wide with fear, tears glistening on their cheeks. Leighth refused to grant her captors the satisfaction of witnessing her beg or cry. If this was to be her end, she resolved to deny these despicable individuals the pleasure of her fear and pain.

Borlden removed the glove from his right hand, revealing a flame tattoo. Pointing it towards her older brother, flames erupted from his palm. The deafening screams that followed were agonizing, accompanied by the nauseating scent of burning flesh that invaded Leighth's senses. Borlden's lips curled into a sadistic grin as he watched his victim writhe and scream until he finally died. He seemed to savor every second of his pain, his eyes gleaming with malicious pleasure. Leighth froze, her body tense. Her heart pounded in her chest, a searing pain enveloping her. Yet she refused to shed tears. In her peripheral vision, she observed the bulwarks cruelly grabbing Kendra's hair, forcefully yanking her head back to witness her son's agonizing fate. The tattoo on Borlden's hand faded from dark black to light gray. Roughly thirty seconds later, the tattoo regained its vibrant black color, and Borlden repeated the same cruel act on her other brother. In that fleeting moment, Leighth realized this might be her only opportunity. With the relentless wiggling of her wrist, she tried to free one hand from its binds as she stared into the soulless eyes of Borlden, who was now directly in front of her.

"Looks like it's your turn," an enormous smile crept across his demonic face.

The desperate twisting of her wrists paid off as Leighth freed her narrow arms, but now she glared at the face of one of the deadliest shrews in the world. Realizing time was running slim, she rolled away from the bulwark that was right behind her and then pushed herself up. As she headed for the front of the stage, something caught the corner of her eye. Her father had got himself to his feet, tears flowing like a river, and rammed his shoulder squarely into the chest of Borlden. Both men tumbled to the ground, Borlden absorbing the blow. She looked at Nalecht, the shard of Hathor on his wrist. *If I could get the shard and take his sword, I could save their lives.*

Her eyes connected with her father as he lay on top of Borlden. "Leighth, you can't take them! Even with the shard, you must live to fight another day. Run!!" he shouted at her. *I know he wants me to escape. No one's ever lost the shard of Hathor, and I'll be damned if we're the ones to bring shame to our family name.* Leighth took a last look at Nalecht, then down at the shard of Hathor now adorning his wrist, before turning to Borlden and etching their faces into her memory.

She jumped off the front of the stage into the thousands of people. The front row of observers separated as she landed on her feet with a thud, rolled, and again picked herself off the ground. Still no tears. She knew this would be the last time she would see any of her family should she escape. She needed to. For her mother, father, and even her annoying ass brothers. Revenge fueled her sight as she snuck under the wooden platform. As Leighth ventured deeper into the maze of wooden beams, the air grew heavy with the smell of decay—rotten food and mold assaulting her senses. Crossbeams intersected above her, entangled with spider webs and layers of accumulated dust. Determined to put distance between herself and the front, she skillfully maneuvered through the labyrinth of wooden structures. The increasing commotion stirred the crowd.

"Kill them now!" They began chanting.

Leighth took a sharp right turn, heading to the side opening. She whipped her head around. The bulwarks poked their heads under the stage but struggled to get fully under because of their armor. She nearly reached the side exit, but before emerging, she removed the leather vest that was over her yellow shirt and tied it around her waist. She removed the pins in her hair, letting it flow down to her shoulders. Leighth took a deep breath in. Poking through the side of the stage, the crowd was so engrossed in what was happening on stage nobody noticed her emerge. She darted through the crowd and got about halfway to the back before making one last glance at the stage. Just in time to see her father's head fall to the floor at the end of Nalecht's blade. The air was thick with the charred flesh smell and the heavy weight of grief as she watched her father's head roll across the floor, a brutal and irreversible finality made painfully real by Nalecht's gleaming blade. Each breath felt like a knife being plunged deeper into her heart, a relentless and searing pain that threatened to break her into pieces. Leighth's chest constricted as if an invisible hand was squeezing her heart and lungs. Leighth's face contorted in anguish. She fought back the tears as she watched her father's head roll to the ground. The sight of his lifeless body, with blood pooling beneath it, burned into her memory. She covered her mouth with her hand to keep herself from screaming.

She could hear the clanking metal armor headed towards the back exit, their presence quickly growing. If it hadn't been for her father's last words, she would've given up.

"There!" Borlden shouted, catching her attention. "Near the back gates! Get her!"

Leighth took off in a sprint when she saw the guard posted just outside the gates give chase. One thing she learned from the stage experience was that with their armor, they would have a hard time keeping up. She pushed her legs as fast as they could muster, ignoring the pain in her chest and now her legs. She flew by house after house.

She weaved between houses, taking many turns while keeping her distance and knocking down a clothesline on the way to slow the guards. Sweat formed as she entered an open alley with a clear path to the merchant district. But a bulwark blocked her way, and she walked on, hoping to go unnoticed. Her head down, eyes staring straight forward. Even with the cover of night, she couldn't lose them. Lost and alone, she forced herself onward.

"You! Halt." The bulwark pointed his weapon at her.

"Shit." She muttered.

She jolted to the right, continuing her frantic pace from before. Until she collided with a stranger, sending both of them sprawling to the ground.

"What the hell?" The man said, pulling himself off the ground.

With each step he took getting up, he moved with an elusive grace. His concealed countenance lay hidden beneath the hood.

The figure stood at an average height. Clad in black pants and sturdy boots, he wore a cloak that draped over his very slender form, its long sleeves concealing his arms and hands. The only exposed part of his visage was his chin, which displayed a hint of blond stubble before disappearing into the depths of the cloak, shrouding any further glimpse of his features.

"Sorry, sir. I got to go," Leighth said.

"What's a young girl like you running from so frantically?" He cocked his head back.

"I really don't have time," Leighth said as she began walking away.

The mysterious person grabbed her shoulder. Holding her in place.

"Is someone trying to hurt you?" his low voice asked.

"Kind of." She nodded.

He shook his head. "I'm going to need more than that."

"Listen, it's a long story, and I really need for you to help me hide or let me go." She pleaded.

His strong grasp held Leighth in place as the bulwark rounded the corner. The man appeared unfazed, exhibiting no signs of fatigue even after pursuing Leighth through the streets clad in full plate mail armor.

"Ahhh, you've caught her. Hand the wench over."

"What did she do?" The man asked. He loosened his grasp, then moved Leighth with his hand, pushing her behind him. *Is he... Protecting me?* Unsure if she could trust him. She began plotting another escape. After all, this was a bulwark among some of the most feared fighters in all of Kalazaar.

"That's not your concern, peasant. Hand her over, or I will use force." The bulwark threatened.

"I don't do threats," said the man, now holding both his hands under his cloak.

"Consider it a promise. You have five seconds. One..." he began counting, withdrawing his sword.

"Very well then." The man took a deep breath in.

Leighth, aware of the inevitable outcome, resumed running, swiftly bypassing the figures in her path. As she sprinted past the man, she noticed his expression remained unchanged—devoid of any smile, grimace, or emotion. In the blink of an eye, his hands moved with astonishing speed, conjuring a dagger that swiftly found its mark in the bulwark's neck, exploiting the sole vulnerability in their formidable plate armor. The sight bewildered Leighth, her mind racing to comprehend the impossibility of the situation before an overwhelming sense of curiosity took hold.

Halting abruptly, Leighth turned to face the enigmatic figure. Her voice filled with intrigue, she asked, "Who are you?"

Chapter Three

S everal minutes after he killed the bulwark and got the guards off their tail, with a quick glance around, the mysterious stranger grasped a handful of Leighth's shirt, propelling her forward as he deftly navigated through narrow alleyways and grassy paths. She needed a place to think, a place to breathe until she could figure out how to get the shard of Hathor back. Her particular company wasn't any help either, pushing her around. Yet, as much as she wanted to get away from him, she couldn't deny she might need his protection yet again, and he seemed to know his way through the city fairly well. They swiftly passed through the entrance of a local pub, only to exit just as swiftly. In her haste, Leighth snatched a piece of paper from a bulletin board, crumpling it and quickly stowing it in her pocket. As the clouds shifted and parted, they revealed a breathtaking canvas of stars and the luminous glow of Luna Novara, casting an ethereal blue hue over the surroundings. Eventually, they arrived at a dilapidated house that appeared long abandoned. Overgrown grass reached a height far beyond what it should have been. *This seems like the perfect hideout for a thief. What did I get myself into?*

A tumultuous sea of thoughts and emotions raged within Leighth as she obediently followed his commands, still choking back the tears from her brother's being burned and father beheaded. Vengeful desires surged through her, longing to exact revenge on Nalecht, Borlden, and their entire families for the pain they had inflicted upon her. It was a searing fire of hatred that threatened to consume her every thought and action.

The stranger surveyed the surroundings once more before forcefully pushing Leighth through the door, causing her knee to scrape against the dusty floorboards when she fell. Taking in her new surroundings, she observed an empty desk, an empty table, and empty chairs—a pattern of barrenness becoming increasingly apparent. It seemed like someone had inhabited the place, but not recently. There were no photographs, no dishes, no glasses. Leighth would be surprised if this run-down dwelling even had running water magically provided.

In each city, they strategically placed large gems, such as sapphires or rubies, to absorb and store magic before releasing it at varying rates. They then connected these gems to massive containers of water, utilizing the expelled magic to push the water through pipes. Thanks to their calculations on gem size per gallon in the tank, they avoided over-pressurizing the pipes and causing them to burst.

The man, once again, seized her by the shoulders, forcibly maneuvering her from her spot and guiding her towards a chair.

"Stay out of the way," he commanded.

"How can I stay out of the way if I don't know where we're going?" She blurted.

He sighed. "Hmph. Just sit there. Don't move."

He clamored around under the desk until she heard a click. Then he slid the table over about two feet, slammed his fist on the floor, popping up a board. He pulled the board, but an entire two-by-two opening came with it.

"Down there. Go," he said, pointing at the new opening.

Leighth vigorously shook her head. "I'm not going down there. You first,"

"What did I say two seconds ago?" He put his hands on his hips.

"Just sit here." Leighth sneered.

"Ugh," he sighed heavily. Leighth felt a sting across her cheek. She didn't realize he'd moved to slap her until her face hurt, and she was now off the chair.

Moving inches from her face, he leaned in. "I will not ask again."

Reluctantly, Leighth climbed down the ladder to the basement of the dump house. *No light, it's pitch black, and he's probably going to lock that damn door as soon as I'm all the way down.*

"When your foot hits the floor, turn around, walk to the wall, and place your palm directly on the wall about the height of your belly button," he called out.

"Is that where I get chained to the wall?" Leighth grumbled.

"You're wearing on my patience quickly. Starting to regret not letting that bulwark have you."

"Fine," Leighth followed his commands. He brought up a good point. He didn't have to help her. Maybe she should cut him a break on the sarcasm. As she placed her hand on the wall, a sizzling noise started on the wall at stomach level, then moved up to the ceiling. There was a faint striking sound, like a match, then a hanging lantern glowed, then another and another, down the entire ceiling.

The room was dimly lit and, like the top of the house, very dusty. Nothing had been used in years, and the scent of old dust and musty neglect filled the room, almost overpowering the faint citrus notes from a long-abandoned cleaning solution. Only two chairs decorated the interior of the dimly lit basement, and the dusty scent tingled her nose.

He quickly descended the steps and glared at Leighth. "Now, who are you?"

Leighth tried not to avert her gaze. "No... I asked first who you are."

He put his dagger at the bottom of her neck. "The one asking the questions is me. I saved your life. I hid you. Who are you? Why are you here?"

"I'm Kendra from Kundry. Queen of the city, my husband Jaynoh will find me." Leighth's arms trembled. *Is he going to kill me now?*

"Pssh." His dagger pressed a little harder. "You've got a lot younger since the last time I saw you, Kendra of Kundry."

Leighth swallowed hard. "Fine. She's my mom. How do you know her?"

"She hired me a few years ago. Why are you out here? Shouldn't you be in your lavish bed?"

What the hell did my mother ever want with him? Leighth furrowed her brow as her thoughts raced. Her mother, sweet and innocent, would have no sort of dealings with someone like him. Not in this lifetime or the next would she believe that statement. She remained silent, not wanting to upset him anymore, as he pressed the cold dagger a little harder against her skin.

Leighth's voice trembled as she uttered the words, "Nalecht killed them," her vision blurred as her eyes welled up with tears. The weight of her suppressed emotions and the intensity of the situation finally overwhelmed her. With no one watching, she could no longer hold back the flood of emotions that had been building within her. The pain, grief, and anguish that she had fought so hard to push aside all came rushing back, and her attempts to restrain the tears proved futile.

"For what it's worth. I'm sorry you lost your mom." He removed the dagger from her neck.

"It wasn't just her. It was my whole family. Dad, Mom, both my brothers." She buried her face in her hands.

"I have some business I need to attend to. I'll leave you in here. There're some clothes upstairs that might fit you. You'll want to blend in." He started climbing up the ladder.

Leighth followed him with her eyes as he ascended. "You're just going to leave me here? What if I leave?"

"You're not a prisoner. You want to chance leaving and facing guards or bulwarks? Have at it. I'm offering you a safe harbor for now. I will help you out of the city, but I have something I must do first. It's also safer down there. If you're going to continue balling and carrying on like that, no one will hear you down there."

"Sure, whatever you say." Leighth's jaw ticked as he climbed the ladder to the exit.

After thirty minutes of straight sobbing, she climbed back up and started rifling through the desk in the lone room of the house. Nothing inside this thing, no paper, no quill's nothing. This has got to be a simple smuggler's safe house. Nobody has a house with absolutely nothing in it. After a thorough search, nothing turned up, so she climbed the stairs to look at these prospective clothes. Luckily, she found a black half-sleeve shirt to put on. This time, instead of the leather tunic, she put on a half-sleeve chain mail shirt over the black one, then changed into a pair of green cloth pants. Using a large bed sheet, she fashioned herself a travel sack and shoved all her clothes in it for the journey out. She wasn't sure if she could even trust him, but right now, there was no other choice if she was getting out of here and taking back the shard.

Leighth sat at the table looking at the wanted paper she grabbed from the pub they ran through earlier. *This has to be him*. A man with scars on his face. No hair. Probably because he had on a hood, the picture didn't look like a masterful rendition of any person. Multiple places throughout Kalazaar wanted this assassin. Leighth had heard of Blank Face but thought he was more of a myth at this point or that she would never have to worry about being in the company of such a person. She was so focused on the paper that after several hours, she didn't hear the door open.

"What's that?" He said, pointing at her.

Leighth rose from the table, extending her finger in his direction. "Not entirely certain, but I'm pretty sure it's you,"

"Where the hells did you get this?" He grabbed it from her hand.

"Stay away from me," she said, backing away.

"Please. If I wanted you dead, you would be there."

"Are you THE Blank Face?" Leighth exclaimed, moving closer and instinctively tugging at the hood concealing his face. Just as she was about to unveil his identity, his hand swiftly intercepted her arm, preventing the hood from fully revealing his features. However, in that fleeting moment, she glimpsed his face. A prominent scar traced its path from under his right eye, extending down to his jawline. Another scar began at the bridge of his nose, curving downward to his upper lip, forming a T intersection just below his right eye. As he firmly gripped her wrist, she could feel the blood flow constricting, his grip tightening relentlessly.

Leighth wiggled her arm, trying to break his grip. "Ow, stop! You're hurting me."

"You ever try that again, I will cut your hand off." He gritted through clenched teeth.

"Sorry, Blank Face. Didn't realize you actually existed." Leighth shot back.

"What of it? Going to run and tell the Anyth? Or some king and get me arrested?"

"You're a killer. A soulless, heartless... I can't even think of the words to describe filth like you," Leighth sputtered.

"Am I the killer or the people who hire me? Like your mom?" He countered.

"Shut your mouth!" Leighth went to punch him but never connected. His hands were impossibly quick. "My mom is a sweet person. She had a heart of gold. Someone like you would never understand."

"Someone like me?" Blank Face let go of her clenched fist, pulling his hood back over his face. "You don't even know me. Like all royalty, you're too busy living your lavish life hiring people to kill whoever bothers you. Getting away with whatever the hell you feel like. You're all the same."

Leighth put her hands on her hips. "Lavish life? This is no lavish life. I'm stuck in a run-down dump with a killer."

"Where were you before you came here to meet the Anyth? Were you out fighting on the front lines? Hunting the various monstrosities that creep too far from The Talon or Mount Harbinger? Were you getting tortured endlessly by an evil overlord?" He quipped.

"No, I was in my castle or out hunting for food. Or hanging out with my best friend." Leighth retorted.

He pointed at her. "Exactly. You had everything handed to you. I worked my ass off to get where I'm at today, and nobody is taking that from me."

"What business did you have to take care of?" She tilted her head to the side.

"Don't worry about that. I told you I'd help you get out, and I'm nothing without my word. So, at the least, I will get you out of the city. Even though I'm a useless piece of shit, right?" He threw his hands up.

The weight of his words resonated deep within Leighth. "I'm sorry. I don't condone what you do or have done. But yes... You saved my life and offered to help me get out of the city. For that, I thank you, but that doesn't mean I have to approve of your life choices."

"I don't really care if you approve or not. Where do you want me to leave you?" He set his bag on the table.

Blank Face began rummaging through his bag. He pulled out a quarter loaf of bread and some cooked meats he must have grabbed on the way back and offered them to Leighth. Leighth shrugged it off, not hungry. Not right now.

She blurted, "I... think... Lantess, maybe?" Leighth thought for a moment, realizing she had nowhere to go. She couldn't go back to Kundry without the shard of Hathor. Anyone who tried to take power there would face an absolute struggle until the shard was returned. Rinawen would probably help her, but unless Blank Face took her there, she didn't possess the capability to navigate her way off Uskela. Her uncle, who would likely take power in Kundry, was violent and deranged. She could not fight him, either. Lantess might be her only option. Maybe she could plead with

King Madislak, and he would help her. Perhaps he could get her to Queen Rinawen. Even then, Rinawen didn't know her well. They were more acquaintances than friends.

"No Lantess." Blank Face shook his head.

Leighth went to put a hand on his shoulder, which he quickly shrugged off, demanding, "Why not?"

"The commoners in the town said that someone destroyed it. There's no one there." Blank Face stared at her.

"I guess that leaves Kirilick as my only option then." Leighth closed her eyes for a moment, taking a deep breath in.

She didn't know anyone in Kirilick, not the queen, not the king, no one. Yet, somehow, she would have to find her way.

"Fine. We leave now." Blank Face tied his pack closed, then put it back under his cloak and headed out the door.

Leighth grabbed her pack and followed him. She had a hard time keeping up with him. His pace was swift, and he moved with purpose, his tall, lanky frame weaving between houses. Most of the houses were rather run-down. Some lacked windows, had broken doorways, or were missing chunks of walls.

"Where are you going? The merchant district is that way?" Leighth said, pointing in the opposite direction they were going.

"We can't be seen. Just follow me and shut up." Blank Face commanded.

Reluctantly, Leighth followed, keeping pace with him now. After several minutes of walking, they came upon yet another abandoned house. Blank Face led her in—same setup as the last place. He unhooked the trap and opened the door to the basement. However, this time, there was a tunnel under this house. They followed the tunnel for several minutes before they came to a fork in the tunnel and a ladder up. Blank Face held up a finger for her to wait where she was. He climbed the ladder and peered out before motioning her to come up.

Leighth took in a large, delicious, deep breath of fresh air. They were in the meadows outside of Ambrosia, beyond the large fifteen-foot-high stone walls that protected it. It was majestic to look at. Leighth reminisced for a moment, taking in the last resting place of her family. Another tear rolled down her cheek as she gazed upon the massive city and its enormous walls. This was more her style, the forest, lush green vegetation. Flowers blooming, a slight breeze tickled her nose.

Blank Face didn't slow down as he kept walking away. "Keep moving. I'm sure they're still looking for you. We go north and you better keep up. I've got a date in Ventessa and a time frame to get it done."

"What are you doing over there?" Leighth asked bluntly.

"Really?" He shook his head.

"Ya, who's the target?" She shrugged.

"Again. Not your business. You should be more concerned about what you're going to do in Kirilick. They might recognize you there," he said.

It was at that very moment, as soon as the words left his mouth. Something popped into her head. *Maybe I can take back the shard. Maybe Blank Face will help me, and I can get my father's shard back and restore our honor.*

Blank Face stopped at a small village that was a few miles from Ambrosia and procured two horses for them. She couldn't keep herself from looking backwards, constantly reminded of the horror that had happened in Ambrosia. *I will kill them.*

"Blank. Stop." She called out.

"What?" He said, bringing his horse to a stop. "We need to go. Stop stalling."

"Take me with you. Teach me. I want nothing more than to see Borlden's face when I plunge a dagger into his rotten heart. Nalecht too." She pleaded. "I don't know anyone in Kirilick or anywhere, really. If I'm going to get that shard back and revenge, I'll have to do it on my own."

"So, it's revenge, then?" Blank Face cupped his chin. "I don't have time to teach you. You will slow me down."

"No, I won't. I kept up with you in town. I've kept up on horseback. I'm skilled with a bow and a dagger." Leighth added.

"Pssshhh." He rolled his brown eyes.

"Okay. I'm not *you* skilled, but I'm better than average. If I'm not good enough, then help me. I'll pay you when we take back Kundry. Whatever you want. Help me get the shard of Hathor back and at least kill Borlden." She pleaded. "Please."

Blank Face rubbed his cheek, deep in thought. She opened her mouth to talk, then stopped. Her stomach burned with a vengeance. She didn't want to feel like the helpless little girl who witnessed her family's demise. She would learn to fight like Blank Face, and when the time came, she would relish seeing Borlden's face and body go limp at her hand.

"No, I won't take back Kundry for you. And there's not enough gold in the world to throw me off this next target. As far as getting the shard of Hathor back, I can't commit to that, but I will offer you maybe." Blank Face locked eyes with Leighth. "If you go with me, you do as I say when I say."

"Yes sir," Leighth pointed at Blank Face. "You're the king."

"We're running out of time, and I prefer to travel at night like it is right now," Blank Face expressed his concerns. "If we hit the road now, we can travel for a day, cross by boat, and reach our destination within two days, with no interruptions."

Curiosity and anticipation filled Leighth's voice as she inquired, "What's our assignment?"

"My assignment is Zonoh. Your assignment is to observe and learn." Blank Face kicked his horse into a sprint.

Blank Face's response caught her off guard, causing her to choke on her own saliva, coughing as she struggled to regain her composure. "King Zonoh!?" she exclaimed.

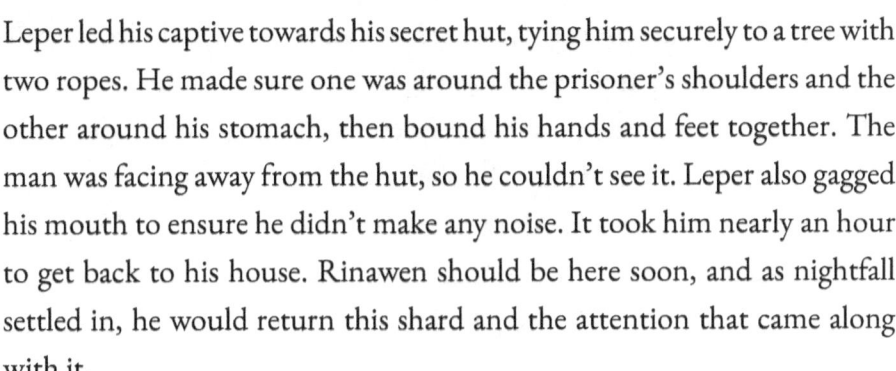

Leper led his captive towards his secret hut, tying him securely to a tree with two ropes. He made sure one was around the prisoner's shoulders and the other around his stomach, then bound his hands and feet together. The man was facing away from the hut, so he couldn't see it. Leper also gagged his mouth to ensure he didn't make any noise. It took him nearly an hour to get back to his house. Rinawen should be here soon, and as nightfall settled in, he would return this shard and the attention that came along with it.

The sky was clear, and Luna Novara shone brightly among the stars. Leper tried to open the door to his hut, but it wouldn't budge. After some rustling, Kelindra opened the door for him. He entered and locked it behind him.

"Is the mean man gone?" Kelindra asked as she pointed at him. "Next time, don't lie to me!"

Leper nodded and went over to Zanera, who was staring at three pictures on the wall. "Are you okay?" he asked gently, wrapping his arms around her as she sobbed.

"I thought they were going to take me. I was so scared. I'm so glad you were there," Zanera said through tears.

Leper brushed her hair out of her face. "I would let nothing like that happen to you. I promise."

Another wave of frustration and anger washed over Leper. What kind of person would harm a child? What kind of monster would kidnap a child just to use them as leverage for a shard? Leper wanted nothing more than to go back out there and punch the bandit in the face. He already had doubts about Nalecht, and this only added to them. Why did the Anyth want to collect other divine shards? What's their purpose? Leper knew Nalecht had his own shard, just like many other places did. Kundry had

Hathor, Nalecht had Ryollin, and Rinawen had Theora. King Zonoh kept the shard of Obidiah because he was the eldest royal and a pinnacle-five shrew who understood magic better than anyone else.

The dwarves who possessed the shard of Kasherri were secluded in their desert home, making it the most logical place for it to be hidden. Rumors of the shard's corrupting powers reinforced this, along with its potential to raise an army of the dead. That left two more shards unaccounted for—Aisha and Amarook. Aisha possessed the ability to heal wounds and sickness and control the weather. Amarook had the power to bring someone back to life once but required a long recharge time of years before it could be used again.

Leper paced back and forth, trying to understand why Nalecht would want to take this shard away from Rinawen when it was crucial to provide food not only for their people but for the entire world.

"Maybe he just wants a different shard," Zanera suggested.

The door jiggled again, and Rinawen's voice rang out from the other side, demanding to know what was going on. Both girls rushed to open the door and hugged their mother tightly, babbling all at once about what had happened in the woods.

Rinawen listened with relief and then concern furrowing her brow. Leper could tell something was wrong just by looking at her face.

"What's wrong?" He asked sternly.

"We need a moment alone," she said, turning to Zanera and Kelindra.

"I'm not going out there alone at night," Zanera protested, stamping her foot. "Especially after what just happened."

"I know. I shouldn't have suggested that. Just... don't tell your father any of this," Rinawen said, pinching the bridge of her nose.

Leper placed a comforting hand on Rinawen's shoulder and asked, "What happened?"

Rinawen shared the news with a grave expression, "They executed the royal family of Kundry. Our ally in the capital informed me just before I came here. Nalecht and Borlden orchestrated the execution to get Jaynoh's shard."

Leper's chest tightened. "All of them? Even the children?" His eyes turned red. *Thank Theora, I could rescue Zanera before it was too late.* The thought of what could have happened to her sent shivers down his spine. It was like a swarm of spiders crawling up his spine, each one leaving a cold, prickling trail of dread in its wake.

"King Zonoh is calling for a meeting in Wen-Tath for all royalty. It's far for some of us, but it will be safer there from Ambrosia and any spies Nalecht may have," Rinawen suggested.

Zanera spoke up. "And what about Kundry? They need our help to establish a new regime without the shard of Hathor to determine their ruler."

Rinawen placed a reassuring hand on Zanera's shoulder. "Exactly. We need someone to assist them during this transition period, which could take quite some time."

"You go to Kundry. Let me meet with the others in Wen-Tath," Leper declared fiercely. "I can't sit by while Nalecht attempts to harm my only family." He handed the shard back to Rinawen and urged her to keep it. Not wanting a magical beacon around his neck anymore. He let out a deep sigh of relief.

But Rinawen was quick to oppose. "You can't go out there! If you're caught, they'll kill you! Consider this an order!" She placed her hands on her hips in a stern stance.

Leper knew she would not easily allow him to go, to venture beyond the safety of their home and into the larger world. He was determined to leave this house, this forest, these plains.

Chapter Four

Leper's gaze locked with Rinawen's as she stood her ground, refusing his offer for help. There was no scenario he could imagine where she would let him leave this place alone or even if she went with him. But he saw this as his chance to get off this island. Maybe even prove to society that he is not a destructive agent of chaos. The stories and rumors about the Chernzerk were just that - false tales. The scent of lilac incense lingered on Rinawen from her flying chariot. He couldn't help but smile, knowing how much she loved the smell and how it always filled her chariot with its overpowering yet pleasant aroma.

"Lep!" Rinawen snapped her fingers in front of his face. "I know that look. If you leave, I swear to Theora, you will regret it. I'll lock you in the darkest dungeon I can find. I will never forgive you."

"Fine." Leper bit his lip, holding back a snarky response.

"Good," Rinawen sighed. "Now I'm going to get some rest before leaving for Kundry tomorrow morning. With any luck, I'll make it to Wen-Tath in time. I'll send guards to take the prisoner back and lock him up."

"He saw me, Rinawen," Leper said through gritted teeth. "I think you should send a message to Nalecht or whoever sent him. And maybe have some people deliver his dead body to Nalecht's doorstep. We can't let them think they can come here and push us around after attacking your children." Spit flew from Leper's mouth as he spoke with anger.

Rinawen agreed, and Leper showed her where he had tied up the man. They tried to extract more information from him. Still, he refused to talk and appeared ready to die with his secrets, including any knowledge of someone named Xartazza, which he claimed he knew nothing about.

After saying their goodbyes, Leper hugged everyone and returned to his house, blowing out the candles. He grabbed his large green hat and tried to make it more secure on his head, knowing he may have to be seen in public soon. But that was a problem for tomorrow; for now, he tossed the hat back onto the counter and lay down, trying to calm his racing thoughts.

The sound of raindrops hitting his wooden roof jolted Leper awake, followed by a loud knocking at his door. Zanera shouted from outside, complaining about getting drenched and demanding to be let in. Leper jumped out of bed and rushed to open the door, welcoming Zanera inside. Her long blond hair was soaked with rainwater. *She looks so much like her mother.* The cool, crisp scent of rain filled Leper's small cabin, mixing with the earthy aroma of wet wood and damp soil. The air was fresh and invigorating.

"You took forever!" she scolded him.

Leper grabbed a towel and chuckled, "You smelled bad anyway. It's about time you got cleaned up."

Zanera playfully punched his shoulder and laughed, "And to think I came all this way just to bring you that stupid blueberry tart I forgot yesterday."

Leper's eyes went wide, "you're the best!"

She pulled a slightly soggy blueberry tart from a burlap sack that wasn't very good at keeping water out, but it didn't matter. Leper devoured the delicious blueberry treat with crumbs and filling spilling out of his mouth. The tart was a perfect balance of sweet and tart, with the fresh, tangy taste of blueberries mingling with the rich, buttery crust.

"Hey, before we do anything else, I need your help with something," he said between bites. Some crumbs flew onto Zanera's shoulder.

"Hold on. I have to go back outside and wash all your gross food off me first, you pig. Then maybe I'll help you," she teased.

"Sorry about that. Where's Kelindra?" Leper suddenly realized that she hadn't come in with Zanera.

"She went with my mom to Kundry."

"Oh, did they leave already? We need to hurry, then." Leper grabbed his hat from the counter.

"Why? What are we doing?" Zanera followed him into the bedroom.

"You're going to sew this thing onto my head," Leper said, grabbing some thread and a needle from his dresser.

"No way, I'm not doing that. You're not a criminal," Zanera protested. "Actually, I didn't even come here to bring you that stupid tart. My mom wanted me to make sure you didn't leave."

In the Elven kingdoms of Kordry and Kundry on the island of Sartina, the elves considered placing a gaudy hat upon someone's head as penance. Attaching the hat to his head would serve as both a punishment and a reminder of his responsibility to seek forgiveness within Kordry society. Their culture believed in visibly carrying the shame or guilt of one's actions as atonement.

Leper grabbed Zanera's shoulders and gazed into her eyes. "Zanera, please listen to me. This is my chance to prove myself to the world and make things better so I can visit you instead of the other way around. If I can stop Nalecht from doing whatever he's doing and save this world, maybe they'll finally accept me. Please, I'm begging you."

Zanera's gaze flickered around anxiously. "I don't know, Leper. It's dangerous, and if something were to happen to you... I couldn't live with myself. And Mom would never forgive me."

"That doesn't matter, Zanera. I'm leaving with or without your help, but it would mean a lot if you could make it a little easier for me." Leper pleaded.

After glaring at him for a moment, Zanera reluctantly agreed to sew the hat on his head. Her delicate hands trembled as she pushed the needle through his skin. The needle pricked at his skin, its sharp tip piercing through the first layer of flesh, then digging deeper as Zanera pushed it through. Leper could feel the stinging sensation and the small droplets of blood that formed around the needle's entry point. Despite the discomfort, he stayed still, not wanting to cause Zanera any more anxiety. He knew he'd have to come up with a story for what he was seeking atonement for. Still, he had plenty of time to think about it as he embarked on his journey - first by boat to Uskela, then by horseback to Wen-Tath, a one or two-day journey at best.

"You're really leaving?" Zanera's eyes welled up with tears, and a single drop rolled down her cheek.

"Yes, I am. But I promise I will come back and see you again. Please tell Kelindra that I love her and say goodbye for me." Leper wiped her cheek and kissed her forehead before turning to leave. "Try to keep my vial case full in case I need them, please?"

"She's going to be mad when she finds out you left without saying goodbye." Zanera chuckled nervously.

Tucking the book in his pack, Leper closed the door to his hut for what might be the last time in a long time. He was nervous and scared, but he couldn't pass up this opportunity. He had been searching for a way to be accepted, and this could finally be it. Maybe along the way, he would uncover more about his past - who his parents were and where he came from.

King Madislak Idelth's entourage pressed onward under the scorching sun, their steeds carrying them swiftly towards the Bay of Disdain. Their task was to find the elusive shard of Aisha, believed to be hidden in this vast, desolate wasteland. Nalecht's request was clear: Madislak must gather a small team and search for the shard without delay. The urgency confused Madislak, but he didn't want to arouse any suspicions about King Zonoh's plans or cause any trouble. So, he complied and formed a small expedition, promising to keep the team safe on their dangerous journey. While he agreed to search for the shard, he didn't specify how much effort he would actually put into finding it. *Why the sudden rush to locate it just a day after the penta-annual meeting?* King Zonoh had just organized a tournament in Wen-Tath to select the finest warriors for the perilous journey to The Talon in pursuit of the shard of Amarook. Madislak shook his head, knowing he couldn't be in both places at once. He decided to finish searching for this shard quickly and make haste to Lantess, then Wen-Tath.

The relentless heat caused their clothes to grow damp with sweat, clinging uncomfortably to their bodies. In this barren land devoid of tree cover, only dry, cracked earth stretched as far as the eye could see, filling Madislak's nostrils with the scent of dust.

Harmony, the skilled practitioner of magical arts and Madislak's esteemed protégé, proved to be an exceptional shrew. At the young age of 22, she had already completed trials for two spells, surpassing the average progress of her peers.

Harmony's face had a harmonious combination of delicate features and striking allure. Her eyes, a mesmerizing shade of blue, exuded an intensity that captivated and drew you in. They sparkled with liveliness. Her flawless complexion seemed to radiate a natural glow, effortlessly showing her youthful charm.

A slender nose and softly curved lips completed her facial composition, the latter often adorned with a captivating smile that emanated warmth and charisma.

"How the hell are we supposed to find a tiny ass shard in the middle of this wasteland?" Firmin's frustration reverberated through the group as his clunky armor squeaked.

Madislak shifted his gaze towards Harmony. "These shards emit a distinct magical energy. I had hoped our resident expert could assist us."

Madislak had been bound to Harmony for three long years, their relationship tethered by duty and obligation. But as much as he tried to push her away, he couldn't help the potent feelings he had for her. He knew it was wrong, especially since he'd been married to Gwen since the young age of fifteen. And yet, if given the choice, Madislak would have chosen Harmony over any other woman in a heartbeat. His heart and mind were in constant turmoil over this forbidden love.

"I've been keeping my senses open, but I have detected no surges of magical essence," Harmony admitted, beads of sweat forming on her forehead as her curly blond locks grew wet.

"This is miserable. It's sweltering... I'm drenched in sweat. We should take a moment to rest," Martin suggested. He wore a practical ensemble comprising a leather sleeveless shirt, pants, and a wide-brimmed black hat that shielded him from the relentless sun.

"I concur. This armor is ill-suited for this kind of expedition. It's too bad you can't use some of that ice, Harmony, to cool us down," Firmin, Madislak's trusted bulwark, chimed in.

Harmony placed her hand through the gap in the neck of Firmin's bulwark armor, and a slight mist emanated from her hand as Firmin let out a sigh of relief.

"That feels so much better. Can you keep your hand there?" Firmin chuckled.

"Unfortunately, I have to keep my magic reserves up, but I'm glad I could give you a minor break from the heat." Harmony smiled as she took her hand away. "I'm only pinnacle two at the moment. I don't have a lot, not like Borlden, who's pinnacle five. He can cast much larger spells that last longer and recharge faster. Someday, I'll get there."

"Get where? How far exactly do you plan on taking it? Pinnacle five's the highest ever reached, so I don't know why you're in such a rush," Martin remarked.

"Yes, Martin, pinnacle five is the highest for now. But what's beyond five? I will tell you when I get there," Harmony fired back.

"Look over there," Madislak pointed to a building in the distance, though its details remained unclear at their current distance. "Perhaps we can find shelter there."

"That random house? It seems to be at the base of Mount Harbinger," Martin wiped his brow, his eyes darting nervously.

Harmony held the carry bag strapped to the side of her horse up for Madislak to see. "I brought some research along. I can review my notes; they might contain something useful."

"Let's move quickly then," Madislak spurred his horse, urging it to quicken its pace.

"To Mount Harbinger?" Martin's voice rose in pitch, sounding almost childlike in his fear.

"Martin, you're my proxy. You should be able to lead the town in case anything happens to me or my wife, Gwen. If this intimidates you so profoundly, then it appears I've made the wrong choice." Madislak's tone held a mixture of disappointment and resolve.

Martin's jaw tightened. Madislak had made a promise to his wife, Gwen, to take care of her brother Martin and appoint him as his proxy. It was a promise he intended to keep, no matter how difficult. However, Martin's timidity, lack of intelligence, and absence of noble qualities made it an arduous task for Madislak.

They continued their journey for another half-hour, their spirits dampened by the daunting presence of Mount Harbinger in the distance. The mountain loomed ominously, spanning an immense stretch of land and standing as the second tallest peak in all of Kalazaar. Even from miles away, they could sense the ever-present malevolence that emanated from its core. Dark clouds swirled around the jagged rocks formed its base while sporadic bursts of colored smoke emerged from its various crevices. Haunting howls, menacing growls, and echoes of undead moans permeated the air, surrounding the mountain in an aura of foreboding.

"There's no chance all four of us will come out of there alive," Martin's voice held a tremor of fear.

Madislak shot him another glare, his sweat multiplying with each passing moment.

"Let's check the house for cover," Madislak directed, his finger pointing at the door.

Firmin stepped forward, his fist pounding against the door. "Anyone inside?"

"No response." Madislak's grip tightened on his weapon. "We're going in. Stay vigilant."

Harmony positioned her palms toward the door. "I'm ready."

"Same here," Martin's words wavered, his sword displaying a slight quiver in his grip.

"I'll lead, Your Highness," Firmin nodded, and Madislak reciprocated with a nod of approval.

The door groaned open, and Madislak moved close behind Firmin. The interior revealed a dusty dining room to their right, a solitary table surrounded by four chairs.

"Clear," Firmin's voice echoed through the room.

Madislak nodded, gesturing to the left. As they moved down the narrow hallway, they passed by a modest kitchen on one side, complete with a sink and a row of cupboards lining both the top and bottom. Across from the kitchen, they encountered a small, unoccupied bedroom. Continuing their path, they reached another bedroom at the end of the hallway. With no signs of any occupants or threats in sight, Firmin signaled the all-clear, putting Madislak's mind at ease. So far, their journey had been relatively peaceful, providing a much-needed respite. Madislak knew, however, that more challenges and obstacles lay ahead, but for now, they were fortunate to have encountered a relatively merciful passage, aside from the relentless heat they endured. They removed their travel bags from the horses positioned outside the abandoned hut, placing them on the floor of the living area.

"The place looks abandoned," Harmony reported, her voice echoing a sense of emptiness. "Cobwebs and dust all around."

"We'll sift through this mess; you focus on your notes," Madislak ordered.

Harmony nodded in agreement, then settled herself onto the bed in the first bedroom. As she sat, a cloud of dust erupted from beneath her.

"I need a moment to rest and get out of this gear," Firmin declared, turning to Madislak.

"You deserve it, Firmin." Madislak's hand found its way to Firmin's shoulder. "I'll see how I can help Harmony."

A dusty bookshelf lined the wall. Madislak trailed his fingers across the top shelf, leaving a line in the grime, before continuing to the closet. Inside, a collection of old clothes still hung, showing signs of age but not complete decay.

"Anything useful on this shelf?" Madislak inquired, gesturing towards the bookshelf.

"A quick look tells me no," Harmony responded, her focus remaining on her notes.

"Wait, here!" Harmony's excitement caught Madislak's attention. "Pasileveo H'xeon, Nalecht's grandfather, mentioned the last known location. He said that it was lost while he was being carried in a dragon's talons. He dropped it to the ground mid-flight."

"Where exactly?" Madislak snapped his fingers at Harmony.

"Um, I think it's here. He mentions two miles northeast of Mt. Harbinger. It was during his flight that he lost it."

"That's a broad area," Martin chimed in from the doorway.

"Can you detect any magical presence?" Madislak turned to Harmony.

"Nothing," she replied, her brows furrowing in concentration.

"Perhaps someone already found it," Martin suggested dismissively. "Seems like we're wasting our time."

Madislak's head snapped towards Martin with a swift intensity. "If you're not contributing, I suggest you remain quiet and out of the way." His gaze narrowed sharply.

The house trembled mildly, followed by thuds echoing from outside. Madislak's heart raced as he exchanged a quick glance with his companions, their eyes reflecting the same mixture of surprise and concern. The sudden shaking of the building sent an involuntary shiver down his spine, a sense of foreboding settling over the room.

"That sounded large," Firmin's voice rang out from behind, his concern clear.

Madislak's attention shifted to Martin, who was now standing by a window in the dining room, his gaze fixed on something beyond the glass.

Madislak hurried to the window, his gaze locked on the sight before him. Standing just outside was a fearsome looking creature resembling a massive black cat, roughly six feet in height and stretching fifteen feet. Its front paws featured two menacing eight-inch talons, while the back paws showcased four. Spikes adorned its back, tracing a path from its head to the tip of its tail, which ended in a menacing, mace-like formation. Two fangs dangled from its upper lip, surrounded by an array of gleaming, dagger-like teeth. Its maroon-hued eyes pierced through the air, and its body emitted a faint, ethereal purple smoke.

"What is that thing?" Madislak looked over his shoulder for anyone to answer. Firmin emerged from the back, putting back on the last of his plate armor.

"Think we can wait it out?" Martin's voice trembled with fear.

Madislak let out a sigh. "We are likely the first prey this creature has come across in quite some time. It won't simply disappear. In fact, I'd wager that if we wait long enough, it will tear down this entire structure to reach us."

Harmony, ever composed and knowledgeable, positioned herself between Madislak and Martin, offering her insight. "I believe that creature is what's known as a shaded panther. It is native to Mount Harbinger and The Talon and is known for its ferocity. We must proceed with caution."

"What the hell is a shaded panther, and how would you even know that?" Firmin asked, befuddled.

"They are one of the many incredible creatures that inhabit Mount Harbinger and The Talon," Harmony explained. "Their hide is so resilient that ordinary iron weapons won't pierce it. To defeat them, one would require the strength of Idelthian steel or a precise strike through the roof of their mouth, thrusting up into their brain."

Madislak and Firmin absorbed this crucial information, realizing the grave challenge that lay before them.

Harmony took a breath in. "I know that because I read books. Madislak told me to know everything about this place, and, unlike some people, I do my job." She looked towards Martin.

"Okay. We can take it. We know it's weakness." Madislak said, drawing his great sword, Skyrunner. "My sword can pierce it. Firmin, if you distract it, I will stab it. Harmony, you hang around the doorway. Try to hit it with your magic..." Madislak thought for a moment. "Will magic even work on it?"

"Yes," Harmony replied quickly.

Skyrunner, a rare and renowned magical weapon in the realm of Kalazaar, held a place of distinction among the few that were given a name. The skilled dwarves of Costin meticulously forged Skyrunner under specific elemental moon phases, imbuing the sword with mystical powers while miraculously maintaining a weight equivalent to that of a conventional blade. Even in the faintest of light, the blade's pristine surface glimmered. A runic symbol adorned the hilt, which also featured three spikes, each approximately two inches long.

Firmin took a deep breath in and out. Gripping his sword and shield, he then flung open the door, plunging himself into harm's way. The panther raced around to the door, taking a swipe at him. Firmin deflected it with his shield. Now, the two enemies circled each other in a stare-down. Firmin's sword began to shiver. Madislak charged through the door, twirling his sword above his head, gathering momentum. He summoned every ounce of strength within him and channeled it into a powerful downward swing, unleashing his full might upon the creature's shoulder. The impact resonated with force, the collision reverberating through his body.

The creature's agonized howl pierced the air, its shoulder seeping black blood from the inflicted wound. In a retaliatory act, the spiked mace-like tail swung towards Madislak, striking him with a powerful blow to the chest. The impact sent him hurtling backward, soaring through the air. However, his firm grip on Skyrunner remained unyielding, and his fortune held as the pleated chain mail he wore absorbed much of the impact. Grateful for this protection, Madislak braced himself. *Time for this ugly beast to taste Idelthian steel.*

"My King!" Firmin shouted. He glanced at the doorway. "Martin! Harmony! Do something!"

The relentless beast charged recklessly towards Madislak, disregarding Firmin's valiant effort to divert its attention. Madislak's head swam. His vision blurred, but he discerned the looming black mass hurtling toward him. As his vision gradually cleared, he saw the shaded panther's jaws wide open, aiming directly for his face. In a desperate, instinctive move, Madislak thrust his arm forward, attempting to block the impending attack. But just as the creature was about to make contact, a large shard of ice abruptly collided with the side of its head, altering its trajectory. The impact jarred the panther, causing it to emit a deep, earthy growl from its throat.

Madislak nodded to Harmony standing in the doorway, that icicle tattoo now a dull gray color. It snapped its head towards the doorway, with a five-foot leap, landed, and continued its pursuit. Martin shoved Harmony outside, then slammed the door shut.

Firmin sprinted as fast as he could in plate armor to intercept the panther. His size wasn't enough to stop the beast, but as he crashed into its neck, he altered its path, and it sped away from Harmony.

Grasping Skyrunner tightly, he propelled himself forward, charging headlong towards the menacing beast. In an unexpected turn of events, Firmin became an unwitting passenger as the creature reared up on its hind legs, using its formidable front paws to penetrate Firmin's sturdy plate armor. A shiver ran down Madislak's spine as he witnessed the life draining from Firmin, his grip weakening as blood pooled around the fatal wound inflicted by the creature's ferocious assault.

"Firmin! Noooo!" Madislak cried out, his hand instinctively rising to shield him from the devastating reality before him.

Firmin uttered his last words, "I'm sorry, my King. I have failed you."

With his final reserves of strength, Firmin drove the jagged edge of his bracer into the beast's eye, causing it to shake him off its neck to dislodge the agonizing pain. Undeterred, the creature clamped its jaws around Firmin, crushing through his armor and sealing his tragic fate.

Now solely focused on Madislak, the panther advanced with deadly intent. Madislak, however, remained undeterred, pointing the tip of his sword down to the ground and then flicking it upward. A small but growing light emerged from the hilt of the sword, rolling up the blade before exploding in front of the panther. The blinding light rendered the creature temporarily blind, unaffected by its futile attempts to shake off the affliction.

Aware that this blindness would only last for a fleeting five seconds, Madislak wasted no time. Closing the distance swiftly, he held his sword high in his right hand, arcing it backward for a decisive strike. The creature's tail swooped towards him in a feeble attempt at an attack, but Madislak deftly rolled past it, positioning himself strategically. With swift precision, he thrust his sword upward, driving it through the bottom of the panther's chin and straight out the top of its head.

A low, primal growl escaped the dying creature as it crumpled to the ground, its dark blood staining Madislak's blade. He stood, triumphant yet somber, amid the aftermath of the fierce battle. The air was overwhelmed by the metallic tang of fresh blood, blending with the pungent, putrid stench of the panther's dark secretions. His stomach turned from the suffocating combination. The taste of battle clung to Madislak's tongue, a mixture of salt from sweat and earthiness from the dirt that covered him.

"Harmony, Martin, it's dead. Come help with Firmin!" He commanded.

Harmony rushed over, brushing the dust off her robes, "Martin's inside. He kicked me out like a coward and locked the door behind him."

Madislak tenderly lifted Firmin's head off the ground, his gaze fixed upon the lifeless face of his fallen companion. Regret weighed heavily upon him, knowing that no healing salve or magic could reverse the grievous wounds that had claimed Firmin's life.

Chapter Five

He took one last glance at Firmin and closed his eyes before he muttered the words, "Serenity be with you."

Harmony quickly repeated the same sentence. Madislak got to his feet. He didn't have time for Martin's petty games and cowardice. They needed to get moving towards his kingdom, Lantess so they could grab his flying chariot and head to Wen-Tath. The blistering sun was finally going down, and Luna Novara shone brightly in the dusk sky. *To hell with Nalecht and his damned shards. I don't know what made him think I'd give it to him if I found it, anyway.* The scorching, arid air sucked all the moisture from his mouth, leaving it as parched and rough as sandpaper. Every breath felt like swallowing dust, and every movement sent a wave of heat radiating through his body. He took a swig of water from his canteen.

Rage overcame Madislak. His stomach burned, and he could feel the blood rushing to his face. He stomped over to the door and, summoning all his might, blasted it off its hinges. Martin tried to run and slam the door to the first bedroom. Madislak overpowered him and knocked him off balance as he tumbled into the small bookshelf and knocked everything over. Madislak grabbed him by his shirt and yanked him up off the floor, then bound his hands and shoulders with rope.

"You are the epitome of worthlessness, Martin, and I shall have you punished for treason," Madislak growled as he tossed him onto the bed.

"Is it because of my actions? Or because of who I pushed out the door?" Martin snapped.

Madislak just grunted, then slapped him across the face.

As Harmony bent down to pick up the mess, a piece of paper slipped from the bookshelf, catching her attention. Her eyes widened, the weight of what she saw clear on her face.

"What is it?" Madislak reached for the paper.

"I... I don't know... it's... Just look." She handed it to him.

Madislak's eyes widened in disbelief, his heart sinking with an ominous sense of malice. Before him lay a chilling revelation—a vivid picture portraying a child, maybe five years old, with prominent horns, an unmistakable symbol of a Chernzerk. As he gazed upon the image, a growing sense of dread coiled tightly within him, twisting his insides with a profound unease. *What did this mean? Was it a harbinger of their return?* And the haunting question that loomed above all others: Who had dared to depict this unsettling truth?

"Look, there's a date at the bottom, year 614," Harmony paused. "That's only eighteen years ago. Does that mean...? Is it possible...? Nalecht's grandfather Pasileveo didn't kill them all?"

Madislak cupped his chin in his hand. "It might not be a person. It might just be someone trying to play games."

Harmony's voice was stern, "Who plays those kinds of games?"

"I don't know. People like Martin?" Madislak mouthed, and the bookcase completely collapsed.

A sudden, unmistakable object rolled out from underneath it—a horn. But not just any horn—this was the glossy, pitch-black horn of a Chernzerk male, sharp and gleaming in the dim light. The texture was smooth, like fine glass against the skin. Female horns have the same sleek feel, but they are always white. The horn arced in a crescent moon shape at the base for a few inches, then bent ninety degrees upward before tapering off into points.

"Madislak, that's a..." Harmony trailed off.

Madislak shot her a glance. "I know what it is. Can you tell how old it is? Better yet, with your psyrenth magic, can you find the location of the person?"

Harmony flicked her eyes to Madislak and nodded to him. Then she sat down beside Martin on the bed. Holding the horn in her hand, she closed her eyes, and the tattoo of the brain on her other hand faded to gray. Moments later, she opened her eyes and shook her head no.

"I can't seem to locate him. It might be too old, or I'm not high enough a pinnacle to locate the person," she offered.

Several minutes later, her tattoo regained its color, so she tried again. When she finished, blood ran from her nose.

"It's hard to discern exactly Madislak, but the horn appears to have experienced about five to ten years of withering." She handed it back to him. "I can't try anymore. My body is fatiguing. I'm saving what little magic I have left for any complications."

Madislak nodded to Harmony. The Chernzerk. A storied past. A tyrannical past. Despite not being seen or encountered in a hundred years, people still spoke and whispered about their histories.

"I can't imagine what it must've been like back then. Constantly living in fear, worried if one of them would ride their dragons to your house or kingdom. Wherever you might be, and level the place for dictatorship." Harmony scratched her neck.

Madislak's brow furrowed. "It adds a whole different level of danger when there's a chance they're still among us," he said. His eyes darted around the room as if searching for hidden enemies. "What if they're biding their time, growing in strength and numbers, waiting to strike back at the civilizations that tried to eliminate them?" He sighed and rubbed his temple, feeling the weight of responsibility resting on his shoulders.

"Why worry about a problem that isn't a problem? There's no way they are alive between Pasileveo and Yusef, Nalecht's grandfather and father. I'm sure they got them all." Martin added.

Madislak shot him a direct glare.

Harmony sat up on the edge of the bed, her curly blond hair frizzy as the sweat had dried. As she spoke, her eyes lit up with passion, and her hands moved animatedly. "Have you ever heard of the legend of Enoch and Ghendala? They were powerful dragon riders, each with a dragon over a hundred years old. Together, they conquered and enslaved the entire Bay of Disdain, once a thriving metropolis." Harmony gestured to the desolate landscape outside the window. "This place used to be bustling with life before they destroyed it all." Her voice dropped as she continued. "After defeating the dragon slayers, their only threat, Enoch and Ghendala, turned their wrath towards the northern kingdoms, destroying a dozen cities and enslaving anyone who refused to bow down to them."

"That's when Pasileveo intervened, right? After they enslaved the south and started marching north. He got the people to turn on them, killed the dragons, and, from that point forward, set out to eradicate the race." Madislak added, putting the bookshelf back.

"Exactly. That's when he intervened. Though, who knows if all of them are like that? That's two people who were unfit to be rulers. I mean... Look at Nalecht, he's not exactly fit to be the Anyth, I don't think." Harmony put the rest of the books back.

"C'mon, Harmony, let's get back to Lantess. Put that stuff in your bag. We need to show that to the others." Madislak placed his hand on her shoulder. "You're right about Nalecht. He's not fit to be a ruler. But someone that can command a dragon... That is worse."

The tiny hairs on his neck stood up and prickled with a sudden cold sensation, almost like miniature hands brushing against his skin.

Madislak let out a heavy sigh as he tied a leash to Martin's ropes and led him outside. To make matters worse, the abrupt departure of their horses, spooked by the fearsome panther, left them stranded in the desolate wasteland. They now faced the arduous task of traversing this treacherous terrain on foot, their journey even more perilous than before.

Leighth found solace leaning against a sturdy tree, her weary body supported by its comforting presence, as her gaze fixed upon the distant walls of Ventessa. Four days had passed since their daring escape from the capital, Ambrosia. Leighth needed him to train her so she could eventually take back her kingdom. The treacherous journey to Ventessa was further complicated by the necessity of traveling discreetly, concealed from prying eyes. Blank Face had guided her to the outskirts of the city, where they established a hidden camp, intent on gathering crucial intelligence: guard schedules, Zonoh's whereabouts, and any valuable information that could aid their mission. Somehow, Blank Face said he was going to kill King Zonoh, a pinnacle-five shrew and one of the most respected men in all of Kalazaar. Not to mention, King Zonoh possessed the shard of Obidiah as well. *Right.*

"Come on. You want to learn? We need to start with your skills. If you're traveling with me, it is imperative you can at least defend yourself," Blank Face said, tossing her a dagger-length stick. Leighth plucked it from the sky with one hand.

"Show me how you hold that," Blank Face commanded.

Leighth deftly manipulated the stick, positioning its bladed end to extend from the back of her hand. Holding it before her face, she assumed a crouched stance and cautiously circled Blank Face. The sun beat down on the Supta jungle, casting dappled light through the canopy of leaves. The air was thick and humid, but a gentle breeze carried the scent of exotic flowers and damp earth. Despite the heat, the temperature was surprisingly comfortable, thanks to the cool relief of the wind.

"Can I hit you with this? Or do you want me to hold back?" She made a couple of quick jabs towards him playfully.

"If you can hit me once with that, I'll tell you something true about my past." He nodded.

Leighth's eyebrows arched in surprise as she swiftly started a slashing motion, aiming for Blank Face's neck. However, he deftly intercepted her attack by catching her wrist and redirecting its trajectory. In a display of astounding speed, he swiftly jabbed her abdomen and the side of her neck, drawing a trickle of blood from the superficial wounds.

"Ouch, you jerk," she said, regaining her balance. She touched her finger to her neck and looked at the blood on her finger.

"The enemy will not hesitate," Blank Face whirled his stick around in his hand, matching Leighth's grip.

Leighth swiftly elevated the stick to eye level, adjusting her stance for enhanced stability by widening her feet. Faking the same stabbing motion as before, she cleverly sidestepped to the left, causing Blank Face's hand to reach for her wrist in vain. Seizing the opportunity, Leighth lunged towards his face, confident that victory was within her grasp. Yet, to her dismay, she found herself abruptly sprawled on the ground; her swing evaded as Blank Face deftly ducked. Employing his shoulder, he leveraged his body to lift under her arm, sending Leighth tumbling backward and landing on her back.

Leighth's head spun from the impact, a sense of injustice welling up within her. Blank Face stepped over her and extended his hand, helping her to rise. *How can I get revenge when I can't even hit this guy with a stick? I will bring shame to my entire family name as the girl who couldn't.*

After sparring for the next thirty minutes without landing a single blow, Leighth's frustration boiled over.

"This isn't fair," she whined.

He looked down at her with his inscrutable expression. "Life rarely is. I faced far harsher trials than this when I was your age."

Leighth's eyes widened with a mix of surprise and skepticism. "You? But how did you even learn to fight like this?"

"I learned through necessity, not choice." He aimed the stick at Leighth again.

She matched his grip and circled him. "Who taught you, then?"

"No one. I had to teach myself." He went to jab her.

Leighth sidestepped the attempted jab, pretending she had given up. "You mean to say you were already this skilled when you were my age?"

Blank Face's lips quirked in something resembling a frown. "Actually, no, I was even younger. Not all of us had the luxury of growing up in a castle." He whirled around, walking back to his starting spot.

Surprisingly, Leighth experienced a twinge of empathy towards him. It was an unexpected sentiment, one she never thought possible. Intense curiosity welled up inside her, urging her to uncover the secrets that lay beneath his perplexing facade. *Who was he, and where did he come from? Who was he before assuming the guise of Blank Face?*

Taking his advice about the enemy, not hesitating, as Blank Face turned his back, Leighth ran up and jabbed him in the back of the neck with her stick. "Got you!"

"That doesn't count. You stabbed me in the back!" Blank Face retorted.

"You said the enemy doesn't hesitate, and life's not fair... Well..." Leighth argued.

"Okay, cheater, what do you want to know?" he let out a sigh.

Leighth tapped her chin. "Where did you grow up?"

"I didn't have a place to grow up. Nowhere was home. I was a slave, a tool you royal cowards exploited for labor and amusement. But to answer your question, Xaneth Harbor."

Her eyes widened at the revelation. "Your parents... did they sell you into slavery?"

He scoffed bitterly. "Parents? I never knew them. If I ever uncover the identity of the cursed soul who brought me into this world, I'd take pleasure in ending their life myself." His intense gaze locked onto Leighth's.

In a fleeting moment, Leighth perceived a glimmer of sorrow within the depths of those dark brown eyes. It was a subtle nuance that struck her as peculiar and out of place. Her gaze shifted momentarily to the scars that marred his visage, prompting her to contemplate a different perspective. Perhaps he wasn't merely an assassin for the sake of being one. *Maybe, just maybe, the world had shaped him into the person he had become.* Though circumstances may have played a role, everyone had choices to make. And it was in those critical moments, when his dagger met flesh, that he exercised his agency.

"Why are you doing this? Straight vengeance? Why not just go back to your protected castle?" Blank Face glanced back over his shoulder.

As Leighth reflected on her objectives, she acknowledged that her primary goal remained unchanged: to exact vengeance upon Borlden and Nalecht and get the shard back. However, there was an inexplicable tug within her, a faint inclination to extend a helping hand to Blank Face. Her parents were unjustly taken from her. Perhaps he suffered the same fate. It wasn't a sinister desire to aid an enemy but a genuine aspiration to guide him towards a better life, one he might not have deemed possible.

With a hint of raspiness in her voice, Leighth opened up about her family dynamics. "My uncle has become somewhat unhinged and twisted. Returning home would only invite more problems unless I can kick his ass." Her words carried a weight of pain and determination. "But Borlden... He set my brothers on fire. The haunting image of that atrocity is forever burned in my mind. Vengeance drives me to keep going with you."

"Well, that's one thing I do very well," Blank Face half smirked. "C'mon, we need to get to a better spot."

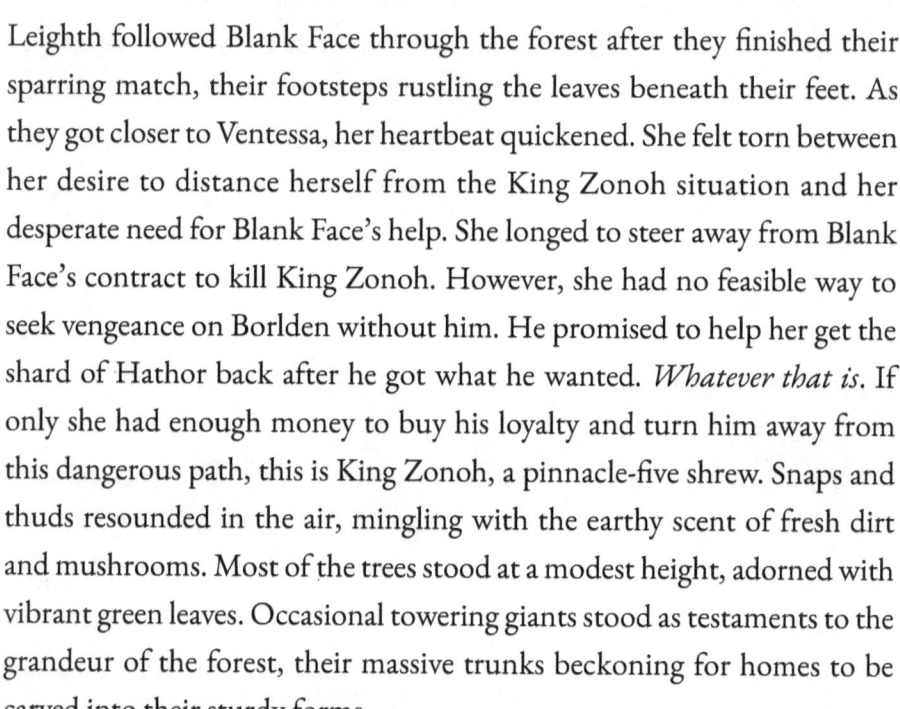

Leighth followed Blank Face through the forest after they finished their sparring match, their footsteps rustling the leaves beneath their feet. As they got closer to Ventessa, her heartbeat quickened. She felt torn between her desire to distance herself from the King Zonoh situation and her desperate need for Blank Face's help. She longed to steer away from Blank Face's contract to kill King Zonoh. However, she had no feasible way to seek vengeance on Borlden without him. He promised to help her get the shard of Hathor back after he got what he wanted. *Whatever that is.* If only she had enough money to buy his loyalty and turn him away from this dangerous path, this is King Zonoh, a pinnacle-five shrew. Snaps and thuds resounded in the air, mingling with the earthy scent of fresh dirt and mushrooms. Most of the trees stood at a modest height, adorned with vibrant green leaves. Occasional towering giants stood as testaments to the grandeur of the forest, their massive trunks beckoning for homes to be carved into their sturdy forms.

Ventessa, known for its dense and lush forests, was one sanctuary of the Elven race. The other Elven cities, Kordry and Kundry, shared this affinity for nature. Although Leighth's proximity to the city's wall limited her view, she could discern certain features. The formidable stone wall stood approximately thirty feet tall, fortified by jagged wires that ran along its crest. Towards one end, the wall gradually decreased in height, providing access to the main gates. Above the wall, three prominent turrets rose from the castle, creating a distinctive silhouette against the sky.

"Here's good enough. We'll set up camp, and I'll head in for some reconnaissance. You stay put and guard the camp," Blank Face directed.

Leighth raised a concern. "I think we're too close. They might spot the campfire."

"No fire. I've got a blended blanket that will serve as our cover," Blank Face explained.

Curious, Leighth asked, "What's a blended blanket?"

"I'll show you. It adapts to colors and shapes, making us nearly invisible from a distance."

Leighth furrowed her brow, admitting, "I've never heard of anything like that before."

"It comes in handy," said Blank Face.

Leighth prodded further. "Where'd you get it?"

"That's not your concern," Blank Face replied, undisturbed. He cleared space by moving leaves and made room for a makeshift pillow and blanket. From beneath his robe, he produced a small pouch, tossing a piece of jerky to Leighth.

"Thanks! I'm starving!" Leighth exclaimed. The jerky was salty and savory, with a hint of spiciness that lingered on her tastebuds. Its texture was tough and chewy but still satisfying.

"I'll grab more food once I'm in town and observe the guard patterns," Blank Face mentioned.

"I should go with you. I need to make sure you don't do anything stupid or get caught," Leighth insisted.

"That's a hard pass." He scoffed.

Leighth shrugged. "Why? I've followed your advice and orders so far."

"You're a princess. Don't you think someone might recognize you?" Blank Face pointed out, gesturing at her.

"I can wear a hood or put my hair up," Leighth suggested.

Blank Face's gaze sharpened as he scrutinized her from head to toe. After a moment, he conceded, "You're right."

Leighth instinctively recoiled as Blank Face reached for her long, flowing hair that fell to her shoulders. Her voice trembled with a mixture of fear and defiance. "No. No. No. Don't you dare!" she scolded, pulling away from his grasp.

"It's one of the quickest and most drastic changes. Just chop off some hair. You have plenty," he insisted.

She held deep personal significance for her hair, nurturing and growing it since her childhood with only occasional trims to maintain its health. It was not merely a physical attribute but a defining feature of Kundry women, a symbol of their heritage and identity. Their hair, known for its slower growth compared to other elves or humans, often became a lifelong commitment for the women of Kundry. In a moment of desperation, Blank Face brandished his dagger and stepped toward Leighth, causing her to swiftly seek refuge behind a nearby tree.

"Please," Leighth pleaded, her voice tinged with desperation.

"I'm begging you, don't do this. It will take forever for it to grow back. I'll do anything else." Her words carried a genuine plea, filled with the weight of her attachment to her cherished locks.

"Fine, stay here then." He turned away, going back to his cleaning.

Leighth quickly put her hair up into a ponytail using a tie band.

"See? Looks entirely different from before." She whipped her ponytail around.

Not acknowledging her at all, Blank Face began hanging a transparent blanket on the trees, using nails as anchors. Leighth could smell the tree sap emanating as he pounded the nails in. She watched as he pointed the face of the blanket towards the city, although she did not know how he could tell which side was which.

"From here, it looks like they can see right through that." She pointed at the blanket.

"Runo wo, ayed qdimo," He muttered.

The blanket rippled, its surface undulating with mesmerizing waves of colors that seemed to dance and flow. Leighth's eyes widened in awe as she witnessed the extraordinary transformation unfold before her. The once ordinary blanket now mirrored the very environment they were sitting in, blending seamlessly with the surrounding forest. She marveled at the intricate details and precise replication, struggling to distinguish where the blanket ended and the forest began. Curiosity getting the better of her, Leighth extended her finger and whisked it against the blanket's surface. To her amazement, a small imprint formed around her touch, creating a temporary disruption in the camouflage before seamlessly blending back in. It was a remarkable display of its adaptive capabilities, leaving Leighth in both fascination and appreciation for the incredible enchantment woven within the fabric.

"Incredible," she muttered. "What did you say?"

"Runo wo, ayed qdimo."

"Ya, I heard that. What language is that?" Leighth squinted at him.

"You don't recognize it?" his face contorting.

"Should I?" Leighth's gaze shifted to the ground, a faint blush tinting her cheeks. She realized that she should have been familiar with the language spoken around her, yet she found herself unable to comprehend its meaning.

"It's the secret language of your island, Sartina. Kordrarian. figured a princess of the city and island would know." He pointed at her. "It is ancient, though few people know or speak it anymore."

Leighth took a seat on a log, seeking the safety of cover as she pondered the mystery before her. As she observed him smoothing his bedroll, she remained in the night's darkness, her mind racing to find answers. Peering up at the vast expanse of the sky, adorned with Kalazaar's dual moons, four moons in total, but only two visible for one night, and countless shimmering stars. Mere moments passed before she fell asleep, and the light of the sun awakened her.

The morning sun was humid. She was running out of time to convince him to give up this crazy plan. "Hey, why don't you just come with me? Help me get my family's honor and kingdom back? I promise I will keep you safe. I'll be a queen; you can stay in Kundry, where no one will ever torture or bother you again."

Blank Face shook his head, "because you can't offer what I'm after."

"Maybe, if you'd tell me what exactly that is, I could!?" Leighth spat.

"I'm doing this whether or not you like it. Stay here or come with me. It doesn't matter to me, but I'm going into that city." Blank Face demanded.

"I'm coming with you," Leighth promptly hopped up to follow. She couldn't stop him from entering the gates, but perhaps she could stop him from killing Zonoh and creating an even larger target on his back. *Why is he so damned stubborn about this? Maybe I can sneak in and steal Zonoh's shard and get them both to listen to her.*

"Are you certain?"

"Yes!" Her eyes were wide, and she nodded enthusiastically.

Blank Face spun around with remarkable agility, catching Leighth off guard. She felt his grip tighten around her wrist, followed by a swift kick to her calf, causing her to lose balance. As she fell to the ground, her gaze returned to the fallen leaves, but before she could react, Blank Face sat on top of her, pinning her down. In horror, Leighth watched as he withdrew his other hand from behind her head, clutching a substantial chunk of her hair that slipped through his fingers. The realization hit her hard — he had cut off at least six inches of her precious locks. Fury and panic surged through Leighth's veins.

"You son of a bitch!" she exclaimed, her voice filled with anger and desperation.

Chapter Six

Leper sat against the sturdy trunk of a tree, reveling in the earthy scent that permeated the air after the rain had subsided. It took him three days to get here once Zanera finished stitching on the hat and applying the magical holds with a sapphire. With a careful, calculating gaze, he scanned the dense woods around him. He knew he needed to head north to reach Lantess, but getting there would require taking a winding path through the trees. Once in Lantess, he would have to navigate his way around the city, avoiding any unwanted attention as he made his way further north towards Wen-Tath. Rinawen had told him that this was where the royal parties would be meeting, and he couldn't afford to arrive late or draw any unnecessary attention to himself if he were to keep his identity a mystery.

Droplets of water glistened on the surrounding leaves, reflecting the sunlight that filtered through the canopy. He reached into a folded leaf pack, retrieving a container of thick moss-green salve. Carefully, he applied a generous portion to his finger and then to the area where the stitches were sewn on his head.

Leper's heart skipped a beat as he observed the approaching figures through the corner of his eye. His mind raced, trying to assess the situation. With cautious movements, he wiped off the remaining salve from his finger on the ground and got to his feet. The distinctive sound of a snapping twig echoed through the forest, followed by muffled voices. *Stay calm. Deep breath. Steady.* Leper strained to glimpse the individuals, staying hidden behind a tree.

One figure, a man with a substantial brown beard cascading down his chest, commanded a sense of importance, clad in pleated chain mail. Walking alongside him was a woman with short, curly blond hair. Leper's pulse quickened. Encounters with people from distant cities or other continents were a rarity for him. He remained still, his senses alert, keenly aware of the need to maintain his cover until he could determine their intentions.

Leper's hand slipped from the tree, betraying his presence with an inadvertent noise that caught the bearded man's sharp ear. The bearded man's head snapped in Leper's direction, his eyes narrowing. His fingers trembled as he tried to steady his breathing. The tightness in his chest constricted with every beat of his frantic heart.

"Who goes there?" his voice resonated with a deep and authoritative timbre.

"No one. Umm..." Leper stammered, searching for the right words.

"Your name, and seeing's you're from either Kordry or Kundry, what crime did you commit?" The man approached slowly.

"Leper, I'm called Leper." Leper cautiously extended his hands outward, palms open, distancing them from his chakrams.

"Why, Leper, are you lurking around these woods?" His hand inched closer to his sword hilt as he eyed Leper intently.

"I'm en route to Wen-Tath," Leper answered.

"For what purpose?" The man's head tilted slightly while his hand rested on his sword.

"My purpose is my own," Leper mumbled, his gaze dropping to the ground.

"This doesn't sit well with me." His nostrils flared as if sniffing for something more. "Do you smell that?" he asked the girl.

"Yeah," she responded, pointing northward. "It's smoke rising from Lantess."

He turned abruptly toward Leper. "What have you done?"

"Nothing, I swear." Leper's frustration tinged his words. "I've just come from Kordry on Queen Rinawen's orders."

"I'm losing my patience. Why would a messenger for Queen Rinawen be heading to Wen-Tath? And of all people, why send a criminal?" his voice held an edge of suspicion.

"I have business with King Madislak," Leper blurted out, using the king of Lantess's name. Considering his proximity to the city, he hoped it held weight.

"That would be me," Madislak confirmed. "And this is Harmony, my shrew." He motioned towards the girl.

Leper's gaze scrutinized the man, piecing together the clues. The purpose behind the pleated chain mail became clearer now. He observed the man's muscular physique and strong jawline. He took great care of his appearance. Leper estimated his age to be in the late twenties or early thirties. Although Madislak seemed slightly relieved, Harmony's lingering side-eye revealed suspicion.

Madislak, a name that carried the weight of authority and respect. His neatly combed chestnut brown hair framed a strong and noble face, accentuating his piercing brown eyes, which exuded both wisdom and determination. Madislak stood tall. The chain mail, meticulously crafted, boasted intricate engravings and decorative patterns along its edges, a testament to the skilled artisans who forged it. The armor clung to his well-built physique, accentuating his muscular frame and serving as a shield against any adversary.

"So why, Leper, do you have the hat of shame?" Madislak's exasperation echoed once more.

Leper prepared for this exact question. "It's quite a long story, but the important part is I took the blame for burning down a field of grain for a friend of mine."

"Kordry's customs seem so weird. Is it really necessary to wear that gaudy thing just to pay for a crime?" Madislak's disbelief contorted his features.

"Yes, it's a form of penance. In Kordry, we believe in carrying our shame or guilt as a means of atonement. It's both a punishment and a constant reminder to me and everyone else that sees me. I must seek redemption." Leper hastily explained.

"How does one accidentally burn down a field... exactly?" Harmony squinted in his direction.

"It was my job to tend the field for the day and ensure proper growth. My friend, Kelindra, an eight-year-old girl, didn't realize that putting blazeleaf and emberbloom together caused fire. We had collected some earlier that day for making some vials of medicine and salves, and I forgot to tell her not to put them in the same pouch." Leper shook his head.

Madislak looked to Harmony, "That seem right? Do those plants interact like that?"

Harmony nodded yes. "Far as I know, they do. Honestly, he sounds like a terrible teacher. I actually feel quite bad for the little girl."

"Fine. Get to the point. I'm in a hurry to reach Lantess," Madislak urged.

"It's about Nalecht," Leper began. "Rinawen believes he's plotting something with the shards. He even sent assassins to steal Theora's shard and abduct her children. He also murdered the royal family of Kundry."

Madislak's eyes widened. His once-vibrant complexion paled as he struggled to process the shocking revelation.

"Her children?" His voice barely rose above a whisper. "By the gods." Leper nodded solemnly.

"We need to investigate that smoke immediately!" Madislak's urgency propelled him into a sprint towards the source. "Harmony, tie Martin to a tree. We'll return for him later," he commanded.

"What? Noooo!" a shriek echoed from behind a tree, revealing Martin's protest.

Madislak distanced himself rapidly, his chain mail clinking as he moved with purpose. Harmony swiftly unfastened Martin's bindings and secured them around a nearby tree.

"Are you planning to gawk or offer some help?" Her gaze bore into Leper, her eyes intense with determination.

Leper felt a surge of frustration and helplessness wash over him as he faced the intense gaze of the beautiful woman before him. He wanted to help but wasn't sure if he should help with the prisoner or follow Madislak. Her eyes bore into his, demanding action. He stumbled over his words, his mind racing to find a way to be of help.

"Uhh, right..." Leper stammered, his voice filled with uncertainty. "Do you need any help or...?"

"No!" she snapped, her voice dripping with anger. "Go with King Madislak," she ordered, her tone leaving no room for argument.

"And don't you dare try anything," she warned, her bright blue eyes piercing into his with a fiery intensity.

Leper held his gaze a moment longer. As fate would have it, something went right for him today. He would make it to Lantess after all. He let out a sigh of relief. *That went much better than expected. Now, as long as I can keep the curiosity off my head. Just act normal.* The only unfortunate part was Leper didn't exactly understand what acting normal even meant. He shook his head, clearing his thoughts as he ran off after Madislak.

As they emerged from the tree line, the sight that greeted them sent a shiver down Leper's spine. The outer walls of Lantess loomed before them, smoke billowing out from inside. The once majestic city now seemed marred by destruction and chaos. Leper's eyes flicked to Madislak, whose face still held the pallor of shock and disbelief. A great tragedy had unfolded within those walls, and now they had the daunting task of assessing the extent of the devastation.

Madislak's gaze pierced through the billowing smoke, his heart heavy with anguish and fear. His beloved city, Lantess, was now engulfed in flames, a haunting sight that tore at his soul. It had been four days since he was here last. If Nalecht hadn't sent him on that goose chase, he would've been here to protect his city. Thoughts raced through his mind like a torrential flood, a mix of worry, regret, and a desperate need to find his family. The pungent scent of smoke stung his nose, mingled with the sharp tang of burning wood and the sickly-sweet undertones of charred flesh.

Turning his attention to Leper, a man with an extravagant hat that seemed at odds with the gravity of the situation, Madislak couldn't help but question how anyone could take him seriously. The eccentric appearance of his newfound ally stood in stark contrast to the dire circumstances they faced. Yet, in this moment of desperation, he had no choice but to place his trust in Leper. Dark, heavy clouds had gathered in the sky, casting a deep shade over the landscape. A low rumble of thunder could be heard in the distance.

The fate of Lantess and the safety of his children depended on his ability to trust in unconventional alliances. As they embarked on their journey together, Madislak hoped his skills would overshadow Leper's peculiar hat.

Leper's imposing stature, towering slightly above him, hinted at his physical strength and resilience. He possessed a rugged frame and broad shoulders, suggesting a natural athleticism and physical capability. His vibrant hazel eyes, large and round, held a certain intensity. Madislak couldn't help but wonder about the stories hidden within those eyes.

The intriguing runic tattoo on Leper's arm, peeking out from beneath his brown shirt, captivated Madislak's attention. Leper maintained a short goatee, which added to the air of ruggedness that seemed to emanate from him.

"I'm here to help you. Whatever you need, if I can assist you, count me in," Leper assured him, gesturing toward the city.

"Let's see what's unfolding. I need to locate my family—my wife, Gwenyvere, and my two children, Rylin and Alissia."

Leper gave a nod. "We'll find them. You have my service until we do."

"Thank you." Madislak quickened his pace toward the front gate, his weapon drawn.

Just in case, best to monitor him. Might be another setup by Nalecht. Unlikely but possible. He expected Harmony's imminent arrival, knowing she could help keep Leper's actions in check as well.

Madislak's heart sank as he surveyed the devastation that greeted his eyes. The once bustling market district now lay in ruins, consumed by flames and chaos. Standing as solemn witnesses, the charred remains of buildings testified to the destruction that had occurred. The acrid smell of burnt wood mixed with the metallic tang of blood filled the air, assaulting Madislak's senses and making his stomach churn. Fire still crackled amongst the rubble.

With a sense of urgency, he rushed towards the fallen bodies scattered amidst the debris. The sight of lifeless forms sent a wave of despair crashing over him, but he refused to give in to hopelessness. With trembling hands, he gingerly rolled over the bodies, desperately searching for any sign of life. His heart pounded in his chest, matching the rhythm of his racing thoughts. Each body he encountered fueled a surge of emotions, a mix of dread and grief. Beads of sweat formed on his brow, mingling with the dust and grime that coated his skin. These were his people; he was sworn to protect them as king of this great city. *I failed them. I failed them all.*

With every pulse of his heart, he clung to the possibility that amidst the tragedy, he would find survivors. He felt the weight of the shattered lives with every breath he took, and the burden of responsibility grew heavier with each passing moment. He knew he had to press forward to find answers and to bring justice to those responsible for this heinous act.

The shattered lion insignia served as a stark reminder of the destroyed lives and the desperate fight that lay ahead. *I am the King. I must go on.* He repeated to himself over and over.

The path to uncover the truth and restore order would be fraught with challenges, but he refused to waver. As the smoke billowed into the cloudy sky and the flames continued to dance, he pledged to rebuild what was lost and guarantee that those responsible would face the consequences of their actions.

"Who would do this?" Leper's head looked around the city.

Madislak squinted his eyes. "I don't know for sure, but after what you told me, I have a solid idea."

The scenes of destruction that unfolded before them were almost too much to bear. Fire consumed everything in its path, reducing once-vibrant streets to smoldering ruins. As they made their way towards the castle, Madislak's gaze shifted to the stone walls that stood tall and resilient amidst the chaos. The damage inflicted upon them was evident, with sections torn apart and windows shattered. Yet, the flag atop the Lantess insignia continued to flutter defiantly, a symbol of hope amidst the devastation.

Madislak rushed through the front door, his voice echoing through the once grand halls. "Rylin! Alissia! Gwen!" he called out, his voice filled with urgency. The silence that greeted him felt suffocating, amplifying his worry and driving him to search every corner of the castle. The interior reflected the external devastation as if someone had crushed the very heart of Lantess. Flags and insignia lay torn and discarded, strewn across the crumbled walls. The castle's halls, stripped of their former glory, marred its grandeur. The weight of loss pressed heavily upon Madislak, his eyes welling up with unshed tears.

He would not rest until he had answers, until he had found his family, and until Lantess had risen from the ashes to reclaim its rightful place as a beacon of hope and strength.

"Anyone!" Madislak's cry echoed through the chaos.

Leper's reassuring hand landed on Madislak's shoulder.

"Dad!" a voice cried out from the rubble near the back hall, where the stairs once stood. In unison, both their heads jerked towards the tiny voice.

"Alissia!" Madislak rushed over, attempting to peer through the tumbled debris.

Alissia poked her hand through the crumbled wall, "Dad! I'm so glad you're here."

"What happened? Who did this?" Madislak grabbed her soft little hand.

"Goreldea's armies appeared just two hours after you and Mom left for the meeting and started attacking us." She blubbered through tears. "I was so scared."

"Goreldea?" Madislak's gaze shifted toward the distant turmoil. "But why?"

Certainly, the queen of Kirilick had her reasons. Madislak had defeated her armies long ago, including the death of three of her sons at his hand. But it was Goreldea who attacked Lantess. He was merely defending his father's city. She may have had reason long ago to seek vengeance but to form an alliance with Nalecht...He shuddered at the thought of both those armies uniting.

"I don't know. Dad, I'm scared. We can't find Mom." She sniffled.

"Where's Rylin?" Madislak tried to peer through the rubble.

She pulled her hand back in. "Here with me. We're trapped."

Madislak flicked his eyes to Leper, then the stone rubble. "Leper, lend me your strength."

Madislak's heart swelled with relief as he and Leper worked tirelessly to clear the rubble. The weight of the rocks seemed insignificant compared to the weight of his fears and worries. With every stone they moved, hope flickered brighter within him. Finally, after what felt like an eternity, they created a path through the debris, revealing a room hidden behind the rubble. Dusty and disheveled, Rylin and Alissia emerged, their once fine clothes now torn and dirty. Their faces dirty and Rylin's long brown hair ruffled. Madislak's eyes welled up with tears as he gathered them in his arms, holding them tightly against his chest. The feeling of their warmth and safety brought a profound sense of gratitude and joy. He wiped Alissia's dirty, wet hair out of her face.

Harmony's voice chimed in from behind them, joining in their collective relief. As Madislak listened to the children recount their harrowing experience, he couldn't help but feel a renewed determination to protect and guide them through the tumultuous times ahead.

"I knew you'd come back." They heard an ominous voice from the other hallway.

Leper didn't know from the tone of voice who just said that. The thunder grew closer. They had just found Madislak's children and pulled them from the rubble. Emerging from the dining hall with a knife to Madislak's wife's throat, tears rolling down her cheeks, was Nalecht—the man who tried to kidnap Rinawen's children and take her shard—now threatening the lives of Madislak's family. *This is it. This is my opportunity. If I can help them out of this situation.*

"Mom!" Rylin yelled.

"Stay there, honey," her voice choppy.

Her tear-streaked face, smeared with dirt, revealed the anguish and fear she endured. The golden strands of her long, tousled blond hair cascaded down to her shoulders, tainted with grime and dust. Leper's throat tightened as he glanced at Madislak, then at Gwen.

Madislak stepped forward, unsheathed his cherished sword, and gently placed it on the ground before him. His actions spoke volumes, a gesture of vulnerability, as he showed he would negotiate and sacrifice to protect the ones he held dear.

"Whatever you want, it's yours," he said firmly, his voice laced with a mixture of determination and compassion. "You don't need to hurt anyone else."

"Well, at first, it was just that I wanted you removed from the equation. That Goreldea still holds grudges against you was just a favorable coincidence, for me anyway," a grin showing on Nalecht's face.

"I've been informed that you killed Jaynoh, although my sources are questionable," Madislak's gaze shifted briefly toward Leper. "And I've also heard about your attempt to abduct Rinawen's children. Why are you involved in all of this? Pursuing shards, kidnapping innocent children, even slaying royalty! Your actions defy the law!" Madislak's voice strained.

"Your comprehension of the shards pales compared to mine, great and mighty Madislak," Nalecht responded, taking a step closer while holding Gwen captive. "Once I've dealt with you, there will be no one left to challenge my supremacy, provided Zonoh is taken care of as well."

One glance at this man and Leper knew he was serious. They needed to defuse the situation.

"Even if you are the Anyth, you will face trial for your crimes. That includes your assault on my city, as well as Goreldea's actions!" Madislak retorted. "They should throw both of you into prison,"

"Who, exactly, is going to aid you in this?" Nalecht sneered. "Goreldea is certainly not on your side. That leaves Brebian and Theodamar. But they are too fearful to oppose me. I refuse to let anyone take away everything I've worked so hard for. I have invested too much time and patience into executing my plan."

Madislak picked up his weapon. "You killed your entire family! The only reason you're not in a dungeon rotting right now is because, somehow, you've convinced all of Ambrosia and Xaneth Harbor you were wronged! Well, you weren't! Brebian confirmed that himself."

Nalecht's eyes burned with intensity as he pointed his knife at Madislak. "My family's death was a necessary sacrifice to ensure my ascension as the Anyth."

Leper's mind drifted back to the traumatic events surrounding Madislak's accusation against Nalecht. It happened about three years ago when the rulers of Kordry sought aid from Brebian to stop Yusef, Nalecht's father, from taking over their island. However, upon Brebian's arrival, he claimed Nalecht had murdered his own family. Brebian's armies had attacked and destroyed Nalecht's stronghold, Axeladdle. But when they went to apprehend Yusef, he was already dead, along with Nalecht's children. His wife, Adalyn, had died a while back before Leper was born. Leaving Nalecht the sole survivor. Leper knew both men had different versions of the story, and neither could be proven true or false. Interestingly enough, Borlden Gruzca served as Brebian's shrew at the time but later switched allegiances to become Nalecht's shrew - a move that raised suspicions. Despite all this happening a while ago, it seemed like old grudges still lingered between the two opposing sides, with only two people truly knowing what really happened on that fateful day.

The timing of this event, just months before Yusef would have taken over as Anyth at the end of Zonoh's reign, seemed too convenient for Nalecht's benefit. Yet here stood Nalecht, openly admitting to slaughtering his family to Madislak, confirming the truth for once.

"You weren't there. You do not know what I was going through," Nalecht retorted sharply.

"Exactly. I had nothing to do with any of that. You can just leave me out of it." Madislak countered sharply.

"Sadly, your lack of involvement won't save you, Madislak. You, the mighty king of Lantess and renowned warrior, destroyer of armies, pose a threat to my quest for the shards," Nalecht declared coldly. "Letting you live now would only come back to haunt me. I can't have you amassing an army and challenging my authority."

"Please understand, Nalecht, the shards can't grant the power you're seeking," Madislak implored. "Regardless, I don't even have any shards! Why go after me?"

"With you and Zonoh gone, who will be left to oppose me? Brebian? Theodamar? The farmers of Kordry and Kundry?" Nalecht retorted, pressing the knife against Gwen's throat once again. "I will have the shards and the power they hold. You and Zonoh are the last two obstacles that stand in my path to total dominion."

Madislak hung his head. "I can't give you what you're asking for. Please, just let them go. I'll do anything—disappear, abandon my kingdom if that's what you want."

Nalecht's gaze locked with Madislak's for a fleeting moment.

"And who might this be, the eccentric stranger with the ridiculous hat?" Nalecht's voice dripped with disdain. "I didn't realize you kept criminals from Sartina in your company."

"I'm Leper Xentoth," Leper responded, his voice steady despite the tension in the air.

"Of Kordry? You wouldn't be the nuisance that killed my errand boys Borlden was telling me about?" Nalecht grinned.

"They shouldn't have been trying to kidnap children." Leper glared back at Nalecht.

Nalecht retracted the blade from Gwen's neck once more, circling around her to face Madislak directly.

"Stay still, all of you," Nalecht's warning hung heavily in the air, his words a chilling reminder of the danger they were in.

Leper couldn't help but notice the trident-shaped shard on Nalecht's hand, which cast an eerie illumination with its blue glow. Simultaneously, a red glow emanated from the spear-shaped shard on Nalecht's necklace—the shard of Ryollin, a token taken by Nalecht from his father. Ryollin increased his strength and speed, while Hathor enhanced his battle knowledge with any weapon he wielded.

"Please, just leave, Anyth. We'll vanish. You have my word," Madislak implored, his voice edged with desperation.

Nalecht's chuckle reverberated with an unsettling mix of amusement and bitterness. "Heh... You couldn't possibly fathom the depths of my motives, the reasons behind my goals."

"You're right. I may not understand them fully, but I can respect the pain that drives you," Madislak offered.

Nalecht's grin widened, a dark intensity gleaming in his eyes. "I believe I can enlighten you, King Madislak."

Leper's heart pounded as he witnessed the horrifying act unfold before him. The realization that Nalecht had crossed the threshold of reason struck him with a profound sense of urgency. At that very moment, Nalecht's twisted intentions took a devastating turn. A dagger flew, finding its mark in Gwen's chest. A spreading pool of crimson immediately tainted the vibrant blue of her gown. Leper's throat tightened as he covered his mouth. As Gwen gasped for air, her hands desperately clutching at the hilt of the dagger, she sank to her knees, her life slipping away. The anguished cries of their children, Rylin and Alissia, pierced the air, their youthful voices filled with shock and grief.

Leper felt his face get hot and flush. The piercing screams of the children drove him to hastily grab his chakrams. Madislak let out a low, guttural cry. His eyes locked on Nalecht, he seemed focused like a hawk and ready to rip him limb from limb.

Leper glanced at Madislak and nodded to him.

Madislak gripped Skyrunner, the legendary sword. He turned to his kids. "Get out now!"

Rylin and Alissia glanced one last time at their tearful mother before swiftly making their way towards the stables. Madislak's gaze fixed on Nalecht, and their eyes locked like those of a hunter and his prey. Just as Madislak prepared to confront Nalecht, Leper stepped forward and positioned himself between them.

"I'll do everything I can to buy you as much time as possible," Leper offered Madislak, his hand resting on his shoulder.

"This is my fight and I fully intend on being part of it," Madislak assured Leper.

"Your kids need you right now. Both of us can see he has two shards. We need more help. I'll buy you time to get out. Go..." Leper tried to push Madislak towards the fleeing kids.

"They know what to do," Madislak gritted through his teeth.

Leper glanced into Madislak's deep brown eyes and saw the hurt and the anger. At that moment, he knew there would be no quelling his rage.

Nalecht bolted incredibly fast towards Harmony.

"No!" Madislak yelled, looking towards Harmony, standing helplessly.

Harmony raised her hand, conjuring an ice bolt that surged forth from her palm, aimed directly at Nalecht's face. But his speed, augmented by the shard, allowed him to effortlessly dodge the attack. Unsheathing his sword, Nalecht swung it downward, intending to cleave Harmony in two. Just as the blade was about to connect, a resounding clash reverberated through the city as a gleaming chakram collided with the sword. Madislak's gaze shifted to Leper, who stood with his hand outstretched, the bracelet on his wrist emanating a humming energy, pulling the chakram back to him. With a swift motion, Leper snatched the second chakram and hurled it towards Nalecht. However, this time, Nalecht was prepared and effortlessly swatted the projectile aside. The chakram sailed past Nalecht, traveling about fifteen feet before landing on the ground.

"Shit," Leper said.

"Fine. I'll deal with you first," Nalecht began pacing towards Leper.

Madislak angled his sword downward, swiftly followed by an upward flip aimed directly at Nalecht. As the blade ascended, a radiant beam of light emanated from its tip, momentarily blinding Nalecht. He furiously rubbed his eyes, halting his movements, blinking repeatedly in disbelief.

"It only lasts roughly five seconds. If you're going to do something, now's the time." Madislak looked to Leper.

Madislak's first strike landed on Nalecht's torso, drawing blood but not inflicting a deep gash. Nalecht's eyes shot open, gasping, his grip tightening on his sword. He retaliated fiercely, swinging at Madislak with such aggression that he was forced to backpedal. His arms moved as fast as he could muster, but he was still losing ground. The shards Nalecht possessed granted him an overwhelming advantage.

Suddenly, Nalecht's sword connected with Madislak's shoulder, but the pleated chain mail absorbed most of the impact, preventing any serious damage. A forceful kick struck Madislak in the stomach, sending him careening backward until he crashed into the rubble. Leper collected his other chakram and intercepted Nalecht as he charged towards Madislak, who was collecting himself from the ground. Swinging for all he was worth, his muscles strained and swung, not making any progress.

"Look out!" Harmony's warning came from behind.

Leper rolled to the side just in time, evading an incoming ice shard that struck Nalecht's chest, sending him staggering backward. He winced in pain, momentarily dropping to one knee. Leper unleashed another relentless barrage of attacks on Nalecht. Madislak joined him in their assault, and they were actually pushing Nalecht backward. Steel clanging reverberated off the walls.

However, their momentary victory was short-lived as Nalecht struck Leper's torso, drawing blood. Leper felt the sting of Nalecht's blade lacerate his torso and immediately dropped his chakrams as he opened up his pack, searching for a healing vial. The deep gash leaked blood and burned so intensely that his fingers trembled handling the vial.

Quickly applying the vial of yellow liquid, the more potent one, to his abdomen, he winced in pain as this one stung. The liquid smelled of damp earth and decaying vegetation, with a hint of spiciness like ginger or turmeric. It had a deep, musty aroma. The warm blood soaked into his pants and covered his hands as he tried to hold it in for the few seconds it took the liquid to build a clot.

"Now," Harmony's voice echoed, catching his attention.

Leper glanced towards the ongoing battle. In a seamless display of co-ordination, Madislak miraculously rolled out of harm's way, narrowly evading the impending danger. At the same moment, Harmony extended her other hand, casting a binding spell that trapped Nalecht in place. She then brought her second hand forward, conjuring an even larger ice bolt. A trickle of blood streamed from her eyes as she released the powerful projectile. The enormous ice block collided precisely with the weakened point of the archway, causing it to come crashing down upon Nalecht, imprisoning him beneath the debris.

"Dad! C'mon, we got horses," Leper heard the children calling.

"Leper, can you walk?" Madislak flicked his eyes to him.

Chapter Seven

Frantically, Leighth let her fury out, unleashing a barrage of punches with all her might right after he chopped off her hair. Her strikes targeted his stomach, hoping to weaken him. Simultaneously, she kicked her legs, aiming to push him off her. The frustration and anger within her erupted in a blood-curdling scream as she tried to retaliate.

"I'll kill you myself!" She reached for a weapon, anything.

"Quiet! Are you trying to give away our position?" he put his hand over her mouth.

Leighth bit down as hard as she could, forcing him to withdraw his hand, shaking it vigorously. The teeth marks had a small visible amount of blood traced around them.

"What's wrong with you?" he smacked her. The impact wasn't forceful, but it held a certain weight. "It's just hair."

"Not where I come from! It's our culture. It takes Kundry elves longer to grow their hair out! Many of us females never cut our hair at all! It still only grows down to the butt!" She gritted.

"Consider it a fresh start then... let's go." Blank Face pushed her back to the ground and started walking away.

Leighth took a fleeting kick at his legs to trip him and connected with his ankle. He stumbled a bit, and his hood peeled back ever so slightly. Leighth finally had the chance to gaze upon the visage of Blank Face. It was the first time she saw him clearly, and in that instant, she couldn't help but notice the sorrow hidden within his brown eyes. The scars that adorned his face puzzled her; she wondered about the stories behind them, the pain he had endured. One prominent scar started at the forehead and went back as far as she could see. This man had endured unimaginable hardships, and a part of her believed he may be irreparably broken.

Blank Face's eyes locked with Leighth as he quickly fixed his hood, "and you are worried about your stupid hair."

A surge of conflicting emotions swept through Leighth as she momentarily entertained a hint of sympathy for Blank Face. However, that flicker of compassion quickly dissolved, replaced by an overwhelming desire to punch him. Anger seethed within her.

His unpredictable nature made it impossible to discern his true character. Sometimes, he displayed kindness and sweetness, only to abruptly transform into a total jerk. The inconsistency left Leighth perpetually bewildered, struggling to make sense of his behavior. However, amidst the confusion, there was one unwavering aspect to Blank Face's persona: his complete disregard for the feelings and opinions of others. He operated on his own terms, unapologetically asserting his will whenever he pleased, without concern for the consequences. Rarely would his face exude any emotion. A half-cracked smile was all she'd ever seen. Which triggered something she had forgotten.

"I'm pretty sure today is my birthday," a smile tugged at the corners of her lips.

"Happy birthday, then. Let's go," Blank Face turned back around, his tone unimpressed, and continued walking toward the gates.

"I'm eighteen now! Finally, adulthood. Although I've got no one to celebrate with me now. You've just chopped off my hair." Her smile faded as quickly as it had appeared. "Maybe we can celebrate?" Her voice carried a raspy hope.

Leighth braced herself for what would undoubtedly be a challenging birthday. Kundry, known for its vibrant celebrations, was an ideal place to mark such an important milestone as turning eighteen. It should have been a joyous occasion. However, the shadow of Borlden's heinous act loomed over her, casting a dark cloud on what should have been a day of celebration. Her family, tragically taken from her by his hand, would no longer be present to share in this special moment. The absence of their love and support was an immeasurable loss, felt acutely on this day.

Even her brothers, who often teased and taunted her relentlessly, held a special place in her heart. It was an unexpected revelation for Leighth to realize that she would miss their antics. Never in her wildest imagination had she expected to long for their presence, but the truth remained undeniable. Amid her grief and longing, Leighth yearned for the familiar bickering and banter that had once defined their interactions. The void left behind by their absence made her realize the depth of the bond they shared as a family, imperfect as it may have been. *The girl who couldn't.*

"Happy birthday," Blank Face patted her on the back. "Now, let's move on from the hair thing and do what we came here for."

"Fine, I suppose if you can handle whatever happened to your face, I can put the hair chopping behind me," Leighth muttered.

Leighth couldn't ignore the subtle shifts in Blank Face's demeanor whenever she was around. It intrigued her, leaving her with a nagging sense that she held some kind of influence over him. The reason behind this connection eluded her, but she felt a glimmer of hope that she could somehow help him redeem himself and turn his life around.

The intense, golden rays of the sun filtered through the lush canopy of leaves, casting intricate shadows on the forest floor. The brightness was almost blinding, causing her to shield her eyes with her hand and squint in its brilliance. With no one else to turn to and nowhere else to go, Leighth contemplated the idea of offering him a chance at redemption, envisioning a future where they could return to Kundry together.

A lot of that hinged on whether he wanted redemption. *Could they get the shard of Hathor back from Nalecht? Maybe he doesn't even want redemption. Perhaps he just wants to remain a cold-blooded killer.* Leighth shook her head. Before any of that could happen, she knew they needed to deal with Borlden, and for that, they had to finish Blank Face's insane contract to kill Zonoh—only one of the most powerful men in the entire world.

Leighth stealthily trailed Blank Face along the perimeter of the wall. They moved cautiously, using the cover of the trees to avoid raising any suspicion. Trapped in a dangerous situation, she couldn't bring herself to accept Blank Face's proposition of assassinating Zonoh. But she couldn't bear to lose the only person who could help her retrieve the shard of Hathor. Leighth feared that Blank Face wouldn't survive facing Zonoh, one of the most powerful figures in all of Kalazaar. Yet, this was also her chance to be in the presence of someone who might aid her in retrieving the shard. She felt torn between her moral compass and her desperate need for help.

Leighth walked the six-foot-wide dirt path leading up to the main gates, monitored by two guards. In a moment of anticipation, Blank Face adjusted his hood, partially concealing his face, and turned to face Leighth. The relentless sun beat down on them, and she wafted her shirt a bit to cool down.

"Okay, just walk normal through the gates. Don't do anything to cause suspicion or be obnoxious." He reached inside his cloak. "Take this."

Leighth swiftly snatched the unremarkable dagger, securing it discreetly at the top of her pants before smoothing her shirt to conceal it. Her heart rate quickened, and her palms grew damp. With determined focus, she fixed her gaze straight ahead and proceeded towards the entrance. Blank Face trailed closely about five feet behind her. She could feel the beads of sweat beginning to form on her head and face.

Leighth's heart raced as she locked eyes with both guards stationed at the large wooden double-door gate, fearing they might recognize her. The insignia of Ventessa, a shrew's staff holding a crystal with flames engulfing it, adorned the gate, surrounded by intricate runic symbols in the official colors of Ventessa, brown and green. *Don't panic. Don't panic. Act normal.* Despite her fear of being recognized, it was too late to turn back now, for they had already established eye contact.

Leighth focused on maintaining a composed facade, offering a simple nod to the guards.

"What's your business here?" One of the guards called out.

"Uhh...Just passing through." Leighth mumbled, her voice barely a whisper.

"Say again? Didn't quite catch that, girl." He demanded.

"We're just passing through. We're heading south to The Rim, just stopping for food." Blank Face interjected.

The guards eyed him up and down for a moment and, with a glance between them, nodded to each other. "Don't overstay your welcome. We'll be watching you."

Leighth nodded back and hustled into the city.

"Good. Now we make for the castle." She heard Blank Face call from behind her.

"Food first?" She patted her stomach. "It's my birthday."

Blank Face let out an exasperated sigh and turned away. Leighth followed closely as they made their way further into the city, eventually arriving at the bustling market district. It was a scene she had encountered in many towns before. The market district served as a central hub, providing weary travelers with the essential needs of food and rest. The rulers of Kalazaar had cleverly designed their cities, ensuring that the markets were easily accessible upon entry, diverting strangers' attention from the residential areas unnecessarily.

The enticing aroma of freshly cooked meats, combined with the vibrant scent of peppers and onions, filled the air, tantalizing Leighth's senses. Her stomach responded with a low growl of hunger while her mouth watered uncontrollably in anticipation of indulging in the mouthwatering delicacies that surrounded her. As the sweat from the relentless heat became more bothersome, she wiped her brow using her shirt.

"Don't waste this birthday girl. It's not cheap." Blank Face handed her a plate with a fresh, fire-cooked steak topped with onions, peppers, and mushrooms.

Leighth acted swiftly, seizing the plate from Blank Face's hands without hesitation. The steak had perfect consistency, juicy and tender, with a smoky char on the outside. The vegetables burst with flavors of garlic, herbs, and butter. As she eagerly stuffed a portion into her mouth. Satisfied, she settled down on the ground beside Blank Face, feeling the heaviness of her satisfied appetite. After devouring the entire meal, Leighth couldn't help but express her discomfort from overindulging, emitting a mild belch. A small, fleeting glimpse of amusement crossed Blank Face's otherwise inscrutable expression as a sliver of teeth appeared.

He got to his feet. "Hopefully, you can still function."

"I'll figure it out," she said, getting back up to her feet. "Let's check this place out."

"Your name is Alissia, and I'm Rylin. Got it?" Blank Face instructed.

"Sure do, Rylin." Leighth recognized Madislak's children's names.

Leighth trailed behind Blank Face, her gaze drawn to the awe-inspiring castle walls that towered an additional fifteen feet above the surrounding walls. Her mouth fell open in astonishment as she took in the sight of the entire structure made completely of stone. The beauty before her eyes was mesmerizing. Three distinct points jutted up from each sector of the castle, reaching towards the sky. Atop each point, flags adorned with Ventessa's insignia and colors fluttered in the wind. These points reached at least seventy feet into the air, a stark contrast to the wooden castle she had grown up in back in Kundry.

Nature had gracefully intertwined itself with the stone walls, creating a mesmerizing blend of man-made and natural beauty. Lush green ivy climbed the sides of the castle, forming a living tapestry that harmoniously melded with the brown stonework. It was as if nature had embraced the castle itself. Within the castle grounds, a serene courtyard beckoned, serving as a sanctuary of tranquility. Towering trees and vibrant gardens flourished, creating an oasis of serenity.

"You know what? Maybe instead of recon, we can just get this done now," Blank whispered into Leighth's ear.

"What!? Why? I'm not ready for that!" Leighth whispered back.

"You've got much to learn." Blank Face retorted as he approached the guards. "Good day."

"Good day," one guard replied.

Both guards wore green and brown-colored chain mail, a metal helmet, a shield on their back, and a sword at the side. From what Leighth noticed, they all wore the same uniform attire.

"We seek an audience with King Zonoh. Immediately," Blank Face commanded.

"Psh, under what premise?" the guard inquired.

"It's about Nalecht. Fresh developments have unraveled. That's all I'm allowed to say." Blank Face shot quickly.

"What is your name, stranger?" The guard arched his head back.

"I'm Rylin Idelth of Lantess. This is my younger sister, Alissia," Blank Face pointed to Leighth.

The guards' faces quickly changed from mockery to serious. Panic even as he fidgeted around uncomfortably. Idelth was a name that held significant weight and recognition, lending credibility to their claim.

"I uhh...uhh," he looked to his companion guard. "Wait here, I guess."

The guard rushed off to the castle as his partner stepped into the center, reluctant to let them through. Moments later, he came rushing back out of the castle.

"Go ahead in." He pointed to the large double doors of the castle entrance.

The imposing doors swung open, revealing a grand foyer area that sprawled before them. Leighth's eyes scanned the space, taking in the sight of several closed doors leading out of the foyer. Straight ahead, another intimidating bulwark stood guard, donning the pristine armor that all the bulwarks wore. Banners adorned the walls, and a painting depicting the family ancestry hung proudly on the left wall.

Anxiety crept up within Leighth as Blank Face deviated from their planned course of action. She unconsciously rubbed at her arms, feeling a slight prickle of anxiety and discomfort spreading through her body. The bulwark at the back motioned for them to enter, swinging the door open. Stepping forward, Leighth entered the room first. It became apparent that this was some kind of planning or war room. Dominating the space was a large oval table surrounded by twelve chairs. Above, a grand chandelier hung from the ceiling, its eight lit candles casting a warm glow. On the table lay a map marked with various cities and placeholders. A group of horse figurines placed near the city of Ambrosia caught Leighth's attention.

The bulwark followed them in, closing the door behind him. Standing at the head of the table was an old elf man clutching his staff.

"Welcome, I'm Zonoh," he gestured for them to take a seat.

Zonoh was a middle-aged Elven man with a warm and wise demeanor, his age reflected in the lines etched upon his kind face. Despite his extra weight, he carried himself with grace and confidence. His long, silvery-white hair flowed down to his chin, complementing the full white beard that framed his gentle smile.

He was dressed in a flowing brown robe that draped elegantly around his form. The fabric featured intricate, runic symbols embroidered in gold and silver thread. His eyes, a deep shade of green, gleamed with intelligence and compassion.

"Tell me. What are your names, and what is so important?" he asked, staring at Leighth.

"I'm Rylin Idelth of Lantess. We have news of Nalecht's treachery," Blank Face pointed to the two bulwarks in the room and two guards. "I don't think I should discuss this matter so openly," he pointed toward the door, gesturing they leave the room.

"Don't lie to me, Blank Face. I know more than you think." Zonoh held his hand up to his bulwarks. "My guards may not understand that Madislak and his wife are both human, yet somehow birthed an elf girl, but I do."

As Leighth's eyes widened and her mouth fell open, a profound wave of despair washed over her. *We're so dead.*

"So, you're aware of why I'm here?" Blank Face gestured towards the shard hanging from Zonoh's staff, a small green axe-shaped crystal.

"Why are you aiding Nalecht?" Zonoh questioned, his hand lowering onto the table.

What!? I'll kill him. I'll kill him for helping that piece of shit. What can Nalecht offer that anyone else can't? Leighth's face heated. She knew her tanned cheeks would be the color of iron melting if she had a mirror. As mere moments passed, something else crossed her mind. Maybe he can be my way to get close enough to Nalecht to get revenge and take the shard of Hathor back. Leighth's mind raced. Torn. Lost amidst this sea of turmoil.

"That's not your concern. I'll ask you for that shard once, politely." Blank Face threatened.

"So, you believe you can stride into my kingdom, issue threats, and act with impunity?" Zonoh's hand shifted to his staff as guards and bulwarks readied their weapons. "Let's face it, Blank Face, for five years, you've sown terror, evaded capture, and remained a phantom. Slippery Death, they call you. But now, I've got you."

Blank Face tucked his hands into his cloak. "You handing over that shard, or just talking in circles? I don't give a damn about your opinions or anyone else's on who I am or what I've done."

Zonoh glanced at Leighth. "And who might this young companion be? The innocent one you've brought along?"

Leighth's eyes darted around the room, desperately searching for a way out, a glimmer of hope to cling to. The walls seemed to close in, suffocating her spirit. She pondered the tough choices before her, torn between adhering to the law and not wanting to make an enemy of Zonoh while also dreading the possibility of Blank Face facing a deadly fate if they should capture him.

"She's my apprentice," Blank Face replied curtly.

"My name is—" Leighth began before Blank Face's backhand struck her across the face. The sting was so intense she instinctively rubbed her cheek, her gaze locking onto his.

"She's not your concern. The shard," Blank Face demanded, taking two strides toward Zonoh.

"She's the missing heir of Kundry, isn't she?" Zonoh mused, prompting the bulwarks to shift, ready to intervene if necessary.

"I can offer you both assistance. Eradicate your wanted status. Your talents are too valuable to squander in a life of crime," Zonoh proposed.

"Turn me into a weapon to serve your ends? No, thank you. You're all cut from the same cloth. You don't give a damn about anyone except yourselves," Blank Face retorted, jabbing his long, slender finger at Zonoh.

"Why are you out here doing Nalecht's bidding, then?" Zonoh mocked.

"I'm leveraging Nalecht's knowledge and his network to find something for me while I get something for him." Blank Face's demeanor remained unchanged.

What knowledge? Dammit, why won't you tell anyone!? Leighth glared at Blank Face for several seconds as she tried to comprehend his motives.

"Let me help you. I have a plethora of resources. I can find that which you seek," Zonoh offered.

"Then what? Say you can help me. After I have my answers, I want to be done with you. No strings." Blank Face shrugged his shoulders.

"You should take that deal," Leighth said to Blank Face, who ignored her sentiment.

"Once you fulfill your end of the deal and I fulfill mine, we go our separate ways. You'll never have to lay eyes on me again," Zonoh proposed.

"That's where you're mistaken. After I complete a job for you with exceptional results, you'll conveniently find a reason not to hold up your end. You'll keep me firmly under your thumb. Nalecht has already held up his side of the bargain. I retrieve this shard, and I'm finished dealing with him," Blank Face retorted.

"You believe he'll just let you walk away? Your naivety astounds me. He just executed Jaynoh and took his shard. When push comes to shove, he won't hesitate to eliminate you, too." Zonoh's face turned brighter shades of pink.

"I'm not scared of Nalecht or the damned shards. This is your last chance. Hand over the shard now." Blank Face's hands produced his daggers.

"Very well. So determined to meet your end today, aren't you?"

Leighth's heart pounded in her chest, on the precipice of fighting against the most powerful shrew in the world and his bulwarks. A battle they could not win, no matter how skilled Blank Face was. Suddenly, a guard swiftly approached, pressing a cold sword against her neck. She was forcefully pulled backward, making the threat obvious. Her chest constricted.

"Now," Zonoh's voice was flat. "I've had enough of this resistance. Stand down, or she dies!"

"And you say I'm the dumb one. You're going to hold a hostage against someone you call Slippery Death? You think you know everything when you don't. I'm getting that shard. Go ahead, kill her." Blank Face nodded towards Leighth.

Leighth's gaze shifted towards Blank Face, desperately seeking any hint of his true intentions. But, as always, his expression remained impassive, his face a mask of inscrutability. She longed for some sign, a glimpse into his thoughts, a flicker of emotion that would provide reassurance. In the depths of her being, she held onto a glimmer of hope, hoping against hope that he was merely bluffing, that he wouldn't dare gamble with her life as the stakes.

"Scum, that's all you'll ever be, Blank Face. Scum!" Zonoh twirled his staff with fluid brilliance.

Have I been just a pawn in this game to him the whole time? Was I really reckless enough to throw my life in the hands of an assassin just for a chance of revenge? To think I ever felt sorry for this asshole.

Leper urged his horse to its limits, matching the pace set by Madislak and Harmony. The children's sadness weighed heavily on his heart. As they put a few solid miles between themselves and Lantess, Madislak signaled for the group to seek refuge in a small, secluded area amidst dense trees and shrubbery. Ahead lay the Uldridge Mountains, the last obstacle separating the south from the north. He knew there was no time to waste—he needed to uncover Madislak's plan of action and figure out how best to assist him. Every act of kindness, every moment of support during Madislak's struggles, will prove Leper's loyalty and absolve him from the shadow cast by past tyrannical Chernzerk. Failure is not an option.

Madislak dismounted his steed and set his hand on Leper's shoulder.

"Thank you for your help back there. I..." Madislak struggled to keep his voice from cracking. "Harmony could remove your hat for you. Far as I'm concerned, I consider your shame and atonement complete."

"No!" Leper instinctively shouted.

Madislak scowled. "Okay. It was just an offer."

Harmony shot him a glare. "Wow, seems a bit defensive there. Why so jumpy?"

"You don't understand. If I take this off without Rinawen's approval first, I will have to wear it even longer when I get back home." Leper said sheepishly.

"Whatever you say, hat man," Harmony mocked.

"I don't even know what to do at this point. Nalecht has clearly made his motives known. Zonoh needs to move quicker on him. How long will it be before Nalecht tries to attack Zonoh? And if Zonoh gets overrun, we lose a very vital piece to our resistance. Plus, there's this hor..." Madislak stopped immediately and looked at Leper.

"The what now?" Leper locked eyes with Madislak.

Harmony sifted around in her bag. "This." She held up a horn, one that looked exactly like the horns on his head right under his hat.

Leper's throat tightened. Fear gripped him. *This can't be happening. I thought Nalecht catching up to us was a bigger problem. All this time, I thought I was the only one. I'm not alone. There's more out there.*

"I wasn't exactly going to divulge that to him right now. We don't even know if we can trust him." Madislak palmed his forehead.

"You're the one that blabbed." Harmony chuckled.

Leper nearly reached for his head but caught himself as he squeaked out, "Is that what I think it is?"

Harmony put it back in her bag. "Exactly! That look, right there. This isn't an old horn. They're out there, Leper. Nalecht might not even be our biggest threat."

"We're going to need people like you to step up. Cause if that horn tells us anything, and this truly is the return of the Chernzerk. We will have to look under every rock, search every corner, and cave to root them out." Madislak continued.

Leper shook his head. "Troubling news indeed. However, there's no concrete evidence there. Whereas Nalecht has just destroyed your city and killed your wife. I think we should focus on that."

Anything he could think of to break their stares at him. Leper could feel them glaring at his hat as if they could see right through the thing. He would give anything to become invisible right now—anything to take the attention off his head. One kid tugged on his shirt as Madislak stormed over towards a tree to take out his frustrations.

Rylin and Alissia, wide-eyed and filled with sorrow, gazed at Leper's hat, their innocent fascination momentarily distracting them from the weight of their current situation. *Of course, they want to look at the hat. Why the heck would anyone not want to look at the hat?*

"You like my hat? Or is it overbearing?" Leper smiled at them. Pushing aside the panic.

"Umm... what's it like, Mr.?" Alissia asked, her voice merely a whisper.

"Leper, just Leper." Leper glanced at them.

Harmony had taken a seat crisscrossed on the ground. Her chest compressions increased as she struggled to keep pace with breathing. Her eyes still trickled a bit of blood from the amount of energy she used to conjure that large ice shard was taking its toll. While not a magic user, Leper knew overdoing it could lead to serious exhaustion and, in more cases than you would expect, death.

"Harmony? Hey, are you okay?" Leper rushed to her side, his hand brushing her forehead. "You're burning up."

"Everything... Hurts..." Panic etched across her face, the color rapidly draining from it.

Leper's hands darted to his trusted pouch of vials, his search ending with the discovery of the pale green liquid he sought. Uncorking it, he moved to pour it into Harmony's quivering mouth. She averted her gaze.

"Come on. Do you really think I'd be here trying to save you if I wanted you dead?" His plea held urgency.

Harmony slowly turned her head back to him, focusing despite the pain. "What... is it?" Her words came in labored breaths.

"It's a concoction of roots and herbs, infused with magic, to aid in recovery from exhaustion," he explained. "I can't guarantee it'll work for magical fatigue, but it's better than the alternative, right?"

Leper tipped the vial once more, offering it to Harmony, who accepted it with a skeptical expression. As soon as she consumed the potion, Leper observed the almost immediate effects. Harmony's breathing steadied, and a healthy hue returned to her once-pale face. The trickle of blood in her eyes ceased and dried on her skin. Satisfied with her improved condition, Leper shifted his attention back to the children, hoping to offer them the same relief.

"Want to play a game?" Rylin and Alissia enthusiastically accepted Leper's question.

"Yeah!" their voices harmonized.

He retrieved a pouch of dice from his pack, containing four ten-sided dice for each of them.

"Here's how it goes," Leper explained, shaking the dice vigorously in his cupped hands. "You toss them on the ground like this and then add up the numbers."

"I'll go first," he announced, scattering the dice on the ground. "I got 18."

"Hey, I got 21!" Rylin's excitement was palpable.

Alissia's shout followed, "I have 32!"

"Wow, that's an impressive roll!" Leper praised, patting her brown hair.

Leper engaged in several more rounds of the game with the kids, momentarily diverting their minds from the haunting sight they had just witnessed. He kept their attention on the dice and the ground, anything to keep it away from his head.

"Can we touch it?" Alissia asked, glaring at Leper's hat.

"I'm sorry, but the stitches aren't quite healed yet, and every time it moves, they have to heal again, which causes a lot of pain. After that fight and all the bouncing on the horse, it is very sore. I'm sorry, but I'd rather not right now." Leper tried to convince them otherwise.

"Awww. I won't push hard! I promise." She pleaded with her sad brown puppy dog eyes.

"How can I say no to that?" Leper blurted.

He grabbed her hand and nuzzled it along the side of his head to make sure she didn't get close to the top. *Whose horn was that?* His mind wandered absently until Harmony hopping up caught his attention. Leper could now hear Madislak slamming his fists against a tree, muttering something at it.

"Thank you." Harmony expressed softly.

As she attempted to place a hand on his shoulder, Leper jolted, his head quickly drawing a furrowed brow from Harmony's face.

"Sorry, thought you were going to push me over." Leper stood up and followed her over to Madislak. "But you're welcome."

"Leper, I don't know you well, but I want to thank you sincerely for your assistance back there. From the depths of my shattered heart," Madislak's eyes mirrored his genuine gratitude and sorrow.

"It's truly not a problem. I came over to help, and I'm glad I could," Leper replied humbly.

"Well, it means a lot. I apologize if we seemed hesitant; these past few days have been chaotic," Madislak's gaze shifted to Harmony, his expression fraught with concern. "Damn it. We forgot Martin in the woods."

"Let him rot. We have enough filth like him in the world." Harmony's voice resonated with unrelenting condemnation.

Amidst the lingering tension, Alissia's childlike innocence cut through. "What do we do now? Our home is gone."

Madislak enveloped her in a comforting embrace. "We make our way to Wen-Tath."

Leper's gaze fixed on Madislak, seeking guidance. "Do you think they'll be able to help?"

"Let's keep our hopes up. Zonoh is powerful and the mastermind behind this entire operation. Perhaps they've had some breakthrough in finding people willing to explore The Talon and seek the shard of Amarook," Madislak responded his tone a mixture of optimism and uncertainty.

"They're heading to The Talon?" Leper mused aloud, a contemplative hand cupping his chin.

Leper had only encountered stories and read countless books about the legendary Talon. An island boasting the tallest mountain in the world, rumored to be the domain of mighty dragons and steeped in immeasurable magic. The tales whispered of its wondrous allure, yet they also carried a haunting truth: those who ventured to The Talon never returned. Ever. Despite this foreboding reputation, Leper's desire to set foot on that mystical land remained unquenched.

"Nalecht sent me on a goose chase. I'm pretty sure he, or someone, already has the shard of Aisha, and he sent me down there to attack Lantess in my absence," Madislak shared with Leper, recounting the past. "They had intended to hold a tournament to identify the mightiest warriors for the task."

Leper's gaze met Madislak's, determination in his eyes. "I'll volunteer to go to The Talon."

Madislak's expression reflected gratitude and consideration. "Let's focus on getting to Wen-Tath first. Zonoh will know what to do."

"Regardless, we need to move and get past the Uldridge Mountains. We've been sitting here for a couple of hours already." Harmony added.

The group mounted their horses, resuming their northward journey. Leper's heart ached for Madislak, but he knew they couldn't afford to dwell in sorrow or grief. Nalecht's relentless pursuit of the shards left them with no time to spare. Previously, they based their conclusions on speculation, surmising that Nalecht had an unknown reason to collect these shards. However, the current revelation left no room for doubt—they were unequivocally certain that his intent was to get them. As the sun surrendered to the incoming clouds, the breeze gained strength, sending a chill through the air. Amidst the changing weather, Leper's gaze caught something in the sky, drawing his attention. It appeared to be an object, growing larger as it approached their location.

"Is that a giant bird?" Leper pointed to the spectacle.

"The flying chariot of Lantess!" Harmony cheered.

Chapter Eight

B lank Face sprang into action, displaying a level of skill that took Leighth by surprise. From beneath his cloak, he swiftly retrieved two shurikens, launching them with remarkable speed and accuracy. One found its mark in the neck of the bulwark standing beside Zonoh, while the other struck true, connecting with the guard standing next to Leighth's captor.

Leighth felt a subtle shift in the guard's grip on the sword against her neck. The strong, musky scent of well-worn leather filled her nostrils. The weapon trembled, betraying a hint of uncertainty as if the sudden turn of events had rattled his resolve. Her heart raced, teetering on the edge of hope and trepidation.

Zonoh's staff twirled effortlessly in his hand. Leighth's eyes widened as his hand extended, revealing a distinct tattoo of a brain on his palm. The symbol sent a chill down her spine, as it could only mean one thing: psyrenth magic. The realization struck her with a mix of awe and dread. Psyrenth magic was renowned as one of the most formidable and elusive disciplines among the shrews. A dark form of magic that included mind control, telekinesis, and other forms of dark manipulation. From a young age, Leighth had been told tales of aspiring shrews who perished in their pursuit of harnessing the power of psyrenth magic. Now, at just eighteen years old, she stood face-to-face with Zonoh, the only person she had ever seen bearing that tattoo. The weight of their impending doom settled upon her. *Happy birthday to me.*

"Stop moving!" he commanded to Blank Face. The color of his tattoo slowly drained to a dull gray.

The ring on Blank Face's right hand, middle finger, lighted with a dull green glow. He held it up in Zonoh's direction.

"You didn't think I came to this unprepared for your trickery, did you?" He mocked.

Blank Face moved with astonishing speed, his actions blurring before Leighth's eyes. However, her vision was hindered by the tightening grip of the guard holding her hostage, making it difficult to fully witness the unfolding confrontation. She tried to muscle free, but the guard just pressed the blade harder. Blank Face delivered a powerful boot to Zonoh's stomach, sending him reeling backward. The impact caused Zonoh to lose his staff, which held the precious shard of Obidiah. The clatter of the staff hitting the ground reverberated through the room.

Meanwhile, the other bulwark closed in, attempting to strike Blank Face with swift and precise attacks. Blank Face deflected the first strike and effortlessly evaded the second swipe. Leighth couldn't help but feel a momentary pang of sympathy for the bulwark. Although they were highly trained fighters, Blank Face's exceptional abilities gave them no chance. At that moment, as she witnessed the seemingly unstoppable prowess of Blank Face, Leighth believed that there was no one in the world capable of defeating him.

Leighth noticed a flicker of distraction in the guard's grip as he, too, became captivated by the unfolding spectacle before them. It was her chance. Leighth mustered her strength and abruptly pulled down on his arm, creating a split second of opportunity. She swiftly tucked and rolled away, freeing herself from his grasp. Her hand found the grip of the dagger that Blank Face had entrusted her with earlier. Circling the guard, she remained focused and composed, recalling the lessons imparted by Blank Face during their time together. Waiting for the right moment, she patiently watched for his movement, following the teachings she had absorbed.

As the guard launched his attack, Leighth sidestepped, deftly evading his strike. She lunged forward, her dagger finding its mark on his leg with a quick and precise jab. The guard staggered back.

"Ahh... bitch," he groaned.

Now, with a sense of resurgence, he charged at her. Leighth dodged to the left, then again left. The second attack nearly caught her shoulder. Her dagger trembled in her hand.

"That's right. Bit off a little more than you could chew, huh?" He taunted.

"Bring it," her jaw clenched.

Leighth's instincts kicked into high gear as the guard advanced towards her, his blade aimed for a straight stab. She dodged to the right, throwing off his intended trajectory. She brought her elbow down with force on his arm, causing the sword to clatter to the ground. The metallic clang echoed through the room, capturing the attention of the other three combatants who had been engaged in their own intense battle. Her gaze shifted to Blank Face, gracefully evading the relentless attacks of the bulwark, his movements like a well-choreographed dance. Meanwhile, Zonoh unleashed his formidable power, casting lightning from his other hand, sending electric currents towards Blank Face.

The room crackled with tension as the battle raged on, each participant locked in a fierce struggle to gain the upper hand. Leighth could only hope that their combined efforts would be enough to get out of here.

"Enough!" Zonoh yelled, aiming his hand at Leighth.

Leighth's muscles constricted with an overwhelming sense of helplessness, her body refusing to obey her commands. Panic surged through her veins as she tried desperately to move, to fight back, but her limbs remained paralyzed as if held captive by an unseen force. Even her fingers refused to respond, causing her dagger to slip from her grasp and clatter to the ground. Her throat trapped the words she desperately wanted to speak, rendering her voiceless in the face of impending danger.

Her heart pounded in her chest as the guard picked up his sword from the ground, closing in. The intent to end her life was unmistakable, and with each step he took, Leighth's fear escalated. She struggled against the invisible restraints, willing her body to move, to resist the inevitable fate that awaited her.

"Don't kill her! Do your job and restrain her. She is royalty and not to be associated with this filth." Zonoh spat, sweat dripping off his old face. "Then get over here and help us end this treacherous fool."

The guard didn't make it two steps toward her before a shuriken came arcing over the table, lodging in his neck as he slumped to the ground.

Leighth felt the magical bind slowly giving way. She could slowly move her fingers now.

As Zonoh bent down to retrieve his fallen staff, Blank Face continued to navigate the fierce battle with the bulwark, his movements fluid and precise. He swiftly extended his leg, tripping the bulwark, causing him to stumble forward. With lightning-fast reflexes, Blank Face capitalized on the opening, thrusting his dagger into the vulnerable spot at the neck of the bulwark, bypassing the pristine armor that had seemed impenetrable. The bulwark slumped over, collapsing to the ground.

Leighth's breath caught in her throat. In that moment, Blank Face's mastery over combat was undeniable.

Upon turning around, Blank Face encountered the sight of Zonoh holding his staff with unwavering focus. Without a moment's hesitation, Zonoh unleashed a powerful blast of wind, sending Blank Face hurtling backward. The force of the impact propelled him into the wall, causing a resounding thud to reverberate through the room. Papers scattered in all directions as he landed on top of a nearby desk, the weight of his impact revealing a prominent crack in its center.

Struggling to maintain his composure, Blank Face swiftly rose to his feet, readjusted his hood, and fixed his gaze upon Zonoh once more. The shard of Obidiah, humming with power, emitted a vibrant green glow, its presence casting an ethereal aura within the room. The renewed focus in Blank Face's eyes indicated he was not ready to back down.

Zonoh's lightning struck Blank Face, whose pursuit abruptly halted. As Blank Face was wrapped in lightning, time slowed down for Leighth. Crackling emitted around him. She glanced at Zonoh, sweat dripping from his face as he maintained his hold.

"Zonoh! Don't kill him." Leighth pleaded.

His brow furrowed. "What business do you have standing up for this disease?"

Leighth inched closer, hoping to get the shard from Zonoh's staff to defuse the situation. "He saved my life. I don't know what he's been through or why, but he can fight. Truthfully, I don't know there's anyone that could beat him. If you let him go, we will take the shard to Nalecht, and Blank can kill them. Both of them. They'll never see it coming."

Zonoh chuckled. "Do you really think this man here will do that for you? You don't understand what happens if Nalecht gets ahold of those shards, young girl. You don't understand..." Zonoh's response was interrupted.

In one swift movement, Blank Face threw his dagger deep into Zonoh's chest, eliciting a gasp of pain. Leighth's breath caught in her throat. Blank Face's dagger piercing Zonoh's chest sent a surge of mixed emotions coursing through her veins—relief, triumph, regret, and a tinge of sorrow for the consequences of their actions. At that moment, the gravity of their mission and the price they had paid for their freedom weighed heavily upon her.

"See, you're not all-powerful." Blank Face held Zonoh as he fell to the ground.

"You can't continue this path," Zonoh glanced at Leighth. "You will all be dead."

"Even with your bulwarks, guards, and the shard of Obidiah, you still lost. Perhaps it's you that overestimates your worth," Blank Face reiterated.

Blank Face plucked the shard from the staff, concealing it within his cloak.

"C'mon, we have to go. Drink this," Blank Face handed Leighth a small vial.

"Why would you do that? He was considering helping us, Blank Face! Why would you kill him? He would've listened to me! Now you're going to alert the entire world, and I'm going to be an accomplice to your murder!" Leighth spat as rage surfaced within her.

"Just drink it. Turns you and your possessions invisible for three minutes, and we need to go." Blank Face downed his vial.

Leighth's heart pounded in her chest as they hastily consumed the vial of grayish liquid, their bodies fading into transparency. She felt Blank Face's hand grasp hers, urging her towards the exit. Leighth reluctantly agreed to accompany him, aware of the consequences of staying behind. If the guards arrived and found her alone, she would be the prime suspect, even if she told them that Blank Face had done it.

Sure, he might have killed them all, but why was she the only one alive when he killed everyone else? There were no good options. Stay here and defend yourself against their trials, or go with him. Every day caught up in a trial would be one day less she would have to seek her vengeance on Borlden. However, there's one thing you can take from something like this. If there is a dog to have in the fight—that person fighting for you—it needs to be Blank Face.

Together, they hurriedly made their way through the front door, swiftly navigating towards the back of the castle. Leighth followed Blank Face's lead, trusting his instincts as they reached a landing pad where an unoccupied flying chariot awaited. Climbing the ladder, they ascended to the platform and swiftly jumped into the chariot, ready to make their escape. The pungent stench of stale food and decay assaulted her senses. Each breath left a sour taste on her tongue, a reminder of the expired and rotting items that lingered in the space.

Once settled, Leighth couldn't suppress her curiosity and concern. Turning to Blank Face, she asked,

"Do you know how to fly this thing?" Her voice trembled with a mix of anticipation and trepidation, knowing that their chances of escape depended on their ability to navigate the skies.

His response was brief but honest. "No."

Leper quickened his pace as he took in the sheer size of Wen-Tath after taking a day to rest and recover after the events in Lantess. He was unaccustomed to being surrounded by so many people, let alone so many guards. People seemed to be everywhere he looked, and the sight made him yearn for the comfort and familiarity of Kordry, where he could be with his only friend.

Hastily making their way through the castle courtyard, Madislak and Harmony set the pace as they raced towards the meeting, not wanting to be late.

Leper was determined to contribute and offer his help during the meeting, hoping it would earn him a chance to visit The Talon. Showing his cooperation and usefulness in any way possible would benefit him if the hat suddenly came off.

The warm morning sun provided some comfort after a long, frosty night. Madislak's father had picked them up in the flying chariot of Lantess moments after they escaped the clutches of Nalecht in Lantess.

Constructed of timeless stone, the castle stood tall and proud, commanding admiration from all who beheld it. This palace featured a unique design with five distinct points. Each point of the stronghold aimed skyward like the fingers of a grand hand reaching for the skies. The stone walls, expertly crafted, exhibited intricate details and carvings that tell tales of bygone eras and noble lineage. The stonework, weathered by time, carried an aura of strength and endurance, hinting at the castle's enduring legacy.

Tall, narrow windows with intricate tracery and colorful stained glass littered the stone wall. Sunlight filtering through created a breathtaking display of light and beauty inside the castle.

Elegant turrets and a ballista adorn the castle's five points. These vantage points offer panoramic vistas of the surrounding fields and forests. There were approximately fifty thousand residents living within Wen-Tath's walls, which stood sixty feet high. Beyond the castle, there seemed to be an endless row of buildings stretching for miles.

"C'mon, you're already a criminal. If you don't want to be the mocking point of this meeting, move your feet!" Harmony hollered as her lips curled upward.

"Hey, it's not every day you get to see a spectacle such as this," Leper retorted.

Harmony stopped briefly. "I mean, this place is nice, but have you never been to the capital?"

Leper glanced at her, then at the floor. "No. Why would I leave Kordry?"

"I just kind of figured as an ambassador of the queen, she might want you to at least be familiar with some other cultures..." Harmony trailed off.

"We're going to be late," Leper took off after Madislak again. He could feel Harmony still glaring at him.

Leper followed Madislak, taking in the sights of an enormous castle. Its inside halls were a mesmerizing blend of history, artistry, and lavishness. They evoked a sense of wonder and transported visitors to a realm where dreams intertwine with reality, where the splendor of the past lives on in every meticulously crafted detail.

The halls were expansive, their soaring ceilings gilded with intricate moldings and decorative motifs that catch the light. Gleaming chandeliers hung from above, casting a warm, golden glow that danced upon the polished floors. The scent of age-old stone and the faint fragrance of candles tinged the air, creating an atmosphere of timeless elegance. As they moved deeper into the hallway, a door opened to reveal a grand chamber. High-backed chairs with plush upholstery beckon guests to rest and engage in lively conversations. One large central, rectangular, and imposing table capable of accommodating maps, charts, and various documents essential to strategic decision-making.

His gaze wandered around the room until it settled on a figure seated at the head of the table. It had to be King Theodamar, he presumed. The king was a short elf attired in elaborate silk garments with orange and white stripes, representing the colors of his city. Standing beside the king was a captivatingly beautiful girl.

Leper's attention shifted to the girl, whose face had a slightly heart-shaped contour. The most striking aspect was her large, beautifully shaped eyes, tinted with a unique shade of green. Her nose was slender and elegant, perfectly complementing her facial features. A sprinkle of freckles covered her cheeks, and the defined arches of her eyebrows framed her captivating eyes.

"Leper!" A familiar voice cut through the tumult of the room, jolting him from his thoughts.

Could it be? Leper swiftly pivoted on his heel, his heart racing as he laid eyes on his lifelong friend, Rinawen. She stood there, dressed in a leather tunic, white undershirt, and brown pants.

"Rin!" Leper's feet moved without hesitation, carrying him across the room to her. "I've missed you soooo much."

Rinawen's eyes squinted as she looked at his hat.

Leper reacted swiftly, placing a gentle finger over her lips, a silent gesture to maintain discretion. "Don't say it." He whispered in her ear. "Nyxg fia ug. Uvv okzviux gro rig vigod sefg qy jugr jrig u fia."

"Aye riho fywo okzviuxuxq gy ny," came her reply.

Leper nodded. Using the ancient language known as Kordrarian, he told her he would explain the situation to her later, only for her to let him know he had a lot of explaining to do.

"So, why, tell me, do we have a criminal in our midst? Do we have no honor left?" the man at the head of the table interjected.

Rinawen leaned in and whispered to Leper it was King Theodamar of Wen-Tath.

Leper never expected the need to reveal the fabricated story he had concocted on his own. And now, he had no opportunity to disclose it to Rinawen. His toes curled up in his shoes as he looked at Theodamar's cherubic face. "I b..."

Theodamar waved his chubby hand, dismissing Leper, then pointed at Rinawen. "I want her to tell me. I'll get my answers from the queen, not her errand boy."

Leper shut his mouth and glared at Theodamar. *Such disrespect.* He felt Rinawen's hand land on his shoulder.

Rinawen looked at Leper. He could see the disappointment in her face as she beckoned him for an answer. Leper made his hands into a ball and pulled them apart, trying to signal fire as he stretched his facial muscles apart.

Rinawen cocked her head to the side. "He...He uhh...broke..."

Leper shook his head no.

"Okay, what the hell's going on here?" Theodamar sat forward in his chair.

Leper turned back to him, "Am I allowed to talk now, your highness?" he quipped.

Leper felt the back of his head sting as Rinawen smacked him. "Respect your superiors, boy."

From out of the corner of his eye, Leper noticed Harmony kick Madislak in the shin and nod their way. Madislak scratched his head. "He burned down a field, but it wasn't his fault. This isn't a matter of importance. Let's just move on already. The enemy is moving, and we're arguing over dumb shit."

Thank Theora. It was bad enough he had this beacon on his head; now everyone was staring. But he didn't miss Harmony's extra-long glare at him, staring, staring, staring... He could tell by the look on her face she knew something was wrong. But he appreciated her saving his ass. Maybe she did it because he helped her with her recovery. Hopefully, that's why she did it...

"I'm Lillian Armana. I won the tournament," the girl beside Theodamar pointed to herself with her thumbs.

What truly captured Leper's gaze was her radiant red hair, which cascaded in natural waves, serving as a vibrant and eye-catching frame around her face. Depending on the lighting, the shade of red could vary, ranging from a fiery hue to a softer, more subtle tone.

"And I am Brebian Urdent, the King of Tudela," the man at the far end of the table proclaimed.

Brebian sported a short beard and salt-and-pepper black hair on top. Clad in leather attire, Brebian proudly displayed the crest of Tudela—a triangular shield outlined in gold. Within the shield, a bear's maw prominently featured, with two white axes positioned behind its head.

Leper involuntarily shifted his gaze towards the woman sitting alongside Brebian, and he couldn't help but be taken aback by her stunning beauty. The coincidence of having two captivating women in the same room struck him. *Are all the women this beautiful outside of Kordry?* His attention lingered longer than intended. But before he could delve deeper into his musings, Rinawen playfully jabbed him in the ribs, swiftly bringing him back to the present moment.

"I'm Petrovana D'leon. Though I'm no king or queen, I'm a representative of Terynsipple. Here to make sure you idiots don't burn the world down." She grinned.

Leper strained to glimpse the tattoos adorning the woman's hands, sensing she was a shrew. Her elegant dress, partially revealing, featured a base color of forest green with scattered brown splotches.

Leper found himself entranced by her eyes, an enchanting shade of deep purple exuding both depth and soulfulness. Her slender and elegant nose perfectly complemented the contours of her face. Her radiant smile was infectious.

Leper's attention shifted to her long, glossy, flowing black hair, which cascaded down her back, resting at the midpoint. Two braids hung down along both sides of her head, falling straight down. He also noticed intricate runic tattoos on her arms, peeking out from beneath the sleeves of her dress, one of them cut off by the fabric. She gave him a playful wink.

"Well, I believe that's everyone that's supposed to be here, with a few extras. Now that we've been introduced, we're all acquainted except for you, criminal," Theodamar pointed his finger in Leper's direction.

"I'm Leper Xentoth, representing Kordry alongside Queen Rinawen," Leper introduced himself with a nod.

Petrovana's voice carried a playful tone as she chimed in, "I must say, I love yer hat!"

Leper offered a modest smile, his fingers touching the rim of the distinctive hat. "Thank you, but it's more for shaming than for looks."

Petrovana's response was swift and effusive. "Well, it suits you perfectly, so I'd say it should be yer signature look!"

Leper was tired of this damned hat. It garnered entirely too much attention and in all the wrong places. Everyone looked at his head like it was some kind of spectacle. His chest tightened as he glanced at all the eyes meeting his gaze. He swallowed hard. *Just act normal. Just act normal.*

"Let's refocus on the matter at hand," Madislak interjected, his tone suggesting a sense of urgency that surpassed the topic of Leper's hat.

As the group began discussing and recollecting the events that had unfolded in Lantess, along with Nalecht's treacherous attempts, Leper settled into a seat at the table. Pouring himself a glass of water, he attentively listened to the debates and conversations swirling around him. However, a lingering sense of unease persisted, making him acutely aware of feeling out of place once again.

The topic shifted, and Theodamar's cautionary words captured Leper's attention. "One more thing to be wary of. Anyone who has a shard, be on the lookout for Blank Face. Got a magical message. He may be collecting them for Nalecht." Theodamar's warning reverberated through the room. "King Zonoh is dead."

Madislak slammed his fist on the table. "HOW!? We cannot lose any more leaders. Zonoh was the strongest shrew in this world. How does Blank Face waltz in and kill a man as strong as Zonoh? We have to find out what Nalecht's intentions are, and we need to stop them immediately."

Just as Nalecht had said when Leper was with Madislak in Lantess, he wanted to eliminate any threats, and now he has eliminated a very powerful ally of theirs.

"Exactly what's he doin' with all the shards?" Petrovana's voice broke into the conversation.

"Not entirely certain, but we need to unravel it. While he was in Lantess, he mentioned some sort of collective power the shards hold but kept the details to himself," Harmony offered.

"Perhaps capturin' Blank Face could yield some answers." Lillian's suggestion hung in the air.

Theodamar nodded at Lillian, instructing her to safeguard Rinawen.

"What news is there of Kundry?" Theodamar waved a hand towards Rinawen.

Rinawen squared her shoulders. "They are under the control of Crux Or'armwell and stable. Hopefully, it remains that way."

"We must organize our efforts strategically," Theodamar suggested, leaning forward as he addressed the assembled group. "Given the threat we face, we should send a team to head to The Talon while we dispatch reinforcements to Tudela. Our assessment shows that Nalecht's next move could be Tudela before targeting Wen-Tath."

"Indeed," Madislak chimed in, his fingers tapping on the table's surface.

Brebian's voice carried a determined note as he leaned back in his chair, arms crossed. "I've decided to return to my home kingdom. None here can defend it with the same efficiency as I can."

Rinawen, her gaze steady, asserted her contribution. "I agree with Brebian. Tudela is a critical point, and I can offer both my leadership and a contingent of troops. Lep and I will head to Tudela."

Leper's eyes shifted towards Rinawen as he got out of his seat and walked over to her, his expression resolved yet tinged with concern. He understood the potential danger of The Talon and the significance of his unique abilities. "Actually, I can go to The Talon," he added, his gaze meeting Rinawen's. "My knowledge of Theora and nature could be invaluable."

"You will do no such thing." Rinawen stomped her foot and glared at him.

Leper grabbed her shoulders and met her gaze. "Rin, I'm not a child. I've managed on my own until now."

"Fine, do as you please," she stuck her nose in the air, avoiding his gaze. "You've already shown your disregard for following orders."

Leper felt the weight of everyone's eyes on him and Rinawen as their argument unfolded.

Petrovana's voice cut through the atmosphere. "Reckon I'll join you on the journey to The Talon," she declared. "We've had to deal with wanderin' creatures that find themselves on our shores a few times." Her gaze met Leper's once more, a playful wink accompanying her words.

"Of course you will, slut," Lillian retorted, her words cutting through the air with a melodic yet biting tone.

"Jealous, are we, street filth?" Petrovana shot back, her gaze a glaring challenge.

Leper watched the verbal sparring unfold as he curled his toes in his boots. Theodamar's voice intervened, breaking the escalating tension. "Ladies, let's keep this civil. So Rinawen and Brebian to Tudela. Leper and Petrovana to The Talon. Who else is going where? I'll send troops and go with Brebian as well," Theodamar's intervention shifted the focus away from the confrontation.

"Harmony and I will go to The Talon. I'd rather get away from this place for a while. As long as my father and children can take refuge here?" Madislak looked at Theodamar, who nodded in approval.

"I'll be goin' with Brebian too," Lillian added, her voice carrying a note of defiance. "I'll keep an eye on Rinawen. Reckon I'd rather not be around that tramp either," she stated, pointing a finger directly at Petrovana.

Theodamar's voice reasserted itself. "Okay, so four to The Talon and five to Tudela with Brebian."

Harmony spoke up, and Madislak gave his tacit approval. "In fact, that's not all. We stumbled upon a drawing at an abandoned shack near Mount Harbinger... and this." Harmony plopped the cut-off horn on the table as a collective gasp escaped nearly everyone's lips.

His chest stopped moving as he glanced around at everyone's shocked faces. He tried to say something, but his throat caught the words. He slowly started backing away until Rinawen's reassuring grip told him he would be alright.

"What... The...Fuck." Brebian mouthed. "We have to go after them. It is imperative that we do not give them time to organize and plot. We must face this Nalecht threat but also keep our eyes open. If we see one, we deal with it right away."

Theodamar nodded back to Brebian in agreement.

"I think we need to focus on Nalecht and go from there," Rinawen offered.

"Why would you stick up for the Chernzerk!? Do you hate living free? No. Anyone who sees one is to kill it immediately and report it to the rest of us so we can take out the hive before they grow to power again! Who knows how long they've been secretly amassing numbers, waiting to get revenge!" Brebian seethed.

Leper could feel his eyes turning watery. The corners of his mouth turned dry, and the taste of salt lingered on his upper lip, mixed with the sweat that had formed from the anxiety. *Is this really how they view me? Is this really what they think of my kind? He has such hatred in his heart. How can I ever change that?*

Chapter Nine

Leper grabbed ahold of Rinawen, bracing himself after what Brebian said at the meeting. He felt like a massive target had been put on his back. His legs nearly gave out, so he used her for momentary support. None of them even knew a Chernzerk, yet they would kill on sight. Leper nodded his head for the door as he felt his lungs constricting.

He needed to distance himself from the monarchs to prevent further scrutiny of his hat until they departed for The Talon in search of Amarook's shard. He wished they could leave now, but that might rouse even more suspicions about his hat and sudden urgency to leave. Madislak and Harmony already voiced their doubts; he didn't need the others insisting he remove it.

Leper's mind was reeling as Brebian and Theodamar's words echoed in his head. He barely registered Rinawen, leading him out of the castle and into the courtyard. The meeting had gone on for six long hours, the sun now sinking low in the sky. Leper collapsed onto a bench, feeling the warm rays soothe his weary body. He took a deep breath, relishing the fresh air filling his lungs. His hands were shaking. Was it anger? Fear?

"I can't believe you." Rinawen took a seat beside him. "What in Theora's name were you thinking? Running off like that, and now you're going to The Talon with them?"

"Did you not hear them in there, Rinawen? They hate me. They absolutely despise me, and they don't even know me." Leper brushed off whatever she just said.

"Shut up! Don't let anyone hear you say that." Rinawen shook his shoulder. "This is what I was afraid of, Lep. I'll tell them you can't make the trip to The Talon."

"No, I'm going. I can't quit just because it seems a little difficult, Rin. I'm going to The Talon, and I will continue to show them they can trust me. Like they did in Lantess." Leper added. "When it's time. I'll show them the real me."

Rinawen huffed. "You are a stubborn fool, you know that?"

"I need a drink," Leper muttered as he got back up.

They strolled through the residential district, passing by opulent mansions and lavish homes. The streets of Wen-Tath were bustling with people as they made their way to their accommodations, a luxurious inn in the city's heart provided by King Theodamar. He still couldn't help keeping his eyes from darting everywhere, watching every single person's move, fearing they were coming after him.

"Care if I join y'all?" they heard right before they crossed the threshold. Leper turned around to see Lillian hot on their heels.

"Sure." Leper nodded.

"Goin to The Talon, eh?" she poked him in the arm playfully.

"I'd like to go, but reckon I'll go help Brebian. Plus, bein' the person recognized fer endin' Nalecht would be a remarkable notch on my sword," her green eyes twinkled at the sentiment.

"Seemed like you cared little for Petrovana, too?" Rinawen interjected.

Lillian glared at Rinawen. "No."

"You guys have an unpleasant history or something?" Rinawen pried.

"Nah, not exactly, she just..." Lillian looked to the ground, then back to Leper. "Never mind, she ain't worth yer time." She shook her head. "Just be careful around that one?"

"Sure." Leper offered. *If only she knew how careful I had to be around everyone.* Leper tried to shake it out of his mind but could feel everyone staring at the hat. Imagine them finding out who he truly is and the consequences he would face.

"I'm serious. You seem like a nice guy, barrin' that ridiculous hat. Why is it stitched on like that?" She pointed around his head.

"Just a Kordry way for me to carry and show my shame for accidentally burning down a field of grain." Leper glared intently at Rinawen.

"How does one accidentally burn down a field?" Lillian furrowed her brow.

"I know how that sounds. It's not what it seems. But it's in the past. Right now, I want to get to The Talon and get that shard before Nalecht does." Leper walked through the doors of the inn. Trying to change the subject immediately.

Stepping into the Proud Elf Bar and Hotel, Leper marveled at the pristine cleanliness that greeted him. Every surface seemed to glisten, from the sparkling glassware in the cupboards to the impeccable dishes. To the right, he noticed a well-appointed bar area with tall tables and stools, inviting guests to relax, indulge in food and drink, and enjoy the soothing melodies played by a local bard. The gentle plucking of the stringed instrument created an atmosphere of ease and tranquility, providing a respite from the day's tensions.

The tantalizing aroma of mead and cooking meat filled the air, evoking a wave of nostalgia within Leper. It had been a while since he had last encountered such scents, not since he left Kordry, and the fragrance was mesmerizing.

"Y'all thirsty, or ya headin' to bed?" Lillian raised an eyebrow.

"I could definitely go for a drink and something to eat." Leper licked his lips.

Lillian sucked in the air through her nose, "care if I join ya?"

"Feel free. Rin, are you hungry?" Leper turned to Rinawen.

"No, not really. I need to go to my room and contact Larnadix, make sure all is well at home and that he's getting the troops ready," came Rinawen's response.

They walked over and grabbed a seat on one table that had high-back chairs around it. Leper went to the bar, got two glasses of mead, and brought them back to the table. But before he could get to his seat, a drunk stranger approached the seat across from Lillian.

"Mind if I join you?" the stranger belched loudly as he sat.

"That seat's taken. I reckon you better disappear before they find yer body in the garbage," Lillian motioned for him to leave.

"Yeah, taken by me. Say, what's a good-looking girl like yourself doing in a bar like this all alone?" He slurred.

"She's not alone. Get lost," Leper interjected, unable to stay quiet any longer.

"Hahaha. So, you'll hang out with Stupid Hat Man, but not me? I can offer you more than just a gigantic head." His grin grew across his face.

"Last chance, mister. Leave, or yer gonna get beat up by a girl." Lillian's hand moved to the hilt of one of her scimitars just behind her head.

Reluctantly, he got up to leave, slurring and stumbling back to the barkeep.

"Some people," she sighed, taking a sip of her large glass of mead.

"You must get that a lot. In Kordry, it's nothing like this. Just a small town." Leper flicked his eyes to her.

"Terynsipple is kinda like that. But we got so many gosh-dang shrew eccentrics over there. Ain't too many folks come around unless they wanna practice magic," Lillian winced. "Or push their power to its absolute limits."

"I see. We don't have too many shrews in Kordry."

"So how long you gotta wear that hat," she chuckled as she glared at it. Cocking her head to the side.

"A year. Just happened a little over a week ago. So, I have a while to go yet." Leper smiled nervously. *I wonder how she feels about the Chernzerk. Should I even bring it up at this point? She keeps glaring at this hat.*

"Can I get you anything?" An Elven server, her brown curly hair cascading to her shoulders, approached Leper and Lillian.

"I'll have the steak with green beans and corn," Leper ordered as Lillian shook her head no.

"Coming right up!" she hastily retreated to the kitchen.

"So, you won the tournament? Must be pretty good with those," Leper pointed to the scimitars crossed like an X on her back.

"Indeed, I am. Wanna fight?" She taunted playfully.

"Not really. I've had my fill of that lately," he chuckled.

"Well, don't start gettin' comfortable. According to the doom and gloom crew, there's about to be a widespread war. And if Nalecht gets his hands on those shards... well, I'm sure you get the point."

"Yeah, any idea what he wants with all these shards?" Leper grabbed his cup.

"Not exactly. Reckon they got some stupid magical ability to them he's after." She countered, grabbing her glass.

Leper lifted his glass, offering a toast as he clinked it against hers.

"To the winner." He proclaimed.

Lillian effortlessly kicked back her glass, swiftly emptying it without hesitation. Leper, not one to be outdone by anyone, followed suit and finished his drink. Almost instantaneously, he felt the effects of the mead coursing through his veins, the warmth spreading from his belly.

"Wow. Must be potent stuff. I think I'm already feeling the effects." He let out a belch.

"Haha... You lightweight." Lillian burst out laughing.

Leper looked down at the table. "Guess I am. So... what do you make of," he leaned across the middle of the table, "you know... the horn thing?" He rolled his eyes.

Lillian glared at him for a few moments before she leaned back in her chair, staring at his hat. "I think we don't know. Reckon killin' them on sight is a little hasty. Why do you ask? That hat hidin' somethin' else?"

Leper could feel her staring now. He signaled for another drink, maybe two or three. A lump caught in his throat. His pulse went from normal to a gallop instantly.

"No, of course not..." He chuckled awkwardly. "I was just curious if you shared the same viewpoint as Rinawen and I on the subject."

She leaned forward again, still looking at the hat. "What viewpoint is that exactly?"

Leper swallowed hard, hoping for a distraction. *Why even say anything? This was going well. Idiot. Fool*

"Well, that stuff happened hundreds of years ago, you know. How do we really know what they were like? Maybe Pasileveo is like Nalecht... Just a total asshole." Leper shrugged his shoulders.

Lillian erupted in laughter. "You should see the look on yer face."

The server approached their table, carrying a sizzling plate topped with a juicy steak accompanied by sides of green beans and corn. The delectable aroma wafted through the air. Not wasting a moment, he eagerly began devouring the food before him, relishing each bite. In a display of politeness, he extended a forkful of steak to Lillian, who willingly accepted the offering. The steak was perfectly cooked, tender, and juicy, with a savory seasoning that added a burst of flavor. The green beans were fresh, while the corn was sweet and buttery. Leper savored each bite, letting the flavors dance on his palate before swallowing and reaching for more.

"That was scrumptious," he wiped his mouth.

"Must've been. So... Where you from exactly? I know Kordry and all, but you don't look elvish. Is Rinawen your wife or girlfriend, or what's goin' on there?" Lillian raised a curious brow.

Feelings he hadn't experienced in a long time surfaced, but he quickly pushed them down as far as possible. Back to the pit where they needed to stay... forever. Leper found himself drawn into Lillian's large, captivating green eyes, their beauty mesmerizing him. Whether it was the influence of the mead or simply his own nature, he couldn't help but feel an unusual sense of trust towards her. There was an unexplainable comfort he felt in her presence, something that made him instinctively at ease.

"It's kind of a long story," Leper said.

"Well, we got til mornin'," Lillian smiled playfully.

"She's not my blood relative, but her mother took me in at a young age, and yeah, she's more like a sister to me now. But definitely not married or girlfriend," Leper chuckled, saying that. If only.

"So if she's not yer blood relative, who's yer parents?" She blurted.

"Well..."

Leper's gaze shifted downward, his thoughts turning to a distant and painful memory—the abandonment by his parents when he was just a baby. It had been a while since he allowed himself to dwell on those thoughts, and the flood of emotions caught him off guard. The weight of that past event resurfaced, reminding him of the lingering pain and unanswered questions that still haunted him.

"I don't really know who my parents are. I was plucked out of the ocean by a crew of fishermen off the coast of Kordry. Rinawen was on board. Apparently, they took pity on me, and raised me as their own," Leper's voice was hoarse.

"I'm sorry I asked. I didn't realize." Lillian placed her calloused hand on top of his on the table.

"Ya, kind of another reason I'm doing this. I want to know what piece of shit dumps their baby in the ocean on a boat and leaves," his voice choppy. "What about you? Why are you helping?"

"I'm usin' this opportunity to get out of Terynsipple. I'm so sick and tired of shrews." Lillian grinned as she glanced at the table. "Plus... Never mind, not important right now."

Leper took another sip of mead. "Are they really that bad in Terynsipple?"

"Those dumb sumbitches put themselves through the wringer just to do it," Lillian gazing deeply into Leper's eyes.

"Can I tell you something? Without you getting weird about it?" Leper squeezed her hand.

"Sounds weird already." an enormous grin crawled across her face. "I might like weird."

"I have this odd sense of comfort around you. Maybe it's the mead talking." Leper said as he realized he hadn't even thought about what Brebian and Theodamar had said at the end of that meeting.

"That's not weird at all. Can I tell you somethin'?"

Leper nodded. "Sure."

"Oddly, I reckon I feel the same. Even with that goofy ass hat." She chuckled, glancing at the hat again.

Both Leper and Lillian burst into laughter. As the evening wore on, they found themselves engrossed in conversation, accompanied by continued indulgence in their drinks. Lost in the moment, Leper suddenly realized the darkness that had enveloped the surroundings. The realization struck him he needed to rest, as he had an early morning ahead of him. Reluctantly, he acknowledged the need to retire for the night despite the reluctance that tugged at his heart.

Leper grinned at Lillian, appreciating the depth of their conversation. "Well, Lillian, this has been quite an excellent conversation," he remarked, his voice tinged with a touch of playful regret.

"I wish I were going with y'all." Their laughter erupted once more as Leper amusingly attempted to imitate Lillian's distinctive accent.

"Me too, we'd make a good team," Lillian said.

Leper got up to go to his room, the mead making him wobble slightly as he stood.

"Easy there. Think you can find yer room?" She held her hand out.

"Ya, I think so," Leper started wobbling towards the stairs. He felt a rough hand grasp his elbow.

"Let me help you," Lillian looked him in the eye.

"Thanks."

Lillian helped him up the stairs and to his room. After fumbling with the key a few times, the door flung open.

"Well, this is it," Leper began, his words trailing off as he prepared to bid Lillian farewell. However, before he could finish his sentence, Lillian surprised him by leaning in and planting a kiss on his lips. Instantly, a mixture of emotions overwhelmed Leper. His initial instinct was to pull away.

Yet, after a moment of hesitation, something within him shifted. Leper reciprocated the kiss, his hand gently cupping Lillian's cheek. As their embrace deepened, panic crept into his thoughts. Being a Chernzerk, he worried she might inadvertently reach for his head and grab a handful of horn. Though a part of him yearned to push through the fear and seize the moment, he ultimately realized that it went against his true nature. Leper pulled back, breaking the kiss.

"I can't." He shook his head.

"What!?" Lillian crossed her arms across her chest.

"I'm sorry. This was a lovely evening. I feel like we got to know each other a little. But you don't know me. I don't know you." Leper looked back at the bed.

"Yer certainly raised different in Kordry, ain't ya?" Lillian's words lingered in the air, echoing in Leper's mind.

He searched for the right response, his mouth opening, but no words forming on his tongue. Silence hung heavy between them, leaving Leper feeling vulnerable and unsure.

As if sensing his struggle, Lillian spoke again, her tone tinged with resignation.

"Maybe it's fer the best. Good luck to y'all... Don't come back without that shard." With those final words, Lillian turned and walked away, leaving Leper standing there in a bewildered state. The sound of the door slamming shut reverberated through the room.

How could I be so stupid? Leper perched on the edge of his bed, the gentle rays of a new day filtering through the partially drawn blinds. Although he didn't feel his best, he also didn't feel terribly ill, considering the previous night's indulgences. He had experienced many mornings where the aftermath of drinking had left him feeling far worse. As he contemplated the events with Lillian, a sense of remorse washed over him, and he buried his face in his hands, wondering if she would ever find it in her heart to forgive him.

As he readied himself for his journey on The Talon, a small smile crept onto his face. Perhaps this would be an opportunity to deepen his bond with Madislak and Harmony and earn a place within their group as a valuable member. Slowly but surely, he hoped to gain their trust and prove his worth. Still, a small part of him couldn't help but wonder if there was more Chernzerk on The Talon, along with the dragons, and what complications that would bring should they encounter another like him. A knock on the door disrupted his concentration, drawing his attention away from his internal musings.

"Come in," his voice groggy.

Rinawen burst through the door, closing it tightly behind her.

She pointed an accusatory finger at him. "What were you doing last night?"

"Just shared some drinks and a conversation with Lillian." Leper shrugged.

"You sure you shared nothing else? I saw you guys all googly-eyed with each other. I also heard her slam the door when she left here." Rinawen steamed.

"Well, that's your answer, isn't it?" Leper's tongue still tingled with the sweet tang of mead from the night before.

"You have GOT to be more careful, Lep." She put her hands on her hips. "You can't be out here traipsing around with all the females until it's safe for you to take that stupid hat off!"

"Then give me a reason to not want to do that!" Leper roared, rising from the bed.

Immediate regret... He knew better. He knew it never would've worked between him and Rinawen. They had already had this discussion years ago. But he didn't stop thinking about it since Lillian asked him about his relationship with Rinawen.

"You know that's not possible." Her face turned pink as she gritted her teeth. "I can't believe you said that to me right now when we agreed to..." the words trailed off as she shook her head, rubbing her forehead.

"I know, I'm sorry. I shouldn't have said that, but I don't want to be stuck by myself wondering when the next time you, Zanera, or Kelindra will come along... You know?" his voice was dry and raspy.

Rinawen pulled him in for a hug. "I know. When I was your age, I was going to other cities, meeting kings and queens. I just don't think you understand that if you mess up or say the wrong thing or take off that hat, you are likely dead."

"Well, it shouldn't be that way. I swear that's going to change. I don't know how yet, but I will change it!" Leper puffed his chest.

Rinawen smiled, gazing up at him. "I seriously hope you can do just that. But until that point, you cannot parade around like some normal person. Even with that hat. You can always come back, and I promise once this war is over, we will work on Chernzerk acceptance."

"Fine. I got to get to the chariot. Madislak and Harmony are probably waiting." Leper locked eyes with her, then kissed her forehead. "And no, I'm not going back now. Love you, Rin."

"Love you too, Lep." She squeezed her arms around him.

Leper embraced Rinawen tightly, cherishing the warmth of their parting hug before swiftly making his way through the doorway. As he glanced towards Lillian's door, he noticed it remained closed, leaving their unresolved conversation hanging in the air. Even at this early hour, the bustling streets were alive with the presence of numerous people going about their daily routines. The tantalizing scent of eggs, sausage, and pancakes wafted through the air, teasing his senses and causing his stomach to growl in hunger. A pang of regret for not grabbing a bite to eat at the inn before leaving tugged at him.

As he approached the gates, the sight of Madislak, Harmony, and Petrovana already settled inside the chariot greeted him. They had expected his arrival, ready and waiting to embark on their next journey. The morning sun blazed brilliantly, causing him to squint and shield his eyes from its harsh rays. The effects of last night's drinking lingered with a vengeance, pounding through his head and making him regret his choices.

"Mornin' sleepyhead," Petrovana smiled at him. "Long night?"

"Yup." Leper marched straight to the chariot, hopped in, and sat down at the back.

"Guess you're ready, then?" Madislak glanced at Leper from the driver's bench.

"Yup." Leper quipped.

Petrovana settled herself beside Leper, catching his attention with her noticeably different attire from the previous day. She now donned a green long-sleeve shirt beneath a sturdy leather vest paired with fitting leather pants. Very tight pants. He couldn't keep his eyes from wandering to her long, beautiful legs and backside. Holstered on her side were two daggers.

Madislak, having completed his own tasks, tossed a couple of bags he had set beside him on the floor. He opened one bag and threw some items towards Leper.

"For you." He grinned.

"What is it?" Leper started unfolding the cloth.

Madislak tapped it with his finger. "Hardened leather for protection. I noticed you don't exactly wear much for protection, so I got you a few things. Plus, we might need it if we run into the owner of that horn over there."

Harmony scoffed. "Right. Can never be too safe, and unfortunately, we got to walk around with that ridiculous beacon on your head. Perhaps we should see if Rinawen will let us take it off really quick?" She stared at his hat.

"Thank you." Leper looked through the items. "And no. That's okay."

Among the items Madislak had given him was a hardened leather vest designed to offer protection to both the front and back. There were thigh guards and shin guards intended to safeguard his lower limbs. Leper wasted no time in securing each piece of armor, carefully strapping them into place. He understood the importance of equipping himself.

"Why? It's almost like you want to keep it on?" Madislak scowled.

I do want to keep it on because I don't want to die here. His pulse quickened again with the constant questions about the hat.

Leper shrugged, trying to play it cool. "Nah. It's really not that bad once you get used to it. Plus, aren't we running late?"

"I think it looks amazin'. Leave it." Petrovana grinned.

Leper locked eyes with Madislak. "Sorry for my shortness. I just had a long night last night. Then Rinawen this morning... Never mind. How'd you guys do last night?"

"I guess if you don't mind being the target, then let's get going." Harmony blurted. "But one day, Leper, we're going to get a glimpse of what's beneath that hat!"

Leper's throat tightened as he lied. "That won't be an issue."

The chariot began its ascent to the skies to latch on to an essence thread. Rays of moonlight struck the gemstone attached to the bottom of the chariot that controlled the flight pattern once airborne. The sapphire anchored to the bottom hummed to life.

"Considering the recent events, I slept as well as I could," Madislak nodded.

"I feel completely recovered from my overuse of magic the other day," Harmony nodded to Leper.

Leper flicked his eyes to Petrovana. "And you?"

"Lil ole me?" Petrovana put her hand on her chest. "I slept just fine."

Leper found himself unable to resist the allure of Petrovana's captivating, large purple eyes. In their depths, he felt an unspoken connection, a bond that threatened to unravel the walls he had carefully built around his heart. However, he reminded himself of the consequences of letting his emotions consume him once more, the painful aftermath of his encounter with Lillian still fresh in his memory. Determined not to repeat the same mistakes, Leper fortified his resolve, vowing to keep his emotions in check and maintain his composure.

"Damnit!" Harmony erupted.

"What?" Madislak jerked the buggy.

"I needed to visit the shrine of Theora and meditate. I haven't visited in a while, and I feel I'm ready for my next challenge," she sighed heavily. "Suppose I'll have to wait until we get back. Last night would've been perfect."

Petrovana let out a sigh. "Reckon it gets very exhaustin'. Which pinnacle are you at, if ya don't mind my askin'?"

Harmony glanced at Petrovana. "I'll be moving up to three if I pass."

"How old are you?" Petrovana glanced at Harmony.

"Twenty-two." Harmony quickly replied.

"Damn, yer ahead of where I was, and you have psyrenth magic, too."

Harmony grinned. "Well, I have Madislak to thank. I've been his shrew for four years now, and he's made sure I've had everything I needed to study and learn the ways of the moons."

Leper understood the reference made by Harmony, the magical influence exerted by the four moons that encircled Kalazaar. Each moon held the power to give a distinct type of magic to the world. He was confident in his knowledge of four types of magic granted by the moons: elemental magic, the ability to manipulate and control the natural elements; healing magic, which remained exclusive to the dwarves; and psyrenth magic, a domain where mind manipulation and necromancy reigned supreme. Lastly, vitalis magic is used to call protective shields or shells and talk to animals. These were the known manifestations of the moon's magical energies, each holding its own allure and potential for both light and darkness.

"How long does that take, Harmony?" Leper turned his gaze to her, hoping this would be an opportunity to show his worth again.

"Oh, maybe thirty minutes for the actual process, depending on the challenge Theora gives me. It's the recovery period that takes the longest. I could manage on two or three hours of sleep, but eight hours is best for full recovery," Harmony explained.

Leper glanced towards the front of the chariot. "Well, I think I can help you meditate if we have the time to complete it, Madislak?"

"Huh?" Madislak turned around briefly, unaware that anyone was addressing him.

"How long's the trip?" Leper chuckled.

"About three or four hours, depending on the weather and any other obstacles," Madislak confirmed.

"It's up to you, Harmony." Leper looked back at Harmony.

Harmony's face scrunched together. "Seriously, you can do that? You don't use magic, so how do you have access to her trials?"

"I don't have access to her trials. We worship Theora in Kordry. She's kind of our patron deity. We're native farmers, after all," Leper clarified.

She bobbed her head up and down. "Umm... yeah, that sounds outstanding, if you don't mind."

"You're not going to accidentally blast off an ice shard and derail the ship, are you?" Leper grinned.

"Haha, no, that's not how it works. I'll be here physically but with Theora consciously. It gets pretty intense inside her trials. I might sweat, shake, bleed." She trailed off.

"Alright then. Sit on the floor and take my hands," Leper settled onto the chariot's floor.

"Wait," Harmony demanded as she lowered her voice almost to a whisper. "Judging by Rinawen's lack of knowledge about your crimes the other day, it doesn't seem like she even knew you were a criminal?"

Shit. She noticed.

Leper swallowed hard. "I... Larnadix demanded the punishment when she went to the penta-annual meeting." He lied.

Harmony's scrutinizing gaze made Leper's heart thrum so loudly he could swear they could hear it.

Finally, she let out a sigh. "Fine." was all she said.

Leper gently laid his chakrams on the floor of the flying chariot, positioning them at the center between himself and Harmony. These remarkable weapons were a cherished gift from Rinawen, bestowed upon him when he was just twelve years old, soon after he had embraced the honor of becoming a disciple of Theora. While he primarily employed them as his trusty weapons, they held a more profound significance to him—they served as a conduit for communion with Theora, the revered goddess of magic and nature. Whenever he sought guidance or wished to communicate with the divine, the chakrams became his spiritual anchor, bridging the gap between him and the realm of the goddess.

"Okay, close your eyes and imagine where you would normally see her," Leper instructed, and Harmony followed his every instruction.

"Our lady Theora. Your student Harmony seeks an audience with your undeniable presence." Leper felt Harmony's hands go limp in his.

Leper silently reassured himself, feeling a sense of completion after placing his hands in Harmony's for the brief communion. Slowly, he withdrew his hands from hers, rejoining Petrovana on the back seat of the chariot. Observing her closely, he noticed her eyes twitching under her closed eyelids, a sign of the magic taking hold. In mere moments, beads of sweat formed on her brow and upper arms, gradually spreading across her entire face. Leper knew Harmony was delving deep into the magic, tapping into its potent forces, and he maintained a watchful eye, ready to offer any support she might need during this profound experience. Yet he couldn't shake his curiosity about what she might endure.

"What's it like in those trials?" Leper turned to Petrovana.

"Depends, really. Some of them test yer fortitude by makin' you run from somethin' you can't kill. Some yer strength, intelligence, candor, could be anythin' really."

"I see. What spells do you have?" He gazed at her palms.

Petrovana turned her hands over, offering Leper a glimpse of the unique symbols etched on each palm. On her right hand, a fiery emblem caught his attention, and he instantly recognized it as a symbol of fire magic. On her left hand, another distinctive symbol appeared, resembling an ice spike similar to the one Harmony possessed.

He pointed to her hands. "Fire and ice, opposites. Do you choose, or is it just given to you?"

"You get to choose. The power or types of powerful spells only become an option, dependin' on yer performance in those trials."

Leper tilted his head. "What's the hardest one to get?"

"Psyrenth magic. Which I reckon, other than Harmony here, I've only seen it from Zonoh and Borlden." She pointed to Harmony.

Leper gazed into her eyes. "Yeah, seems like a suitable type of magic to keep locked away. And does the magic come from Theora for you shrews or from the moons?"

"Reckon it comes from the moons. Though each moon isn't always visible, the magic from them still travels to us via light. Our skin absorbs it, converts it to the magic you see us sendin' out of our palms. It's the conversion from light to magic that wears on shrews."

"Ahh... Okay... So, the moon refills your magic aura when you use it. That's why the tattoo goes gray?" Leper mused, cupping his chin in his hand. "We have these small devices we use to filter the magic from the moon's phases when they're most prominent. Then we use that magic to create useful potions and such."

"Reckon it works the same way for us. I'd love to go to one of the moons and stand on the surface. See how all that wonderful magic is made." Petrovana's eyes lingered on the sky outside the window.

"Ahh, that's right. Shrew eccentrics. Are you folks really that obsessed with magic?" Leper wondered aloud.

"Ain't nothin' wrong with lovin' the idea of magic or appreciatin' what you can do with it. Just like when Harmony here showed that Chernzerk horn. Ain't nothin' wrong with them. In fact, I think they might hold the key to understandin' why society fell apart durin' their time," Petrovana sweetly explained.

"Sure, they might hold the key to why society fell apart—because they were tyrannical dragon-riding killers with no empathy for life," Madislak interjected, his voice laced with anger. "They enslaved an entire nation and marched them north to destroy the other half of the world. How are you not fearful they could do that again? I don't want to be a damn slave!"

Petrovana's expression shifted from curiosity to irritation. "How do you know that, Madislak? Have you ever seen one? Spoken to one? No. All we know is what's written in those books, and someone like you could've penned those tales. I believe the answers lie within the mountain we're headin' to."

"Other than Enoch and Ghendala, what did they do? Nalecht isn't much different right now from their actions. Should we kill all the elves?" Leper inquired.

"Well, no..." Madislak stammered. "That's different. Elves can't talk to and manipulate the dragons for their own musings. Or at least if they could, they didn't. Don't tell me you think like she does? Just let these people roam free and unchecked?"

"I mean. If they don't act like Nalecht, I don't see why they need to die just because some of their ancestors were bad people," Leper countered.

"Madislak, let me ask you this," Petrovana interrupted. "Do you think that because Nalecht removed yer father from the throne and put you on the throne of Lantess, we should do that when yer son is old enough to rule?"

Madislak's head whipped around. "How did you know..." The buggy wobbled out of control before he turned back around and regained control. "That's family business and you have no right sticking your nose in it. I suggest you stand down right now before I have you thrown in prison."

"Like I said. Reckon it's different when yer the one bein' targeted." Petrovana quipped.

Madislak slammed the front panel. "Everyone just shut the fuck up. Let's finish this ride in peace."

As Petrovana's comment hung in the air, an uncomfortable silence settled over the chariot. Leper sensed that the conversation was heading towards an argument, and he decided it was best to stay out of it. Amid the silence, a small glimmer of relief washed over him. Petrovana had openly expressed her stance on not harming a Chernzerk if she encountered one. It was a reassuring revelation that there were people who didn't believe in the wholesale eradication of his kind. This realization lifted a weight off

Leper's shoulders, offering him some comfort and hope that perhaps the world wasn't as hostile as he had initially perceived.

With a deep breath, he allowed himself to relax a little, knowing that he was among a diverse group of individuals, each with their own unique perspectives and beliefs. Leper found solace in knowing he wasn't alone in seeking understanding and acceptance of his kind.

Chapter Ten

L eper noticed Petrovana looking at his hat again. If only he could get rid of this dumb thing and these horns and not have to constantly worry about all the looks and glares. The last thing he needed was for this thing to come off after the conversation they'd just had with Madislak not thirty minutes ago. Leper desperately wished they were on The Talon already, searching for the shard of Amarook. Yet he remained cooped up in this chariot with all the attention on him. With the window open, he heard the gentle rush of wind, accompanied by the distant cry of seagulls. The ocean breeze carried with it the aroma of briny saltwater, mingling with the clean, crisp scent of fresh air.

"I know it's dumb. I wish I could take it off," Leper admitted sheepishly.

"We're not in Kordry right now. No one would know." Petrovana reached out her hand to touch it, but Leper quickly pulled his head back.

"I just want to feel the stitches," she explained.

"Just don't push too hard or tug. It hurts a lot more than you'd think when it moves." Leper put his head a little closer to her.

As Petrovana's fingers delicately traced the stitches of the hat that Leper had sewn onto his head, a curious mix of sensations washed over him. It was an unusual feeling, yet surprisingly comforting as if her touch somehow connected with the very essence of who he was. Her gentle exploration continued, moving all the way around his head. He couldn't help but marvel at the tenderness with which she handled the stitches. Strangely, the act of feeling those stitches seemed to have an unexpected effect on the pain he had been enduring. As her fingers moved, it was as if a subtle magic emanated from her touch, soothing the discomfort and easing the ache that had plagued him lately.

At that moment, as Petrovana's touch continued to caress his head, he felt a deep sense of connection with her. It was as if she understood the significance of those stitches, of the hat that had become a part of him. He felt a surge of gratitude towards her for acknowledging and embracing this peculiar aspect of his identity. With a newfound sense of calm, Leper closed his eyes, allowing himself to fully immerse in the comforting sensation of her soft touch. In this shared moment of intimacy, he felt a special bond forming between them, one that transcended words and embraced the unspoken understanding of kindred spirits.

"Well, what do you say?" Petrovana gazed deeply into his eyes.

"I say that's enough," Leper stated firmly.

She giggled. "No, dummy. Why don't we take off yer hat?"

"I can't do that. I've never lied to Rin and never will. Plus, I'd have to sew it back on, and that hurts." Leper shook his head no.

"I think you should just take the hat off and leave it off." Madislak interrupted.

"Someday," Leper agreed, his eyes filled with hope as he looked out the window. He envisioned a future where he could live among his friends without this ridiculous hat, hoping they would openly accept his Chernzerk features.

Harmony gasped, awakening in apparent distress. Her face was flushed and glistening with sweat, and he noticed a small trickle of blood coming from her eyes. Concern etched his features as he offered her a cloth to wipe away the discomfort.

Her legs trembled beneath her as she attempted to stand, but they betrayed her, leaving her unable to rise on her own. Leper stepped forward, lending a supportive hand to help her back into her seat. He understood the toll that magic could take on her, and he wished there was more he could do to ease her pain.

From his trusty pack of vials, he retrieved a carefully prepared concoction designed to assist with exhaustion. He opted for a more potent mixture. He set the pouch on the bench where he was sitting. Uncorking the vial, he handed it to Harmony with a gentle smile, hoping that it would provide her some relief.

"Here, take this. It should help," Leper said softly, offering the vial to Harmony.

"You sure you're not trying to poison me?" She joked.

"Trust me, if I wanted to poison you, it would've been the first vial I gave you. This one is just a little more potent." He grinned back at her.

"I know. I'm just joking with you. I trust you." She smiled softly at him.

Harmony bravely chugged down the potion, her initial smile fading as the taste hit her senses. Leper couldn't help but chuckle at her reaction, finding humor in her brave attempt to finish the entire vial despite its unappealing taste.

"Oh, I should have warned you about that," Leper said between fits of laughter. "It's disgusting."

Harmony shot him a playful glare, rolling her eyes at his amusement. Despite the bitter aftertaste, she seemed relieved that the potion might bring some much-needed relief to her exhausted body. Feeling a sense of camaraderie with Harmony, Leper couldn't help but smile warmly at her.

"Well, I think I'm already feeling rested…" She looked at Madislak. "Still, I'm going to rest my eyes."

Leper nodded in agreement as he listened to Harmony's words. The next three hours were silent as they approached The Talon. An enormous mountain captivated him, its majestic presence stretching from one end of the island to the other, almost touching the clouds. The jagged cliffs and stone pathways encircling the mountain only added to its imposing aura. Leper couldn't help but feel a mix of excitement and trepidation. The

Talon held so much mystery and danger, and he was eager to uncover its secrets, yet he also knew the risks that lay ahead.

He couldn't shake the feeling that destiny was calling him to this place to confront the truths hidden within The Talon's depths.

"You keep notes in here?" Petrovana said as she pulled out a piece of paper from Leper's trusted pack of vials.

Shit. I knew I shouldn't have asked Zanera and Kelindra to keep the container filled.

"No!" Leper strained to get the paper as Petrovana smiled and tugged it out of his reach.

"Is it a love note?" She teased. "Let's read it out loud."

"Petrovana..." Leper glared at her. "Just give me the paper, please."

"C'mon. Yer no fun. Where's yer sense of adventure?" She winked at him.

Leper didn't want her to read whatever was on that paper. Yet, he didn't want to make it painstakingly obvious that he was indeed hiding something. Depending on who wrote it, it could have some very unfortunate information.

"Fine. But why don't you let me read it to you guys?" Leper suggested.

"Nope. I think she should read it." Harmony joined in the teasing.

Leper winced.

"Mr. Leper, how dare you leave without saying bye! I will have to teach you a lesson in manners when you return. Zanera and I will keep your container full. I hope you come home soon. Until then. Horn shake." Petrovana read aloud and then giggled. "Doesn't look like they added anything to the case, it's only got five left."

Leper's chest constricted quickly.

Harmony burst out laughing, "What on earth is a horn shake? And what manner of friends do you have?"

Leper swallowed hard. "Well, that was Kelindra. She is eight years old. She made up this horn shake thing where we take bull horns and..." Leper trailed off, tired of trying to explain it. "It's just our special type of hand-shake. Can't I leave some parts of my life out of our discussions?" He grabbed the note and tossed it back in his bag as he huffed. Leper hung his head. A liar. That's all he ever would be with this hat, with himself. Everything...Everything he did and said was nothing but a filthy lie.

"Calm down. We're just messin' with you. It's cute she looks up to you like that," Petrovana squeezed his forearm as he sat back down beside her.

"Let's just land this damn chariot and do what we came here for." Leper glared at them.

As the flying chariot descended towards The Talon, Leper couldn't help but marvel at the breathtaking beauty of the island. The trees and vegetation displayed a mesmerizing array of colors unlike anything he had seen before. Shades of purple, pink, blue, and vibrant oranges and yellows adorned the landscape, creating a surreal and enchanting scenery. The forest below was unlike any he had encountered in his few travels, with trees that soared to towering heights. Their leaves were colossal, large enough for the entire group to use as a hammock, and still have space between them. Leper's amazement grew as he observed the sheer size and magnificence of these trees, which stood like ancient guardians of the island.

But what truly captivated him was the interconnected network of leaves high in the air. Some of the large leaves joined together, forming a magical pathway suspended amidst the canopy. It was as if nature had created its own enchanting bridges, inviting travelers to explore this wondrous realm. For someone who cherished nature, like Leper, the sight was a dream come true. The vibrant colors and extraordinary vegetation ignited a sense of excitement and wonder within him. He was eager to immerse himself in this new world, to explore the mysteries that awaited them within The Talon's heart.

"I don't recognize a lot of these plants and trees," Leper pointed out, indicating several on the ground.

"Uh oh," Madislak blurted.

"What?" Petrovana quickly rose to her feet.

"We've got company." Madislak nodded his head toward the base of the mountain.

"Xaneth Harbor... Tamara. That bitch is workin' with Nalecht for the shard," Petrovana seethed.

"Damn it." Madislak scanned for a suitable landing spot.

"Hopefully, they haven't seen us. Quickly, choose one of those entrances and land. We need to get out of the sky," Leper instructed.

Petrovana's sharp eye guided them to a flat area on The Talon's surface, marked by two cave entrances. As the chariot landed, Leper couldn't help but feel a mix of anticipation and nervousness.

Leper jumped out of the chariot first, holding the door for the others. Madislak and Petrovana had already taken out their spyglasses. They rushed over to the cliff edge, intently peering down at the base of the mountain to monitor Queen Tamara's activities. After searching for about two hours, they finally found a suitable spot to land and hide where they could observe the people on the surface of The Talon below. The vibrant and abundant vegetation provided them with some much-needed cover. Though Tamara being here certainly complicated matters, now they would have to race against her to find and acquire the shard of Amarook. Rumored to revive one person or thing. All of Kalazaar trembled at the mere mention of Tamara, knowing she was Nalecht's chosen and unwavering right hand. The presence of the shard in her possession could only mean one thing: it belonged to Nalecht, and with it came unspeakable power and influence that sent shivers down the spines of all who dared to oppose them. Leper waited for Harmony to step out of the door before grabbing her arm, seeking a private moment away from Madislak and Petrovana's ears.

"Here, take this," Leper dug into his bag of vials again.

"What is this one? How do you keep all these on you?" She asked, smiling back at him.

Leper handed her a vial with a vibrant yellow tint. "This one is sort of a revival potion. It's imperative you pour this either on the mortal wound or in their mouth before three minutes go by, or they're dead."

"Leper, I don't know if I can accept this. That's very generous of you, but I know how long those take to make, and it takes years." She pushed his hand back.

Leper placed it in her palm and closed her fingers. "No, you take this one. I have one more. I trust your judgment the most out of anyone here. Just please take it, and if something happens, use it when you feel it's needed."

"Well, thank you. I won't let it go to waste." Harmony tucked the vial into the pouch on her side. "You never told me where you keep all these."

"Right, I have a magic bag. It's connected to my vial case at home. I just open this thing up, and if there are still vials in my house, they're here for me to grab. So, they're not actually in the bag itself." Leper smiled. Hoping this would deepen the connection he worked tirelessly to form with Harmony and Madislak.

"You have some tricks, I see." Harmony flicked her eyes at him.

"They're funnelin' in, lookin' for the shard. It must be in the mountain somewhere," Petrovana called out.

Leper peered through his spyglass, carefully assessing the situation below. The once bright sun had disappeared, swallowed up by thick, dark clouds that hovered ominously in the sky. The air was heavy with anticipation as the threat of rain loomed overhead, ready to burst forth at any moment. He estimated approximately two thousand troops, some making their way into the mountain, while others had established a camp on the ground where Queen Tamara likely stayed.

Curiously, several colossal beasts roamed the area, but they seemed to coexist with the camp without attacking. One creature caught his attention with its unique triangular face, rectangular eyes, and long, scrawny arms ending in razor-sharp talons. Its pitch-black eyes exuded an aura of menace, resembling the embodiment of death itself. As he continued observing, Leper inhaled deeply, savoring the crisp scent of spring water and the essence of the mountains. The natural beauty of the surroundings juxtaposed with the presence of danger and intrigue, heightening his senses and focus on the task ahead. Guard's approaching footsteps created a pounding sound as they marched about.

"Whoa, would you just look at the size of those beasts? But why the hesitation? Why aren't they tearing into them?" Madislak's finger pointed at the looming creatures.

The very ground quivered beneath them, sending shivers up Leper's spine.

"Wait, a second. Is this some kind of live volcano we've stumbled upon?" Harmony's eyes swept the horizon.

A deepening rumble echoed, jolting Leper into a frantic search for cover. His heart raced, each tremor intensifying his pulse. He struggled to keep his footing as the earth roared and convulsed. Desperation etched across his face as he scrambled for a safe haven, a place to shield himself from the growing maelstrom.

"Come on, let's make a swift retreat to the chariot and bolt from here. We'll scout out a safer location," Madislak urged, already making his way toward the waiting chariot.

Leper's heart pounded as he followed Madislak, the fear rising within him. Suddenly, the world erupted into chaos, and the mountainside burst open with a deafening explosion. The ground shook violently, throwing them all to the ground amidst a shower of rocks and debris. The mountain trapped the chariot, lodging it against its side.

But what emerged from the newly formed chasm was far worse than any volcanic eruption. A monstrous dragon flew by, its bronzed scales gleaming despite the lack of sunlight. Leper's breath caught in his throat as he beheld the immense creature, its catlike eyes a mesmerizing deep gold with a menacing red outline. Spikes ran down its back and tail, while deadly horns on its head curved forward like spears. A thundering roar followed that sent shivers down his spine, scattering all creatures below in terrified retreat. The very sight of the dragon sent waves of fear through Leper's body.

Like a shimmering bronze spear, the magnificent dragon flew down to the encampment, swerving gracefully around the trees and plowing over the small ones it couldn't get by. All of them grabbed their spy glasses. Leper peered through his spyglass, his mouth agape at the spectacle. Not at the dragon this time, but at what was riding on top of the dragon. A Chernzerk, just like him, jumped off its back, wielding the shard of Amarook and two axes across his back.

"That must be the one from the picture," Harmony muttered. "Working for the enemy. Just as you suspected, Madislak."

"Gods damn it. He's already got a dragon, and he's working for Tamara. This is just like Brebian said: if only we'd gotten here sooner, maybe we could have killed him and not had to worry about this entire situation." Madislak seethed.

"No..." Harmony shook her head. "He's not missing any horns, though... Does that mean?" She rubbed her temples. "There's more than him? How many are there?"

"Reckon you don't understand his circumstances there, mighty King. How do you know he isn't bein' forced to do that?" Petrovana quipped, paying no heed to Harmony's musings.

"How the hell do you force someone who can manipulate dragons to join your side?" Madislak countered sharply.

"We can't linger long, guys. They have the shard of Amarook. There's about two thousand people down there, a dragon, a Chernzerk. The dragons have an innate sense of this island and likely already know we're here. At least, that's what I understand from what I read about them. I didn't realize they were still alive and well." Harmony sputtered. "Besides, even if we could get the shard of Amarook, it doesn't exactly give great destructive power. It can bring someone back to life, but I don't think it's worth risking a try for."

"What do you think, Leper?" Petrovana asked, setting her hand on his shoulder.

"Unbelievable..." Leper mouthed, not realizing he was talking out loud. "I'm not the only..." Catching himself, he quickly closed his mouth.

He heard a commotion beside him. Turning to face Madislak, he saw the warrior with his sword drawn, pointing it directly at his heart. The intensity in Madislak's eyes was hard to ignore, and Leper knew he had to tread carefully.

"Finish that fucking sentence." Madislak's intense gaze blared through him.

Leighth swiftly hopped into the chariot, taking her position on one side to make space for Blank Face. As he joined her with a nimble leap, she stole a quick glance in his direction. A nod of understanding exchanged between them. To get this chariot airborne and wherever Blank Face needed to claim his reward.

"C'mon, start pushing levers." He began moving things around.

Leighth's heart raced as she fumbled with the levers, trying to maneuver the chariot into action. She first pushed the middle lever up, but to her dismay, the chariot only crackled and groaned, remaining stationary. Undeterred, she quickly put it back in its place and turned her attention to the closest lever within her reach. She shoved it upward, and a soft hum resonated from beneath the chariot.

The vehicle lifted slowly, its initial ascent wobbling like a rocking chair. Leighth held her breath, pushing the handle with all her might, coaxing the chariot to take flight. The humming sound grew, echoing through the air as the chariot responded to her efforts. In that crucial moment, she gave it her all, pushing the lever to its maximum point. And then, suddenly, the chariot shot upwards, soaring into the skies. The rush of adrenaline and accomplishment flooded through Leighth as she piloted the chariot, guiding them to the expansive realm above.

"There! We're in the air," she proclaimed, smiling at Blank Face.

Guards swarmed below them. The tolling bells reverberated through the city, intensifying the chaos that erupted in their wake. Leighth gritted her teeth and focused on steering the chariot amidst the rain of arrows that clinked against its sides. Taking a moment to steady herself, she inhaled through her nostrils, calming her nerves. As she guided the chariot through the tumultuous flight pattern, she couldn't help but imagine how erratic it must have appeared to those below.

"We need to move now! They're aiming the ballista our way." Blank Face commanded with urgency in his voice.

"You're not offering any help here. Stop sitting around and start doing something!" Leighth replied, sarcasm dripping from her tone.

Collectively, they figured out the general controls and sped away. With the chariot now sailing away, a surge of panic flooded her mind, overshadowing Leighth's immediate sense of relief. She couldn't ignore the weight of her actions—the murder of King Zonoh, a member of royalty, no less. The gravity of the situation dawned on her as her thoughts raced and her eyes blurred with anxious tears. *I'm no better than Borlden.* Her heart pounded in her chest, and she felt the weight of the consequences closing in on her. The realization that she was now an accomplice to such a serious crime filled her with an overwhelming sense of unease. It was a reality she couldn't escape.

"I'm nothing more than a wretched killer, just like you," Leighth's voice trembled.

"You've never taken a life. I'm the one who snuffed them all out." Blank Face's retort remained unchanged, his demeanor an unmoving mask.

"But I was with you! Therefore, that makes me—"

"We'd be locked in his dungeons, awaiting our execution!" Blank Face's interruption sliced through her words.

"Why couldn't you stick to thievery? Why did you have to become this... this abomination?" Her frustration burst forth. "You were ready to let them take me! You told him to go ahead and kill me!"

"Different upbringings forge different souls." He shrugged. "And I never would've let it get that far."

"Really? You would've surrendered?" She shook her head.

"No. I'm saying the moment they tried to harm you, I would've intervened. Zonoh would not hurt a harmless bystander." Blank Face nodded towards her.

"Well, Now I'm your burden to hide. A lifetime of evading guards awaits me. By the gods, if Borlden hadn't crossed my path, none of this shit would've happened! Next time I see him, I will kill him." Her anger seethed.

Leighth felt her cheeks flush with heat as her emotions intensified. The turmoil within her was palpable, her chest burning with a mixture of anger, fear, and guilt. The weight of her actions and the consequences that lay ahead weighed heavily on her shoulders. As doubts clouded her mind, she couldn't help but question the path she chose. Continuing on this perilous journey seemed daunting, and a part of her yearned for a more honorable course of action. The inner battle between her conscience and the desire for revenge tugged at her soul. Yet, deep down, she knew that turning back might not be an option, that the choices she had made had set her on a path that couldn't be undone.

Blank Face leaned in an air of finality in his words. "Well, the gears are turning now. One step closer to my destination."

A pause, then a probing question. "And what's that goal, really? Spare me the money spiel. Who are you truly after?"

Blank Face's eyes held a secret. "Just someone specific."

"Family, perhaps?" Leighth's voice softened.

"Nope. But here's something real: I stumbled upon a picture of a horned man, a Chernzerk, in a deserted shack by Mount Harbinger. That's what I'm chasing." Blank Face's voice held a hint of truth.

Leighth's reaction was explosive. "What the...!? I thought they were all wiped out, hunted down, and slaughtered by Nalecht's grandfather, Pasileveo."

A grim nod from Blank Face. "All I came across was that image. Can't say whether it's from the past or if there's still a bunch around."

Leighth's curiosity hung heavy in the air. "And why on Kalazaar does that matter so much to you?"

Blank Face's silence echoed in the air, and Leighth sensed the weight of his thoughts as he gazed out the window. Below them lay the mysterious sea of confusion, a body of water that had earned its enigmatic reputation. Its eerie aura was enough to deter any boats from crossing its surface, for the very touch of its water or breath of its air could consume one's mind, leaving them disoriented, with no memory left.

"Because my freedom came at a price. I agreed to kill this Chernzerk man for someone to help me escape. However, he is both elusive and tough to track down. I'm hoping Nalecht can help me find the cherno so I can be done with Nalecht and with the other contract for my freedom. It's been five years, and I need to clear that debt before he comes back to collect on the risk he took to set me free." Blank Face's gaze shifted to Leighth.

Leighth's voice was a mix of disbelief and derision. "Why is Nalecht the only one who can help you find him?"

"If my instincts are right, Borlden can track down anyone... I've spilled more than I usually do already. Maybe I should leave you somewhere. I prefer to work alone." Blank Face's words carried a hint of cold detachment as he glanced at the floor.

Leighth's retort dripped with playful mockery. "You wouldn't be lying to me, would you?."

A sliver of teeth peeked out from under Blank Face's hood. "Nope."

Leighth's tone turned aggressive. "Sounds like a bunch of bullshit to me."

Leighth was sure she was missing something but couldn't quite put the pieces together. *Why would him killing a Chernzerk free him from captivity? Who would've given him that deal? I need to figure out who got him out of captivity.*

His features reverted to their usual stoic state, his face as unyielding as ever. The next several hours were quiet.

"We're on the brink of Ambrosia's landing pad. Both Borlden and Nalecht will be there. If they spot you..." Blank Face's voice trailed off.

A spark of excitement ignited within Leighth. "Maybe this is the opening I've been waiting for."

A measured response from Blank Face. "Trust me, you're not ready to face Borlden. He's a mastermind."

Leighth's determination remained unshaken. "I can stay hidden, observe. If I can get that shard. You handle your business. I've already been tangled in this web far too much."

As the chariot drew closer to the capital city of Ambrosia, Leighth's awe was clear. The grandeur of the residential district spread out before her, a bustling metropolis teeming with thousands of people going about their daily lives. The sheer expanse of the city seemed to stretch infinitely, with streets weaving through the intricately designed buildings and towering structures that reached towards the heavens. Yet, it was the sight of the majestic castle that truly took her breath away. Near the back of the city, the massive stone wall encased the seven-pointed wonder, standing an impressive hundred feet tall. Lengthy windows adorned the majestic towers, spaced evenly about twenty feet apart, offering a glimpse of the splendor that lay within. Blue and yellow tapestries adorned the exterior of the castle.

Beyond the stone walls, a lush and expansive garden sprawled. The visible courtyard within the walls was equally magnificent, offering a serene sanctuary amidst the bustling city. The castle stood as a testament to the city's rich history and its place as the heart of Kalazaar, a symbol of power and elegance that left all who gazed upon it in awe. Every guard she saw was wearing plate mail armor like the bulwarks. As Blank Face took over piloting the buggy, guiding it towards the landing pad where Nalecht and Borlden awaited, Leighth couldn't shake the gnawing sense of unease that crept into her thoughts. How did they know they were coming? The question lingered in her mind, casting shadows of doubt and suspicion. She fidgeted nervously in her seat, careful not to draw any attention to herself through the windows of the chariot. *Hopefully, with my new haircut, they won't recognize me.*

A whirlwind of thoughts filled her mind, her imagination spinning scenarios of betrayal and danger. Did Blank Face lead them into a trap? Is he planning to hand her over to them, along with the shard of Obidiah? The fear of being double-crossed loomed ominously, and the possibility of facing the wrath of Nalecht and Borlden sent shivers down her spine. As the chariot landed with a thud, Blank Face stepped out, and Leighth couldn't help but feel a pang of apprehension. She hesitantly cracked open her door just slightly, trying to eavesdrop on their conversation, desperate for any clue to the truth behind this encounter. Right now, he was the only hope she had at recovering her father's shard. After witnessing his skills against one of the most powerful people in this world, he might be the only one who can help her. With her heart pounding in her chest, she steeled herself for what lay ahead, ready to face whatever challenges awaited, but also hoping against hope that Blank Face wouldn't turn her over to them. It was a risk, but one she was willing to take to get the chance to kill Borlden.

Chapter Eleven

L eighth listened intently from inside the cabin of the chariot as she immediately recognized Borlden's annoying voice. Just hearing his voice sent a surge of boiling anger coursing through Leighth's entire body. They just landed on Ambrosia's landing pad, where both Nalecht and Borlden waited outside. While she had agreed to stay hidden at Blank Face's request, if presented with the chance to kill Borlden and retrieve her shard or negotiate for its return, she wouldn't think twice about taking it. Or, at the least, get Blank Face to commit to helping her get the shard of Hathor back.

"So, you were successful, then?" Borlden's high-pitched squeal sliced through the air, a sound akin to an unshakable itch.

"I've got the shard right here," Blank Face stated, his voice steady.

Impatience laced Nalecht's words as he cut in, "Hand it over already."

Blank Face held his ground, resolute. "And what about my demand?"

Nalecht's voice dropped, a dark undercurrent beneath his words. "The Chernzerk you seek is currently under my employ. I can't tell you where to find him right now."

A challenge sparked in Blank Face's response. "That's bullshit, and you know it."

A wry skepticism tinged Nalecht's words. "What do you want with him so bad, anyway? Is it just to kill him?"

Blank Face's retort was sharp. "What concern is it of yours?"

Nalecht's response held a shadow of patience. "I already told you. He's working for me. Like you, he's chasing after the shards."

Blank responded. "No, I want to know his whereabouts. Where does he live?"

Leighth couldn't see what was happening, but she didn't like what she was hearing.

"You inquired about the Chernzerk, and I've provided the information. Now, give me the damned shard," Nalecht's demand hung heavy in the air.

Borlden's voice cut through a mix of curiosity and suspicion. "And who accompanies you on this venture?"

Blank Face's defiance was curt. "None of your concern."

Borlden's tone sharpened. "Ah, but it is my concern. Don't hide, reveal yourself, you coward."

As her hands trembled, she knew she couldn't stand by idly and let others dictate their fate. After a five-hour flight, she stepped onto the landing pad and felt the stiffness in her limbs. Summoning her courage, she pushed open the door, revealing herself to Nalecht and Borlden. Seeing Borlden's sneer was rage inducing.

"You!" Borlden screeched. "Hahaha... what a pleasant surprise. You are just too good at what you do, Blank Face."

Leighth's heart pounded in her chest. Her eyes locked with Blank Face's, silently pleading for his support again at this critical moment. Though his expression remained unreadable, she hoped he understood the gravity of the situation. As Borlden raised his hand, wielding the flame tattoo, Leighth couldn't help but feel a surge of dread and anger. She recognized this symbol all too well—it was the same tattoo Borlden used when he mercilessly burned her brothers alive. The memories of that horrifying day flooded her mind, fueling her determination to put an end to this menace once and for all. She tried to steady her hands, but all she could picture was her father's head falling to the floor. All she could hear were her brothers' agonizing screams as they slowly died that day. She balled her hands into fists, clenching them tightly enough to hurt.

"You know I can still hear them screaming, burning, just so agonizing right until they stopped screaming," Borlden's mouth curled into a wicked grin.

"Shut up, you ruthless bastard!" Leighth gritted. "Shut the fuck up!" she screamed.

Patience, Leighth, father would say. Patience. I need to get away from these people and get this pompous man out of my sight before I get myself killed. Leighth's face contorted, her brow furrowed, and her breathing intensified. She took a deep breath, trying to calm herself. It didn't work.

With her grip tightening around her dagger, Leighth bolted straight towards Borlden. Right before she got there, Nalecht's arms grabbed her shirt and yanked her backward.

Blank Face sprang into action with remarkable speed and precision. In a blur of motion, he dashed towards Borlden, slicing his wrist with a calculated strike. Then, with a deft maneuver, he locked Borlden's arm above his head, holding another dagger to his throat. *Is he finally sticking up for me?*

Leighth snarled, "Let me go." she yanked and pulled to no avail.

"The emotionless assassin has feelings, does he?" Borlden teased.

"I would be careful with your words, shrew. Or do I need to remind you who has the dagger to your neck?" Blank Face's voice was cold, his grip tightening slightly, drawing a bead of blood from Borlden's neck.

"Stab him, Blank! Stab him in the neck right now!" Leighth growled.

"Let's dial it down a notch. Blank, release him. And Borlden, I've no intention of harm coming to the girl," Nalecht's authoritative voice rang out, reclaiming control of the scene as he tossed Leighth on the ground and stood between her and Borlden. The thud caused her to bite her tongue, and she tasted the metallic tang of blood.

Borlden's voice screeched, akin to nails on a chalkboard. "Oh, don't you recognize her, Anyth? She's the one who slipped away when Jaynoh refused to hand over the shard!"

"I'll kill you!" Leighth seethed. "I assure you. I might not be able to do it now, but I will kill you!"

Nalecht shifted his gaze to Borlden, his words cutting through the tension. "What exactly do you think she'll accomplish? Are you frightened by her, or does her mere presence gnaw at you, a constant reminder of your own incompetence?"

Leighth couldn't suppress her laughter, a bubbling chuckle escaping her lips. She watched Borlden storm off, a satisfied grin on her face as she envisioned driving her dagger into his black heart someday.

"Blank Face, Leighth," Nalecht addressed them both. "I have another proposition for you."

Blank Face's response was dry. "What is it this time?"

Nalecht added the shard of Obidiah to his necklace, along with the ones he already had, which were Ryollin and Hathor. Leighth's eyes lingered on the shard of Hathor a little too long, and Nalecht put them back around his neck. *I should just grab it. Just grab it and run.*

Nalecht grinned at her. "I know what you're thinking, and that wouldn't be a smart move. I may have let you live. Don't take that for granted." He warned her, then turned back to Blank Face. "I've got someone working on getting the shard of Amarook and Kasherri. Aisha is guarded closely by Tamara but is mine when I request she bring it to me. However, that leaves one more piece to the collection."

Blank Face's arms crossed over his chest. "And you want me to get it? After the less-than-stellar reward last time?"

Nalecht's gaze shifted, pointing at a rather unassuming chariot nearby. "Do you see that vehicle over there?"

Leighth's eyes followed his direction, and she noticed the chariot's unique features. Unlike the ornate designs they were used to seeing in the capital city, this one didn't have an insignia but sported a sleek camouflage color on its body and sails.

"I had that specially made for you. To help you blend in and get around faster. Inside, you will find twenty thousand gold pieces." Nalecht grinned.

Leighth's mouth fell open in astonishment. Her family never encountered monetary hardship, but twenty thousand gold was an incredible amount to hand out. She turned her gaze to Blank Face, who, as usual, appeared unfazed by the sight before them. His inscrutable expression gave nothing away, leaving her to wonder what he truly thought.

"I'm prepared to divulge information on another Chernzerk I've located along with the one in my employ. By the time I'm through with his services, you'll have all you need," Nalecht's assurance hung in the air.

"Yet another one? Your well of knowledge seems inexhaustible. And let's be clear—when you possess this last shard, our debt is settled, correct? We assist you now, and you'll keep your distance later," Blank Face sought clarification.

Nalecht's grin spread, an unsettling reassurance that held no sway. "Of course."

"Including her." Blank Face nodded towards Leighth.

"Sure. Including her." Nalecht agreed.

Trusting this long-haired elf was as likely as trusting a viper not to bite. He was a harbinger of death, targeting families and children alike.

"Very well. Who is it, and where?" Blank Face's question cut through.

"Rinawen Xentoth. Last seen in Wen-Tath," Nalecht answered.

"We need lodgings for the night. We'll set off at first light. Can we secure a fortified room? I'm not interested in your shrew stirring up more shit," Blank Face's demand was assertive.

"He wouldn't dare cross me. But indeed, you're welcome to the guest quarters just over there," Nalecht pointed toward the opposite end of the landing pad.

Blank Face led the way to the room, and Leighth hurried to keep pace with him. They finally arrived at the grand guest room, which exuded splendor in every detail. The room was spacious and square, adorned with luxurious furnishings. A small, elegant coffee table took center stage on top of an intricately designed area rug, while two sumptuous couches flanked it on either side. There were several lit candles in the room. Hints of rose, lavender, and jasmine intermingle with notes of honey and vanilla.

A magnificent chandelier hung gracefully from the high ceiling, casting a warm glow over the room. As they entered, Leighth noticed four open doors, each attended by a maid, ready to cater to every guest's needs with impeccable service. The atmosphere was one of indulgence and refinement, befitting the grandeur of a capital city. In the presence of such opulence, Leighth couldn't help but feel a sense of wonder and admiration for the lavishness that surrounded her. The capital city's extravagance captivated Leighth as she found herself in a world unlike anything she had ever known.

"Let me know if you need anything," the maid called out to them as she shut the door.

Leighth explored a little more and looked out the window, overlooking the ever-bustling city life. As the sun sank below the horizon, the sky became a canvas of vibrant oranges and fiery reds, with a touch of cool blue from the emerging moon. People all over the place, guards everywhere. The high stone walls had amazing graffiti on them. Another doorway in the room led to a bathtub and washroom, complete with a mirror. The smell of roses from the soaps filled her senses.

"I'm definitely getting myself one of those," Leighth declared, nodding towards the tub.

Blank Face's offer held a hint of consideration. "You don't have to accompany me this time."

A scoff escaped Leighth. "Are you kidding? I'd rather endure anything than stay here with that lunatic."

"I can arrange for you to go somewhere else," Blank Face suggested.

Leighth's response was firm. "Are you serious? Where would I go? Once word gets out about Zonoh, we'll be hunted. I can't survive that on my own, and you promised you'd help me get my shard back after this... Remember?"

"Sure. You've helped me quite a bit, and you deserve it. My past may be a little more tortured, but I think that's what makes me pity you." Blank Face sat on the bed. "Yes. I remember I said I might help you for the right price. But you realize each shard we give him, the stronger he gets, right?"

"Pity me?" Leighth rolled her eyes, and she sat beside Blank Face on the bed, leaning closer to him. "Do you think? Instead of getting the shard for Nalecht, we could get the shard and kill them both?" her voice barely above a whisper.

Blank Face flicked his eyes to her, turned, laid down, and huffed. "Saying shit like that is what gets people killed. You need to understand we are two people. Yeah, maybe we could kill them, but that still leaves Tamara, who is in league with Nalecht, and don't forget there's a cherno under his thumb as well, who likely has a dragon. Following the rule of odds, we're farther ahead to keep the peace with him."

I'm getting there...Slowly. He will come around.

However, they might have a larger problem on their hands if Nalecht didn't keep his promise. That was another problem entirely, and Leighth knew in her heart that he wouldn't keep that promise. Somehow, she had to convince Blank Face the same thing before it was too late. If he possessed all seven shards, who would stand up to him? Especially if he had the Chernzerk on his side, the dragon riders that used to rule with their dragons as weapons. A shiver ran down her spine at the thought.

As Lillian settled into the back of the flying carriage with Rinawen the morning after the meeting, she admired the intricate details of Rinawen's chariot. After a brief discussion with the other members of royalty, Lillian offered her services to protect Queen Rinawen and the shard of Theora. The rising threat of Blank Face grew even more, especially since he just killed King Zonoh and took his shard. Zonoh was one of the greatest kings this realm has ever seen. A wise and powerful old man. Her lips curled upward at the thought of being the one to capture Blank Face, putting an end to the threat he posed.

The dark green exterior resembled a charming log cabin, enhanced by delicate vines trailing gracefully down the sides. The windows featured tiny leaf imprints, enhancing the vehicle with a touch of nature's beauty. A striking silhouette of a fern graced the top right corner of the front windshield. The craftsmanship and artistry displayed in every aspect of the chariot fascinated Lillian.

Lillian sighed as the overwhelming scent of lilacs filled the carriage. Opening one of the side windows, she hoped to let in some fresh air to counter the strong fragrance. The sun had just risen over the ridge, painting the sky with hues of orange and pink, signaling the beginning of a new day. The events of the last few days still lingered in her mind—winning the tournament in Wen-Tath.

Her thoughts then drifted to Leper, the intriguing man she had met the night before. Despite his unconventional hat, there was something about him that drew her in. His large, striking, hazel eyes. His towering, muscular frame. She nearly drooled. However, at the last moment, he pushed her away, leaving her to wonder about his true intentions. Confused and uncertain, Lillian couldn't help but question the type of man who would act in such a way.

Lillian tried to push the lingering anger aside, but it seemed to claw its way back, wrapping around her thoughts like a suffocating vine. Perhaps if he knew her, the real Lillian, he wouldn't even want to be with her.

Her eyes absent-mindedly fixated on the floor of the carriage, lost in her inner turmoil until the soft murmuring of voices within the cabin drew her attention. Glancing up, she met Rinawen's curious gaze, causing her to straighten up in her seat.

"Lillian?" Rinawen called again.

Rinawen's outfit perfectly complemented her adventurous spirit. Lillian admired her fashion sense as she donned a sleeveless green leather vest, which stressed her lithe figure. Underneath, a black long-sleeved undershirt and brown pants provided practical warmth for their journey. Lillian's gaze drifted to the satchel tied to Rinawen's side. But it was her Elven ears that fascinated Lillian the most—delicately pointed and adorned with two glistening ruby-studded earrings. She fit the image of a queen and was entirely beautiful.

"Are you okay?" Rinawen patted her on the shoulder.

"Yeah, I'm fine."

With a piece of paper in hand, Rinawen chanted incantations that Lillian couldn't decipher. In a flash, the paper vanished, transformed into a translucent message that drifted effortlessly through the walls of the chariot.

"What in tarnation was that?" Lillian's finger pointed at the hovering paper.

"A magical note," Rinawen responded with a regal air.

"How in the world does that work? The receiver just hears what you said?" Lillian's head tilted inquisitively.

"Well, you recite the incantation and then convey your message. The paper turns transparent, then reappears before the intended recipient," Rinawen explained.

"I see now. You got any more of them yer plannin' to share?" Lillian's curiosity was clear.

"I'm afraid not, my dear. Acquiring them is rather challenging," Rinawen said softly.

"It's a darn shame. Was that note aimed for Leper?" Lillian sat forward in her seat.

"No. It was meant for my husband, Larnadix, to remind him where to bring our small army. Although you seem a bit too nosy," Rinawen replied with her composed demeanor.

"Reckon that's just me," Lillian shot.

Lillian's mind swirled with conflicting emotions as she replayed last night's encounter with Leper in her thoughts. She couldn't deny the powerful connection she felt with him, a connection that seemed to transcend time and reason. It was as if they had known each other for eternity, and yet, in reality, they had only just met. Her heart tugged at her, urging her to reconsider her reaction to Leper's sudden departure. Perhaps she had been too quick to judge, too guarded with her heart.

The memory of his scent lingered in her senses, the musky fragrance of the dark forest wrapping around her like a warm embrace. The mead taste on his lips when they'd kissed was sweet and honey-like, with a hint of warmth from the alcohol. It was a scent that reminded her of the wild, untamed beauty of nature, and it had left a lasting impression on her.

"Maybe once this entire ordeal's done, I could offer an apology. Maybe we can give it another shot," Lillian confessed.

"He's not keen on girls. Believe me," Rinawen's retort was swift and pointed.

"Then boys, perhaps? He gave off a mighty different vibe last night." Lillian's smile radiated.

Rinawen's exasperation was evident. "No, he's into girls..." A heavy sigh escaped her. "Could we shift topics? What about you? What's the trouble with Petrovana? How are you going to protect me from Blank Face? Zonoh was powerful and had the shard of Obidiah on him. How are you going to stop him?"

Lillian couldn't help but notice the change in Rinawen's tone, a subtle shift mirrored by the blush that tinted her cheeks—a sign of the frustration lingering from last night's events. Was that a hint of jealousy in her expression or perhaps the instinctive concern of a mother? Despite her burning curiosity, Lillian suppressed the urge to ask the question that begged to be voiced.

Lillian's frustration bubbled to the surface, and her voice tinged with bitterness as she spoke.

"Reckon she's already stole one man from me. Probably gonna do it again. Tramp," she muttered, clenching her fists in frustration. Her cheeks flushed. "You leave that worthless assassin to me. I'll show you exactly what I will do to stop him. He might think he's all-powerful, but he ain't takin' that shard. I can promise you that."

It wasn't just about Leper leaving without a proper goodbye. It was the fear of losing something precious, something that had briefly lit up her world amidst the darkness. Something she didn't realize was possible after... *No!* She shook her head as distant memories from long ago tried to surface, but she pushed them back down, back down so far that they would remain in that black hole within her forever. She felt vulnerable and exposed, and her heart ached with a mix of longing and resentment.

"So, she's a mite promiscuous, you say? Appears there's more to it," Rinawen probed.

"Hell, yes, she sure is. I've lived my whole life watchin' her foolish antics. Always puttin' on that act of dumb bitch. Don't let it fool ya, though. She knows exactly what she's up to. Stumbled into bein' the heir of Terynsipple," Lillian rolled her eyes.

"Oh? How does one stumble into something like that?" Rinawen's gaze remained fixed on Lillian, her interest clear.

"It's a long story, but Zonoh put her there when she was young. I think six years old." Lillian huffed.

"Where did Zonoh find her from then? Who's her real parents? They must have names." Rinawen set her hand on Lillian's arm.

Lillian's eyes followed the movement on the ground below as Theodamar marshaled his army, forming an impressive force of about five thousand men. They needed to reach Tudela before Nalecht's forces arrived. The fate of the kingdom hung in the balance, and Lillian's heart raced with the weight of responsibility. *What if Blank Face beats me, too? What happens if he kills me, Rinawen, and then takes the shard?* Goosebumps prickled at her neck. *I can't lose. I won't lose.*

"I don't know, nor do I care. All I know is she was a good kid until her adult life. Now she's a backstabbin' tramp." Lillian seethed as she glared at Rinawen. A writhing in her gut told her not to ask what she was about to ask, but she couldn't help it. Holding it in wasn't her style, and she wasn't about to let a queen intimidate her into silence. "You're in love with him, aren't you?"

She'd never seen the shade of red on anyone grow so quickly. Rinawen pulled her hand off her arm. A look of utter rage. Was it because she was right? Or was it something else entirely? Something she most definitely decided she would not be asking anytime soon.

"I think that's enough personal talk for now. We need to focus on the task at hand. Is there anything you need, anything I can help you with?" Rinawen gritted through her teeth.

Rinawen's anger radiated so intensely that Lillian felt a powerful impulse to shrink away from her. She must have struck a nerve, a realization that left Lillian regretting her decision to broach the subject of Leper again.

"Reckon you just stick with me, and when he shows up, I'll show you what I'm goin' to do." Lillian tapped the hilt of her scimitars.

The rest of the two-hour ride was silent. Tudela, an average-sized city housing tens of thousands of people, presented a mix of gold and white colors adorning every door frame. The castle, with only one peak and the kingdom's proud insignia soaring above it, welcomed King Brebian's arrival with open arms. His wife and three children eagerly embraced him as his chariot landed shortly after Lillian and Rinawen. The halls within the castle lacked the grandeur one would expect from a capital city in Kalazaar. Cobwebs draped the corners, and the absence of family pictures or ancestral trees left the place feeling barren.

Maids guided them to their rooms in Tudela.

"Excuse me." Rinawen's voice was clear and concise. "I'd like a room next to Lillian, please."

"As you wish, my lady." The guards moved her stuff to the room next to Lillian. She barged through the doorway like she owned this castle, too.

What was that all about?

"Come here," Rinawen grabbed Lillian's wrist, pulling her into her room.

"What in Amarook's name are ya doin'?" Lillian spat.

"I just want to be closer to you. If Blank Face truly killed Zonoh, I might be the next target... I don't want to take any chances." She demanded.

"I'm right here, yer highness?" Her lips curled upward.

"I don't think you're taking this seriously enough. Zonoh was a pinnacle-five shrew." Rinawen locked eyes with her.

"Psh, I ain't scared of no man that hides behind a hood." Lillian scoffed.

"Don't let your arrogance be your downfall," Rinawen warned.

Lillian furrowed her brow. "Please."

Perhaps Rinawen had a point; perhaps Lillian had been too arrogant to confront the assassin. Especially one who had just killed a pinnacle-five shrew amidst guards and bulwarks. What set this assassin apart from others? How did he evade detection, capture, and never lose, even against formidable opponents like a king and his guards? The spotlight on him only seemed to intensify, yet Blank Face remained elusive, his methods and weaponry shrouded in mystery. *How am I going to fight against him?* She pondered.

Lillian surveyed the room with a keen eye, assessing potential entry points and threats that could arise during the night. With a decisive motion, she secured the windows tightly shut and reinforced them with glue.

Placing a small bell above the doorway, she rigged it to chime at the slightest movement, providing an alert to any attempted entry. While she may not have witnessed Blank Face's methods firsthand, she was determined not to let him sneak in, steal the shard, and escape without a confrontation.

Lillian held no fear of facing him; she had heard rumors of his prowess, and she relished the prospect of bringing him to his knees. The challenge of defeating formidable foes like Blank Face or Nalecht fueled her spirit, driving her to seek the adoration and respect that victory would bring. Embracing the trials openly, she welcomed the opportunity to prove her strength and skill to the world. She closed the door, making sure the bell rang, as Rinawen settled on the bed. *Blank Face will not touch Rinawen or that shard.*

Chapter Twelve

"I 'm not the only one who saw that?" Leper said sheepishly, looking to Madislak.

Madislak's narrowed gaze fixated on him, his magnificent sword Skyrunner pointed directly at his heart.

"Bullshit, I think it's time we see what's under that hat," he snarled. "There's been far too many instances where I've questioned your reactions and what you say."

"Madislak, you know me. I've done nothing against you." Leper put his hands up.

His pulse throbbed in his temples, loud and insistent. Leper could feel the adrenaline coursing through his veins, making him jittery. As he looked at Madislak's face, twisted in anger and frustration, Leper couldn't help but wonder if anything could console him if this hat came off. He hoped that Harmony and Petrovana could somehow calm him down, their soothing voices and gentle touch helping to defuse his rage like water poured over hot coals. The air was suffocating. Dark clouds filled the sky, and a light breeze blew.

"Take off the hat. If there's nothing to hide, then it won't be a big deal, or let me feel that hat properly." Madislak advanced one step towards Leper.

Leper's eyes darted from the ground to Harmony, silently pleading for help. However, no help seemed to be forthcoming. Harmony appeared less insistent about him removing the hat, but he couldn't find any support there either. Turning to Petrovana, he saw a comforting smile, which offered some solace amid the tension.

"Fine. Can someone help me?" Leper mouthed, defeated.

"Don't you dare try anything," Madislak's steady hand extended Skyrunner. Harmony and Petrovana started cutting the stitching around his head, causing a slight pulling sensation on the threads. But what troubled Leper the most was the sudden change in Madislak's demeanor.

As they finished cutting out all the threads, they attempted to remove his hat, but it halted. Leper's horns were preventing it from coming all the way off. He reached his hand around the lip of the hat, feeling for where Zanera had sewn it to fit his head, and ripped those stitches out. All of them were glaring at his head except for Petrovana, who had a whimsical glint in her eye. Leper couldn't shake the feeling that something significant had changed between him and Madislak, who stared at him, his mouth agape.

"Exactly what I thought. Not only a worthless teacher but a dirty liar as well. Is anything you've told us true?" Madislak grumbled.

"Yeah, everything. Matter of fact, the only lie I've told was about my race and the lie I made up to put the hat on. Know why? Because before you knew about these horns, I was your friend and ally!" Leper glared at Madislak, ignoring the weapon aimed at him. "Suddenly, that's all changed."

Madislak scrutinized him, then glanced around before settling his eyes on Leper's horns. His noble upbringing seemed to clash with his sense of what was right in this world—mixed with what Petrovana had said in the chariot about his father being removed from the throne. Leper could empathize to some extent; after all, his ancestors had brought chaos and ruin to Kalazaar. However, he knew he was not his ancestors, and he had no intentions of repeating their mistakes. He hoped Madislak would eventually see that too, that not all Chernzerk were alike.

"So, what now? We're no longer allies? We get ourselves stuck on the side of this mountain... Madislak, I'm still the same person you met outside Lantess." Leper pleaded.

"No, you stay on the side of this mountain. We leave so we can tell the others what you are. I should kill you like Brebian said, but since you helped me save my city, I'll offer you this mercy once." He gritted through his teeth.

"Madislak, I think you need to take a moment. I understand you've lost a lot, but your kids and we would not be alive right now if not for him," Harmony put her hand on his shoulder. "Put the sword down, please."

"You know how much I loathe dirty liars. This is not a mere fib! The horn, that picture we got in that house. He knew when we showed it to him," Madislak huffed. "He knew and didn't say a damn thing!"

"Reckon yer reaction and what was said at that meetin' about them had somethin' to do with that," Petrovana stood beside Leper. "You know good and damn well he ain't goin' to hurt anyone."

"I'm only trying to prove we are not the chaos seedlings depicted in all the texts," Leper shrugged.

Frustration boiled over as Madislak took a step towards Leper, who quickly jumped back.

"I don't want to fight you, Madislak, but I will defend myself." Leper set his hand on the leather portion of his chakrams. "The enemy is down there!"

"Yeah, that's exactly what you want, isn't it? To distract us so you can talk with your buddy down there and kill us all?" Madislak seethed.

"Hey. Madislak, need I remind you, he has helped us every step of the way here. Had he wanted to kill us, I'm pretty sure it would've been with one of those vials or in the chariot and one of any dozen other times where he had an opportunity!" Harmony snapped. "Think for two damn seconds. Now, we've got an army down there, a dragon rider, a dragon, and Queen Tamara. We do not have enough people to fight them all. We spent five hours flying towards another failure. Not a total failure, though. We at least know where the shard of Amarook is and can prepare better."

"Get the carriage. We're leaving." Madislak pointed at Petrovana and Harmony.

Leper could sense the reluctance in Harmony's expression. She clearly wasn't ready to leave, but duty-bound her to obey the orders of her king. Resigned, she walked over and skillfully dislodged some debris from the chariot's wheels via her psyrenth magic, freeing it from the rocks. Leper admired her loyalty, even in the face of her own desires. The distant roar of a dragon, followed by the far-off noise of whooshing wings, caught their attention.

"Stay put," Madislak ordered, walking backwards.

Leper's voice carried a note of concern. "So, you're just going to abandon me here?"

"That's your best bet for now," Madislak's response remained resolute. "C'mon, Petrovana, let's head out."

Petrovana's defiance flared. "I don't take orders from the likes of you. Leavin' him here alone is the sort of heartless move only a chaotic asshole would make."

"Your call. You eccentric shrews are a peculiar bunch, that's for sure," Madislak retorted.

Petrovana's face turned red as she gritted. "We're unconventional because we refuse to accept that the tried-and-true path is the only one. I've spent a day with Leper, and I can sense the kindness in him. But perhaps that's my eccentricity speakin'."

"A kindness cloaked in deception. Don't be surprised if he collaborates with that dragon rider, and they decide to cut you down without reason! From the sounds of it, he's on his way up here right now." Madislak's brow furrowed.

Madislak swiftly leaped into the chariot, taking control of it with practiced ease. Leper glanced at Harmony, who hesitated outside for a moment. He nodded to her. It was a wordless assurance that they would meet again and everything would be alright. With a forced smile, Harmony joined Madislak in the carriage as it began takeoff.

"I'm sorry I got you into this, Petrovana. I don't know if we'll make it out of here alive, but for what it's worth, thank you." Leper put his arm around her.

"You have nothin' to be sorry fer. Now, c'mon, we got work to do." She pointed over the cliff. "Not to mention a dragon on its way up here."

Leper looked out over the cliff's edge and could hear the whooshing of wings headed their way. Madislak had just lifted off in the chariot with Harmony and left him and Petrovana here on The Talon. Leper's heart pounded in his chest, and at that very moment, the majestic beast soared past them with astonishing speed. A powerful gust of wind whipped around them, and before he could react, his cherished hat tumbled over the edge of the cliff.

"Shit! They're going after the chariot!" Leper instinctively grabbed his chakram. Mustering all his strength, he heaved it at the dragon.

"You realize we can't outrun that beast, right?" Petrovana scowled at him, unimpressed.

"Into the cave, quick pick a path." Leper pointed and gently guided Petrovana towards the mountain.

Leper watched his chakram soar through the air, striking the dragon's underbelly but causing no significant harm. The creature roared in response, and the chakram fell, now out of his reach. He desperately reached out his hand, activating the magical bracelets, but the distance was too great to retrieve it. His trusted weapon was now lost.

Leper and Petrovana rushed into the cave entrance on the right, their steps echoing through the passage. As they ventured deeper, they gradually discovered a mesmerizing sight: the walls of the tunnel were adorned with glowing quartz, emitting a soft, ethereal light. The distant drips of water also echoed throughout the tunnels. Leper felt an instinctual tug at each intersection as if something or someone were guiding him through these tunnels. *Must be Theora.* They continued to run until the tunnels opened up into a large circular room. In the dead center of the room was a shrine-like structure elevated on a platform about three feet high. Four statues, slightly larger than human size, stood upon the platform, all depicting Chernzerk like Leper.

The room's floor was no longer rough mountain rock; instead, it was smooth stone, as if someone had carefully crafted this space. Despite the hint of iron in the air, Leper couldn't help but be captivated by the soft glow of the quartz illuminating the chamber. The mesmerizing light danced across the Chernzerk statues, giving them an otherworldly presence. It was a sacred place, and Leper could feel the ancient energy coursing through the room. A sense of awe washed over him as he realized they stumbled upon something extraordinary deep within the heart of the mountain.

"What is this place?" Petrovana muttered, her eyes darting all over.

"I don't know." Leper mouthed.

Leper and Petrovana cautiously circled the platform, their eyes fixed on the distinct Chernzerk statues, each one uniquely crafted. However, Leper immediately noticed the statue at the back. Hanging gracefully from its majestic horns were two chakrams, their surface glimmering with an otherworldly radiance. They were like no weapon he had ever seen before. The blades of these chakrams were unlike any traditional design. On one side, they curved gracefully like a scimitar, while on the other, they bore serrated edges. A single handle connected both blades at the center, making them appear almost like a pair of uniquely interconnected weapons. Instead of forming a complete circle, they extended three-quarters of the way around. At the ends, the blades curled outward before tapering to a sharp point.

Leper's eyes caught sight of a magnificent round shield leaning against the wall behind them. Bright red, gold, and black runic symbols adorned it.

He had encountered nothing like these chakrams before, and their presence in this sacred room only deepened his sense of awe and reverence for this place. It was as if the statues themselves were guarding a well-kept secret, waiting to reveal their mysteries to those worthy of their knowledge.

"Look," Leper pointed to the chakrams. "I just lost my other chakram. Is that a coincidence or what?"

As they walked around to the back, two lifeless bodies lay on the ground, surrounded by pools of blood. As Leper rushed over to them, his heart sank with the realization of the tragedy that had occurred here. Both Chernzerk appeared to be very old, possibly in their eighties or nineties. Thinning white hair covered their frail bodies. One had a beard; the other did not. It was the slight differences that made him wonder - could one of them be his father? His mind raced with uncertainty and emotions, but he knew he had to find out the truth. He gently shook each of the bodies, hoping against hope that one of them might still be alive. But the silence that followed confirmed his fears - they were both gone.

Leper's heart ached as he knelt beside them, realizing that if one of them was indeed his father, he would never get the chance to know him. The weight of his past, the abandonment he had felt as a baby, resurfaced with a vengeance. In this sacred room, surrounded by Chernzerk statues and the mysteries of his people, Leper faced the haunting question of his origins. Now he knew where that iron smell was coming from. The humidity in the chamber tasted stale and damp, like musty air trapped in a closed space. It left a slightly metallic aftertaste on the tongue.

"Hey, Leper. This one resembles you if you look closely enough," Petrovana pointed at the one with the chakrams hanging off it.

The impressive glossy black horns were even shaped like his. They began at the front of its head, gracefully arcing backward towards the crest before branching outwards for a few inches. From there, they took an upward curve before coming to a point. The one beside it, with the axes, resembled the Chernzerk they had just seen on the dragon.

"Step onto the platform in front of you," a voice reached Leper's ears.

He turned to Petrovana, seeking confirmation. "What did you say?"

She responded with nonchalance, her shoulders lifting in a shrug. "I didn't say anythin'."

Leper's confusion grew. "Someone clearly said to step onto the platform."

Petrovana jerked her head towards the platform.

Leper's hand trembled as he reached out and contacted the glimmering chakrams. In an instant, a surge of energy coursed through him, and his surroundings blurred into a blinding white light. It felt as if he was being pulled through the very essence of Kalazaar itself - a torrent of emotions and memories flooding his mind. In the whirlwind of images, he witnessed a Chernzerk man with a beard engaging in a dark and disturbing act with a human woman, forcing himself upon her. Her features were clear in his mind - shoulder-length black hair, a round, cherubic face, warm brown eyes, and a distinct necklace that read Ana on it. The scene flashed again. This time, the woman was pregnant and preparing to give birth. But something was terribly wrong; the babies that emerged from her womb had horns, just like Leper's, and there were two of them—twins.

Confusion and shock overwhelmed him. These memories were not his own, yet they felt oddly familiar. The revelation hit him like a thunderbolt - one of the fallen Chernzerk was his father. The pieces of his identity, like shards of a shattered mirror, came together, forming a haunting picture of his past. Torn between conflicting emotions, Leper stepped back, trying to make sense of the truth he'd just glimpsed. Although the answer he'd sought for so long lay unveiled, any joy was tainted by the darkness and complexity surrounding his people. Confusing images flooded his mind, including his father's face and the knowledge of his sibling. The woman passed away, unable to survive the damage caused by the horns of the babies, both boys. *Where is my sibling?*

As the images flared again, the tapestry of history unfolded before Leper's eyes. He saw his people, fierce warriors riding majestic dragons, brave souls fearlessly slaying the very beasts they rode upon. The leader of their Chernzerk community, a figure of wisdom and justice, guided his kin with a steady hand. Then there was the shapeshifter, a guardian of nature, morphing effortlessly into various animals, creatures, and even other beings. They weren't the monsters portrayed in the books but a diverse and complex civilization with a rich heritage. Yet, the visions didn't stop there. Another Chernzerk, without the beard, emerged in the memories—the father of two more twins, a boy and a girl. But this story was different; this time, love enveloped the Chernzerk. The woman, his mother, cherished their union and their children. The boy's horns took the shape of the man riding the dragon they just witnessed, and Leper's mind raced with a myriad of questions.

With each revelation, a tangled web of emotions flooded Leper's heart. So many answers were now unveiled, yet even more mysteries remained. Where were the other two siblings? Who was his mother? Where is his brother?

Fluttering back to the present, Leper's focus returned to the statue he stood before. But before he could fully comprehend the surge of emotions within him, a powerful burst of energy erupted beneath his feet, causing Petrovana to tumble to the ground. The floor beneath him quaked fiercely for five seemingly endless seconds before finally coming to a rest. The experience left him breathless, his heart pounding in his chest as he tried to make sense of the profound connection he felt with the ancient Chernzerk figures before him.

"I am... Maka... Kura." The voice sounded ghostly or spiritual.

"Who? Show yourself." Leper demanded.

"You grasp me in your hand."

Leper looked down at the shiny chakrams within his hands, white knuckles.

"You can talk?"

"I'm a sentient being. Born within these chakrams. I am bound to you and only you. When you perish, I shall return to the dust as well."

"Why me?" Leper realized his mouth was not moving, and he was having a conversation.

"You are the slayer of dragons. Every Chernzerk here gets their magical ability. You get the legendary Maka Kura."

"All I do is kill dragons? How are we talking?" Leper shook his head.

"That is up to you. Your horns are your specialty. With the powerful magic within this shrine released, you, along with the others, now have your abilities restored. However, it comes with one caveat. The men who are slain are no longer protected by the magic and will die for real this time. They will not receive any resurrection."

"What abilities? I'm so confused. You can bring them back?"

"You have me Maka Kura. You control my flight via our connection through your horns. But I must recharge daily. While I can fly and be controlled by you and cut through anything. It is not endless energy. Before the magic was released, it offered them protection from dying. Now that it's released, they will not be brought back to life."

"Leper?" he heard from behind him.

"Huh?" he turned to see Petrovana on the ground still, the dragon rider standing to her side, aiming his axe at Petrovana's neck.

"Who are you?" Leper studied him curiously.

His grin widened. "So, you've seen into the history, I presume? I've been waiting for you."

Leper's eyes narrowed as he stared at the Chernzerk standing before him. The man wore the distinct colors of Xaneth Harbor, a combination of yellow and brown, on his hardened leather chest piece. His mismatched green undershirt clashed with the color scheme, making him appear somewhat disheveled. His shaggy red hair framed a round-shaped face, and his nose, slightly larger than average, seemed out of place amidst his features. The beady proximity of his eyes and his bushy, almost orange eyebrows added to the man's eccentric appearance. Freckles dotted his nose and cheeks. As Leper observed the man's arms, he noticed the prominent veins visible through the short-sleeve shirt he wore under the leather armor. A tattoo of a dragon adorned his left arm, while the right arm bore a mysterious, runic symbol. The two axes crossed behind his head.

"I'm Ace," his voice balanced depth and pitch. "And who might you be?"

"Leper," he introduced himself simply.

Ace's attention shifted to Petrovana. "And what about the lady?"

Her reply came without hesitation. "I'm Petrovana, hailin' from Terynsipple."

Leper cut to the chase. "Did you kill these two men?"

"Sure, if that's what you want to believe." Ace's grin took on a chilling edge. His glossy black horns started just beyond the forehead and arced gracefully over his head.

Leper's gaze remained fixed on the Chernzerk before him. Something was unsettling about this man, an air of arrogance that oozed out with every word exchanged. His ragged appearance, along with the pungent scent of sweat mixed with dirt and grime, wafted off him, put Leper more on edge.

"Why are you waiting for me?" Leper's arms folded defensively across his chest.

Ace's explanation flowed forth. "With you having finally triggered the magic within the shrine, I can now communicate with the dragons. This place has been steadily amassing magical energy, waiting for distribution among us. The other two arrived before you. You were the last piece of the puzzle."

Concern etched Leper's features. "What happened to the other two?" His gaze involuntarily drifted to the lifeless bodies nearby, a fleeting worry for his sibling's safety surfacing.

Ace's response was cryptic as he grasped both axes. "Who's saying I had any part in their fate?"

Leper scowled. "Why are you doing this? You're only making it worse."

Ace's tone held an unsettling mix of logic and malice. "Well, if you die, the power intended for you from the shrine becomes mine. It's our role, our destiny. Ultimately, a single, unquestioned leader will emerge."

Leper's objection was swift. "That doesn't seem right. The power should be shared. It's far too much for a single person."

Ace's nonchalant response carried a note of indifference. "Eh, we'll cross that bridge when we get to it."

With lightning reflexes, Leper swiftly sidestepped the incoming axe hurled by Ace. The blade clashed against the stone wall, filling the air with a resounding clang. Strangely, as Leper evaded the attack, he sensed an unfamiliar sense of instinctual prowess, as though he'd been honing his combat skills for a lifetime.

"I share my knowledge with you." Maka Kura said in his head.

"Then help me restrain him." Leper's jaw clenched as he focused on Ace.

With Maka Kura firmly in his grasp, Leper swiftly launched one of the chakrams towards Ace, who expertly deflected it with his other axe. As the chakram hit the ground, Leper concentrated, commanding it to return to his hand. To his delight, the weapon responded with a brief vibration before whizzing back into his waiting palm. The rush of adrenaline and newfound control over his weapon left Leper exhilarated, a grin forming on his face as he savored the moment.

"This is going to take some getting used to," Leper's thoughts directed towards Maka Kura.

"Indeed, but the effort will yield rewards. I stand as the pinnacle of weapon craft, and I am now yours to wield." Maka Kura's response resonated within Leper's mind.

Leper's heart pounded in his chest as he faced off against Ace's relentless assault. Their weapons clashed with a resounding clang, the sound of steel reverberating through the room and tunnels. Leaping and dodging, Leper parried Ace's powerful attacks, pushing him back momentarily. Ace rolled to the side, quickly retrieving his other axe, and Leper seized the opportunity to strike. With calculated precision, Leper hurled another chakram at Ace, guiding it around a nearby wall to catch him off guard. Ace turned and batted the chakram away, only to witness it return to Leper's hand, unaffected by the blow. A grin spread across Leper's face.

Ace lunged forward once more, unleashing a barrage of swings. Leper's reflexes kicked into high gear as he feverishly parried, matching Ace's speed and strength with skill and determination. The dance of blades intensified.

"You're not coming out on top here, Leper! I've got a dragon stationed outside, along with many more within this mountain and an army just beyond these walls." Ace's words dripped with hostility.

Leper laced his retort with nonchalance. "As you say, we'll cross that bridge when we get there."

After a brief pause to catch their breath, then they both rushed towards each other, ready for round two.

"That's enough, boys," Petrovana called out.

As Petrovana stood there, hand extended towards Ace, she called upon her ice magic, summoning a large block of ice that hurtled towards him with tremendous force. The frozen projectile collided with Ace's chest, sending him careening backwards. Seeing the opportunity to gain the upper hand, Leper swiftly moved forward, seizing Ace's arms and locking them behind his head in a powerful hold, effectively restraining him.

"Now, some actual answers," Petrovana walked over, keeping her palm aimed directly at Ace. "Since you seem to like to murder everyone, reckon it's time we repay the favor."

"You're all fools. Once you're lifeless, the full power of the shrine will be mine to command. Not even Nalecht, with the talisman, can dare to challenge me!" Ace's voice reverberated with menace.

"So, you did murder the other two?" Leper prodded, his eyes seeking closure. Ace's response was an ear-to-ear grin, chilling in its implication.

Petrovana interjected, her voice laced with curiosity. "What talisman are you referrin' to?" Her brows furrowed.

"The Talisman of Runes," Maka Kura's voice resounded in Leper's thoughts. "The book, in your possession. Look at that page again."

Gritting his teeth, Leper pressed on with urgency. "What's Nalecht's next move?"

"It's too far, and your timing is futile. They're likely at Tudela, ready to obliterate Brebian's forces and claim the shard of Theora. All that will be left is to decimate the remaining resistance. When I arrive with Voldahyl, the bloodshed will be unstoppable." Ace recounted.

"Voldahyl?" Leper's head tilted, seeking clarification.

Ace's sneer was clear in his tone. "My dragon, you moron. One of many on this mountain and out in the world."

"Where?" Leper squeezed.

"Wouldn't you like to know?" Ace grinned.

Ace squirmed and struggled to break free, but Leper's grip was unyielding, as strong as that of a cave bear securing its prey. Leper tightened his hold and delivered a swift knee to Ace's back, eliciting a pained whimper from him. As the impact reverberated through the mountain, rocks from the ceiling dislodged, falling around them. Leper glanced up—it had to be Voldahyl, Ace's dragon, trying to reach him. The cavern trembled with the dragon's power, and Leper knew they needed to act swiftly. He kept his focus on restraining Ace while also keeping a watchful eye on the surrounding situation. The mysteries of the Chernzerk history and the secrets hidden within this ancient place could wait. Right now, they had a formidable opponent to deal with, and it was time to make their move.

"We need to get out. We are outnumbered," Maka Kura popped into Leper's mind.

"I know. I'm working on that, but we have no means of transportation, and we can't outrun a dragon." Leper snapped.

"This place is your home, too. Not just his. Get outside and whistle. Your mount will come."

Leper looked at Petrovana and then made a side-eye motion towards the exit. Her face scrunched for a second before it looked like the lights came on. Leper squeezed a little tighter, drawing strength from Ace as you would squeeze juice from a lemon. Right before Leper let go, Petrovana unleashed another ice shard at his head, and he fell unconscious to the ground.

"I'd like to bring him in as prisoner, but we don't have time," Leper grabbed Petrovana's hand. "We need to go now."

"Agreed." She nodded.

Leper's heart raced as he strapped Maka Kura to his side and grabbed the magnificent shield from the wall. With the chakram guiding them, they swiftly navigated the labyrinthine tunnels, emerging on the opposite side of the mountain from where they had entered. As Voldahyl continued to claw and dig in desperation, Leper let out a loud whistle. A majestic griffin appeared in the sky. Feathers of many colors, shimmering, adorned its large wings. Its sharp beak and lion-like paws exuded a sense of power and grace. Utterly amazing.

The wind blew wildly now, and rain fell heavily from the dark clouds. Leper shielded his face from the rain and couldn't believe his eyes as his griffin glided gracefully towards him. Its majestic figure and vibrant plumage caught him off guard. Fighting the urge to let out a triumphant cry, he watched as it landed before him.

Overwhelmed with a tumultuous mix of emotions, Leper struggled to make sense of it all. He felt a surge of joy rushing through him as he realized he was more than just an average man and that the Chernzerk were not the mindless beasts they had been painted to be. But his heart thudded with disappointment as Ace's actions mirror the negative stereotypes perpetuated by history books, potentially solidifying the Chernzerk's unjust reputation. Leper quickly retrieved the book that Maka Kura reminded him of, flipping it to that page that was purposefully mutilated. As he glanced at the pages, he could read some descriptions and interpret the runes, thanks to Maka Kura's assistance.

He read the passages aloud to Petrovana. "It stands as the most potent relic in this realm, created by the gods for the gods. Yet, ages ago, humanity chanced upon this artifact, bestowing upon them the power to shape, to obliterate, to grasp eternal life. When the virtuous rose against the tyrant Eden Sarsnip, they sundered the amulet of its might, shattering it into seven shards."

"Reckon we should get that information to the others." Petrovana offered.

"If they'll listen to me now. In case you forgot, Madislak was heading back to tell them what a piece of shit I am, remember?" Leper glanced at the ground.

"Leper, let's just go. We have more pressin' concerns right now." Petrovana motioned towards the griffin.

Leper extended his hand, allowing the griffin to investigate his scent. When it lowered its front legs, he took it as a sign of acceptance. Without hesitation, Leper hopped on the griffin's back, feeling the strength of the creature beneath him.

"I hope this thing is fast," Leper said aloud.

Chapter Thirteen

The flying chariot struggled to keep up its speed, and Madislak's heart pounded in his chest as he held onto the controls. They had just lifted off, leaving Leper and Petrovana there as dark clouds began swirling in around The Talon. With the machine groaning and teetering, he pushed it to its limits, desperate to create distance between them, the island, and the relentless dragon chasing after them. They crossed the point of no return, and it was now all-or-nothing. The veins in his neck heaved. The imminent danger of crashing in a fiery blaze lurked in the back of his mind.

Madislak's focus briefly shifted to Harmony, who was frantically moving back and forth, peering through the windows with a terrified expression. Her hair looked frizzled, and her face appeared as pale as a ghost. *I can't believe I just left them there. What kind of king abandons people that helped him escape certain death?* They were in dire straits, and he needed to keep his wits about him to navigate this perilous situation. Madislak couldn't escape the shadow of his father's downfall, constantly haunted by the fear of becoming just like him. The thought of being seen as a failure like Nelaan and removed from the throne like him was enough to make him shudder. But he couldn't deny the drive to prove himself and not bring more shame upon their family name. Knowing Leper is a Chernzerk and aiding him would only make Brebian and Theodamar question his judgment as king.

"I think it stopped," Harmony's face pressed up against the window.

"Why would it do that?" Madislak snapped.

Harmony kept peering out the window. "I can't tell, but I saw a reflection come off what looked like one of Leper's chakrams."

"Why would he do th..."

"Because he's your damn friend," Harmony smacked the window.

Madislak couldn't see out the back of the flying chariot, but he trusted Harmony to monitor their pursuer. Even though he left Leper on that mountain with no apparent escape, he still couldn't shake the guilt that crept into his mind. The weight of his actions hung heavy on his shoulders as he continued to fly, the dead silence around them deafening. History books and his father's beliefs depicted Chernzerks as chaotic and vengeful beings thriving amid turmoil. But there was something about Leper that didn't entirely fit that mold, and the conflicting emotions within Madislak were hard to reconcile.

"Doesn't it bother you that he lied to us? To everyone?" Madislak's voice broke the silence.

"Apparently, not as much as it bothers you. I'm pretty sure Rinawen knew," Harmony responded with a hint of frustration. "And to tell you the truth, I knew he was one at that meeting. His reaction to the horn, dodging questions, Rinawen had no clue about his crime, Madislak. It was right there. You just missed the clues."

"How could you have deduced that and not told me? What else are you lying to me about?" Madislak scowled. "It gets harder and harder every day to know who you can trust, Harmony, and you're one person I didn't expect to be on that list."

"You're right, my King. Forgive me for not saying anything when I knew you would react this way." Harmony said as she sat down on a bench, crossing her arms.

"So, you're suggesting we should have them both imprisoned until we can decide what to do?" Madislak stated firmly.

"You can be so exhausting sometimes. Just once, can you put aside your commitment to law and order?" Harmony let out an exasperated sigh. "It's against Pasileveo and Nalecht's law."

"What do you mean by that?" Madislak turned to face Harmony.

"I mean exactly what I said. He might be a Chernzerk, and Rinawen may have protected him in Kordry all this time, but he has committed no crimes. He's helped us, and now you've left him stranded on a mountain to face a dragon," Harmony let out a dejected sigh.

"Petrovana is with him, and her magic is an advantage against the dragons," Madislak explained.

Harmony shook her head. "Whatever you call it, Mad, if Rinawen discovers what you've done..." she shook her head.

"I am your KING!" he shouted, his face mere inches from hers. "You will treat me with the respect I deserve, or I'll have you thrown into the dungeons!"

Frustration boiled over in Madislak. Despite the logical sense in Harmony's words, he'd been belittled by an understudy. He was the king of Lantess, and he demanded respect. His mind acknowledged the wisdom of her advice, but his pride pushed back against it. He wanted to prove himself, to show that he was a capable leader, not just someone who relied on others' guidance. The conflict within him simmered, and he took a deep breath, seeking a balance between humility and asserting his authority.

"Yes, my King," Harmony replied, her gaze shifting to the floor. She avoided eye contact, fixing her stare on the ground.

Madislak took his seat at the front of the carriage again. Maybe he was being a huge asshole, but as a king, he knew that sometimes tough decisions were necessary. Aiding a Chernzerk carried penalties that Madislak wasn't willing to pay.

Ten years ago, Madislak took an army of five thousand and defended Lantess from Goreldea, winning the battle. When Nalecht became Anyth eight years later, he removed Nelaan Idelth from the throne for incompetence. Ever since that moment, it made Madislak edgy and uptight. His mind churned with conflicting thoughts as guilt took hold. He was torn between his duty as a ruler and the moral weight of Leper's plea for help. *What kind of king abandons his people to face a dragon? What kind of king leaves two to die—especially when one saved him and his children?*

Two hours of flying later, as they neared the city of Wen-Tath, they could see the walls. Suddenly, a resounding boom echoed from behind them. At first, Madislak feared the dragon had returned, but his fear intensified as a beam of pure energy shot out from The Talon. The energy's wrath engulfed the flying chariot, causing it to become unstable and rattle violently. The powerful force tossed both Madislak and Harmony from their seats as the chariot fought against it, causing them to struggle to hold on. In the chaos, Madislak desperately tried to regain control.

"That's not good," Madislak muttered.

Madislak feverishly shoved levers up and down, to no avail. Their descent from the sky intensified with no relief in sight.

"Harmony, help me, please!" he pleaded.

"Why so you can turn your back on me when I need you most?" she glared, not moving a muscle.

"Stop being so stubborn, woman! If this thing crashes, we both die. That includes you."

Harmony rolled her eyes. "Okay, I don't know if it's a good idea, but when we get closer to the ground, I'll bind us and the chariot. That's all I can think of."

"It gives us a better chance of survival," Madislak held Harmony by the waist. "I'm sorry for yelling at you."

Harmony stared at him. "It takes a life-threatening situation to get a man to apologize."

As the ground rapidly approached, Madislak's heart pounded in his chest. To halt the chariot's descent, Harmony stretched out her left hand, using her binding magic. However, her magic didn't stop the chariot's descent, and it continued its plummet toward the earth. Madislak opened the side door to the chariot before they hit the ground. Holding Harmony, they jumped together out of the side door as Harmony used her magic, and the brain tattoo slowly faded to gray. They remained suspended in mid-air while the chariot crashed.

"How do we get down?" Madislak looked at Harmony.

With a grin, she replied. "We fall and hope for the best."

With their descent unyielding, Madislak frantically searched for something to hold on to once Harmony released her binding spell. But there was nothing within reach, and he resigned himself to the possibility of a grim fate. He exchanged a nod with Harmony. As the moment of impact approached, Madislak acted on instinct, pulling Harmony over him, hoping to shield her from the worst of the impact. With an enormous thud, they landed on the soft ground, then tumbled around for a few feet before finally halting. Madislak landed face down. Thankfully, the terrain was not hardened or dry, which softened the impact and spared them from more severe injuries. They lay there for a moment, catching their breath, Madislak's heart still racing from the near-fatal fall. The damp dirt had a heavy, musty odor that lingered in Madislak's nostrils. The dirt tasted earthy and gritty, with a touch of bitterness. It left a dry, powdery residue on Madislak's tongue that was hard to swallow. He spat out chunks of grass and dirt.

"Ugh," Madislak groaned.

"Thank you," Harmony said as she stood and dusted herself off.

"Here, take this," she opened her side pouch and handed him a vial.

"What is it?" Madislak inquired.

Harmony glared at him. "Leper gave me some. It aids in recovery. Works like a charm."

"He's still helping us," Madislak's hand hit the ground. "Perhaps I'm as blind and foolish as I feel."

"You're neither blind nor foolish. I also apologize for my earlier words. It must be a constant struggle to know who can be trusted when you're a king. That goes for anyone. Elves, Dwarves, Human, Chernzerk." Harmony offered.

Madislak got to his feet. "Regardless, we must make our way to Wen-Tath or Tudela. They need to be informed about the dragon and its rider. We also need to let them know the enemy has the shard of Amarook."

Harmony peered through the trees. "What about Leper?"

"I don't know yet. I need time to think. Right now, the important part is we need to get to Tudela and let them know the enemy is approaching. We have to be ready to defend against these major threats." Madislak pinched the bridge of his nose.

"Well, well, well, how the tables have turned," a high-pitched voice echoed.

Madislak's eyes widened as he faced Martin, accompanied by a small host of fifteen orcs. Despite their diminished numbers, the orcs had always preferred staying underground, their pride and stubbornness preventing them from forming a significantly organized army. Madislak's mind raced, trying to comprehend how Martin could exert control over them. Steeling himself, Madislak gripped his sword tightly, ready to defend Harmony and himself.

"This isn't the right time, Martin. You should move along. I won't be as forgiving as before." Madislak drew Skyrunner from its sheath.

"It's two against... how many are here? I think it's me who's about to call the shots." Martin's words were strained through clenched teeth.

"What are you doing here? And why are you with the orcs?" Madislak questioned.

Martin puffed his chest. "Well, after you left me to die, one Queen Tamara saved me."

"Queen Tamara? From Xaneth Harbor? She's neither kind nor young. She's using you," Madislak responded.

"At least she provides me some protection, unlike certain people," Martin glanced at Madislak.

"Protection! You shoved me outside the door during a battle with a shade panther. Then, locked yourself inside and hid! You're despicable. A cowardly slime that drains life from everything around you." Harmony's anger flared.

Madislak's heart sank as the shadow of the dragon loomed above them, a sight they had hoped not to encounter so soon. The uncertainty of Leper and Petrovana's fate weighed heavily on his mind, and he could feel the rage building within him. The urgency to confront the enemy and discover the truth fueled his determination.

"No more Mr. Nice Guy," Madislak declared, his voice filled with resolve. He couldn't afford to be held back by Martin and the orcs any longer. With a swift motion, he raised his sword. Harmony nodded in agreement, her eyes reflecting the same determination. With Martin and the orcs in their way, Madislak prepared to unleash the full force of his abilities.

"Well, I guess they're going to find out about the dragon soon," Harmony's voice dripping sarcasm.

"Move or we go through you, Martin. I'm done pissing around." Madislak lowered his head and began marching toward Martin.

Leighth utilized the cover of Blank Face, uncertainty gnawing at her as she faced the precarious situation ahead. It took them two days to travel to Tudela. She hoped to convince Queen Rinawen to let her borrow the shard of Theora so she and Blank Face could attack Nalecht. Maybe Leighth could convince her Blank Face would be an excellent ally. After all, he doesn't lose many battles. Maybe he can even fight Nalecht for them. That would require him to agree, though. *Right.*

She and Blank Face never spoke again about what she asked him the other night in Ambrosia. Maybe he wasn't ready, or maybe he just wasn't ready to admit it. Something in her gut told her Blank Face isn't all evil.

She remembered Rinawen from her childhood as they neared the door. Their families ruled and maintained peace on the island of Sartina for decades. Rinawen was much older than her, so they were not close friends, but she was always kind. Despite her hair being cut short by Blank Face, Leighth was almost certain Rinawen would still recognize her. The thought of having to ask for the shard was frustrating, as she wished it could be a simpler, more straightforward task.

The door swung open, revealing a red-haired woman with two scimitars on her back. Leighth's heart raced. The confusion on the woman's face betrayed her inner turmoil.

"What the shit?" the red-haired woman muttered, her eyes scanning Blank Face from head to toe.

"I have someone who wishes to speak with Rinawen," his voice devoid of emotion.

"Who might that be?" the commanding woman inquired.

Leighth leaned into the doorway, glimpsing Rinawen perched on the bed's edge of the pristine guest room of Tudela.

"Merciful Theora, is that really you, Leighth?" Rinawen's face lit up.

"Yeah, it's me." Leighth half grinned.

With a rush of enthusiasm, Rinawen closed the gap to embrace her. "It's okay, Lillian. Leighth is Jaynoh's daughter and rightful heir to Kundry."

"I heard about what happened. I thought you were dead. Please, come in and have a seat." Rinawen walked back to the bed, taking a seat.

Leighth took a seat on the bed beside her. The burning candles emitted a floral scent. "Alright, Queen Rinawen."

"Just Rinawen is fine, Leighth."

Blank Face stood firm at the doorway, his gaze locked onto Lillian's with unwavering intensity. The tension in the air was electric, as they seemed to be engaged in a silent battle of wills. Leighth motioned for him to come over, but he remained immobile, refusing to budge. She sighed and shrugged, accepting his decision, and settled herself on the bed, waiting to see how the situation would unfold.

"What... What happened to your hair?" Rinawen's fingers brushed through Leighth's now-short locks. She glanced at Blank Face, then back to Leighth. "And who is this skulking figure you've brought along?"

"He helped me escape and alter my appearance to avoid detection by Borlden's men. He's also saved my life multiple times... Right?" Leighth looked at Blank Face.

"Yep," came the reply from his statue-like stance.

"Well, thank you. Your service won't go unrewarded. You'll be honored throughout Sartina," Rinawen offered.

"I don't need your charity now, and I didn't then," Blank Face's voice cut through, his gaze fixed on Leighth.

"Right. Rinawen, I need to ask you a favor," Leighth said, her tone sheepish.

"Wait, what did you mean by that last remark? Have we met before?" Rinawen turned her attention to Blank Face.

"Apologies, I misspoke," he retorted, his tone neutral.

Rinawen shifted her focus back to Leighth, her face displaying a mix of thoughts. "Well, regardless of all this, whatever you need... Is it about Kundry? We can handle that."

"Not exactly," Leighth replied, her gaze dropping to the ground. "They took the shard of Hathor from my dad. We need the shard of Theora to get it back," she lied.

"Why do you need that? You know it's a family heirloom, passed down like your father's..." Rinawen's words trailed off, her expression showing a mixture of concern and curiosity.

Leighth watched as Rinawen's eyes darted back and forth, piecing together the puzzle before her. The defensive stance and the probing questions revealed her suspicion, and Leighth knew they had to act fast to prevent the situation from spiraling into chaos. Time was of the essence, and the stakes were high. She needed to improvise, to defuse the tension before it erupted into a potential bloodbath. Leighth's heart pounded in her chest, fully aware that every move they made now could determine the outcome of this crucial encounter.

"I'm not a fighter, but if I had the shard of Theora and with his skills, I could reclaim my shard and take back the throne of Kundry," Leighth urged.

"You're well aware I can't comply with that." Rinawen remained steadfast. "Nalecht has made his intentions clear. I will not give him another shard to add to his collection."

"Told you diplomacy is dead," Blank Face chimed in, gesturing at Leighth.

"What's his name?" Rinawen scrutinized Leighth. "And why are you associating with this... filth?"

"He's saved my life on more than one occasion," Leighth defended. "Not to mention, he's the only one who's promised to help me retrieve the shard of Hathor. Nobody else has even hinted at an offer to help me. I don't care about Nalecht collecting them or whatever... I want my damn shard back. It's the only piece of my family I have left!"

Blank Face attempted to move past Lillian, but she swiftly blocked his path, brandishing a scimitar that halted him in his tracks. She firmly pressed the cold steel blade against his chest, clarifying that any further attempts to bypass her would be met with resistance. A large grin crawled across Lillian's face.

"Oh, I don't think so, Mr. Face. Reckon I'll be sendin' you to meet yer maker today," her grin widening. "So, when they ask who defeated Slippery Death itself, y'all can tell them it was Lillian."

"Don't flatter yourself, girl," Blank Face drew his daggers, swatting her scimitar off his chest.

Lillian's face flushed red. "My name ain't girl. It's Lillian, and after today, you will remember that."

Lillian's scimitar sliced through the air with deadly precision, but Blank Face proved to be a master of evasion, gracefully sidestepping both attacks. Undeterred, he attempted to slip past her once more, only to find Lillian blocking his path with her body.

Her eyes blazed with defiance as she declared, "To get to her, you go through me!"

Blank Face's retort was cold and unwavering. "Fine, if you want to forfeit your life, I'll gladly be the one to take it."

Leighth watched anxiously, her heart pounding, knowing that every move from this point forward could lead them down a treacherous path. As the tense standoff continued, Leighth noticed the unmistakable thrill of battle etched across Lillian's face. Despite the gravity of the situation, there was a spark of excitement in her eyes, and Leighth realized Lillian was just as eager for the confrontation as Blank Face. The realization sent a chill down her spine as she understood they were dealing with someone who reveled in the chaos of combat.

Leighth's eyes widened. Blank Face's swift and precise attacks were usually enough to render any opponent incapacitated, but Lillian proved to be an exception. Each strike from Blank Face met with equally skillful parries from Lillian, and the resounding clang of metal filled the air, echoing through the halls like a symphony of combat.

Intrigued and slightly apprehensive, Leighth began rubbing her arm nervously as Lillian matched Blank Face's every move with expert precision. She didn't want either of them to die since Rinawen wouldn't help her directly. She just wanted to take the shard so she could use it to get her shard and kingdom back. Leighth glanced over at Rinawen, looking for the shard of Theora, but didn't see it on her.

"Please, Rinawen." Leighth set her hand on the queen's arm. "Give me the shard. We can stop this madness right now."

"I'll do no such thing. You are not thinking clearly." Rinawen pulled her arm away and separated herself from Leighth.

It was like witnessing a mesmerizing dance of blades, and she could hardly believe that anyone could keep up with his lightning-fast strikes. Lillian's exceptional agility and reflexes allowed her to sidestep and counter Blank Face's attacks with ease.

Leighth's eyes went wide as Blank Face executed a brilliant feint, luring Lillian into lowering her defenses. With lightning speed, he deftly maneuvered around her, catching her off guard and landing a swift strike to her side. Lillian staggered back, momentarily caught off balance by the unexpected attack. The two skilled combatants continued their intense dance of blades. Leighth's heart pounded in her chest, akin to a drumbeat increasing in tempo. Blank Face's cunning and agility were on full display, and she couldn't help but admire his tactical brilliance.

"I grow tired of your resistance," he snarled.

"Sucks to be you cuz I ain't done," said Lillian re-energized from the strike.

Lillian's agility and adaptability were truly remarkable, and she caught Blank Face off guard with a well-timed sweep of her foot, sending him slightly off balance. In that critical moment, she seized the opportunity, delivering a powerful strike across Blank Face's chest with her scimitar. Her lungs constricted.

Blank Face rolled back twice, creating a small gap between him, and then he grinned at Lillian. He placed his hand on his chest and then examined the red blood for a moment.

"Told ya! Today, yer reign ends, boy!!" Lillian mocked, pointing a scimitar at him.

"Don't kill him!" Leighth cried, catching Lillian's attention. "Both of you combined could easily kill Nalecht and Borlden and end this whole thing right now!"

"Reckon I don't work with criminals, princess." Lillian sneered.

"Look at me, Lillian." Blank Face aimed his dagger at her. "I'll not have a distraction win this fight for me. I want you to see the end coming." His face scrunched together slightly, giving off a deep sense of anger. Leighth had never seen his face change before.

Blank Face's fury was clear in the ferocity of his attacks as he relentlessly pushed Lillian backward, his blades moving like a blur. Leighth could see the determination in his eyes, and she knew he was now truly angry. Lillian fought with all her skill and strength, but even her impressive agility couldn't match Blank Face's relentless assault. In a desperate attempt to gain some ground, Lillian stumbled near the edge of the bed, but her determination kept her on her feet. However, Blank Face's speed seemed to have intensified, and he delivered a series of precise strikes to her leg, arm, and waist in rapid succession. The sight was both mesmerizing and terrifying, and Leighth's heart clenched.

Then, with a swift and powerful kick, Blank Face sent Lillian flying back into the wall, causing her to drop her weapons. The room echoed with the sound of the impact, and Leighth felt a surge of fear and concern for Lillian's well-being.

"Like I said, girl. Don't flatter yourself," Blank Face taunted back at her.

A resounding boom echoed through the sky, reverberating through the ground and the very walls of the castle. The intense vibration sent shivers down Leighth's spine, and she feared that the entire castle might collapse around them.

"What was that?" Rinawen looked at Lillian, who was picking herself up off the ground.

"The shard, now elf bitch," Blank Face pointed to Rinawen with his dagger.

"No, Blank, they can help us. She's just as good as you are. We can take on Nalecht and get my shard back!" Leighth interrupted. "You said you'd help me, so help me."

"You're too late; backup is coming. Are you going to kill them all wounded?" Rinawen taunted right back.

Blank Face clutched his chest, grimacing in pain. "This isn't over. I'll be back." He glanced over at Lillian. "I commend your ability. You are leaps and bounds above anyone else I've ever fought."

"Ya? Well, you can shove yer commendation straight up yer ass, murderer." Lillian gritted.

"Rinawen, you have to see things from my perspective. I have lost everything: my family, my kingdom, my shard. You and the others have never helped me, but he has. He may not be the most noble or the cleanest, but you cannot deny that he would be a powerful ally. He can kill Nalecht and Borlden, the ones who took everything from me. And I want them dead." Leighth huffed. "I want them dead more than I want anything else in this world."

"Are you genuinely thinking about joining him? You have allies here, Leighth. Don't make a foolish choice," Rinawen begged.

"I've grown beyond being a naive girl, Rinawen. Just because you don't understand him doesn't mean he shouldn't at least be offered a chance," Leighth responded, casting one last glance at Rinawen before swallowing an invisibility potion. The potion had a thick, sticky texture that coated her entire mouth with its sweet taste.

Her eyes scanned the room frantically, searching for Blank Face's figure to slip out and tend to his wound. Her mind raced with thoughts of revenge as she vowed to kill Borlden, no matter what it took. Bloodthirst fueled her every move as she prepared to take matters into her own hands. *If nobody else will help me, then I will become an assassin myself. Then, I won't have to depend on anyone else to fight my battles.*

Chapter Fourteen

With Petrovana clinging tightly to his waist, Leper skillfully guided the griffin down into a lush cluster of trees. The vibrant foliage provided some cover, hopefully enough to keep them hidden until both Ace and Voldahyl moved on. Even though their clothing clashed with the brilliant colors of the forest, it was their best chance of evading detection. *Hopefully, this relentless rain will wash away our scent.*

Silence enveloped them as time dragged on. They left Ace unconscious in the cave an hour ago. Voldahyl circled the area, his keen senses detecting the scent of the forest. Leper's heart pounded in his chest, knowing that a confrontation with a dragon was no small feat. Ace, too, was a formidable adversary. After a series of failed attempts to locate them, the dragon seemed to grow impatient and sped off toward the west. The drops of rain pelting on the ground grew smaller as the dark clouds seemed to give way to clear skies. He could hear the drops echoing off the leaves and ground.

Leper let out a breath he hadn't realized he was holding. "That was too close," he murmured, grateful that they had avoided direct confrontation for the time being.

"Shit. I hope it's not going to Wen-Tath." Leper looked to Petrovana.

Leper couldn't help but be captivated by Petrovana's beauty, even during their perilous situation. Her wind-blown, wild hair and dirt smudges on her face seemed to enhance her allure. But it was her captivating purple eyes that truly held his gaze as if they contained an entire universe of mystery and wonder. The flowery scent of her hair wafted through the air, a delicate and sweet aroma reminiscent of a lush garden in full bloom. Despite the surrounding chaos, he found himself lost in those mesmerizing depths, grateful to have her by his side.

"I think that's exactly where they're goin'," Petrovana said.

Leper's mind was a whirlwind of emotions, trying to process all the information he learned in the cave. His heart raced, and his breathing became erratic as if he couldn't catch his breath. His vision blurred slightly, and he felt overwhelmed by the weight of everything he discovered. The truth he sought for so long was now before him, and it was more than he could handle at that moment. He took deep breaths, trying to calm himself, but the flood of emotions was too much to bear all at once. For a moment, he felt like he couldn't control his own actions.

"Leper, are you okay?" Petrovana put her hand on his shoulder.

"I... Ugh... Damnit!" he slammed his fist into a nearby tree.

"What's wrong?" she said, gazing into his eyes.

"Everything. My dumb father. Ace. Everything!" he rested his head against Petrovana's head.

"Tell me about it." She reassured him.

"I literally exist because my father raped my mother," he seethed. "He was a total dick. Then Ace... I have a brother..."

"Well, had a brother who Ace killed, maybe? I don't know. Ace had a sister." Leper mumbled.

"And he killed her too?" Petrovana pulled her head back, gazing at him.

"Yes. Apparently, when you kill a person from that shrine, you inherit their power or magic our fathers stored for them."

Petrovana shook her head. "Dear gods, that's why he wanted you dead so bad."

"Ya, exactly." Leper nodded.

"Who was your mother, then?" She stroked his cheek.

Leper pointed to his neck. "A human woman named Ana, I think. At least that's what was on her necklace. Dark hair, brown eyes, hair was to the shoulders."

"Ain't no one I know." Petrovana's eyes darted around.

Leper placed his hand on her shoulder. "So, who are your parents, then? The king and queen of Terynsipple?"

"I... uhh... honestly, now's not the time for that discussion," Petrovana mouthed.

"Wow, sorry, I don't know what came over me there. It felt like I couldn't control myself for a minute." Leper expressed, wrapping his arms around her in gratitude. "And for staying here, with me, after they left. Even in the face of danger."

"My pleasure," Petrovana replied, her smile radiating warmth.

"There's one more thing Maka Kura told me," Leper continued, holding her hands.

"Who's Maka Kura?" she tilted her head in curiosity.

Leper shifted his gaze to his weapons, then back to Petrovana. "Maka Kura is my sentient weapon. Once forged, he doesn't know of a way to break the talisman back apart. Petrovana, we can't let them reforge that talisman."

"Then what are we sittin' around fer? We need to get back to the others. They need to understand what's at stake here." Petrovana pulled on his hand.

"Right, and if he has three of them. Ace and Tamara apparently are working with him, and they have Amarook now. That leaves Theora, Kasherri, and Aisha." Leper glanced off into the distance as his thoughts wandered towards Rinawen.

"He can't get them, Leper. Reckon if he does, Kalazaar will become a dark oblivion." Petrovana took a quick breath in. "If that talisman holds that kind of power and Nalecht is seekin' to reforge it. C'mon, we have to go now."

Their eyes locked in a magnetic connection, and Leper felt an irresistible pull towards her. Her charming personality was infectious, drawing him closer, and he leaned in to kiss her. Their lips met in a moment of shared intimacy, but as quickly as it began, Petrovana pulled back, breaking the spell between them. Her lips had a delicate, fruity sweetness, like freshly picked blueberries and ripe strawberries. Confusion and disappointment washed over Leper as he searched her eyes for an explanation.

"Sorry, but we kinda have a dragon on the loose," she said.

"Right, ugh, I'm so stupid. Sorry," Leper started walking towards their new mount.

"Don't be sorry. Didn't say I didn't like it, we just got shit to do, ya know?" She giggled.

"Yep, now's not the time." Leper turned and headed for his griffin.

Leper's joy and excitement were clear as he helped Petrovana onto the griffin, but his grin faded as memories of his night with Lillian flooded back. He felt a twinge of guilt, knowing she had warned him not to be swayed by Petrovana's charms. He couldn't deny the strong connection he felt with Petrovana. Still, he didn't want to hurt Lillian or jeopardize their friendship. Leper's emotions tangled into a web of conflicting feelings, unsure of what path to take. He took a deep breath, trying to push the turmoil aside and focus on the immediate task at hand.

Yet here he was, falling for her beauty, wit, and personality. He was happy when she was around him. *Rinawen*! If Ace is headed to Wen-Tath or Tudela, she will be there. Time to get a move on.

"C'mon Ghost, make haste westward!" Leper called out as he mounted the great griffin.

"Ghost?" Petrovana scrunched her face together.

He grinned. "That's what I named him."

"Weird name for a pet." She mused.

"I have a weird name, so it works." Leper smirked. "He'll be Leper's ghost."

"Indeed, you do, Leper," she purred.

The wind rushed past them as Ghost, the griffin, soared through the skies with remarkable speed. Leper could feel the raw power of the creature beneath him, and he marveled at how effortlessly it glided through the air. The fresh air and aroma of the forest vegetation as they took off filled his nostrils. Petrovana held on tightly, her face close to his, and he could feel her warm breath against his neck.

The landscape below them blurred into a colorful mosaic, the lush forests and rolling hills transforming into a patchwork of green and gold. Leper couldn't help but admire the beauty of Kalazaar from this vantage point, even amid their urgent pursuit.

"I hope Ghost is fast," Petrovana said confidently, her voice carried away by the rushing wind.

Lillian's muscles ached from the intense battle that just concluded with Blank Face. The surrounding room was in disarray, evidence of the fierce fight that had just taken place. Books covered the floor, and the walls bore scorch marks from their clash of weapons. Despite her injuries, Lillian focused her eyes on Rinawen, who appeared stunned and frightened. Probably from the battle or perhaps from the fact they still hadn't made it outside yet to assess the battlefield like Brebian had requested. He could wait a little longer. One day wasn't much to ask for.

"Are you alright?" Lillian asked, concern lacing her voice as she approached. Rinawen nodded, her hand clutching the shard of Theora tightly. Lillian could sense the fear emanating from Rinawen, which only fueled her determination to protect her.

"That bastard won't get away with this," Lillian growled, her fists clenched in anger. "I won't let him harm you or take that shard."

Rinawen's eyes met Lillian's, gratitude and trust evident in her gaze. Lillian knew she had to stay strong, not just for herself but for Rinawen as well. The shard of Theora was a powerful artifact, and they couldn't let it fall into the wrong hands.

"Here, take this. I've got a salve that'll hasten your recovery. Those wounds will be a memory in a day," Rinawen extended her offer.

"It ain't the wounds. It's the reality that piece of trash bested me," Lillian fumed.

"If it provides any consolation, it appears you'll have another chance," Rinawen offered.

"Fuck him. If he crosses my path again, I won't hold back," Lillian seethed, settling down beside Rinawen.

Lillian winced as Rinawen applied the healing salve to her cuts, relieved that it wasn't as painful as she expected. That lilac smell still poured off Rinawen as she got close. She sighed, feeling a mix of frustration and disappointment in herself for not defeating Blank Face. Losing was a bitter pill for her to swallow, as she prided herself on her skills as a warrior. She looked over at Rinawen, who seemed to be lost in thought. She wiped the blood off her mouth, the taste still fresh on her tongue.

"So, who is Leighth exactly?" Lillian studied Rinawen's face.

"Ugh," Rinawen shook her head. "She is a really nice young lady. King Jaynoh's daughter, her whole family, was killed in Ambrosia about a week ago."

"How'd they die?" Lillian tilted her head to the side.

Rinawen looked down at the shard of Theora. "Nalecht killed them for the shard."

"How'd she get away?"

Rinawen shook her head. "According to her, Blank Face helped her."

"He's got her brainwashed for sure. I wouldn't blame that one on her," Lillian rested her arm on Rinawen's shoulder.

Rinawen huffed. "I don't blame her for his actions. I just wonder what she could do to help by running around with the enemy."

Lillian paused a moment before an idea popped into her head. "She could be a good snitch. Might be a way to take advantage of that, I reckon. She seems motivated enough to kill them as well. Honestly, can you really blame her? Especially if they killed her family... I'd be pissed."

"I couldn't put her in such danger." Rinawen shook her head.

"Sometimes you gotta let folks be who they're gonna be," Lillian shrugged.

"Meaning?" Rinawen looked at Lillian.

"For instance, Leper. You can't protect everyone all the time. Sometimes they gotta learn themselves." Lillian flicked her eyes to Rinawen, then to the floor.

Rinawen furrowed her brow. "And sometimes experience knows best."

Lillian hopped up. "I'm just sayin'. Some people grow tremendously when they see what the world is like. Other's not so much."

"Well, let's just leave it at that. I don't want to get into an argument." Rinawen got up beside her.

Lillian tried to avoid arguments, especially with Rinawen, who seemed to hold strong to her queenly nature. To Lillian, it felt like Rinawen needed to loosen her grip and allow people to find their own paths of growth. Perhaps it was the influence of Terynsipple's upbringing, where shrews often pushed the boundaries of magic and paid the ultimate price. The memories of horrific experiments gone awry sent shivers down her spine, like the shrew whose eyes popped out or the one who choked on his own blood. She couldn't shake the irony of their reckless pursuit of power leading to their downfall. For Lillian, it was a reminder of the importance of balance and responsibility when wielding magic or any form of power. Too many terrible memories of that place.

"I have to go assess the battlefield and make sure Tudela is ready for any attack. Though if anything I've noticed is any indication, it will not be good," Rinawen suggested.

"Well, I sure as shit ain't lettin' you out of my sight now," Lillian remarked. Her wounds had already closed thanks to the healing salve. She marveled at its effectiveness. "This salve works wonders. What's it made of?"

"It's a secret recipe from Kordry. Surprisingly, it's not too complicated to make. We have some variations that involve specific moon phases for crafting." Rinawen led her out the door.

Lillian and Rinawen made their way through the mostly empty halls, occasionally encountering guards hurrying past or barking orders. The urgency in the air signaled that Brebian had indeed ordered preparations for an imminent attack. Stepping outside, they found the atmosphere even more frantic. People were scrambling to secure their homes, reinforcing defenses, and arming themselves.

"This place looks in dire straits, Lillian. They are not ready for an attack. Look at them, they're afraid. Guards are scrambling around barking orders they don't understand, and King Brebian is nowhere to be seen. We need to get a better vantage point, but from what I see, they won't survive thirty minutes in an attack." Rinawen gritted.

Lillian glanced around. "This ain't good. Where is the structure? The bulwarks? The generals? Does he not have some sort of chain of command?"

"Let's head over to the watchtower and check out our surroundings from above. We need a better view of the entire situation," Rinawen pointed toward the tower.

The watchtower stood near the castle's front doors, a symbol of vigilance in the face of danger. A guard stationed at the bottom of the watchtower greeted them.

"Can... Can I assist you?" The guard's surprise was apparent in his rapid blinking and nervous fumbling.

"Are you alright?" Rinawen's concern was genuine.

"I'm, well, yes. Just worried about the potential attack." His voice trembled.

"We have allies en route. Help is on the way, so there's no need to be afraid," Rinawen reassured him gently.

He turned to Rinawen, his eyes filled with apprehension. "We're up against Anyth, my lady, not just ordinary foes."

"We'll manage. We can't be certain they're even coming for us," Rinawen said, attempting to calm his fears.

"Quit wettin' yer pants. Grow a spine. Do I look scared?" Lillian stepped in, confronting the guard head-on.

"N... N... No," the guard stuttered.

"Exactly. We're goin' up this watchtower to survey the surroundins'," Lillian declared firmly.

"Alright," he responded, his voice still shaky.

"Pathetic. You'll be the first to die in any type of war, soldier. Get yer shit together." Lillian quipped as she grabbed onto the rung of the ladder.

The watchtower, made of thick oak, was about forty feet high. With a clear blue sky, the sun shone brightly, providing a comfortable temperature. To ensure sturdiness, they added steel brackets to reinforce the braces. Lillian climbed the ladder behind Rinawen until they reached the peak. Inside, another guard sat in the corner, head slumped on his shoulder.

"They're comin'! Nalecht is here!" Lillian exclaimed.

He clambered about, standing up and nearly running off the edge before Lillian caught him.

"Wh... What's happening?" He muttered.

"Nothing yet, but if it were, you would already be dead." Rinawen scolded. "This place is a total disaster. Do any of you take your duties seriously?"

The guard stood straight and saluted, "Yes, ma'am."

Lillian's keen observation revealed the downtrodden state of the defenders. Their morale was low, and she knew that without encouragement and leadership, the situation could turn dire. Where was Brebian when they needed him the most? A king should inspire his men, rallying them for the coming battle. Another bone-chilling roar echoed from the east, but this time, it wasn't the same as before. This one came from the sky, casting a massive shadow that sent shivers down Lillian's spine. She looked up to witness the looming presence of a menacing threat in the form of a fearsome dragon.

"Holy shit!" Lillian pointed to the sky. "Incomin'!!!!" she hollered from the perch.

Tudela erupted in panic with people running and screaming everywhere.

"By the gods," Rinawen muttered.

Lillian grabbed Rinawen and escorted her towards the ladder to let her get down first. "C'mon Queen, get yer ass down there now!"

The guard scrambled for the ladder, heading down just before Rinawen. The dragon flew westward, turned around, then came back east. A mountain of fire erupted from its maw. People screamed in horror. The smell of burnt flesh immediately overpowering anything else.

"It's headed straight for us! Go, go, go!" Lillian panicked.

The colossal creature's wings collided with the watchtower, causing it to crumble to the ground. The beast carried away the guard, who could not escape in time. Lillian and Rinawen were sent sprawling through the air.

The orc's dull purple eyes stared hungrily at Harmony and Madislak. Outnumbered seven to one, Madislak focused his mind on the task at

hand, determined to push past Martin and any other obstacles in his way to follow them. A resounding "screeeee" emanated from above. Everyone looked to the sky, glimpsing a griffin carrying two very familiar people zoom by. Madislak's eyes widened in surprise as he recognized Leper and Petrovana riding the griffin through the sky. The sight of his two companions filled him with relief and concern. Relief that they were safe and alive, but concern about the perilous journey they must have endured. They were on a mission. They were in pursuit of the dragon, notorious for its fierce breath and dangerous ways. Martin and his band of orcs stood in his way, but Madislak was prepared to march right through them.

"Leper," Harmony muttered. "He must be going to fight them!"

"Then let's repay the kindness he's shown us and be there to help him!" Madislak puffed his chest.

"Last chance, Martin," Madislak stopped briefly. "I won't ask again."

Three hours after they had left The Talon, their chariot crashed after a resounding boom, and a dragon had just flown overhead that no one missed.

Madislak turned to Martin, who remained poised and ready for the impending battle. With a swift motion of his wrist, a brilliant bead of light gleamed off Madislak's blade, momentarily blinding Martin. To his surprise, the blinding effect had no impact on the orcs, who seemed unfazed. Martin, acting panicked and uncoordinated, flailed about like a coward. Harmony swiftly launched a sizable ice shard, precisely hitting a group of five orcs, causing them to collapse to the ground.

Slicing and impaling every orc that crossed his path, Madislak wielded Skyrunner with unparalleled skill and precision. With every swing, he effortlessly cut down his enemies, a masterful display of deadly grace. His movements were a seamless dance of strength and agility as he swiftly parried incoming strikes and retaliated with swift, calculated slashes. The clash of metal echoed through the air as King Madislak's blade found its mark repeatedly, leaving a trail of fallen foes.

As he fought to hack his way through the orcs, the sheer number of enemies overwhelmed Madislak. Martin's blade sliced across his abdomen, but Madislak refused to give in. Warm blood oozed from his wound, but he pushed through despite his strikes becoming weaker and less precise. Meanwhile, Harmony attempted to use her magic to launch another shard of ice, but she missed her mark completely.

"Madislak!" she hollered, her voice strained.

In a moment of distraction, the orcs pounced on Madislak and wrestled him to the ground, trapping him in a chokehold. Desperately trying to breathe, Madislak struggled against their grip as their sausage-like fingers squeezed tighter and tighter.

Martin walked in front of Madislak, grinning ear to ear. "Well, it's past time the mighty Madislak finally meets his end. And at my hand, of all people." He taunted.

Suddenly, the pressure stopped, and Madislak glanced up to see Harmony extending her other hand, blood running from her nose as the brain tattoo faded to gray. He knew her magic wouldn't last long, but he wasn't wasting this opportunity. Martin's face snapped from that of malice to concern in an instant. The orcs gave off the unmistakable stench of darkness and dampness. Like moss-covered stones in a forgotten cave, their odor clung to them, mingled with the putrid scent of stagnant water.

Madislak got to his feet and, with a firm boot, sent Martin sprawling backwards. Then he twirled around a full circle with Skyrunner extended and killed the remaining orcs around him.

Once the last one fell, Madislak turned his attention to Martin.

Martin cowered in fear as Madislak approached him, Skyrunner leading the way.

"I'm sorry, I'm sorry, please!" he begged.

"You know, Martin. Although it hasn't been long since I've been on this journey, it has been pointed out to me that I need to make some changes."

He looked to Harmony. "So, Harmony, we have him in the woods. This man has committed a crime against you and would've done so again, given the chance. What shall we do with him?"

Harmony's face lit up. "I believe he deserves the death penalty, my King."

"Very well," Madislak agreed.

Madislak felt torn inside as he faced Martin, the man who had caused so much chaos and devastation. Every fiber of his being rebelled against the idea of taking another's life. He believed in justice, in giving everyone a fair chance to defend themselves, no matter how vile their actions might have been. This was against everything he'd been taught and what he stood for. But he couldn't dwell on this right now. Leper and Petrovana needed his help, and he would do anything he could to get to them.

With a heavy heart and a deep sense of regret, Madislak raised his sword and prepared to strike. He hoped that in taking this action, he could prevent further harm and protect those he cared about. However, the internal struggle persisted, creating a lingering sense of unease and doubt that Madislak knew would haunt him long after he won the battle—if they won the battle.

Perhaps bending the rules once wouldn't weigh on him forever. Maybe he would come to terms with it, eventually. After all, Martin was a despicable human being. Madislak shook his head and, with a quick stab forward, plunged Skyrunner into the chest of Martin. He watched as his eyes, horrified, rolled back into his head. He used his foot to shove Martin off the edge of his pristine blade. Then, he glanced off to the west, searching for any sign of the dragon or his friends.

"Thank you. I know that was difficult for you, but you have eliminated a threat to me," Harmony rushed over and kissed him on the cheek.

As Harmony's lips touched his cheek, Madislak felt a mix of surprise and warmth rushing through him. It had been a long time since anyone had shown him such a tender gesture. The memory of Gwen's tragic death still haunted him, making him hesitant to open his heart to someone new. But in that moment, he couldn't help but feel a glimmer of hope, a possibility of finding happiness again. Harmony's presence and courage had already made a significant impact on his life, and he knew he couldn't let her go. He wanted to protect her, to keep her safe, and to cherish the moments they shared. Despite the uncertainties that lay ahead, he wanted to embrace this new connection and see where it might lead.

"Harmony," he turned to her.

"Yes, sorry, I shouldn't have done that, my King. It was uncalled for."

"No, that's totally fine. Before we go, there's something I must do." He wiped the blood off Skyrunner. "Please kneel."

Harmony skeptically knelt down on one knee. Madislak placed the blade at her heart.

"For your heart that forgives and accepts without objection." Then he moved the sword to her head. "For your just mind that knows no bounds. Your understanding of fairness and remarkable ability to pass Theora's tests unwavering," he paused once more. "Here, under the gleaming sun, place your hand upon the sword."

She grabbed the sword in the center, and Madislak placed his hands over hers. Then, he squeezed enough to draw blood from his hands and hers and mingle it together—the sign of an oath taken for his city, Lantess.

"I officially appoint you proxy of Lantess. Your wisdom and intelligence shall bring great times upon our city," he smiled at her.

"Madislak, I..." Her eyes were wide and blinking rapidly. "I don't know what to say. I'm honored."

He offered a hand to help her up. "Well, no one's here to see it, but once Lantess is rebuilt, we shall do this in front of every citizen."

"Thank you. I won't let you down!" She grabbed his hand and stood.

"Now, let's go kill a dragon and get to Petrovana and Leper." Madislak sheathed Skyrunner and took off, running westward towards Wen-Tath.

Chapter Fifteen

L eper's heart sank as Ghost soared through the scene of devastation. He frantically scanned the battlefield for any sign of Rinawen.
Where the heck is she? I can't lose the only person I know. His mind raced at
the thought of her dying. Who would he turn to for advice and protection?

The once serene city now bore scars of destruction, with the residential
district in ruins and parts of the castle courtyard charred by Voldahyl's fiery
rampage. Smoke billowed into the sky, and the cries of the wounded and
the mourning filled the air. Amongst the carnage, he spotted Lillian on
the ground. The guards valiantly attempted to defend the city, but the
dragon's power seemed unstoppable.

Leper tightened his grip on Ghost's mane, urging the griffin forward,
driven by a mix of determination and despair to confront the merciless
creature and put an end to the chaos. The journey, faster than a chariot, still
required four hours of following Voldahyl to reach this place. He didn't
want his mount to get eaten within hours of meeting him. This was his
first time attempting to slay a dragon; he wasn't sure how it would go.

"Fire!!" yelled one guard perched by a ballista.

Leper's heart pounded so hard he thought it would explode as he
watched the arrow miss its intended target, the dragon. The situation
seemed dire, but he had to focus on rescuing his friends first. Guiding
Ghost down near the broken watchtower, he swiftly dismounted and
rushed to Lillian's side. Without hesitation, he started clearing away debris

to help her escape the wreckage. His hands worked quickly, fueled by the urgency to get her to safety.

"Where's Rinawen!" He glared at Lillian, who was staring at his head.

"She flew off the tower with me. The dragon came out of nowhere." Lillian explained, her gaze not moving off him.

"Yes, I lied. I'm a dirty Chernzerk. I will not hurt you." He reasoned as he searched the wreckage, finding Rinawen under some rubble.

"We need to get you to safety," Leper pulled Rinawen out from the debris. The deep gash in her leg meant she needed help to stand up.

"I'll be okay. I have some salve left," Rinawen said, clinging to Leper's shoulder. "I see your hat is missing. I'm sure that went over well."

"I don't care about the hat. I care about you, and I care about killing this dragon so that I can show these people who I am," Leper roared defiantly.

Lillian rested her hand on his shoulder, "I knew there was somethin' off about you as soon as I saw yer hat."

Leper glared back at her, not sure if she was okay with his true identity or not. He quickly recounted the events with Ace, Voldahyl, and Madislak, explaining the situation they were now facing with the dragon and about the talisman. As they huddled together, Leper and his friends discussed their options, trying to devise a plan to deal with the powerful dragon wreaking havoc upon the city. They knew they had to act fast and decisively, but the situation was stacked heavily against them. Leper handed Rinawen the shield he found at The Talon to protect her leg and herself.

The sound of raging fire and the stench of burning flesh filled Leper's senses as he bravely faced the dragon for the first time. His heart was pounding in his chest, a mixture of fear and determination pushing him forward. But even with Maka Kura by his side, the odds seemed insurmountable. The armies were in complete disarray, their feeble attempts to defend against the massive creature proving futile. This battle was like nothing Leper had ever faced or seen before—it was pure chaos and destruction.

Dragons were an afterthought for centuries, and now, here was one, laying waste to everything in its path. If they were going to survive this onslaught, they would need a miracle. And there was no sign of King Brebian anywhere, leaving his people to fend for themselves against this ancient threat. It was a fight for survival, for their kingdom, and for their very lives.

Leper glared at the dragon flying over the city, his knuckles turning white as he grabbed hold of Maka Kura. He would be the one to make this dragon retreat or die. As the sun dipped beneath the trees, the dragon's massive shadow stretched across the ground.

Brebian finally emerged from the castle before them, adorned in his regal armor that symbolized the pride and strength of Tudela. Leper let a dejected sigh escape his mouth as the king unsheathed his great sword, pointing it directly at him. Confusion and disbelief swept over Leper's face as he tried to make sense of the situation. Rinawen and Lillian exchanged worried glances. Unsure of what Brebian's intentions were. Leper's mind raced, trying to defuse the tension and convince the king that they were on the same side.

Brebian's eyes bore into Leper, his grip on the great sword tightening. The weight of the moment hung heavily in the air, and the fate of Tudela seemed to rest on the next few moments. Leper took a deep breath, steadying himself, and spoke with conviction, hoping his words would resonate with the king and change the course of their fate.

"I'm here to help you," Leper said.

"I knew you were a liar as soon as I saw you!" Brebian seethed.

"Brebian, we don't have time for this," Rinawen interjected. "A dragon is decimating your city." She pointed to the sky.

Voldahyl was still circling the city, preparing for his next attack.

"I can help take down the dragon," Leper offered.

"Reckon I can try to get people to safety. My swords won't reach it," Lillian looked to Brebian.

"I might be able to hit it with some ice or somethin'," Petrovana added.

"Fine, but once this is over, that one will be locked away until we decide his fate," Brebian pointed to Leper.

Leper's grip tightened around Maka Kura as he prepared for the impending battle. His heart thundered in his chest, adrenaline coursing through his veins. He took a deep breath, focusing his mind and body on the fight ahead. The smoke was thick and acrid, leaving a sharp and bitter taste on his tongue. It was like inhaling burnt rubber and tar with a lingering aftertaste of ashes and charred wood. He needed this. He had to prove his worth, or he would face prison and ridicule. As Voldahyl drew nearer, its massive wings beating the air with tremendous force, Leper readied himself for the attack.

Voldahyl swooped down upon the city, its massive form casting a menacing shadow over the buildings below. People screamed and ran for cover, and he knew he needed to act quickly to protect them. With Maka Kura in hand, he ran to the wall. Drawing upon every ounce of strength and focus he possessed, Leper took aim with his chakrams. The weight of the curved blades felt familiar and reassuring in his hands. He focused on his target, his mind blocking out the surrounding chaos. With a powerful throw, the first chakram flew, followed swiftly by the second. They arced gracefully against the bright sky, slicing through the air with precision.

The first chakram hit the side of the dragon's neck, followed swiftly by the second slashing its shoulder, stifling the dragon's fiery breath. Blood poured from the wounds, and Voldahyl roared in pain, momentarily losing control of its flight. The crowd erupted into cheers, but Leper knew there was no time to celebrate. Voldahyl was a formidable adversary, and the battle was far from over.

Leper took in a deep breath. *If I cannot defeat a dragon, my sole purpose for existence, how will I ever prove my worth?* The fate of Tudela and Leper's freedom rested on his ability to bring the beast down.

Madislak surveyed the aftermath of his actions. The carnage sprawled about him. Martin took up an hour of his precious time. A pang of regret settled in him for ending Martin's life; he had intended to glean insights about the orcs accompanying him, but time was of the essence. A dragon flew overhead towards Tudela, and he intended to be there to stop it. His gaze shifted to Harmony, and with a mutual understanding, they quickened their steps toward Wen-Tath, where he hoped he could get a flying chariot to press on towards Tudela. But, before they could proceed farther, a sudden, searing sting lanced through Madislak's neck. Helplessly, he crumpled to the earth, his limbs rendered immobile. The world blurred around him.

A shadowy, hooded figure materialized in his dimming vision. The voice that emerged carried a distinctly feminine quality. The figure pushed back the hood, revealing a face resembling that of a feline, with prominent bug-like eyes and sharply pointed elfin ears that added to the overall catlike appearance.

"Who are you?" Madislak tried to murmur.

"Say? What's that? Can't quite understand you with your lips not moving. But don't worry, in about an hour, that'll wear off, and we can have a conversation." He cackled.

Gazing at a distant point, the enigmatic man issued a directive for someone to approach, bind them, and transport them to the master. Madislak's knowledge of this master's identity was vague, but the prospect didn't ignite enthusiasm within him. His comrades faced peril, yet he remained incapacitated. Madislak saw more orcs—resembling those in Martin's company—emerging into view. Despite his yearning to call out to Harmony or even turn his head, he remained immobile, strangled by the paralysis.

The taste in his mouth was putrid and bitter from whatever poison was coursing through him as if he had swallowed spoiled meat or rotten eggs.

Eventually, he found himself unceremoniously flung into a cell—a cage secured to the rear of a horse-drawn wagon. The confinement was far from extravagant: it was a simple squared metal structure.

With a sudden movement, Harmony was thrown before him, and her presence provided Madislak with a small amount of solace. Their immobilization waned, permitting them to shift and assume seated positions. Yet, their wrists remained ensnared by metallic restraints, demanding a key for release. Judging from their direction, Madislak surmised they were journeying southward. The procession comprised a formidable assembly, perhaps a hundred or even two hundred orcs, alongside numerous generals and officers orchestrating the advance. The eccentric man popped in front of them.

"Who the heck are you?" Harmony blurted.

"Names aren't important. What is important is that you enjoy the ride to Xaneth Harbor!" his enthusiasm bordered on crazy.

"Xaneth Harbor!?" Madislak scoffed. "Release us at once. We've important business to attend to."

"Now, now, King Madislak, I've already informed the master that you will join us when we arrive." His voice carried an unsettling undertone.

"Who's the master?" Madislak's curiosity sparked, his eyes fixed on the weird man.

"Well, Queen Tamara, of course!"

Madislak's gaze sharpened. "And what shall I call you then?"

He waved his hand dismissively. "Fine, fine, my name is Thessek."

Madislak's expression grew stern. "Well, Thessek, unless you want the full force of Lantess and Wen-Tath unleashed on you, I suggest you let us go right now."

The stench of Thessek's breath was suffocating. The sour tang of bile lingered in his breath, mixing with the musky odor of unwashed hair and clothes. It's a sickening combination that reflects the unkempt, wild appearance of Thessek himself.

Thessek chuckled mockingly. "Oh, such enormous threats. But considering Lantess is burned to the ground, and Wen-Tath just sent a lot of soldiers out of their doors, I'm so scared."

Madislak clenched his jaw, his frustration mounting. The wind grew stronger as they traveled south, through the open plains just beyond the edge of the forest. The gusts whipped around Harmony's hair.

"Now, I need to ask you a question, and I need you to answer honestly. See this ring?" Thessek raised his right hand, revealing a silver ring. "It glows red if you're lying to me."

"Fine. But how about if I answer a question honestly, then you need to answer one honestly for me, too?" Madislak ventured. He couldn't help but think that this was the kind of wild behavior Thessek lived for, based on his current actions and appearance.

Thessek's eyes lit up with excitement. "Ohhhhh, like a game! I love games! Okay, okay, I'll go first." Thessek opened the door to the cage and climbed inside, sitting cross-legged on the wagon floor.

"My first question is... Hmmmmm." he tapped his finger on his lips as he pondered. "The griffin that flew overhead. Who was on it?"

Swiftly, Madislak's gaze dropped to the ground. The question before him was one he wished to evade. Yet, he comprehended the danger in prolonged hesitation—it could spark suspicion. Revealing one of their last remaining secrets wasn't desirable either, particularly the one concerning Leper. Tamara likely remained oblivious to Leper's existence.

"I have no idea. That's why we're in a hurry to get to Wen-Tath," Madislak held Thessek's gaze, his voice steady. The ring on his finger glowed with a crimson intensity.

Thessek's eyes squinted in apparent amusement. "Now you see," he scratched his head. "You can't even answer one question honestly. Do you not like to play this game with me?"

From within the depths of his leather vest, Thessek's hand retrieved a diminutive blade—around four inches, more elongated needle than knife. With disturbing precision, he thrust it into Harmony's leg thrice. Her anguished cries punctuated the air.

"Ouch, you fucker!" Harmony's exclamation echoed through the tense atmosphere.

"No, no, no, don't blame me. He's the one answering the questions." Thessek nonchalantly pointed to Madislak.

Fury blazed in Madislak's eyes. "You want to stab someone with that? Stab me, you coward," he seethed.

A sinister grin spread across Thessek's face. "Answer the questions honestly, then no one has to get poked again."

Madislak's frustration was palpable. "Alright! Geez. His name is Leper."

The band on his finger glowed a soft yellow color this time. Madislak glanced at Harmony's leg, which was turning a crimson red through the pants.

"Better. Who is he?" Thessek's mock applause rang out with a hint of condescension.

"Isn't it my turn?" Madislak shot back his voice laced with urgency.

"Hmmm," Thessek growled, his tone taking on a dark undertone. "Unlike you, I will honor the game's rules."

Madislak's mind raced as he considered the precarious situation. This twisted game, as unsettling as it was, seemed to feed Thessek's malevolent enthusiasm. With a deep breath, he braced himself to answer the next question.

"Why are you and all these orcs going to Xaneth Harbor?" Madislak's expression shifted from cunning to contemplative.

"A fair question," he mused aloud, tapping his chin. Then, suddenly, his gigantic eyes widened as if struck by inspiration. "Aha! We're going to help the queen."

Harmony's curiosity burst forth, "With what?"

"Ah ah ah. That's two questions," Thessek interrupted her inquiry with a devious grin.

Thessek seized the moment. "Is this Leper a friend to you?"

"Yes," Madislak's response was swift and resolute. Once again, the ring on Thessek's finger glowed yellow, affirming the truth in his words.

Amid their predicament, Madislak couldn't ignore the faint smile that graced Harmony's lips.

"My turn. What are you helping Tamara with?" Madislak countered immediately, his determination showing.

"Hmmm... I don't like your questions," Thessek muttered, tapping his chin as he feigned contemplation. "We're helping her with the task she's given us!"

"C'mon, that's not fair!" Madislak protested, frustrated by Thessek's response.

"But I answered honestly, didn't I?" Thessek's voice carried a mocking tone as he displayed the yellow glow of the ring. Madislak rolled his eyes in exasperation.

"What's the best way to attack Tudela?" Thessek inquired, a devious grin stretching across his face.

"Let me take this one, Madislak," Harmony interjected, her voice tinged with pain. "With an army."

"Smart one, are we?" Thessek's attention shifted sharply to Harmony as he drove the needle-like blade into her leg six more times. The pain was clear in her agonized cry. "Asshole!" she spat, her anger boiling over. "I answered you honestly!"

"Yeah, but that's not what I wanted to hear," Thessek countered with a malicious smile, unfazed by Harmony's protest.

"You're cheating!" Madislak growled, his frustration seeping into his voice. "That's not how the game is played."

"You're right," Thessek conceded, his tone dripping with smugness. "But you're the ones tied up, and I'm the one asking the questions, aren't I?"

Four more jabs landed in her side, his eyes gleaming with a disturbing intensity. Madislak witnessed the gradual drain of blood etching its mark on Harmony's countenance. His fury surged, an inferno of rage igniting within him, urging to tear the man responsible apart, limb from limb.

"Knock your shit off! You're going to kill her!" Madislak tried to head-butt Thessek.

His demeanor transformed from twisted playfulness to a frigid, calculated killer as he grabbed Madislak's neck, his face mere inches from Madislak's.

"It's time you began answering, and you'll do it on my fucking terms, prisoner," he hissed. "I'll give you some time to think that over, and when I get back, we'll finish this game. This time, I'll ask all the questions."

Madislak watched him get back out and lock the door. He wiggled himself beside Harmony.

"Are you okay?" Madislak's voice was gruff as he turned his attention to Harmony.

"Yeah. For now," Harmony's response carried a hint of tremor, reflecting her discomfort. "But if he keeps stabbing me, I won't be able to cast any magic, even if we break these restraints."

Madislak's jaw clenched at the thought of Harmony enduring such pain. "Where did they put our weapons?" he inquired, his focus shifting to their potential means of defense.

Harmony closed her eyes momentarily, her brow furrowing as she concentrated. "Somewhere near the back of this wagon, I sense Skyrunner's magic."

Madislak pivoted, confirming his suspicions: a general had materialized, an unforeseen presence during their earlier engagement. The man looked tall, a cascade of untamed blond hair falling roughly four inches. Pity welled within Madislak for the steed, burdened by the general's substantial frame. However, what truly captured his attention was the remarkable weapon affixed to the general's side—Skyrunner, his magnificent sword extending beyond the horse's belly.

"I see it," Madislak's voice was hushed as his eyes settled on the location of their weapons. "When he opens the door, if we can break free, I'll charge out and retrieve Skyrunner."

Harmony's eyes flicked to her side. "I think I have a hairpin in my side pouch, but I can't reach it," she suggested.

"Let me try to get it," Madislak replied, positioning himself beside Harmony as if seeking support. His fingers cautiously explored the area, trying to locate the elusive pouch at her side.

"That's my butt. Try higher on the waist where a normal pouch would be," Harmony quipped.

"Sorry," Madislak whispered, a sheepish smile on his face.

After a couple of minutes filled with fumbling and the occasional clatter of dropped items, he located a hairpin. "Can you pick locks?" he inquired.

"I've never tried, but I understand the mechanisms," Harmony admitted.

"Here, take the pin and see if you can unlock my restraints. I'll return the favor," Madislak suggested, passing the small tool to her.

Several minutes passed as Harmony persisted in her attempts to loosen the restraints. In a fleeting moment, Madislak caught sight of Thessek, who was now making his way back from the vanguard of the convoy.

"Hurry, he's coming. We're going to miss our opportunity," urgency laced Madislak's words.

"What do you think I'm doing!?" Harmony retorted.

With Thessek drawing nearer to the cage, Madislak detected the subtle loosening of the steel cuffs. However, he exercised caution, maintaining the appearance of being restrained so as not to arouse suspicion. Curiously, none of the orcs or men present, apart from the hefty one guarding his sword, displayed significant concern for the security of this mobile cell. Madislak cast another quick survey around. Apart from the wagon driver, who obediently trailed the procession of horse-drawn wagons, there were two mindless orcs positioned about thirty feet on either side of their wagon, walking in tandem.

As Thessek approached the door, his key poised to unlock it, Madislak's acute hearing caught the faint sound of the locking mechanism disengaging. In an instant, he harnessed the strength of both legs, delivering a forceful kick that nearly tore the door from its hinges. The door clanged against the adjacent bars with a resounding impact, propelling Thessek backwards to the ground in a sprawl. Seizing the opportunity, Madislak sprang into action.

From Petrovana's perspective, she discerned the remarkable effectiveness of Leper's chakrams in countering Voldahyl's presence. Yet, a pressing need arose: a means to neutralize both the dragon and its rider, to apprehend Ace alive for further interrogation. *If they could talk with him, maybe he could lead us to Tamara's motives and involvement with the shards. Maybe he knows what Nalecht's next moves are, and we could get a step ahead of him.* Voldahyl's body, now oozing blood from his neck and shoulder, betrayed the extent of his injuries. A few more strategic strikes could incapacitate his aerial capabilities entirely.

Petrovana's attention shifted briefly to Leper, who was winding up for another assault with his chakrams. Turning her focus back to Voldahyl, she extended her hand, the intensity of her resolve crystallizing in a deep inhale. Drawing upon every ounce of her energy, she gradually clenched her fingers into a fist. The air chilled as frost materialized upon the dragon's wings, their rhythmic motion slowing. Magic ebbed from Petrovana's being, leaving her senses slightly muddled, yet her determination remained unwavering as she continued to channel her power.

The frost quickly built into ice spots, wearing it down as its wings beat slower and slower.

"If yer gonna throw them things, now would be a good time," she called to Leper.

Seizing Leper's subtle signal with a nod, Petrovana watched as he dispatched a chakram toward Ace, the rider perplexed by the unexpected turn of events involving his dragon. In the nick of time, Ace detected the glint of the spinning blade hurtling his way. Acting swiftly, he lunged for his axe. He evaded the projectile by rolling clear of his mount's back, sending him falling towards the ground. The abrupt motion caused Voldahyl to scoop him up in his talons. The dragon began a gradual retreat. The impact of Petrovana's frost magic on his wings compelled a descent to the ground.

Petrovana strained her limits, pouring all her energy into the spell. However, her resolve had its costs. The strain became unbearable, and she could no longer sustain the magic. As blood trickled from her eyes and nose, she relinquished control, the frost slowly dissipating.

"Are you okay?" Leper asked, catching his returning chakram.

"I'm fine," she motioned towards the dragon. "Get over there. Now may be the only opportunity we have to capture him. I'll be right behind you."

"C'mon, let's go." Leper turned to Lillian as they both headed off towards the chaos, followed closely by Brebian.

Petrovana allowed herself a thirty-second pause to collect her bearings. Despite being twenty-nine and a pinnacle-four shrew, she understood the direct correlation between spell size and magic depletion. This recent exertion had taken its toll. The agony of such a grand spell was unprecedented to her; its magnitude and impact were both new and unsettling. Her mental clarity gradually resurfaced, dispelling the haze that had clouded her mind.

With renewed determination, she abandoned her brief respite and sprinted toward the last known location of Voldahyl. Although she couldn't visually pinpoint him, a rough estimate guided her pursuit.

The cacophony of terror-stricken screams and the chaotic stampede of fleeing people served as a gruesome compass, pointing Petrovana in the direction she needed to take. Racing onward, Petrovana arrived at the scene where Leper, Lillian, and Brebian confronted Voldahyl. The dragon loomed over Ace, protective and resolute. It drew a breath, signaling its intent to unleash flames once more.

Swiftly, Petrovana's left hand rose, conjuring a block of ice that hurtled toward the dragon's head. The impact struck with surprising force, prompting the dragon to recoil in disbelief, its head swaying back and forth as if struggling to process the sudden interference. A sudden shock ran through her body, forcing her to her knees. Her head pounded in agony as blood now dripped from her face onto the ground.

Capitalizing on the distraction, Lillian sprang into motion, swiftly clamping onto Ace's legs just as he endeavored to mount Voldahyl once more. Ace swung his axe at Lillian, and she skillfully evaded the swing but wasn't able to avoid the boot she took to the head. Voldahyl rocked his body, and Lillian plummeted to the ground, landing with a thud. The dragon then used its paw to swipe at Lillian, who tried to roll out of the way but wasn't quick enough and got tossed into a building twenty feet away. Leper launched himself onto Ace's back and dragged him off Voldahyl and to the ground, where they got up and encircled each other.

Leper glanced at Ace hesitantly, "Why are you doing this? Join us. We can make the world a better place together," Leper pleaded, holding out his hand.

Ace grinned. "Dumbass. They'll never accept us. They'll always treat us like we're terrorists."

Brebian charged in out of nowhere and slammed Ace to the ground, restraining him. "You idiot! I knew you couldn't be trusted." Brebian glanced at Leper. "Quickly bind this one." Brebian hollered as he put his sword on Ace's neck.

Voldahyl's gaze fixated defensively on them, a deep growl reverberating from his throat. Despite his aggression, he refrained from advancing, held in check by the predicament of his captured rider.

"Enough," Brebian pressed his sword harder. "Tell your beast to leave us forever, or we will kill you right now."

Ace swallowed hard. "Voldy... Go, I'll call for you when I'm ready."

Petrovana understood the profound connection that often formed between a dragon rider and their loyal beast. The bond that developed over time was genuine, forging an unbreakable link that rendered them not only companions but inseparable allies.

Voldahyl huffed and took flight. Once Voldahyl turned his back, Brebian approached Leper. "Kill it! He let his guard down! Kill it now!"

Petrovana couldn't believe what she was hearing. They surrendered, yet Brebian demanded to slay the dragon. The dust and dirt carried by the strong winds from his beating wings smelled earthy and gritty, with hints of dried leaves and musty air.

Ace hollered, "NO!"

Leper sent his chakrams out, and both of them missed. Whether or not he meant to miss as Voldahyl was disappearing into the sky, she wasn't sure, but she was glad he did. It's hard to negotiate in good faith when you do shady shit like that.

"Pathetic," Brebian mouthed. "Bind that one. He clearly isn't here to aid us," he pointed at Leper. "Utterly worthless."

"I did nothing but help you!" Leper's voice carried a mix of frustration and confusion as the guards moved to restrain him, a resistance he offered no fight against.

"Just hold yer horses there, Brebina," Petrovana's voice broke through, playfully toying with his name. "We just saved yer pathetic city from burnin' to the ground, and yer arrestin' us?"

"I'm not arresting you, just him," he focused his glare on Petrovana. "But keep up your witty comments, and I'll throw you in prison with both these psychos."

"Then yer gonna have to take me with him, 'cause I object," Petrovana raised her hand in defiance against the guards attempting to bind Leper.

"Reckon, I second that," Lillian emerged from the rubble, her scimitars poised threateningly in their direction.

"You crazy bastards. Do you not see what they are?" Brebian's anger seethed through his words.

Petrovana's disbelief was clear across her countenance. Much like Madislak, Brebian staunchly rejected the reality before him. Leper's actions bore no trace of malevolence. Yet, Brebian seemed determined to remain blind to this, unwilling to grant him even the smallest chance.

"It's no wonder they burned cities to the ground! With assholes like you and Madislak in charge. Reckon I would do the same damn thing," Petrovana's anger seethed, her words dripping with disdain.

"It's okay. Put me with him. When that dragon comes back with Nalecht, don't ask me for help." Leper's voice was flat, his gaze fixed on the ground. "Besides, once Nalecht reforges that talisman, there won't be anything left."

"What talisman?" Brebian's eyes sparked as they locked onto Leper.

"The Talisman of Runes. We discovered its origins at The Talon when we went. The shards can be forged together to create a corrupt and powerful amulet that wields unimaginable power," Leper stated, his gaze unflinching as he stared back at Brebian.

"His words are true. He read the passage directly out of a book," Petrovana added.

"Regardless, we're all still safer with both of them in the prison!" Brebian scoffed, his conviction unwavering.

"This ain't right." Lillian pointed at Brebian. "We should ask Rinawen for her thoughts. She ain't here because her leg was badly gashed, but we should find her." Lillian sheathed her sword. "You should be a hero to this city, not a prisoner."

"There's been enough lives lost today. If putting me in a cell will make everyone sleep better, then so be it. But for saving your city and the efforts I put forth today to help you, I better get a comfy bed and a good meal." Leper's demand held a hint of defiance.

"I'll make sure you do," Petrovana reassured as she placed her hand on Leper's shoulder.

Petrovana's heart ached witnessing the unjust treatment of a hero. Yet, her resolve remained unshaken in her determination to aid him and show their capacity for peaceful coexistence. The sun was now setting in the sky as they marched towards the dungeons. She discerned, without doubt, that Leper bore no intentions of causing harm. She saw the goodness within his heart, though she recognized that convincing others of this truth would be a gradual process. Particularly challenging would be swaying the minds of the entrenched old-school monarchs, clinging to outdated beliefs.

In her hometown, Terynsipple, they didn't adhere to the teachings of those historical accounts. Their community held a trove of history, documenting the coexistence of Chernzerk, elves, and humans in harmony on their island for countless years. Disparities seemed to emerge in Uskela, taking a distinct turn from Terynsipple's perspective. The former was a realm of tyrannical dragon riders and unrestrained chaos, a stark contrast to their ethos. Petrovana maintained faith in the potential of peaceful cohabitation.

She glanced at Lillian as the guards walked both Ace and Leper towards the castle to be put in jail cells.

"Rinawen is going to be pissed," Lillian smirked.

Chapter Sixteen

Leighth and Blank Face arrived at the northern edge of Tudela several hours after their discussion with Lillian and Rinawen. Blank Face clutched his chest, clearly in pain from the laceration Lillian inflicted on him. Leighth carefully assessed the wound, it appeared to be not too deep. With some cleaning and bandaging, Blank Face should recover. However, Leighth couldn't help but wish she had the time to grab the wonderful salve Rinawen usually had on her. As the sun waned in the sky, a thin layer of clouds drifted in, casting soft shadows over the landscape. The cool breeze picked up, rustling through the trees and carrying with it dried leaves and specks of dirt.

"Let me have a look at that," she said, walking towards Blank Face.

"I'm fine," he muttered. "I don't need your pity."

"It's not pity, you idiot, wounds can get infected." She shook her head.

Leighth's heart sank as she saw the scars on Blank Face's chest and stomach. His body bore the marks of a life filled with danger and violence. She couldn't help but wonder what led him down this path and what caused him to become the feared assassin he was today. Despite his menacing appearance and his reputation, she couldn't ignore the fact that underneath it all, he was just another person carrying the weight of his past. Who would do this to someone? What kind of monster would make a person suffer so badly, and at a young age? Leighth's empathy for him grew, and she realized that there was so much more to him than met the eye. As she tended to his wound, she couldn't help but feel a sense of responsibility towards him. Maybe she could be the one to help him find some semblance of peace.

"What did they, whoever they are, do to you?" Leighth's voice trembled as she gazed at Blank Face's scarred face.

"You don't know the nightmares that exist in this world, princess," Blank Face's monotone voice seemed to carry the weight of his experiences.

"Are all these scars from... people or beasts?" Leighth struggled to comprehend the cruelty that could lead to such disfigurement.

"People. Like you. Royalty just playing their petty games." his words were sharp, filled with a bitter edge.

"Like who? Tell me, Blank, who did this to you? When I become queen, I swear I will have them punished... no. I'll have them executed." Leighth's determination was unwavering, her eyes blazing with a fierce resolve.

"Queen Tamara, Borlden," his response was direct, his gaze meeting hers without flinching. "I was kept in a dungeon, forced to fight warriors, beasts, men. Winning meant I got to live, but it also meant I got another victory scar. At least that's what they called them."

A profound mix of sadness and shock consumed Leighth. The man before her was actually sharing something deeply personal about his past, a level of vulnerability she had never witnessed before. It left her reeling with conflicting emotions and, at the same time, furthering her resolve to kill Borlden for his involvement.

"How do you work for Nalecht and Borlden, then? After Borlden's involvement?" Leighth gazed into his brown eyes. "Are you...Afraid of them?"

"No. They don't even realize who I am. Borlden wasn't nearly as bad as Tamara was. She would, daily, find new ways to make me suffer. Just to heal me back up and do it again." Blank Face grimaced.

"Then let's take her down!" Leighth offered. "You're the greatest fighter in Kalazaar, so go take care of Tamara. You waste your time aiding the enemy when I feel you're afraid to face your fears."

"Maybe you're right," he sighed heavily. "I'm not afraid of Tamara. I'm not afraid of anyone. After I got out, I vowed never to go back to Xaneth Harbor...Ever. But I needed to survive."

Leighth put a bandage over his wound. "So, you had to conceal your identity and take the work that was given to you."

"Right. No one is going to trust or hire an eighteen-year-old man scarred everywhere. I only knew how to fight and am damn good at it. So, I started in Kundry doing work for Kendra, then moved to bigger targets." He glanced to the side.

Leighth finally understood the connections. He started in a small town, away from commotion. That's where he learned Kordrarian and knew about her mother.

"It's not too late. Give up this mission to get the shard. Help us defeat Nalecht, and we'll get justice against Tamara! I promise," Leighth pleaded.

Blank Face scoffed. "Your only true ally is Kordry, and you haven't even accepted regency yet. Tamara's army is large and ruthless."

"I can convince others to help!" Leighth grinned.

"Not after what I've done. I'm too far past the point of no return. Plus, your precious Rinawen..." He looked up at the sky. "Is the whole reason I ended up in Tamara's clutches. Another thing Nalecht helped me discover. So, it's a personal vendetta with her."

"That makes little sense. She is the sweetest..." Leighth shook her head.

Leighth came to an abrupt halt as the echoing roar reverberated through the air, sending a shiver down her spine. The hairs on her neck stood on end as a massive dragon soared overhead, spewing fire from its menacing maw. Panic and terror erupted among the people of Tudela, their screams filling the air. The looming shadow of the dragon cast an ominous presence over them before it veered away and circled back. At that moment, Leighth's attention focused on two shining chakrams that sliced through the drag-on's neck and shoulder, compelling it to retreat. Her heart pounded in her chest, and she wondered who the mysterious savior could be. She inhaled a deep breath. The scent of damp earth and wildflowers filled her senses, carrying with it a hint of moss and bark.

Her eyes narrowed, and Leighth's patience wore thin as she witnessed the terror inflicted upon innocent people. The memories of her family, engulfed in agonizing flames by Borlden's merciless actions, haunted her as flames erupted from the beast's maw. She could still feel the desperation as she pushed through the crowd to escape, only to witness the beheading of her mother and father at the edge of Nalecht's icy blade. The searing pain of loss fueled a raging fire within her. In that moment, Leighth vowed to bring justice to those she lost and to all who suffered under the tyranny of Nalecht's rule. The intensity of her determination left no room for fear or hesitation. Her heart, now set on vengeance and redemption, steadied her resolve to stand against the forces that caused so much suffering. *I can still hear their screams.* Borlden's voice continued to taunt her thoughts.

"Now is the time," Leighth's voice was filled with urgency as she finished bandaging Blank Face's chest. "Make your stand, Blank! Help them! I will not let them turn their back on you. I promise!"

"Again, you're not even queen yet. You can't make that promise." Blank Face's response was flat, his demeanor unchanged.

"Please! They need us! They have a dragon. That Ace guy is right there, fighting them. You have to kill him for someone, right?" Leighth's plea was desperate.

Blank Face didn't respond or say anything.

Leighth's head tilted in disbelief. "What? Then who?" she shook her head. "Whatever. I'm going in there. If I get the opportunity, I'm taking it."

"If you go in there, I'm leaving. I won't be going with you." Blank Face got to his feet.

"Fine. Then be a coward! Hide behind your hood. You could make a real difference in this fight if you weren't too busy being fucking stubborn!" Her words rang out.

"Don't die, Leighth. I won't be there to save you this time." Blank Face's voice was gruff.

Leighth heard his words, but she kept walking anyway, her resolve unwavering. As she picked up the pace, her steps turned into a determined run along the back of the wall. The battle raged on fiercely at the front gates, but she noticed the dragon's wings becoming thick with ice as it descended into the city, unable to fly anymore. She looked over her shoulder, but Blank Face was already gone, nowhere to be seen. Unexpectedly, a couple of tears ran down her face. She wasn't sure why. Perhaps she cared more for Blank Face than she realized.

As she walked towards the city, a hand suddenly covered her mouth with a cloth. She instinctively fought back, trying to grab hold of her attacker, but they were too elusive. The chemicals on the rag had a harsh, chemical taste that burned the back of her throat. There was a strong, almost medicinal undertone, similar to rubbing alcohol, with a hint of bitterness that lingered on the tongue. In a matter of seconds, she stopped struggling and fell into unconsciousness.

Petrovana trailed behind the prisoners as they returned to the castle, her footsteps silent. Her disappointment overshadowed her current disgust as she grappled with the unexpected turn of events. Leper remained on her mind—a friend and perhaps something more, although she wasn't entirely certain. Attraction tugged at her, intensified by his enigmatic, masculine presence, especially with his newly revealed horns. His inch-long dark hair matched the color of the goatee on his face. Tall. Dark. Handsome.

Her type of person. Yet, with the looming specter of war and Kalazaar's potential collapse, her emotions were a complex tangle that made focusing on her feelings for Leper challenging.

Her initial plan involved informing Queen Rinawen about the recent developments and preparing the grounds to confront Brebian. Once that was set in motion, Petrovana intended to position herself outside Leper's cell, guaranteeing his fair treatment and protection from mistreatment.

Yet Petrovana's curiosity about Leper persisted, and her thirst for understanding remained unquenched. Numerous inquiries danced through her thoughts, not only about Leper but also about Ace. She pondered his origins and motivations: *Why did he align himself with Nalecht?*

What did he hope to gain from working with Nalecht? Personal matters or was he just like some of the history books depicted? Evil.

"What's yer plan?" Lillian interrupted her thoughts.

"Reckon I'm gonna let Rinawen know about this and wait outside his cell," Petrovana glanced at Lillian. "Don't want them mistreatin' the one that saved this damned city."

"I can talk to Rinawen if you want to follow them," she said, pointing to Leper and Ace.

"Fine," Petrovana let out a sigh.

Lillian's gaze briefly interrupted Petrovana's internal contemplations with an unmistakable air of disdain.

Lillian's words grabbed Petrovana's full attention. "One last thing," Lillian's voice remained steady, and her gaze turned intense as it locked onto Petrovana's eyes. "You may have his attention for now. But don't fool yerself into thinkin' that's set in stone. And let me make this perfectly clear—I won't stand by and watch you repeat what you did to Alzen. I've got my eyes on you, bitch."

Petrovana's response was swift, her tone dripping with defiance. "I didn't do anythin' to Alzen. It ain't my fault you couldn't keep him happy, and it sure as hell ain't my fault you couldn't do one thing right." *Alzen.*

"Keep tellin' yerself that," Lillian paused for a moment, letting her words hang in the air before she turned and began walking away. "Whore," she quipped as she stormed off toward the castle.

Petrovana struggled to disentangle herself from the deluge of memories that Lillian's words ignited. Alzen—her past—emerged from the depths of her consciousness. He had been Lillian's betrothed, their relationship spanning three years, culminating in marriage. Yet, behind the facade of Lillian's love, Petrovana and Alzen shared a hidden bond, their mutual passion for magic. This connection, however, revolted Lillian, engendering disgust. Through years of friendship with Lillian, Petrovana had grown entwined with Alzen's charms. A forbidden romance blossomed between them, concealed in secrecy. This affair continued until the fateful moment when Petrovana's adoptive parents, the king and queen of Terynsipple, exposed their forbidden love. The consequence was Alzen's execution, which Petrovana's stepparents ordered. Desperation led Petrovana to turn to Lillian, pleading for help to escape with Alzen. In a tragic twist, Lillian's guidance led them into a treacherous trap, where Petrovana was forced to witness Alzen's demise, sanctioned by her adoptive parents. This devastating event severed their friendship irreparably, forever casting them out of Terynsipple's bounds.

Thankfully, a few weeks later, they intercepted Madislak's letters detailing the tournament in Wen-Tath and plans to thwart Nalecht's rulership as Anyth. As Petrovana made plans to leave Terynsipple with no direction in mind, Lillian packed her things, said she was going to the tournament and left. That had been the last time she had seen Lillian until she saw her again at the council meeting about five days ago. Petrovana deceived everyone at that meeting by claiming she had been sent on behalf of the king and queen. She took charge and pretended to be their leader until she could come up with a plan for her future after both she and Lillian were banished from Terynsipple for their betrayal, instead of informing her adoptive parents about the note she found.

This very reason had tethered Petrovana to Leper and the rest. The unpredictable, eccentric behavior of the shrews played a pivotal role in diverting attention from her actions. After all, few would scrutinize the capricious whims of a shrew. Yet, anxiety gnawed at her. If Terynsipple ever discovered her ruse, the potential consequences loomed darkly. Would her punishment mirror Alzen's fate? The uncertainty swirled. What fate awaited her for impersonating the acting king and queen? *Alzen*. A tear escaped her eye as she quickly wiped it away.

Petrovana shook her head as the guards set Leper's and Ace's weapons on the ground outside the cell, then just shoved them in together.

"Hey! Easy on that one. He just saved yer pathetic life," Petrovana's voice cut through the tension like a blade.

"I don't take my orders from you, shrew!" The guard shot back.

"You willin' to back up yer words with action?" Petrovana challenged, raising her hand as if daring him. He swallowed hard, his bravado faltering as he shook his head in retreat. "Thought so," Petrovana taunted, a smirk playing on her lips. The musty stench of mildew and dirt filled the air in the prison cell as if no one had touched it for years. It carried a sharp tang of sweat and bodily fluids mixed with a hint of decay.

"What's your problem, Ace?" Leper interjected, his eyes fixed on Ace as he rubbed his wrists. His gaze held a piercing intensity directed straight at Ace.

Ace didn't respond. He simply walked over to the benches mounted on the walls and took a seat. Petrovana looked at the ragged-looking Chernzerk. She couldn't tell if he was angry, sad, or depressed.

"If you don't start talking, maybe I'll just beat it out of you," Leper threatened.

"You can try," Ace finally replied, his gaze fixed ahead as if staring into the distance of his thoughts.

"Why are you with Nalecht, anyway?" Petrovana inquired, her tone curious yet sharp.

"Who says I'm with Nalecht?" Ace's voice carried a bitter edge. "Can't I make my own choices?"

"So, you're just an asshole, then?" Leper settled into a seat across from him, his gaze unwavering.

"I'd rather be an asshole than a complete fool," Ace retorted with a smirk. "Without your help, this city would have gone up in flames. Yet here you are, locked up, just like the person who was burning it down."

Leper's gaze shifted from Petrovana to the ground, a telltale sign of his contemplation of the situation. She sensed the weight of his thoughts, yet she found herself at a loss regarding how to counteract this sentiment. Ace's words had struck a chord of truth; their shared heritage could offer him a means to sway Leper's allegiance, a perilous outcome that held dire consequences for all involved.

"Don't pay him any mind. He's tryin' to sow doubt," Petrovana interjected firmly.

"Well, he's not entirely wrong. You can't just brush that aside," Leper countered.

"Are you seriously buyin' into this? Think, Leper. I care about you, as does Rinawen, Harmony, Madislak, Lillian," Petrovana implored.

"I'm not so sure about Madislak either," Leper replied, his gaze steady on Petrovana. "His whole demeanor shifted the moment my hat came off. You saw it, didn't you?"

"Give him time. Harmony will set him straight," Petrovana assured, gesturing toward Ace. "This one is just a pawn until Nalecht's done with him. Y'all will see." Ace lunged towards Petrovana, his fingers clutching the bars of the cell.

"I'm not working with Nalecht, you bitch!" he snarled, his anger flared. Petrovana deftly moved out of his reach as Leper rose to his feet.

"Hit a nerve there, did I?" she teased. "I'd like to speak with your manager, errand boy."

She noticed the flush of anger spreading across Ace's face, a reaction she had deliberately stoked to prompt a more revealing response. Her calculated prodding seemed to hit the mark. However, Petrovana's primary worry was Leper's safety, as he was confined within the same cage as Ace.

"When I get out of here and believe me, I will. You'll be the first one Voldahyl burns, and I'll make sure he watches." Ace's eyes flicked towards Leper, his anger simmering. "Or maybe I'll have Fingin freeze you."

"Fingin?" Leper grabbed Ace's arm. "Who is Fingin?"

"You'll find out soon enough, asshole." Ace yanked his arm away. "Don't touch me again."

"Plannin' a grand escape, are we?" Petrovana chimed in, her tone mocking.

"Like I said. You'll find out soon enough," Ace replied smugly.

"Nalecht's your ticket out, isn't he?" she chuckled. "Once again, just a puppet."

"I'll display your head in my room," Ace spat out the words, flecks of spittle flying.

"Enough," Leper's voice rumbled with warning as he grabbed Ace, forcibly shoving him from the bars.

In an instant, Ace's fist connected with Leper's cheek, the impact resounding in the confined space. Leper's hand instinctively rose to touch the spot where Ace struck him, and Petrovana detected a shift in his demeanor. His gaze locked onto Ace, the intensity in his eyes glaring. The cage, once a backdrop of confinement, transformed into an arena of conflict as a brawl erupted between them. The clash of fists echoed in the tight space as they exchanged blows. Ace seized the upper hand, locking Leper in a headlock and delivering a series of punches, targeting his chest and stomach.

"Get off of him!" Petrovana screeched, holding up her hand as she turned to the guards. "Do somethin' you idiots." The guards responded with indifferent shrugs, clearly unmoved by the situation.

Leper elbowed Ace a few times in the stomach before breaking out of the headlock.

"So, we're just going to hang out in here and fight?" Ace stared intently at Leper with a grin.

"Nope," Leper responded, his voice dripping with malevolence.

Petrovana felt something whoosh by her. Leper's hand extended towards the bars as his chakram glided through the cage bars softly into his hand.

"I'll just kill you myself right now," Leper gritted through his teeth.

Ace's face went from a menacing grin to concern instantly.

"No, Leper, stop, we need him alive," Petrovana pleaded.

"He's not right in the head. Something's missing. He threatened your life, and I won't let that slip." His determination was gravely intent.

"Go ahead, kill me. That'll change their mind about you. That's all you care about, isn't it? Having to get their approval?" Ace motioned his head towards the guards.

"What the hells is going on here?" Brebian charged around the corner. "Get that weapon out of his hand! We need the other one alive!"

Leper turned to Brebian, holding out his chakram in his direction.

"I'm not going into another cell. I just defended your fucking city, you ungrateful bastard!" Leper seethed with anger.

Petrovana could immediately tell something was wrong with Leper.

"You're in no position to be making demands, cherno!" Brebian growled, pointing his sword at Leper.

"Drop your sword, or I'll take off your head," Leper demanded as his other chakram floated to Brebian's neck. Brebian's sword fell to the ground.

"You're doing great. We'll be out of here before I thought," Ace smirked from behind him.

Leper turned and jabbed Ace in the stomach with the pointed end of Maka Kura. "Shut up," he turned back to Brebian. "Now get me out of this prison."

"Lep, drop your weapons! What are you doing!?" Rinawen came hobbling around the corner, Lillian right behind her.

"Rin?" Leper turned to her.

Leper's chakrams clattered to the floor, a visual cue that left Petrovana grappling to comprehend the startling turn of events. She entertained theories of possession or some form of bodily takeover.

The man she just observed was starkly different from the Leper she knew. This realization carried an amalgam of intrigue and unease, sending a shiver down her spine. Yet, a thought took root—could this incident provide insight into Ace's perpetual malevolence? That something, some entity, had taken control of Leper resonated within her. It explained Ace's sinister nature. She couldn't dismiss the notion that whatever transpired with Leper might be mirrored in Ace's actions.

"I'm sorry. I don't know what came over me. I was just so angry, mainly at him." Leper's voice held a hint of remorse as he glanced at Ace, who was clutching his stomach on the ground.

"Don't apologize to them," Ace coughed, his voice strained. "That was excellent."

"You threaten a king, an offense punishable by death," Brebian's tone remained flat as he delivered his verdict. "We will carry out the sentence tomorrow evening."

"What? You can't do that," Rinawen's voice held a mix of disbelief and command.

"I can, I will, and you won't intervene," Brebian waved her off.

"Like hell, I won't intervene." Rinawen crossed her arms defiantly. "You'll release him, and I will take him home."

"Or what?" Brebian's tone carried a hint of mockery.

"I'll march Kundry to your doorstep."

"I'm not scared of your farmers and merchants." Brebian mocked.

"I'll bring an army of shrews with them," Petrovana added, her threat hanging in the air.

While the prospect of shrews mustering an army was beyond workable, the mere notion was enough to instill fear even in the hardiest of monarchs. Petrovana recognized that, despite their limitations in physical combat, shrews possessed a potent weapon in their magic. The potential havoc they could wreak, the devastation they could unleash, made them formidable adversaries.

Brebian looked around, trying to assess the threats that were laid before him. "Fine. We'll hold a trial tomorrow to determine his fate. Whatever the outcome, we stick to the decision of the people."

"That ain't fair either. You know how that will go." Petrovana argued. "I say you give him an actual chance to be who he says he is. Let him stay here with me. If he commits any other offenses, then we have a trial. But considerin' he just saved yer ass from him and Voldahyl," she motioned her head towards Ace. "You can let this pass."

"I second that. He's lived his entire life around me, my children, and my people. He's harmed none of them in his life," Rinawen reassured him.

"New deal. I let him out of here. He is your responsibility. If and when he commits another act of violence towards me or any of my people, and he will, he will be sentenced to death. And you must surrender the shard of Theora to me," Brebian demanded.

As Brebian divulged the current location of the shard of Theora, Ace's eyes gleamed with newfound knowledge within the confines of the cage. Petrovana's reaction, however, was one of profound disappointment and disgust. She couldn't help but shake her head, thoroughly disheartened by Brebian's lack of vigilance. A true monarch, especially a king, should exhibit greater awareness of their surroundings and the potential consequences of their disclosures, unlike Brebian's careless revelation.

"You dipshit. You just told him where the shard is. Good goin'," Lillian fumed from behind Rinawen as she stormed out of the room.

"I'll take that deal. I trust him," Rinawen agreed immediately.

"I truly am sorry, Brebian," Leper called to him on his way out of the cell.

To which Brebian ignored entirely and ordered the guards to tend to Ace's wound, who was still chuckling like a complete lunatic.

Madislak erupted from the confines of the cage, with Harmony still cuffed but sitting up despite her weakened state from the loss of blood. The sun glared through the trees as Madislak plowed through the door. Clutching the cage bars for support, Madislak executed a swift maneuver, spinning himself around 180 degrees, and surged towards the figure stationed at the wagon's end. The horseman attempted to evade Madislak's charge, simultaneously signaling for aid, yet Madislak's unwavering resolve prevailed. He seized the moment, vaulting onto the horse alongside the rider. The horse's balance faltered under the combined weight, sending them both tumbling to the ground. In a single fluid motion, Madislak snatched up his sword, Skyrunner, and swiftly dispatched the man, silencing the threat.

He turned around to see Thessek picking himself off the ground.

"You there! Grab the girl. We got a resistant one here," Thessek commanded the driver of the wagon.

The driver leapt from his perch, aiming to apprehend Harmony. With nimble precision, Madislak closed the distance to Harmony, his grip firm on his weapon. Thessek, however, had unique plans. Retrieving a blowgun from his pocket, he readied a small, paralyzing dart reminiscent of those previously employed on them. Meanwhile, the orcs on either side of the wagon began their convergence toward Madislak and Harmony's position.

In a display of resourcefulness, Harmony worked her bindings down around her feet, freeing her hands. Positioned in front of Madislak, her open palm faced Thessek—an unspoken plea, a silent appeal that held potential consequences.

"Stay still," Harmony's voice carried a tone of determination.

Thessek's movements halted abruptly as he clutched the blowgun against his lips. "Seize them! Seize them all!" His cry echoed, laden with a palpable sense of panic.

Driven by an urgent need to escape, Madislak surged forward as the driver closed in on Harmony as she wavered back and forth. In an uncoordinated motion, Harmony unleashed another icy projectile from her open hand, propelling the driver off the wagon and onto the ground below as she collapsed. Capitalizing on the opportunity, Madislak jumped from the wagon, pinning the driver to where he lay. The lethargic orcs finally arrived at the scene, their slow approach elongating the tense moments. Madislak wasted no time employing the pommel of his sword to render the driver unconscious. The escalating commotion drew an undesirable amount of attention to their vicinity.

In a single fluid maneuver, he wrestled Thessek into his grasp and pressed the edge of Skyrunner against his neck.

"Don't you dare move," Madislak's voice resonated with authority.

Thessek's lips contorted as he muttered disdainful words, spittle spraying from his mouth. "Incompetent, sluggish, imbecilic, worthless orcs," he muttered under his breath.

"Where's the key to her restraints?" Madislak shook Thessek violently.

"In my pocket," Thessek admitted begrudgingly.

With the blade of his sword held close to Thessek's throat, Madislak kept a firm control while retrieving the keys and tossing them to Harmony. They landed next to her as she slowly grabbed them, her hands trembling.

"Order your lackeys to stand down and fetch us two horses immediately!" Madislak's tone left no room for argument.

Thessek's wide-eyed expression and trembling demeanor betrayed his deep-seated fear for his own life, laying bare his inherent cowardice.

"How quiet you've become now," Harmony said warily.

Thessek retorted with venom, spitting in her direction. "This isn't the end. We'll track you down, and trust me, my approach won't be as gentle."

"I believe you," Harmony remarked, then disarmed Thessek of the blowgun. She extracted the dart from its chamber. A swift, forceful slap across Thessek's face punctuated her actions. Without hesitation, she plunged the paralyzing dart into his neck.

Madislak helped Harmony onto her horse, put the reins in her hands, and smacked it on the hind leg to get it moving. He glanced at the orcs, who still seemed very docile. Like they didn't want to be there or want to have any part of the violence. Madislak hopped onto his horse as he kept a close eye on the orcs and galloped off after Harmony, hoping she didn't fall off her horse. Madislak's thoughts raced, grappling with the recent events and the elusive motives that might have driven them to this remote location.

"What was that?" Harmony's gaze shifted toward Madislak, her incredulity clear. "That was the most disorganized and uninspired gang of criminals I've ever encountered."

"My exact sentiments. It was as if they barely cared if we escaped. And those orcs exhibited such passivity. It's unlike anything I've seen," Madislak contemplated, his hand supporting his chin in deep thought.

"There's definitely more beneath the surface of that whole situation. Orcs rarely venture out of their subterranean dwellings. It was almost like they were coerced into assisting. As if they had no choice," Harmony said, as her head swayed.

"Hey, are you okay? What's going on?" Madislak looked her up and down. He could see the bloodstains from where Thessek had jabbed her.

"I'm... fine... just.. with the jabbing and the magic." She said through labored breaths.

"The vials take another vial," Madislak commanded.

She shook her head no. "Gone. I'm worried about Le..." Her body went limp, and she fell forward.

Madislak stopped his horse and hopped off it to catch her.

Madislak grappled with a tough decision—whether to establish a camp for the impending nightfall or to press on relentlessly. Harmony needed rest or medical attention. The sun was steadily sinking. The allure of rest tugged at him, but the urgency to reach their destination was equally compelling. Thessek's intervention and their subsequent journey in the wrong direction had undoubtedly set them back by at least a day or two. Their progress thwarted, they now faced the arduous task of retracing their path on horseback, making their way back to Wen-Tath and, hopefully, procuring a chariot to facilitate their westward journey. After securing the horses to a nearby tree, he plucked some ripe apples and sweet berries from the surrounding bushes. He ate some for himself and saved some for Harmony in case she woke up.

The apples tasted firm and crisp, with a refreshing tartness that balanced out the intense sweetness of the berries. Together, they created a delightful blend of flavors, satisfying both the need for something tangy and something succulent.

Harmony's life was more important than getting to the battle depleted and weak. They would have to rest for tonight. But not this close. He needed to get some distance and assess her wounds. If he didn't get the blood to stop, she would surely bleed out. He hoped that, somehow, they didn't get decimated by the dragon.

Under the cloak of night, Madislak climbed on Harmony's horse and held her as he rode on for two hours. The sun had long disappeared, leaving the air brisk and chilly—a gentle reminder of the world's quietude. A gust of wind swept through, its crisp touch carrying the fragrance of untamed wilderness. Relying on his intuition, Madislak eventually identified a level expanse, its modest concealment offered by the encompassing shrubs and foliage. It seemed as suitable a spot as any to rest for the night. Madislak quickly built a fire and laid Harmony down on the ground, her face grow-ing paler by the second. Not a medic in any way, shape, or form, Madislak tried to assess the severity of her wounds and bandage up what he could with anything he could find. Then he sat her up and offered her some water, which she swallowed. *Still alive, that's good.*

Finally, Madislak surrendered to the weariness that weighed on his body, an unfamiliar experience. He lowered himself to the ground, his fingers massaging his temples to ease both physical and mental exhaustion. He held Harmony close to him to keep her warm and put as much cloth as he could over them.

Amidst the quiet of the night, his mind became a cascade of rushing thoughts, tumbling like a waterfall. The safety and well-being of his com-panions, Leper and Petrovana, clawed at his consciousness. Dread loomed large, fueled by the haunting possibility that they might have succumbed to dire circumstances, left to fend for themselves against the formidable might of a dragon. His memory resurfaced the explosive event that flashed through the sky, grounding their chariot and prompting questions. He pondered the ominous shadow cast by Nalecht, who threatened to overrun Brebian's realm much like his own city. The weight of his absence during this crucial juncture pressed heavily on him, a sense of disappointment and self-blame creeping into his thoughts, a bitter taste in his mind. Terror clenched his heart at the thought of losing Harmony. His head shook violently, unable to fathom a world without her by his side. The mere idea of living without her caused a physical ache in his chest. A gnawing emptiness that threatened to consume him entirely. *Failure. Just like father. Failure.*

Morning came, and Madislak woke to Harmony not in his grasp. He shot up, searching feverishly.

"Are you alright, my king?" Harmony interjected.

"I'm fine now," he responded as Harmony grinned. "I thought you would not make it."

"Thanks to you, I'm alive. Although you could use some work on your bandaging techniques." Harmony joked.

"Well, I did the best I could," Madislak huffed. "But. Now that you're okay. I was thinking about last night. Does this all seem like it's been planned all along, and we're just finding out about it?"

Harmony tapped her chin. "It definitely seems that way. Orcs are marching to Xaneth Harbor. The dragon and Chernzerk emergence. The shards. All of it seems like it's connected somehow."

"Exactly. A little over a week ago, I ruled over a city with my wife. We were on a quest for the shards to protect our people at Nalecht's behest. Now Lantess is in ruins, a dragon looms, Tamara is gathering an army of orcs and humans heading south, and Blank Face is gathering shards. The precision is disconcerting; it feels too orchestrated, and I don't like it." Madislak got to his feet.

"It seems unnaturally precise. But Madislak," Harmony walked over and placed her hand over his, "we can only do what's within our power. We must trust that our allies are also fighting with all their might. It's not solely your responsibility to safeguard the entire realm."

"I understand, and your unwavering support means the world to me. Through thick and thin, you've stood by me, teaching me it's okay to lean on others, even if they aren't exactly who we thought they were." Madislak's gaze delved into her captivating blue eyes. And it's true.

"Where would I be without you?" Harmony inched closer. "You offered me the chance to be your head shrew, defended me, rescued me, and put anyone who questioned my intellect in their place. A quality I find quite appealing in a man, if I may say so."

The soft press of Harmony's lips against his abruptly shattered Madislak's reverie. The sensation sent a whirlwind of emotions coursing through him. In that fleeting moment, their shared kiss served as a transient sanctuary from the daunting challenges looming ahead.

Madislak indulged in this passionate exchange with Harmony, a tender reprieve amidst the storm. However, amidst the flickering flames of desire, a shadow of guilt lingered—a remnant of Gwen's recent departure still casting its subtle touch upon his thoughts. He quickly pulled away.

"I'm sorry." Madislak grasped her shoulders. "We need to go."

Chapter Seventeen

L eper's ears picked up the sound of Brebian's voice as he walked out of his cell, carrying his request to Petrovana as they went their separate ways. Several hours after his imprisonment, Brebian agreed to release him for the time being. The words were innocuous enough—just a brief conversation, but they held a weight that stirred unease within Leper. The thought of Petrovana being alone with Brebian in his private chambers roused a mix of uncertainty and anxiety in him. A wave of heat spread across his cheeks. Leper briefly thought about whistling for Ghost and hopping on his back to get out. With an uncertain future ahead, he didn't want his magnificent griffin to face any repercussions for being connected to him.

Leper grappled with an inexplicable surge of impulse that had driven his recent actions. The transition from defending Petrovana to a blind rage was a bewildering whirlwind. It felt as if a switch flipped, and suddenly, Leper found himself consumed by a seething concoction of emotions—hatred, anger, and an overwhelming urge for escape, irrespective of the consequences. The realization that he brazenly threatened Brebian's life, a king and an ally, struck him. He shook his head, attempting to shake off the lingering shock and disbelief. Guilt swiftly followed, settling upon him like a heavy shroud. When Ace threatened Petrovana, he couldn't control himself. All he could picture was killing Ace and getting out of that cage at any cost, regardless of who he had to harm to achieve that. *Perhaps*

I'm more of a danger to my friends than I realize. Maybe Brebian is right. Someone should lock me up somewhere where I can't cause harm to anyone.

"Hey, everythin' alright there?" Lillian's gentle voice reached him from beyond the castle doors.

"I'm not sure. I just did something unbelievably stupid," Leper admitted, his head bowed.

"What? Spent more time with Petrovana?" Lillian teased. "Yeah, that's definitely a bad move," she added, chuckling.

"Come here this instant," Rinawen interjected, grabbing Leper by the ear.

"Oww, owww," Leper protested, his voice tinged with pain. "Where are we headed?"

Rinawen guided Leper to a relatively secluded spot near the shattered watchtower. The surroundings were sparsely populated, with only a handful of individuals moving about roughly forty feet away from them. She looked quite awkward with the large round shield still strapped to her back.

"Forgive my language, but what the royal fuck is your problem?" Rinawen glared intently at Leper.

"Ain't been around Rinawen all that much but reckon she wasn't this pissed even after Blank Face attacked us," Lillian poked playfully.

Rinawen's dagger-like eyes pierced through Lillian momentarily, and Leper's head snapped to Rinawen.

"What?" Leper's eyes widened. "When was this?"

"Thanks, Lillian, your timing is paramount," Rinawen's voice dripping with disdain. "But this isn't about me right now. Where's your stupid hat?"

"I messed up. In front of Madislak. When we saw Ace, I may or may not have said something about not being the only one... Out loud."

"Damn it, Leper!" Rinawen's fists clenched tightly. "I warned you! I told you unequivocally! Look at your surroundings..." Rinawen's gaze bore into Leper's eyes. "LOOK!" she shouted urgently.

Leper observed the individuals in their vicinity, his gaze sweeping over the crowd. Although not their primary focus, most of the people milling around exuded expressions of disdain, loathing, and spite. Despite his lack of involvement in causing the havoc, their contempt was unmistakable. They cast sneers and glares his way, unjustly attributing the blame to him in spite of the actual events.

"I didn't do this!" he yelled.

"Go destroy your own home, cherno!" one person yelled.

"Nobody likes you!" another chimed in as she hurled a spear his way.

Leper moved out of the way as the spear thudded into the ground and stuck there. A group of ten of them started rushing towards him, drawing their weapons. Leper put his arms out in front of him.

Rinawen stepped in front of him, the shard of Theora humming to life as the brown glow emitted from it, forming a dirt barricade in front of the aggressors. "Go back to your homes now! He will be dealt with accordingly. He is not a murderer, and neither are any of you."

Leper's depression set in. Even after his heroic efforts, they still didn't believe in him. The dirt barricade formed around them, keeping anyone out. The scent of damp soil and minerals filled the air, along with the musty aroma of earthworms.

"And then your stupid ass goes and threatens their king!" Rinawen steamed.

"Ya, reckon that ain't your best move," Lillian piled on.

"All I ever wanted was for you to have a normal, peaceful life. I kept you safe, fed, and happy. But no, Leper has to run off on some stupid quest to prove how great he is. 'They'll accept me,'" Rinawen mocked. "'I'll show them.' Now, because of your incompetence, I may have to part with a three-hundred-year-old family heirloom."

Each of her words struck a chord within him, resonating with a resounding truth that cut deep. Leper's heart thudded with the weight of regret, a heavy rhythm of remorse. Raking his hands over his face. What had he unleashed? A wave of self-disgust surged within him, eclipsing any other emotion. The realization that he disappointed Rinawen, the person who held the highest importance in his heart.

"You're right, Rin. I'm sorry," Leper conceded. "I'll just leave this place. Find somewhere where I won't bother anyone ever again. They'll never change their minds. No one will ever accept me for who I am. Who am I kidding?"

Leper's fingers closed around Maka Kura, the weapon's familiarity reassuring in his grip. His eyes traced the intricate contours and impeccable craftsmanship of the blade, absorbing each nuance. With a final, lingering look, he released the weapons, tossing them on the ground amongst the rubble. A heavy sigh escaped him, laden with unspoken emotions, as he pivoted and walked away.

"You have a home in Kordry, Lep," Rinawen offered. "You're always welcome there."

"You ain't seriously lettin' him disappear, are you?" Lillian's voice dripped with disgust.

"No. She's not letting me do anything. You see how they are, Lillian? They don't care. I could have killed that dragon, but I didn't. I can't control my own emotions; I don't know how to deal with adversity." Leper took in another breath. "I'm a danger to all of you guys, and the one thing I was born to do, I didn't even do that. You heard Brebian. I'm pathetic and useless. How can I prove to be a peaceful person when I threaten the lives of kings or innocent people?"

Rinawen just glared at Leper. "Go home, Lep."

Leper shook his head. "I don't have a home. I'm not welcome here. I'm not welcome on The Talon with Ace." Leper sighed. "It appears you were right this whole time. I should've never left Kordry. I should've stayed there and just lived in the woods my entire life, making vials."

"Reckon that ain't right, Rinawen, and you damn well know it," Lillian confronted her, getting inches from her face.

"Get out of my face, Lillian," Rinawen's expression was stern and un-yielding as she lowered the dirt wall.

"You call yerself a queen? I wouldn't want to be associated with any queen who abandons her own fuckin' people in the face of adversity!" Lillian's face turned red as she spat the words.

"It's okay, Lillian. I deserve it. I'm just going to go." Leper turned to-wards the open gates, now that the wall was gone, as Lillian and Rinawen followed.

"Like hell, you deserve this," Lillian's words slashed through the air, her frustration echoing loud and clear for all to hear. Her gaze swept over the onlookers, piercing through them. "All of you bastards wouldn't even have a city to call home or a place to rest yer heads if it weren't for this man," her voice carried a vehement intensity. "So, take yer judgmental, fearful, and ignorant attitudes and hide in yer pathetic corners. He saved yer pitiful existence! Is this how you repay a savior?" Visible strain accompanied the force behind her words, her neck and face veins standing out.

To Leper's astonishment, most of the onlookers seemed to break free from their trance. Slowly, they dispersed, their gazes averted as they re-treated to their respective places. The city was already in chaos, and the realization that many had to rebuild their lives from the ruins seemed to snap them out of their judgmental stupor.

"And you... Queen Rinawen," Lillian gritted. "Call yerself a queen! Yer not better than Nalecht or Borlden. Not supportin' people that don't conform to yer standards. You know what I say to that?"

"Judging from this outburst, I think I know, but why don't you tell me, anyway?" Rinawen mocked.

"Reckon I say fuck you, fuck them! And fuck King Brebian! If he leaves, I'm goin' with him. Have fun fightin' Nalecht, missin' two of yer greatest fighters here." Lillian stormed off towards the gates. She turned her head over her shoulder. "And good luck against Blank Face!"

Rinawen sighed heavily. "You're both young and stubborn. I might lose Theora because of you. And likely Brebian's allegiances as well. Things could've been different. But on the heels of a dragon attack by a Chernzerk. You can see what they think."

Another harsh reality. How can he rally the people's support if he can't even defeat dragons or prevent Ace from causing destruction? These uncontrollable episodes are a hindrance, and they won't inspire anyone to trust him.

"Like I already said, Rinawen, you don't need to keep saying it. You're right. I'm leaving. I don't know where, but somewhere. There's got to be somewhere to go where I won't be a danger to any of you or them anymore." Leper nodded. "What are you going to do about Blank Face?"

"I'll have Brebian send some guards and a bulwark with me. Just go home to Kordry, Lep. Please. You'll be safe, and we can sort this out together when we're done here." Rinawen pleaded.

Leper shook his head no. He had no desire to return to Kordry, not that he disliked the place. However, if whatever took control of him in the prison overcame him there, what would happen to Zanera and Kelindra? He couldn't bear the thought of being a danger to anyone, especially them. Those two girls were the most important people in his life, aside from Rinawen.

Leper pointed at Rinawen. "I always thought I could trust you above anyone else. Apparently, you don't love me as much as I love you. I have other friends now, and I don't need your stupid protection anymore. You obviously care more about that shard than me, anyway!" A single tear escaped his eye.

Tears immediately streaked down her beautiful face. "How can you say that!? I... Lep..." She started sobbing so hard she couldn't speak.

Leper's heart was a wellspring of sorrow as he walked away with Lillian, the weight of his emotions palpable. Bidding farewell to his cherished weapons was difficult, but it paled compared to the wrenching farewell he had just shared with Rinawen. He couldn't help but glance back one more time, worried that someone else might lay their hands on his weapon. But then he quickly pushed that thought away - it didn't matter who picked up Maka Kura, as he didn't deserve to wield such a powerful weapon. Saying farewell to his closest companion and sister was an excruciating task, tearing at his heartstrings and solidifying it as one of the most difficult moments he ever experienced.

"C'mon, Leper, let's get out of this shit hole," Lillian's comforting gaze offered momentary solace.

As they departed from the city in its current state of chaos, Leper was acutely aware of the stares and glares directed their way. The disapproving eyes bore into him, a reminder of the disarray he inadvertently contributed to. His thoughts couldn't help but stray to Petrovana. How would she feel about him after he leaves without saying goodbye? Just one more person who would hate him. *Oh well.*

Petrovana trailed behind Brebian, ascending the stairs and passing through the regal main hall of the castle the morning after Leper's imprisonment. The journey led them to his private chambers. Upon entering, Petrovana's gaze swept across the room, taking in the details that painted a portrait of the man who ruled this domain. Brebian meticulously secured his sword in a weapons case, nestled alongside an assortment of weaponry that included a great axe, a short sword, and a bow. The lavishness extended to the meticulously made bed, adorned with sheets bearing the hues of green and white. To the right of the room, a collection of two dressers flanked his weapons case. Petrovana anxiously scanned her surroundings, her thoughts spinning as she wondered if Terynsipple discovered her deceitful act of posing as their representative. Did he bring her here to punish her or, worse yet, send her back to Terynsipple for punishment?

On the opposing side, two couches arranged in an L-shape occupied the corner, offering a space for contemplation and conversation. An elegant vanity adorned the wall adjacent, a testament to the attention paid to his personal comforts. Rich fabric draped the lone window. Positioned before the couches, a small ottoman provided a touch of coziness in an otherwise dignified setting. Lavender incense burning on the dressers provided a soothing aroma. It carried a hint of sweet floral notes intertwined with the warm, woody undertones of the burning incense.

Two individuals occupied the couch, the first being Brebian's wife, Breann. Her short dark hair framed her Elven face, styled around her ears. A pair of earrings dangled from each ear, and her appearance suggested a woman in her mid to late forties. Seated beside her was another person, robed in the attire of a shrew. Though Petrovana assumed her to be Brebian's shrew, her identity remained a mystery to her. This shrew appeared older than both Brebian and his wife, hints of silver intermingling within predominantly blond locks that grazed just past her human ears. She intertwined her hands, concealing any telltale signs of potential spells she might possess.

"Please take a seat," Brebian pointed to the couch.

Petrovana's heart quickened, a surge of nervousness coursing through her veins as she contemplated what King Brebian might have in store for her, particularly in the presence of his wife and shrew.

"What's this about?" Petrovana's voice was shaky.

"Would you like some tea? Or mead?" Brebian offered graciously as he grabbed a bottle from his dresser.

"Sure, tea, please," Petrovana sat at the opposite end of the couch from the other two.

"Hello, I'm Breann, queen of Tudela. It's nice to meet you." Her voice was soft and melodious.

"I'm Genova. It's a pleasure to meet you." the shrew's dry, raspy voice came out.

"Petrovana, a pleasure. Do y'all know if I did somethin' wrong?" Her eyes flicked between the two women. She could hear the clinking of glass as Brebian poured himself a drink.

"I have no idea," Breann said.

"Hey, honey, can you go grab me another bottle of mead from the pantry, please?" Brebian's gaze turned to Breann. He then handed a chalice to Petrovana, and she took a sip. The tea was bold and strong, with a sharp bitterness that lingered on her tongue. The lack of sweetness only intensified the bitter flavor, almost overwhelming Petrovana's taste buds. Should've just said no.

Breann rose from the couch, responding with a gentle, "Sure thing, dear."

"Thanks," Brebian called after her as he settled beside Genova.

"So, you've met Genova?" Brebian inquired.

"Yes, reckon she just introduced herself," Petrovana replied.

"While my wife's gone, let's get down to business," Brebian's tone grew stern.

"Finally, I've only been askin' what this is about since I stepped foot in here," Petrovana sighed.

"I need you to do something for me," Brebian's request was direct.

"Little ole me?" Petrovana crossed her arms.

"Yes. We are at a critical crossroads in our history. I don't know if you realize what the return of the Chernzerk symbolizes." he sipped his mead. "But we have two in our custody. The one will be easy enough to execute. But the other, well, people did see him help us, and if he gets enough support, I could deal with an uprising here."

"What exactly are you sayin'?" Petrovana cut to the point.

"This is Mortis Nightshade," Brebian held up a vial of dark, smoky-colored liquid. "Made from a plant named after the moon itself. This is potent enough to kill anyone that ingests all its contents."

"Okay, you better start makin' sense here. You want me to give that to Ace?" Petrovana's voice remained tense.

"No, that's the easy one to take care of," Brebian smirked. "I need you to put this in Leper's drink. Get him drunk, and he won't even notice."

Petrovana let out a chuckle. "There's not a chance in this lifetime or the next that I would help yer ruthless ass do that."

"Thought you might say that," Brebian smirked. "Why don't you tell her what she might be missing here, Genova?"

"Certainly, my King. My full name is Genova D'leon of Terynsipple. Sister of your adoptive mother, like you, I was banished as well."

Petrovana's heart raced even faster, her thoughts spiraling as she absorbed the revelation of her aunt's existence. The intricacies of Terynsipple's ways became clear: exile equated to erasure from history. A whirlwind of questions stormed her mind, leaving her wondering what her aunt might hold within her knowledge.

"What of it?" Petrovana squeezed the cushion of the couch. *What if she knows? I hope she doesn't know.*

"When I reached out to the king and queen of Terynsipple to inquire about their absence from the penta-annual meeting in Ambrosia and later the tournament, as well as Madislak's letter regarding the attack on Lantess, I was startled by their complete lack of awareness on these matters," Brebian explained.

"That's got nothin' to do with me." Petrovana lied.

"Genova did some contacting of old acquaintances. Sure enough, we found out you were exiled as well. Would be a shame if they discovered what you did with those royal letters, wouldn't it?" Brebian sat back arrogantly.

Petrovana's heart nearly stopped. *They know. They know. How could I be so reckless to not completely cover my tracks? If they tell the king and queen of Terynsipple the truth, I would be hunted down and executed for meddling in royal affairs.*

"So go poison him. Why do I gotta do it?" Petrovana relented.

"He seems to have some kind of fondness for you," Brebian explained.

"Maybe I'm fond of him, too. He just saved yer city." Petrovana didn't back down.

Petrovana felt a genuine fondness for Leper. Beyond his naturally muscular frame, she admired his compassion and empathy—a rarity in their times. His Chernzerk heritage was a source of fascination for her, as were his eyes, a mesmerizing blend of green and brown. Enhanced by his strong jawline and neatly trimmed goatee. The short, dark hair that framed his horns gave him an air of confidence. His origins and unique appearance captivated her, making her unable to resist being drawn to him out of curiosity.

"You can get close enough that he won't suspect anything," Genova added.

"No, I refuse. I'll tell everyone in this town what an asshole you are." She threatened.

"Thought you might say that too," Brebian smirked, looking to Genova again.

"Don't do it. Then you'll never know your actual parents. Something only King Zonoh knew, and now he's dead," Genova teased.

Petrovana's eyes widened in shock as her most guarded secret exposed itself - not even she knew her actual parents. Zonoh, who saved her life, never revealed her true parents. Something she yearned to know. Zonoh promised to reveal their identities on her thirtieth birthday, a milestone that was now just months away. She never understood why he kept it a secret... And why at thirty? However, his passing cast doubt on whether she would ever know her true origins. And now, faced with Genova's revelation, she felt a painful dilemma—unveil the long-awaited secret or protect the friendships she had forged since her exile from Terynsipple.

Leper walked through Tudela's streets, Lillian accompanying him. His mind was a chaotic storm, torn between the weight of his recent actions. Walking away from Rinawen, a mix of regret and sorrow surged within him. He threatened a king's life, wounded Ace, engaged in an argument with Rinawen, and jeopardized the shard of Theora. He's supposed to be defending the shard's safety, not endangering them. The overwhelming sense of disappointment in himself hung heavy over his thoughts, leaving him unable to escape the self-condemnation that gnawed at his conscience. He needed to get away from Tudela, to find a place where he could be alone and think for a while, away from the chaos and the glaring crowds that put him on edge and far from King Brebian's oppressive presence.

Despite the looming threat of Nalecht obtaining all seven shards and wreaking havoc on this world, Leper knew he couldn't face him alone and emerge victorious. The fear of his other side resurfacing only added to his hesitation. He couldn't risk putting his friends in danger, not after all the progress he'd made in changing the perception of Chernzerks. It would only prove the negative stereotypes perpetuated by history about his kind.

"Hey, chin up, fuck them," Lillian jabbed him in the arm.

"I've lost my best friend," Leper looked at Lillian.

"She'll come around. Rinawen's a stubborn one, but she's got a good heart. She'll realize Brebian is bein' unreasonable. These peckerheads should be bowin' to you."

"Still. I kind of lost it there. When he threatened..." Leper stopped. "Petrovana," his thoughts whirled again at the thought of abandoning her.

Lillian snorted. "She'll be fine. Trust me. That tramp has many tricks up her sleeve."

"You don't give her enough credit. She's very smart and sweet." Leper furrowed his brow.

Lillian slapped him on the shoulder. "That's the problem, Leper. I know her too well."

Leper trailed behind Lillian as they ventured into the encompassing woods to the north. Her persistent talk about Petrovana was a source of irritation, yet it also stirred a deep curiosity within him. The earthy scents of mushrooms and soil embraced his senses, offering a soothing familiarity as they trod over the rustling leaves blanketing the forest floor. The sun's descent on the horizon marked the approaching end of the day.

"Okay, I gotta know what happened over there in Terynsipple?" Leper poked. "You can ask me any question you want, and I'll answer it."

Lillian sighed heavily. "Fine. But yer not allowed to go blabbin' it to anyone else!"

"Deal." Leper turned his full attention to Lillian.

"We were best friends." Lillian sat down on the ground. "Now we ain't. End of the story."

"Oh, come on," Leper said, frustrated. "That's not what I meant."

"Calm down, I'm just jokin' with you," Lillian smirked playfully.

"Hilarious." Leper sat down in front of her, a grin growing across his face.

"So, we were best friends. She's six years older than me, but I've known her since we were little. Anyway, I was betrothed to a man named Alzen, and we were married for three years," she took a breath in.

Leper's eyes widened. "You were married?"

"Just listen. You can comment when I'm done." Lillian gazed into his eyes. "Movin' on. Turns out she was foolin' around with him durin' our last year of marriage. And it wasn't the failed marriage that upset me the most. He was in love with his magic, much like her. Honestly, they were made for each other."

"I'm still not sure I understand," Leper interjected again.

"And not that I didn't love Alzen, either, because I did. But we were meant to be together forever. That's kind of how betrothal works, and I truly tried to love him. But when yer supposed best friend has an affair with yer husband, and she didn't say anythin' about it to me? That's what's unacceptable."

"Yeah, I can see how that would be infuriating," Leper offered.

"So, after they asked me to help them flee the city because they would both be punished fer their affair—which I agreed to help them—I made a deal with Petrovana's parents and led them headlong into a trap. Petrovana and I had to watch Alzen die, and I was no longer bound to Terynsipple."

"That's awful. What kind of person makes another person watch their love die?" Leper said.

"Did you even listen to the fuckin' story, asshole?" Lillian stared blankly at Leper.

Leper burst out laughing. "It was a joke."

"Guess I had that one comin'," Lillian smirked.

"Sorry. But to be serious, that was very crappy of her and also kind of crappy of you as well."

"I know. I was just so disappointed. So angry I didn't care about anythin'. It's not like I got people that will stick up fer me. Not like Rinawen sticks up fer you...That person, I thought, was Petrovana. Makes me wonder if our friendship was ever worth a damn to her." Lillian sulked.

Leper grinned. "I'm sure it was. I will not make excuses for her, but my guess is she said nothing because she fears you."

"Are you scared of me?" Lillian leaned forward, glaring angrily.

"Very. You're extremely intimidating. I wouldn't want to piss you off." Leper chuckled.

"Good. That's what I'm goin' fer."

"But. I also don't have any weapons. That's the main reason," Leper burst out laughing again.

"What an ass," Lillian chuckled alongside him.

Lillian playfully punched Leper's shoulder, and in response, he gave her a playful shove back, sending her falling backwards from her sitting position. Swiftly recovering, they both sprang to their feet, and Lillian sized him up. She lunged at him, wrapping her arms around his waist and deftly sliding down to his legs, which caused him to topple to the ground.

With a grin, Leper got back up, saying, "Oh, it's on."

As Lillian attempted another lunge, Leper swiftly caught her wrist and expertly twisted it behind her back. He leaned in close to her ear and whispered, "Hope you're not ticklish."

"Don't you dare!" Lillian responded. Her tone was a playful mix of warning and challenge.

Leper playfully tickled her sides, causing her to burst into laughter as she squirmed to get away. However, Lillian swiftly retaliated by grabbing his other wrist and reversing his grip. Now she had him firmly by the wrist behind his back, and she leaned into whisper into his ear, "My turn now."

Leper squirmed, breaking free from her hold as he tugged on her wrist, which he still gripped. This brought them inches from each other's faces, their gazes locking as he looked into her captivating green eyes.

"I need you to answer somethin' fer me now," Lillian whispered.

"Right now? Kinda thought we were having a moment," Leper retorted.

"Kind of like in Wen-Tath? Yea, we were then, too," Lillian smirked. "But I need you to know I'm not gettin' into another competition with Petrovana. It's either me or her and I can tell you have feelin's for her, but what about me?"

"You can't tell?" he said, stalling.

Leper grappled with his emotions, torn between his feelings for both Lillian and Petrovana. Each had their own unique qualities that drew him in. Petrovana's laid-back nature, sweetness, charm, and intelligence resonated with him. Lillian's energy, enthusiasm, and playfulness were equally captivating. He cherished their friendships and realized that whatever words he chose next needed to be contemplated so as not to jeopardize those connections.

"Look, I will not sit here and lie to you, Lillian. I have feelings for you. And I have feelings for Petrovana. Honestly, I don't know which is stronger. You're beautiful, funny, and spontaneous, and I feel very comfortable when you're around. But for me to say that I don't have feelings for Petrovana as well would be a flat-out lie," Leper held her by the waist.

"That's better than what happened last time. I appreciate yer honesty. I really do, and I can't say I blame you. She is smart and pretty, much as I hate to admit that, but she also has a deceptive background and can be very snake-like." Lillian glanced at the ground.

The intensity in Lillian's eyes told Leper she was genuinely concerned and not just playing around. Considering their history, she might have valid reasons for her caution. Leper contemplated her words, realizing that he should be cautious and consider seeking Petrovana's perspective on the past. His friendships were becoming more complex than he expected, and he needed to navigate them carefully.

Gazing into her eyes, Leper realized he hadn't seen Madislak or heard from them in quite some time. It had been days since they were on The Talon, and it shouldn't take that long to get here. A knot formed in his stomach as he thought about what could have happened to them. Despite being abandoned by him, Leper couldn't shake off the feeling that something terrible might have happened. Perhaps he and Harmony are facing danger together. Part of him wished they were safe, while another part was resentful of the way Madislak left him stranded.

As Leper was saying, "This is completely unfair of me to ask..." Lillian's plump lips interrupted him.

Their kiss deepened, and Leper pressed Lillian against a tree, a sense of familiarity and shared secrets intensifying the moment. Their passionate exchange was halted abruptly by a piercing scream that echoed through the woods. Leper broke away from the kiss. His gaze locked with Lillian's as they processed the unexpected interruption.

"Damn it, curse my luck," Lillian muttered, her disappointment evident.

Leper gently set her down, his fingers lingering on her arm before they both turned and sprinted toward the source of the scream.

Chapter Eighteen

L eper's heart pounded as he followed Lillian's guidance, slowing his pace and scanning the area ahead. He trusted her instincts. As they moved forward, Leper focused on the figure ahead. In an instant, he realized - it was Leighth from Kundry. Blood trickled down her temple, staining her tanned skin, neck, and green shirt as she struggled against the ropes binding her to a thick tree trunk. Next to her, a hooded figure sat on a fallen tree trunk, his dagger reflecting the faint light of the sun. His clenched jaw and furrowed brow betrayed his deep contemplation. Leper picked up his pace, worry coursing through his veins as he neared the mysterious figure.

Leper's gaze shifted between Leighth and Lillian, confusion clear on his face as he whispered. "Leighth, the princess of Kundry."

Lillian confirmed that she already knew of Leighth's identity. Leper felt a pang of curiosity about how Lillian knew, but he quickly pushed that aside in favor of focusing on the urgent situation at hand. Leighth was in trouble, wounded, and clearly distressed. It dawned on him that he left Maka Kura behind in Tudela. The absence of his weapons made him feel vulnerable, causing his heart to skip a few beats. There was no opportunity to ponder over it at present.

Lillian whispered. "Let's go. Leighth's in trouble and wounded."

The figure sitting on the log beside the restrained Leighth was a disheveled sight, his clothing hanging loosely off his frame. He wore a brown robe that resembled a rough burlap sack. Its hood pulled down to reveal a hairstyle that immediately caught Leper's attention. The man's dark hair flared up on either side, creating a distinctive mohawk-like shape that converged at the top, forming an oval mass of hair atop his head. His clean-shaven face had a long nose that seemed to draw attention to its pointed end, while his beady eyes held an intense and unsettling gaze.

Metal earrings dangled from the man's Elven ears, giving him an eccentric appearance. The robe concealed his body, making it difficult to discern his physique or any other details underneath.

"We going in loud and proud or sneaking up on him?" Leper asked Lillian.

"You know me," Lillian smirked as she hollered, "What's goin' on here?"

His head snapped in their direction, drawing him from his thoughts.

"Oh, I didn't expect to have visitors way out here," he said, his voice even.

"Well, that kind of happens when you're torturing people in the woods," Leper shot back.

Leper's attention focused on Leighth, and her eyes widened with either fear or surprise as their gazes locked.

"Not torture, just a little game," he smirked.

"Where you from, stranger? Don't reckon I recognize you?" Lillian poked.

"Terynsipple, like you apparently," came his reply.

Drawing closer, Leper's keen observation revealed older adult lines etched onto the man's face, suggesting that he was in his mid or early forties, weathered by the passage of time.

"Well, I think yer fun's over. Give us the girl," Lillian drew her scimitars.

"Wow, straight to violence, huh?" he furrowed his brow.

"What's your name?" Leper asked, placing a hand on Lillian's arm.

"Not important, but most call me The Latter," he smiled widely.

"And what are you doin' out here with the princess of Kundry?" Lillian pushed.

"He's after the shard of Kasherri, but he needs Blank Face to run the rain trials for him to get it!" Leighth blurted.

"You stupid bitch!" The Latter hissed as he aggressively rushed towards Leighth.

Leper's muscles tensed as he sprinted after the man, throwing his body forward and tackling him to the ground. As Lillian rushed over to stand in front of Leighth, Leper wrapped his arm around the man's throat, cutting off his air supply. But before Leper could secure the hold, the man transformed into a cloud of black smoke, slipping out of Leper's grasp. The smoke drifted towards Lillian and reformed into a solid being right beside her.

"What the fuck?" Lillian's head jolted as her face contorted.

Lillian's feet moved with precision as she twirled and slashed her blades, the sound of metal meeting metal echoing through the air. The Latter, a skilled opponent, could evade each blow by transforming into a trail of smoke. Leper, missing Maka Kura, attempted to restrain or punch The Latter but failed as he effortlessly dissipated into nothingness.

"What are you?" Leper muttered.

"I'm The Latter," came his response.

Leper observed that whatever this figure was doing was exacting a toll on him. Blood seeped from under his nose and near his eyes, a sign that his actions were straining his body.

"Just keep swinging. He can't do that forever," Leper called to Lillian.

They relentlessly attempted to strike him, but it felt like fighting a ghost. His movements were elusive, transforming into smoke and swiftly altering his attack angles. This man was a master of combat, skillfully manipulating whatever power he possessed. Each time he transformed, the scent of toxic smoke assaulted Leper's nostrils, and he refrained from breathing while in his smoky form. The noxious fumes that invaded his senses carried a sharp, acrid odor reminiscent of burning chemicals, causing his eyes to water and his throat to sting.

"I grow tired of these games. Take the girl," he growled. "I'll find my way to Blank Face, eventually."

"No, I'm not done with you," Lillian spat, ratcheting up her intensity.

The Latter persisted in his charade, morphing into smoke and then solid form repeatedly to strike at them. However, Lillian grabbed hold of one of his sleeves, tearing it from his arm. His narrow wrist revealed a swirling black mist as he shifted back into smoke form. A diamond-shaped gemstone, obsidian-like and glowing purple, pulsed on his arm.

"What the hell is that embedded in yer arm?" Lillian inquired.

"Only those of the rain trials will ever know," he chuckled.

"What the fuck are the rain trials?" she blurted.

The concept of rain trials was unfamiliar to Leper as well, leaving him with questions needing answers. The man's nose was now leaking blood more heavily, a clear sign of the strain he experienced. He transformed into smoke once more, drifting through the trees and vanishing into the depths of the forest.

"Damnit, he's gettin' away!" Lillian pouted.

"Let him go, let's help Leighth," Leper set his hand on her shoulder.

"Don't come near me. Let Lillian untie me!" she barked.

"He ain't gonna hurt you, princess," Lillian reasoned. "Where's yer skulkin' friend at? He abandoned you already?" she smirked.

"No, I abandoned him. Who's your horned friend?" Leighth asked shakily.

"That's Leper. He's nice, not like yer buddy," Lillian reassured her.

"Leper..." Leighth thought for a moment. "As in Zanera's Leper?"

"Yes. That's me," Leper smiled at her. "I've seen you, but, well, with the horns, I'm kind of restricted on how many people can see me."

"Not anymore. It's out there," Lillian stated flatly. "Let's have a look at yer head."

Leper observed as Lillian gently brushed Leighth's hair aside, revealing the aftermath of the attack. Rather than merely cutting her face, the man had chopped off her entire ear.

"What kind of monster... What did he want with you?" Leper spat.

"He wanted Blank Face for those rain trials or whatever. He knew that Blank Face was protecting me somehow and needed him to get the shard of Kasherri for him, which is apparently locked within the rain trials," Leighth panted.

"So, he thought by tyin' you up out here and torturin' you, Blank Face, would help?" Lillian spat. "That man don't care about anyone but himself."

"No, he cares about me, and I care about him. He could've let me die several times, but he didn't. One day, you're going to wake up and realize that we need him to win this war." Leighth clenched her jaw. "He beat you, didn't he?"

Lillian's face turned beat red as she huffed. Leper grabbed her shoulders and ushered her in the other way before she did something she regretted. After that jab, Lillian might need another day to cool down. She'd just calmed herself from Leper's imprisonment the day before.

Leper hoped Maka Kura could still hear his thoughts as he mentally spoke. "I need you."

"You left me lying on the ground," Maka Kura responded with a tinge of disappointment.

"I'm sorry. I didn't realize you had feelings," Leper replied.

"I'm sentient. Of course, I do. I'm also only bound to you and you to me. When you leave me behind, I sit here craving adventure." Maka's voice was stern.

"I'm so sorry. It'll never happen again," Leper pleaded with his weapons.

"Consider this your one and only mistake," Maka Kura's tone was firm.

"Thank you." Leper let out a sigh of relief as he could feel Maka Kura heading his way.

"C'mon, let's get you cleaned up," Leper said, using the last of his healing salve. He then put some cloth bandages over the wound.

Leper led her back to where he and Lillian had set up camp earlier. They spent the rest of the nightfall discussing the events in Tudela, and Leighth shared her insights about Blank Face. As the sun disappeared below the horizon and the temperature dropped, a gentle breeze brought a chill to the night. Leighth shared that Blank Face was going after the shards for Nalecht but not to help his quest for power. There was something else he wanted that she wasn't sure of. That she was using his closeness with Nalecht and his ability to fight to both get revenge on Borlden and potentially get her family's shard back.

"So, what's next for you?" Leper turned to Leighth.

"I'll crawl back to Rinawen, hope she takes me back, and seek my vengeance that way." She tussled some leaves. "What about you?"

Leper glanced to Lillian, then back to Leighth. "I don't know. Fail at something else, I suppose."

"Yer not a failure," Lillian interjected.

Leper shook his head. "I just need to think."

Leper sat down and leaned against a tree, feeling drowsy. He wasn't sure how much time passed when the sound of Lillian's frantic voice echoing through the woods suddenly jolted him awake. "There's people comin'! We need to move."

Leper glanced about and heard rustling in the distance and voices, yet no sign of Leighth.

The day after she met with Brebian, Petrovana's thoughts raced like a tempest as she stood alone in her room gazing out of the window at the bustling city of Tudela. The weight of recent events bore down heavily on her shoulders, a tangled web of emotions entwining her every thought. Today was the day of the trial. The unsettling threats Brebian had cast over her and the tantalizing prospect of uncovering her true parentage all swirled in a chaotic mix. The tendrils of jealousy wormed their way into her heart whenever she contemplated Lillian's closeness to Leper. But then, there was Brebian's mysterious offer—a promise of revealing her lineage, of providing answers she'd longed for, albeit with the looming threat of exposing her to the authorities of Terynsipple. She sipped her coffee; the warm liquid coated her tongue with a smooth and creamy texture. The sweetness of vanilla and sugar complemented perfectly the rich flavor of the coffee, creating a harmonious balance on her taste buds. Just how she liked it.

Time pressed on. With the trial's commencement only minutes away, each tick of the clock urged Petrovana to take action. Leper wouldn't return soon enough to save himself, and she couldn't fathom the thought of him suffering from attempting to shield her from harm. With a surge of determination, she made a resolute decision—she would approach Brebian before the trial unfolded to implore for Leper's safety and to navigate the treacherous threats of being exposed. Taking in a deep breath, Petrovana donned a deep blue gown she had bought earlier. Its fabric flowed around her figure like water. She steeled herself, squaring her shoulders, and ventured towards the castle. Filled with people, the courtyard thrummed with life. Worried glances and hushed tones permeated the green grass arena. The grand stage dominated the space. If these people decided the Chernzerk were too much of a threat, then it would be over before it even got started for Leper.

As she drew closer, her heartbeat resonated like a drum in her ears, a relentless rhythm of determination. Petrovana's gaze locked onto the stage, and her thoughts focused on the conversation she was about to initiate with Brebian. With every step, her resolve solidified, and she hoped her words could sway the king's decision, sparing Leper from the dire fate that seemed imminent.

The courtyard was alive with anticipation as Petrovana stepped into the scene. On the stage, Brebian's wife, Breann, Genova, Rinawen, and two formidable bulwarks flanked him. The trial seemed to be underway, and Petrovana realized that her chances of having a private conversation with Brebian were gone. *Shit*

Brebian revealed his frustration through his demeanor, and he fixed his gaze on Rinawen, demanding answers for something. As she approached the stage, their voices became audible, and she strained to listen to their conversation amidst the growing commotion.

"Where is he then?" Brebian's voice was sharp, his finger pointed accusingly at Rinawen.

"He left. And like I promised, has caused no issues," came Rinawen's sharp reply.

"He wasn't supposed to leave. That wasn't part of the deal," Brebian spat.

Petrovana was glad Leper wasn't here to witness this trial or receive the potential punishment. She remained angry that he never said goodbye. Maybe a little jealous as well since he was probably with... her. She shook the thoughts from her mind and focused on the fact that he was at least safe from the hateful eyes and likely damning outcome of this one-sided trial.

"Reckon that wasn't called out. You said he can't cause any issues. Never said he can't leave. Perhaps that's the best way he thought to not cause problems." Petrovana interjected.

"This doesn't concern you." Brebian scowled.

"You have no leg to stand on, Brebian. He didn't cause any harm to anyone. The problem is handled. Let's move on to the real enemy—Nalecht and Ace, and him reforging the shards into a talisman. We need to get more information on that," Rinawen motioned towards the castle.

Brebian's commanding voice cut through the tension like a blade. "People of Tudela!" he boomed, capturing the attention of the gathered crowd. Petrovana's heart raced. She could sense the weight of the decision that hung in the balance.

"The Chernzerk that threatened my life has fled the city, leaving it up to us to determine his fate should he return," Brebian proclaimed, his words echoing throughout the courtyard. Petrovana's mind raced, and she felt the pressure of the moment. The fate of a man's life rested in the hands of the people.

"Should we put out an order to kill on sight?" Brebian's gaze swept over the crowd. "Or should we punish his heinous acts with servitude?" The question hung in the air, and Petrovana's heart clenched at the stark choices presented. The crowd stirred, whispers and murmurs spreading among them as they contemplated the decision they were about to make.

"He saved the city!" one man shouted.

"They're all evil, though!" countered another voice.

"He can fight the dragons for us. Why kill him?" came another shout.

Petrovana's lips twitched into a small smirk as she observed the crowd's reaction. The consensus seemed to lean favorably toward Leper's actions, an unexpected twist that brought a glimmer of hope. She couldn't deny the satisfaction of seeing the people's support, even if Leper wasn't there to witness it himself. However, Brebian's unyielding stance on enforcing a punishment remained apparent.

"What of the other one?" came another shout.

"Hang the dragon rider! He destroyed a lot of our great city!" followed another.

At that suggestion, the crowd erupted in cheers and shouts, calling for Ace's demise. Petrovana glanced at Brebian, who looked disappointed. He walked to his bulwarks and whispered something to them, and they took off towards the castle.

"All in good time," Brebian yelled across the stage, his voice echoing. He then turned to Rinawen. "About that shard. I think it's time to hand it over."

"That wasn't the deal. I held up my end of the bargain." Rinawen's voice was shaky.

"If you cannot keep your word, then what worth does it carry?" Brebian's reply was sharp.

"She kept her word. Leper never harmed anyone! Even the crowd agrees," Petrovana interjected, drawing a sneer from Genova.

"I think it's best you shut your trap," Genova opened her palm, revealing a brain tattoo.

Petrovana's body tensed, and a feeling of unease washed over her as she considered the situation. She questioned Brebian's true intentions. Was he using this trial to manipulate Rinawen and get the shard of Theora? She considered the situation, suspecting he might be aligned with Nalecht. Her mind spiraled with a multitude of possibilities. The uncertainty of the situation only heightened her anxiety.

"That is uncalled for," Rinawen pointed to Genova. "Just what exactly are you trying to do here, Brebian?"

"I am trying to keep order amidst my city's turmoil and ensure its future safety." He said.

"Then I think you need to re-evaluate your process. Holding a trial for someone is fine. But this should've been about a trial for Ace. And why, by the gods, do you want this shard that's been in my family and Kordry's history for centuries so badly? It is safe in my possession and shall remain so," Rinawen said.

"You shouldn't have the shard just because your ancestors did! Why do Kordry and Kundry get to safekeep one of the most powerful objects of this realm? You've already lost one. Let me use its power to defeat the threats we face. Lantess has already fallen, and Madislak is missing. I can use the power of that shard to defend us all. My army is larger and better trained than any other," Brebian argued.

"As can I, and I will help you every way I can, but you seem to be on a path of anger and vengeance." Rinawen didn't back down.

"My city was just attacked and likely will be again! I will not let these great people suffer the same fate as Lantess," Brebian said, mere inches from Rinawen's face.

Petrovana broke free from Genova's binding spell, her status as a pinnacle-four shrew giving her the advantage to resist and dispel spells with greater ease. She honed her magical abilities to a point where she could overcome magical restraints, and Genova's spell was no match for her expertise. As the day faded into evening, gray clouds rolled in, and a cool breeze blew.

"If yer so concerned for yer city's safety, why would you shove two of the best warriors this realm has seen straight out the front gates? Reckon you need to change yer approach," Petrovana spat back as she walked to Genova. "You do that again, and it'll be the last spell you cast," she whispered threateningly.

Genova glared intently back at Petrovana, who just smirked in response. The bulwarks came rushing back through the doors of the castle.

"My King, we have a problem," one of them looked around.

"Speak, we don't have time for nonsense. Quickly now!" Brebian commanded.

"Ace, the prisoner, he's gone. The two guards stationed outside his cell... Dead." His voice quivered.

"Son of a bitch!" Brebian kicked the air. "Get every guard looking for him right now! Who knows when he got out?"

The bulwarks issued orders in a hurry, which prompted Brebian to disband the trial.

Brebian approached Petrovana, his face contorted in anger as he got inches away from her. "We wouldn't have this problem if you would've done what I asked you! Guess I'll have to send a note to Terynsipple now?"

"Then tell them. Reckon you won't get anywhere threatenin' me." Petrovana scoffed. "You want me to get it done? I need time to be around him. Stop pushin' him away and invite him in." Petrovana lied.

Though she wanted to know her parents and who she was, she wasn't willing for it to be at the cost of betraying Leper. All she needed was for Brebian to believe she was going to help him, just to keep Leper safe for the time being. She could worry about the implications later.

Brebian hissed. "Just remember our deal, or Terynsipple will have your head as well." He turned to Genova. "Start tracking his blood. Unless the cleaning wenches already scrubbed the floors, his blood should be in there."

Genova headed for the castle, and Petrovana followed her closely until someone caught her elbow and turned her around. Rinawen was standing there with a stern expression on her face. "What's their other problem you are helping them with, exactly?"

"Rinawen, now and here is not a good time to discuss that." Petrovana's urgency was apparent in her voice.

Rinawen held firm. "What exactly did he want with you in his private chambers?"

"Not now I said. If Ace is located, he might have gone after Leper. We could get him back here." She urged.

"No. He needs to be out of here. He needs to be away from people," Rinawen argued.

"You heard them at that trial, right? Half of them were on his side," Petrovana pleaded.

"Fine, but I want to know every detail of whatever deal you made with them, got it?" Rinawen glared at Petrovana as they walked.

"Fine." Petrovana conceded. *She is a pushy one.*

Genova delicately crouched in Ace's cell, using a piece of cloth to wipe away the dried blood from his wounds. Afterwards, they all moved to Brebian's war room, where they laid out a map across the table. The scent of ink and paper filled the room, reminiscent of a library with its scattered papers. Genova carefully placed the cloth, still stained with Ace's blood, at the center of the map. Using a needle, she pricked her finger, allowing a small droplet of blood to form. With her palm held over the map, she murmured an incantation, her focus intent on her task.

"Light the way to our enemy," she whispered softly.

The droplet of blood on the cloth transformed, becoming liquid once again, and it glided across the map. As the black hue of her brain tattoo faded to a grayish tone, the liquid blood continued to move, tracing a path until it came to a stop in the woods east of the city.

"It looks like he's headed towards Wen-Tath." Brebian mused.

"Yeah. Right towards the city that just sent half their army here to defend your city." Rinawen palmed her forehead.

Petrovana's chest tightened. "They're missing most of their defenses and their king."

Chapter Nineteen

L eper jolted awake. His heart raced as he scanned the area, searching
for any sign of Leighth. Then, he sought Lillian, his companion and
friend, who was scouring the woods. Countless possibilities flooded his
mind at once. He had to find Madislak and plead with him once more.
Informing him about the shards and Nalecht's scheme would certainly
help. Perhaps if he laid out the whole truth to Madislak and explained
the potential repercussions, he could secure his assistance. Leper couldn't
defeat Nalecht on his own, but he believed mighty Madislak could if he
could persuade him to put aside their differences for now and lend a hand.
Wherever he is.

Leper's eyes darted across the dense woodland, a labyrinth of towering
maple and pine trees obscuring his view. Each breath filled his nostrils with
the sharp scent of pine. His throat tightened. *Where was she?* They had just
rescued her, and now she vanished again like a ghost slipping through the
shadows. Leper's memories of Leighth were distant but vivid, as he recalled
seeing her from a distance during Rinawen's journeys to Kundry. As he
looked around the forest, his thoughts swirled with a mix of concern for
Leighth's safety and the unsettling knowledge that The Latter might still
lurk nearby. A shiver ran down his spine at what the mysterious, twisted
man might do to her. They needed to get away from the guards that were
searching the woods and get a better view to find Leighth.

"Want to see something really amazing? And it'll help us move faster?" Leper turned to Lillian.

"Sure, dazzle me," she smirked.

Leper emitted a sharp whistle into the air, the sound cutting through the silence of the forest. Whistling for his mount that he told to leave Tudela two days ago. He glanced at Lillian, a faint smile on his face, but the immediate lack of response made his gesture appear ineffective. Lillian's playful scold showed her lack of faith in the plan's success, but Leper was not so quick to give up. He raised his finger, signaling for a bit more patience, hoping that Ghost, his magnificent griffin, would heed his call.

Leighth appeared through the trees, walking towards them.

"Where the hell did you go?" Lillian jabbed her finger in Leighth's direction.

Leighth glanced to the ground, then back to Leper. "Nowhere. I'm going back to Tudela now. Before the guards see you, I suggest you start moving. I will distract them for a few moments."

It only took one glance for Leper to realize she was lying about something. She went somewhere, and something happened. He could see it in her face, but he didn't press the issue. "Fine. Get yourself to safety, Leighth. Maybe someday we'll meet again."

Just as Lillian voiced her skepticism, Ghost gracefully descended from the skies above, his presence a spectacle to behold. The sight of the majestic griffin left Lillian wide-eyed. Leper patted the magnificent beast on the head, and Ghost nuzzled into Leper's chest, shaking his neck.

"This is Ghost. A perk of my horns, apparently." Leper stared at Lillian.

"Wow. He's incredible," Lillian said, awestruck.

"Actually, he is she," Maka Kura popped into Leper's mind.

"Correction, I've just been informed he is actually she," Leper repeated.

"Either way, is she yer's?"

"Well, I don't think she's mine," Leper began, his tone contemplative, "But when I was on The Talon, Maka Kura told me something interesting.

He said it was our home, mine, Ace's, and all the others. The animals and the environment, they were our allies, too."

Leper's heart clenched as he caught a fleeting glimpse of agony or perhaps pain flickering in Lillian's eyes. Her gaze flitted between him, the ground, and Ghost. With a swift motion, he leaped onto the mighty back of the griffin, extending a hand to help Lillian up. Their movements hurried as they soared away.

As the sun dipped towards the horizon once more, they realized their efforts had been in vain. He steered Ghost higher above the tree line, ensuring they remained hidden from the searching eyes below. With all avenues of the search explored and the sun setting on another day, Leper headed south towards Lantess.

Leper and Lillian scoured the landscape for any sign of the missing king, Madislak. Perhaps he retreated to his hometown after The Talon incident. But where is he now? Why was he taking so long to reach Tudela? They'd departed from The Talon ahead of Leper and Petrovana. Yet, here they were, days later, with no trace of Madislak.

Agreeing that it was wise to halt their search for the night, they made camp. Leper's mind whirled with terrible thoughts. Maybe Voldahyl circled back and killed him. After all, it was the direction they were heading when the dragon flew away. Leper tried to clear his mind. Tomorrow, they would continue searching to find the lost king and his shrew, Harmony. A gnawing sensation in Leper's gut whispered of ominous possibilities. Madislak may have reservations about working alongside a Chernzerk like Leper, but his sense of duty and honor would compel him to relay such crucial news to the other monarchs. The absence of any word from him spoke volumes, igniting fears of a grim fate awaiting them all. To prevent Nalecht from obtaining all the shards, they would require Madislak's help. People in Kalazaar regarded him as the greatest warrior, and they needed every skilled person for this battle for the shards.

After locating a suitable spot inside the Uldridge Mountains, they huddled within a cave entrance and started a fire that quickly crackled to life. A musty smell, like stale water and earth, permeated the air, mixed with the metallic tang of iron and other minerals. It was a damp, earthy scent that was at once both refreshing and foreboding. The sound of water droplets echoed softly off the cave walls, a consistent and soothing rhythm that offered a sense of tranquility. With concern gripping his heart, he settled in for the night, hoping that tomorrow would bring better news.

As the small fire crackled in the background, its warmth mingling with the echoes of dripping water, a gentle breeze danced through the cave. The flames swayed, casting flickering shadows around them. Leper couldn't help but notice the goosebumps rising on Lillian's arms as she rubbed them for warmth.

Drawing her close, he wrapped an arm around her, feeling the softness of her skin against his own. "We can keep each other warm," he murmured, his voice barely above a whisper.

Lillian leaned into him, her green eyes shimmering with warmth and affection. As she settled atop him, her touch sent shivers down his spine, igniting a familiar longing within him. Despite his uncertainty, he found himself drawn to her, drawn to the comfort and connection they shared.

Her breath mingled with his, their closeness enveloping them in a cocoon of intimacy. "Well?" she whispered, her words sending a jolt of desire through him. "I see who you are, hat man, and I'm not afraid."

Leper's heart pounded in his chest as he leaned in, capturing her lips in a passionate kiss. The sensation of her skin beneath his fingertips was electric, sending sparks flying between them. They broke apart momentarily, their chests heaving with anticipation before surrendering once more to the primal urge that consumed them.

In the dim light of the dwindling fire, they lost themselves in each other, their bodies moving in sync as they explored the depths of their desire. Wrapped in each other's embrace, they found solace in the warmth of their shared passion, igniting like a flame in the chilly night air, momentarily casting aside all doubts and fears.

Beneath the soft glow of a rain-kissed morning, Leper stirred to the soothing melody of raindrops dancing outside.

"Well. Are ya goin' to say anythin' or just slip back into business as usual?" Lillian's hand rested gently on his chest within the confines of their bedroll.

Meeting her gaze, Leper felt a rush of emotion. He reached out, tangling his fingers in her hair. "I'm at a loss for words. Last night was... beyond words."

"Was that...yer first..." Lillian's voice faltered, her curiosity mingled with tenderness.

Her words sparked distant memories that he pushed away... Memories that would negatively affect more than just him, and in a very disastrous way. Leper shook his head *no*, his mind drifting momentarily to the memories of their shared intimacy. But the weight of their mission bore down on him once more. As much as he longed to linger in this moment, the nagging sense of unease regarding his friends, Madislak and Harmony, gnawed at him relentlessly.

With a sense of purpose, he roused Ghost with gentle combs of her neck and resumed their search for Madislak. The rain-drenched landscape seemed to mirror his internal turmoil as he scanned the surroundings for any sign of the missing monarchs. As the rain pelted against his face, he could taste the fresh rainwater on his tongue, and it was surprisingly refreshing.

Their journey led them farther southward, over the mountainous terrain that acted as a natural divide between the north and the south. As they cleared the crest of the first rocky peak and emerged onto a flat expanse, a shocking sight awaited Leper, rendering him speechless as the rain moved out and the sun beamed in the sky. An enormous army, twenty thousand strong, adorned in the colors of Ambrosia and Kirilick, Goreldea's realm, marched purposefully northward. Flanking this formidable force was the dreaded Voldahyl the Rotten, a sight that sent a chill down Leper's spine. The alliance between Ambrosia, Kirilick, and Voldahyl signified a dire threat to Tudela and its surroundings. Madislak still nowhere to be seen, Leper realized that the challenges they faced were far greater than he initially thought. The fate of not just Tudela but the entire realm lay in the balance.

Swiftly, Leper turned Ghost around behind a rocky outcrop, offering cover from peering eyes.

"Look at the size of that army. Tudela is going to get ripped apart." Leper mouthed.

"Good for them." Lillian huffed.

Leper shook his head. "Even if I wanted to. What difference could I make against an army of that size... And Voldahyl."

"Why would you even want to? Brebian was bent on havin' you killed, remember?" Lillian spat.

Leper took her wrists. "Even if that's the case, Lillian, can't you see that army, that dragon, and Nalecht don't intend on stopping at Tudela? It will be widespread. There's nothing I can do to stop it. Even with your help."

"You ever think you don't have to do it all on yer own?" Lillian tilted her head to the side.

Leper gazed into her beautiful eyes and saw the sun reflecting off her fiery red hair. As he thought about what she had just said, he remembered the feeling when he first picked up the shard of Theora when Rinawen had left for the capital. The magic that flowed through him.

"I have to, Lillian; otherwise, they'll never accept me like you do." He kissed her. "You are a genius. Do you know anything about the shards and how they interact with people?"

"No, not really. I think they hold great power, but judgin' from who had them and who has them now, it seems to affect them differently." She grinned. "For instance, Nalecht seems greedy and power hungry. Rinawen seems protective and uses it for food production for her world."

Leper's thoughts were racing. From the moment he picked up the shard of Theora for Rinawen when she left for the capital, he could sense a distinct change in the surrounding air. It was a constant flow of magic, one that surpassed any limitations or barriers to casting or using Maka Kura. If he could get one of these shards, perhaps he could control Maka Kura without worrying about his limits.

"C'mon, we need to go back to Tudela." Leper pulled her arm.

"Why? Let them get overrun. Those bastards and Brebian deserve it." Lillian countered.

Leper ran his hands through her hair. "But Rinawen and others we care about are there."

"Then let's get them and get out." Lillian tilted her head into his hand.

"Let me put it this way. Imagine the accolades and glory you'll get for being the one to defend Tudela against that." He pointed to the army.

Leper observed the wheels of determination turning in Lillian's head, a defiant fire kindling in her eyes. He understood that for her, the prospect of a battle against overwhelming odds was a challenge she welcomed with open arms.

Knowing her well, he recognized the allure of etching her name into history as the one who bested a mighty adversary like Nalecht, who wielded the power of the shards.

"Fine. If yer so damned set on savin' everyone despite their efforts to toss you aside."

"I swear I won't drag you into another fight you don't want to be part of." Leper grinned.

"I'm goin' to hold you to that."

Leaping onto Ghost's back, they soared northward, the wind whipping around them. As they neared Tudela, they gracefully descended, landing on the chariot landing pod. Leper dismounted first, his feet hitting the ground with a purpose. He gave a reassuring command to Ghost, urging the majestic griffin to return home for now.

"What are you doing here?" a guard beckoned to them.

"We need to speak to Brebian, Rinawen, and Petrovana," Lillian commanded as the guard stared blankly in her direction. "Right now!" she yelled, her intensity like a fire.

"Yes, ma'am. Uhhh, wait here with him," he instructed the other guard, who nervously gripped his spear.

Moments later, Brebian emerged with the other two in tow.

"What are you doing back here so soon?" Rinawen demanded.

"We have grim news for you all," Leper stated flatly. Avoiding eye contact with Rinawen.

"Restrain him," Brebian sneered.

The guards encircled Leper.

"Damnit Brebian! You need to listen to us right now. This is more urgent than yer petty grievances." Lillian bellowed. "I won't let you restrain him again." She pulled her scimitars out and stood in front of the guards.

Leper laid his weapons down to show his willingness to cooperate. Petrovana stood beside Lillian, promising the same defiance. Leper could see the pained, hollow look on Rinawen's face. But he wasn't ready to apologize for his words. She's the one who chose her shard over him.

"There's an army out there. Twenty thousand strong and Voldahyl at their side. Marching this way. I can help you defend this city against the dragon and the army. But I don't want you to restrain me or treat me like I'm some kind of murderous criminal." Leper locked eyes with Brebian.

"You threatened my life, you halfwit!" Brebian gritted. "I should have you all hanged for aiding and hiding a Chernzerk all this time."

"Fine. Good luck defending yer city when we leave." Petrovana added.

Brebian pointed at Rinawen. "Our deal still stands, then. He remains out of sight and out of trouble until the war. Should he cause any issues at all that shard is mine?"

Rinawen nodded solemnly. "That's fine. He won't cause any harm to anyone. You have my word." She flickered her eyes to Leper, pleading, but he stood firm as she walked away.

Leper swallowed hard. He had to maintain his mental state and not do anything reckless. While he planned on using a shard to help him win the battle, he had to figure out how to get hold of one and not lose his mind in the process.

Two days after they returned, Lillian glanced out at the massive army marching upon the wall of Tudela. They covered the entire field in front of them. Her heart thumped loudly in her chest as she gazed upon Nalecht's immense army, their banners flying high and adorned with the symbols of both Ambrosia and Kirilick. She could feel a chill run down her spine at the sight of the massive dragon that marched alongside them with Ace, somehow, on his back. Thick clouds loomed on the horizon, carrying with them the rumble of thunder, mimicking the deafening sound of the approaching army's footsteps. Lillian followed Brebian out through the gates, where he had horses summoned for himself, Petrovana, and Lillian. He pointed to the soldier on a horse in the left flank.

"That is Oybeck, my bulwark and general. You can go to his side," he then turned to Petrovana and pointed to the mounted soldier on the right flank. "That is Sevit, my other bulwark and general. You can go with him."

Brebian's eyes scanned the battlefield, his expression serious and resolute. He was a commanding presence, radiating a sense of authority that inspired confidence in his soldiers. Lillian could see why his people respected and looked up to him. As they prepared to face the daunting army of Nalecht, Lillian gripped her reins tightly, her mind racing with thoughts of the upcoming battle. She knew this would not be an easy fight, but she was determined to do whatever it took to protect Tudela and its people.

With a deep breath, Lillian steadied herself, focusing her attention on the path ahead. She felt the familiar rush of adrenaline coursing through her veins, fueling her resolve. Alongside Brebian, Oybeck, Petrovana, and Sevit, she braced herself for the impending clash with Nalecht's forces, determined to face the darkness head-on and fight for the future of Tudela. Rinawen remained within the city walls to hide and keep the shard of Theora out of the reach of the enemy and to nurse her wounded leg.

Lillian urged her horse forward, its powerful form adorned in chain mail that ran down to its knees. She stole a quick glance over her shoulder, watching Leper skillfully hurl chakrams at the dragon. The mighty beast attempted to reduce their numbers and morale before the foot soldiers arrived. While she hoped he had the situation under control, Lillian knew she couldn't afford to lose focus.

The approaching army commanded her attention. Nalecht, adorned in his majestic war apparel, exuded a menacing aura. His imposing presence was enhanced by his steel-spiked shoulder pads and chain mail chest protector. Even his greaves were equipped with small steel spikes. His metal helmet had a face portion shaped like a triangle, covered by a mesh of metal. She needed to remain steadfast and brave for her comrades. The sight of the enemy forces was indeed intimidating, but she knew she couldn't let fear paralyze her.

Nalecht sat astride a formidable bullarik, a large, gray-skinned beast with a single, razor-sharp horn jutting from its snout. A thick bone plate encased its head, rising about two feet high. Behind this plate, a collar rigged with jagged wires encircled its neck. Towering as tall as horses but with the sturdy mass of a rhinoceros, the bullarik exuded an air of power and danger that matched its rider's imposing presence.

Lillian's heart raced as she spotted Borlden, the only pinnacle-five shrew left in Kalazaar, riding atop his bullarik at the front of Nalecht's forces.

She knew he was a formidable opponent, and the sight of his war attire sent a shiver down her spine. Dark black robes with green lines and magical symbols. She glanced over at Petrovana's flank. There in front of her was another general atop a bullarik. Although his armor covered his face, the sight of the menacing scythe was unnerving. With adrenaline coursing through her veins, Lillian rolled her shoulders, knowing that the fate of the kingdom hung in the balance. She took a deep breath, drawing upon her training and determination, preparing herself for the impending chaos of battle.

"I'm Lillian," she guided her horse beside Oybeck.

"Oybeck, nice to meet you."

"Look, I don't want this horse. You can give it to someone who can use it better than me." She gave a nod.

"Are you certain? Chances of survival plummet radically when unmounted," Oybeck cautioned.

"Yes, positive," Lillian jumped down from the noble steed.

Lillian marched confidently to the front lines. Nalecht's army drew nearer, now just a mere twenty feet away, and the intensity in the air was electric. She could feel the tension building, and her heart pounded with each stomp of the army's footsteps. As the dragon vanished into the distance behind Nalecht's forces, Lillian's focus remained fixed on the impending battle ahead. She blocked out everything else, her mind clear and determined. The noise of armor clanking, soldiers chanting war cries, and the earth trembling underfoot filled her senses. With each step, she felt the weight of responsibility on her shoulders. She was no longer just a warrior fighting for herself; she fought for her allies, her kingdom, and the hope of a better future.

"Alright boys, first to a hundred kills can take me on a date. But if I get there first, you have to grovel at my feet!" she hollered, thrusting her sword in the air.

That got a small chuckle and a couple of glares. Oybeck hollered out the order to charge. Without a moment's hesitation, she launched forward with incredible speed, her blades dancing like a whirlwind of steel, cutting down anyone in her path. Steel on steel echoed throughout the air as that prominent smell of blood filled the air.

With every fluid motion, Lillian proved herself to be a master of combat, her blades moving as if they were an intrinsic part of her being. The dance of death unfolded before her, leaving a trail of defeated foes in her wake. Her sights set on Borlden, determined to confront the shrew and sever the head of the enemy force. As she pressed forward, her line surged, pushing back Nalecht's army with the sheer force of her skill. As she cut down enemies, those around her hollered and charged in with confidence. The ripple effect of her prowess on the battlefield was undeniable. When morale soared, the entire army fought with heightened vigor. Lillian's presence alone served as a beacon of hope, inspiring her comrades to give their all and stand firm against the encroaching enemy.

With a quick glance, Lillian locked eyes with Borlden, the pinnacle-five shrew, who charged directly at her atop his bullarik. Instinctively, she shifted her weight, effortlessly rolling to the side, narrowly evading the deadly attack. In a single fluid motion, she swung her scimitar, cutting the rope that held the saddle in place. The disassembled bullarik roared ahead, spearing and trampling its way through the enemy ranks.

Oybeck charged hard at Borlden, who was picking himself up off the ground.

"Insolent fools," Borlden screeched.

Lillian's heart sank as she witnessed Borlden's ruthless attack on Oybeck, engulfing him in a torrent of fire. The loyal general's screams of agony pierced the air, only to be silenced as his lifeless body lay motionless on the ground. Grief and anger welled up inside her. Her eyes locked onto Borlden, his tattoo darkening ominously, signaling his impending spell.

Bracing herself, Lillian expected his move, ready to evade whatever dark magic he might unleash.

"Let me show you true power, wretch!" he seethed.

Borlden's dark magic unleashed unimaginable horror upon the battlefield. With a sinister grin, he revealed the brain tattoo on his left palm and raised both arms to the sky, summoning a spell that caused over a hundred men to writhe in agony. Their bodies grotesquely burst from the inside out, leaving a gruesome scene of guts and blood. As if that display of cruelty wasn't enough, Borlden twirled his right hand above his head, summoning pillars of fire that formed a deadly fifty-foot circle. The pillars connected with beams of fire, and a deafening roar filled the air. Flames erupted from the ground within the fiery circle, and Lillian could feel the searing heat on her face as men inside screamed before succumbing to the inferno, leaving behind the sickening stench of burnt flesh among the fallen.

Lillian's heart pounded in her chest as she faced the horrifying power of Borlden's dark magic. The boom of thunder reverberated through the air like a cannon blast, causing ears to ring and hearts to jump. A hissing crackle followed it as the lightning sizzled through the clouds before striking the ground with a powerful thud. The bright streak of lightning illuminated the dark sky, its jagged edges casting eerie shadows on the ground below. With both spells now recharging, she took her opportunity to strike, swiftly rushing at him, swiping gracefully, trying to chop off one of his hands. She narrowly missed on her first strike as he recoiled his arms. But he couldn't dodge Lillian forever as she gashed him in the leg and kicked him backwards, sending him tumbling away from her.

"Dumb bitch," he squealed.

Petrovana took her place beside Sevit on the right-side flank, her mind focused on the task at hand. With Lillian leading the other flank and Brebian in the middle, it was her responsibility to make sure this side of the flank didn't falter. Otherwise, they would get overrun easily. While Sevit wielded a formidable great axe on his back, Petrovana knew that her intelligence was her greatest asset. She understood that the key to gaining the upper hand in the battle was to target the enemy commanders swiftly, and that was precisely her plan, working in tandem with Sevit to execute it as fast as possible. As the adrenaline surged through her veins, she steeled herself for the coming fight, knowing that their strategic coordination could tip the scales in their favor and lead them closer to victory.

"You make a path to that captain, and let's take him out." Petrovana pointed to the plate armored man riding a bullarik.

"Uhh, okay, who are you again?" Sevit looked at her, cocking his head sideways.

"I'm Petrovana D'leon, and if y'all want to make it out alive, I suggest we get to the commanders as quick as possible." She demanded.

"Yes, ma'am," he nodded to her.

Petrovana strategically employed her fire and ice abilities, using them sparingly to support the troops where needed, all the while conserving most of her reserves for the tougher battles ahead. As a pinnacle-four shrew, she understood that her magical prowess might not match Borlden, but she was not far behind him either.

Glancing to her left, she watched Lillian expertly disrupting the front lines of Nalecht's army, and for a moment, she almost wished to be fighting alongside her. Despite her reservations about Lillian, Petrovana couldn't help but respect the skill and prowess Lillian commanded in physical combat, effortlessly slicing through the endless ranks of front-line troops.

Their forces pushed forward relentlessly, but the tides turned when the enemy commander charged in on the bullarik, wielding a menacing scythe aimed at Sevit.

Petrovana bided her time, patiently waiting for the perfect moment to strike. As the opportunity presented itself, she swiftly conjured an ice spike, driving it through the captain's heart with lethal precision. Sevit wasted no time claiming the fallen captain's scythe for himself. Petrovana spared a quick glance to her left, only to find Nalecht dismounted and charging through the front lines. Taking down the generals and soldiers proved manageable, but she knew the genuine challenges lay ahead with Nalecht and Borlden.

"Sevit, I'm goin' to make my way to Lillian. You continue to close off this flank. Now that this general is taken care of, we need to get the other two." She nodded.

"Yes, ma'am. It will be taken care of!" he saluted her.

Petrovana's heart pounded in her chest as she saw Nalecht change course, heading straight for Lillian. Without hesitation, she urged her horse to greater speed, navigating skillfully between the guards and fighters on the battlefield, determined to reach Lillian's side. Her eyes remained locked on her comrade as she closed the distance rapidly. As she drew nearer, Petrovana witnessed the intense struggle between Lillian and Nalecht. It was a fierce deadlock, with Lillian expertly parrying Nalecht's strikes and delivering her own blows. But the three shards Nalecht possessed granted him an advantage, as he landed a brutal hit to Lillian's face with the pommel of his sword, followed by a powerful kick that sent her sprawling to the ground. Petrovana's lungs constricted.

With swift maneuvering, Nalecht's army encircled Lillian, cutting off any escape and leaving her trapped within a dangerous ring of enemies, including Nalecht himself and the formidable Borlden. Time seemed to slow as Petrovana's mind raced, assessing the perilous situation before her. The skies crackled with another burst of lightning, followed by a booming clap of thunder.

"Now you'll pay for what you did to my leg," Borlden mocked.

"Finish her, Borlden. We have more company," Nalecht said.

On the eastern ridge, King Theodamar and his five-thousand-strong army charged towards the left flank. A sigh of relief escaped her lips as she glanced back at her struggling comrade. Seizing the opportunity, Petrovana launched an ice block at Borlden, knocking him down before he could cast a spell. All of Nalecht's men turned their attention to Petrovana as she conjured a wall of ice around Lillian, protecting her from harm. With precision, she gestured with her other hand, summoning a colossal thirty-foot cyclone of fire that engulfed the soldiers surrounding Lillian. Nalecht and Borlden scrambled backward, seeking safety from the blazing inferno. With a safe distance between them, Petrovana released both spells, leaving devastation in their wake. The battlefield shifted, and Petrovana's display of power breathed new life into their fight for victory. As the rain fell, the earthy aroma of wet soil mingled with the clean freshness of rainwater, coating everything with a damp, musky smell.

"C'mon this way," she shouted to Lillian.

With an awkward glance and her head cocked to the side, Lillian got up and retreated to the front lines with her.

"Guess I should thank you," Lillian looked to Petrovana.

"Consider that, my apology. It's the only one you'll ever get," Petrovana smirked.

Lillian nodded back.

Petrovana flicked her eyes to Lillian. "So we're square then?"

"We'll see." She retorted.

Petrovana shifted her focus back to Nalecht and Borlden. They re-formed their ranks. Now, with two fronts to combat the new threat. Borlden, still gimping, got back to his mount, then moved over to Theodamar's soldiers. They began breaking into the soldiers' ranks, pushing Nalecht's army back farther. Borlden held out the shard of Obidiah.

"Shit, this ain't gonna be good. Maybe it's time to bring out Rinawen and the shard of Theora." Petrovana muttered.

Borlden harnessed the shard's power, unleashing a torrent of elemental forces—lightning, ice, fire, and stone—until the shard reached its limit and could send no more. The devastating display wiped out a significant portion of King Theodamar's freshly arrived army, along with some of their own. Amidst the aftermath, Brebian returned to their side, lending his strength to the fight. The battlefield became a maelstrom of power, and Petrovana knew they had to stand united to overcome the relentless onslaught. Grief washed over her at the sight of poor Theodamar's army getting rendered entirely useless the second it showed up. The deafening clash of thunder reverberated through her body, sending shockwaves of fear and adrenaline through her veins. It was as if the sky itself had split open, crackling and booming with the force of a thousand drummers.

"I don't think we're winning this," Brebian said, looking defeated.

"So yer just gonna give up, then?" Lillian asked.

"What can we do? Nalecht is overpowering everything. Borlden just wiped out most of the reinforcements. There's still a dragon out there somewhere." Brebian pouted.

"What are our options, then? Give him Rinawen and her shard? That's ultimately what he's here fer," Petrovana's voice dripping with sarcasm.

"Just give the shard to him. Not Rinawen. We live to fight another day." Brebian shook his head.

"With Lillian's help, I think she and I can take care of Nalecht," Leper joined them on the battlefield. "And if Petrovana can manage Borlden, that would take care of most of the problem."

"We don't take orders from the likes of you," Brebian snarled.

"Just a suggestion. givin' up won't do nothin'. These people are willin' to wipe out entire families. I don't think givin' them the shard is gonna make them stop attackin'," Petrovana added. "Borlden just killed some of their own men with that shard. Reckon they ain't concerned fer keepin' anyone alive."

"And if the dragon comes back?" Brebian poked.

"Then I'll focus my attention on it again," Leper held up his chakrams.

"Fine, we reform our ranks and load the ballista in case the dragon returns. You two go after Nalecht," Brebian pointed to Lillian and Leper. "You come with me, and we'll advance on Borlden," he pointed to Petrovana.

Petrovana's heart raced as the weight of the battle intensified. Theodamar's charge had been daring, but she couldn't ascertain his fate amidst the chaos. Brebian's army, though depleted, regrouped with a sense of determination to continue the fight. Petrovana knew that this was no longer just a battle for one city or one shard; the fate of the entire free world hung in the balance. Victory was not a luxury; it was the only path forward.

Chapter Twenty

Leper fixed his gaze on Nalecht as both armies reformed their front lines, ready to clash in battle. Now is the time to stop this chaos, and the best way to do that is to reach Nalecht and either restrain him or eliminate him. His grip tightened around Maka Kura.

"Ready to fight this nightmare?" he looked at Lillian.

"Reckon I am! When I land the final blow, yer gonna take me out on a proper date." She teased.

"Deal. When I land the killing blow, make friends with Petrovana again." Leper poked back.

"I ain't guaranteein' that shit, but I will give it an honest effort." She nodded.

Approaching the front lines of Nalecht's army, Leper and Lillian shared a quick, knowing smile. As he began jogging forward, Leper paced ahead of them, clutching Maka Kura tightly in his grasp. Without hesitation, he launched a chakram straight ahead, skillfully guiding its path with the help of his horns. The spinning weapon zipped through the enemy ranks, taking out the first two soldiers standing side by side. Continuing its deadly trajectory, it eliminated the next two, and then the next, until it reached an impressive tally of twenty fallen soldiers before gracefully flipping back into his waiting hand.

Leper glanced at Lillian, and with a wink, he said, "Good luck."

Her excited response was infectious. "Oh, yer on!"

Amid the adrenaline-pumping moment, Leper couldn't help but notice the determination written all over Lillian's face.

They carved through Nalecht's army like it was a knife to butter. During the chaos of war, these two emerged as an unstoppable force. They stood side by side, their unwavering determination etched on their faces. Together, they moved with astonishing precision, their movements in perfect harmony as they faced an overwhelming number of enemies. Brebian's army charged valiantly with them as shouts and hollers spewed forth.

While the clash of metal echoed around them, their teamwork was an art form in itself. Lillian was a nimble, acrobatic whirlwind, gracefully darting between foes with unparalleled speed. Leper's chakrams, an extension of his being. With each swing, he carved a path through the enemy ranks, sending bodies and weapons flying in all directions. The ground trembled beneath their feet as they became an immovable fortress, protecting each other with relentless resolve. Leper became more and more astonished at the sheer force and mastery Maka Kura provided to him.

The seamless coordination between them created a lethal whirlwind, leaving a trail of defeated foes in their wake. As they approached Nalecht, a loud blast from a horn to the west drew everyone's attention. Leper immediately recognized the distinct Kordry banner and colors flying high. It was a sight he had been eagerly waiting for. Larnadix finally came through.

The mounted warriors of Kordry charged into Nalecht's left flank with impressive force, catching the enemy off guard and pushing them back even farther. The timely arrival of their allies infused fresh energy into the battlefield. Leper felt a surge of determination as he continued to press forward, knowing that victory was now within their grasp. The rain fell, and thunder continued throughout the skies with flashes of lightning every once in a while. The scent of damp earth and clean air mixed.

"Yaaaaaa," Lillian hollered at the saviors to the west.

Leper's attention snapped back to Nalecht as the ruthless leader dismounted his bullarik. Using his sword, he smacked it to create havoc among the soldiers directly in front of him. However, the spectacle was short-lived, for within seconds, the great bullarik had charged barely ten feet before a well-aimed ballista spear found its mark, piercing the creature's neck and rendering it useless. The beast let out a pained roar, but the defenders quickly quelled its rampage.

"Guess I just have to do everything myself." Nalecht snarled.

Lillian and Leper circled around Nalecht. Noting the shard of Ryollin, Hathor, and now Amarook draped on his chain necklace. Leper made a mental note of Borlden having Obidiah in his grasp. With four of the shards on this battlefield, Rinawen kept the shard of Theora safely behind Tudela's walls—the other two were still missing.

"Give it up, Nalecht. You're not going to win." Leper pointed his chakram at him.

"Why do you fight for these people? They'll never respect or trust you." He sneered.

"Because several of them are my friends. You may have Ace brainwashed, but it won't be that easy on me," Leper retorted sharply.

Nalecht chuckled. "I'll prove it to you. They'll say they care about you, but they don't."

Nalecht lunged at Leper with three precise strikes, but Leper deftly parried them away. He quickly realized that keeping up with Nalecht's relentless pace, especially with the augmentation from the shards, would be a daunting challenge. However, there was no time to dwell on that as Nalecht charged back, only to be intercepted by Lillian, who skillfully matched his strikes. Leper joined her, and together, they converged on Nalecht, their weapons clashing in a fierce dance. Lillian positioned herself in front of him, and Leper stood firmly behind him, both determined to take down their formidable foe. Yet, Nalecht effortlessly parried or dodged each of their attacks, proving to be an elusive adversary. Their battle raged on, an enticing game of cat and mouse, with all parties locked in unwavering focus. Leper's mind raced as he strategized and analyzed Nalecht's moves, seeking any advantage to gain the upper hand.

Time seemed to slow as they exchanged blows, each movement calculated, every strike meant to seize the slightest opening. Leper felt the adrenaline course through his veins, his senses heightened. Patiently, he waited for the opportunity to yank one of those shards from around his neck.

Until a fateful roar emanated again from the skies. Voldahyl, no longer bleeding, returned to the battlefield, setting the Kordry army ablaze. His presence alone was enough to break the army's resolve. Panic spread like wildfire. Some soldiers turned and fled, their loyalty to the cause forgotten in the face of such overwhelming power. The Kordry army was now reduced to scattered remnants, Larnadix and a few others making haste back the way they came.

"You again," Leper looked at Voldahyl circling overhead.

"Leper, do your thing. I got this scumbag." Lillian nodded to him.

Leper nodded back to her. Backing away from Nalecht, he kept his focus on Voldahyl, waiting for the dragon to circle back towards him. He released Maka Kura, sending both chakrams spinning through the air. One of the chakrams found its mark, opening another gash in Voldahyl's neck, causing the dragon to roar in pain. The other chakram, Leper, aimed at the dragon's wing, attempting to ground the formidable creature. As it sliced through the wing, it suddenly stopped cutting, getting ejected out of it.

Leper's heart pounded in his chest as he tried to comprehend what had just happened with his new weapon. His head hurt as a trickle of blood flowed out of his nose. The tear in Voldahyl's wing caused the dragon to wobble in flight, making it visibly unstable. The realization that his chakram failed to cut through the tough scales weighed heavily on his mind. When the dragon's eyes locked onto him, Leper knew he had drawn the creature's fury upon himself, but there was no room for fear or doubt in this critical moment. He steeled himself, his gaze unwavering, and tightened his grip on Maka Kura.

The beast landed behind Nalecht, examining its wing. Leper heard Maka Kura's voice in his head once more.

"I need to recharge. Our newly formed bond is not strong enough to continue."

"Well, shit." Leper said to Maka Kura. "Looks like it's back to the old-fashioned way."

Leper's eyes swept across the battlefield, taking in the devastating scene before him. Fallen bodies littered the ground, and the smell of blood and burning flesh filled the thick air. The rain poured down again as the thunder and lightning were unrelenting. Smoke billowed from the right-side flank of Brebian's army, evidence of the intense and unrelenting conflict. His eyes flicked to Lillian, still in battle with Nalecht, then back to the massive dragon in front of him. Although Voldahyl couldn't fly anymore because of Leper's previous hit with Maka Kura, the dragon remained a formidable force. The great dragon flapped its ripped wing, trying to endure the blood flowing from its neck. A ballista spear flew by Leper's head, which Voldahyl caught in his mouth and snapped in half. The guards around the dragon flung weapons at it, some of them sticking into the beast as it slowly backed away.

"Keep hitting him! Push him back. I need to help the others with Nalecht and Borlden!" Leper commanded. They glanced at him, then nodded and continued their assault as Leper moved towards the others.

Leper and the guards surrounded Voldahyl, forcing the creature to retreat further away from the battlefield, battered and defeated. Voldahyl sought refuge behind the rest of Nalecht's army. At the same time, Leper shifted his focus to where he could offer more support.

Brebian and Petrovana valiantly pushed forward, trying to reach Borlden, but the relentless opposition hindered their progress. Weariness etched their faces, showing the toll the battle had taken. Leper's heart ached at the sight of Petrovana's nose beginning to bleed from the strain of consistent magic use. Amidst the chaos and the toll on his allies, Leper's resolve remained unshaken. He focused every ounce of his being on turning the tide of the battle in their favor. Despair and fatigue would not consume him, not when the fate of their cause hung in the balance.

Petrovana conjured fire tornadoes on the battlefield, unleashing a devastating display of her power. The flames roared, creating a chaotic scene with Borlden's cage of fire raging on the field. Meanwhile, icicles rained down from the sky under Petrovana's command, piercing through Nalecht's army. But for every gap she created, the enemy swiftly filled in the spots, overwhelming them with sheer numbers. Even Borlden, their formidable foe, seemed to feel the strain of the battle as a trickle of blood formed under his nose and eyes. Leper knew they couldn't afford to give up; losing this battle would mean losing the war. Despite the grim circumstances, Leper refused to surrender to despair. The weight of responsibility weighed heavily on him; he knew they had come too far to turn back.

Leper's gaze settled on Lillian, who fought with all her might against the nightmarish Nalecht. Her blades whirled like a fierce windmill, displaying her incredible skill and determination. But even her impressive prowess couldn't protect her from Nalecht's vicious attack. In a gut-wrenching scene that brought back haunting memories of Gwen's fate, Nalecht parried her blades aside and ran his sword through her stomach. Lillian's scimitars fell to the ground, and she let out a cry of pain.

"Lillian!!!" Leper's heart pounded in his chest as he hollered, rushing over to her side. Panic and fear gripped him, but he pushed those emotions aside, focusing solely on getting to her.

As Nalecht stood over her, Leper used the one chakram in his hand and took a swing at Nalecht. The blow connected with his shoulder, his armor absorbing most of the blow, but it was heavy enough to knock him backwards. He longed to summon his other chakram back to his hand, but the magic had depleted, and he would have to make do with just one.

"Grab her and get her back to the castle!" Leper commanded some soldiers. "I'll take care of this scum!" He turned his attention to Nalecht, who was ripping off the dented shoulder plate and tossed it on the ground.

"You're fighting a losing battle. Give up." Nalecht demanded as he swirled his sword in his hand.

Leper noticed the shards still dangling around his neck. The sword-shaped shard of Amarook glowed bright white in the center.

"I won't give up. I'll send you back to where you came from." Leper charged at him.

Swinging his singular chakram, Leper tried to overtake Nalecht, who easily parried. Nalecht knocked Leper's last weapon out of his hand and then kicked him backwards, and he collided with some soldiers about twenty feet away. *I need more magic.* Leper's stomach reeled in agony as he forced himself to get back on his feet.

Brebian and Petrovana emerged from the guard ranks. Dirty, rugged, and fatigued.

"What's happened?" Petrovana panted.

"Lillian's down—the damn dragon. We need to get her out of here. We need to get out. There's too many of them." Leper pleaded to them.

In the heat of the moment, Voldahyl whooshed in, coming dangerously close to Leper. Nalecht stood right beside the dragon, and Borlden flanked around them, accompanied by a host of soldiers. Leper's heart raced, and he braced himself for whatever was about to unfold.

Borlden's left hand, the one bearing the brain tattoo, swept across the assembled forces. With a commanding voice, he bellowed, "Enough!!" The words seemed to reverberate across the battlefield, momentarily stilling the chaos.

Leper's body tensed, an overwhelming sense of helplessness washing over him. Borlden's powerful magic rendered all of them immobile, preventing them from moving or escaping. The sheer force of Borlden's magic was intense, and Leper felt its grip tightening around him and his companions. Like a heavy blow, they were trapped, with no chance of escape. He felt despair threatening to consume him, realizing that they were outmatched and outnumbered. The battle had taken its toll, leaving them with too few fighters and too little fight left in them. Leper couldn't deny the truth - this was the end of the line, and hope seemed distant and unattainable. The relentless downpour served as a constant reminder of their defeat in the war against Nalecht.

"Brebian," Nalecht called to the helpless king. "I'm going to give you this offer one time and one time only." He walked in front of Brebian. "Stand down your army, what's left of it anyway, and stop fighting against me. In return, I claim the shard of Theora and this Chernzerk life," he pointed at Leper. "What do you say?"

"I say..." Brebian looked to Leper. "Agreed."

Leper's heart sank. After all he'd done to help them in their cause. He fought endlessly to protect this man's home, his town, and his people, and he's willing to trade his life for it.

"No!" Petrovana bellowed. "We do not agree."

"You don't run my kingdom. I will gladly hand over the shard of Theora and a Chernzerk life for the safety of my family and my people," Brebian retorted.

"Do you see, Leper? They do not care for you. Even with the awe-inspiring efforts you showed. Their judgment will never change." Nalecht sneered.

Leper couldn't help but hear the truth in his words. It resonated deeply with everything he said earlier and with the turmoil he felt inside. He knew he had chosen a challenging path, attempting to rewrite history itself. *Perhaps changing hundreds of years' worth of history is too difficult. He's a fool for thinking he could accomplish that... A complete fool.*

"One cowardly man does not speak for the masses," Leper muttered, looking around for support from more than just Petrovana. "And you're not touching that shard."

Leper instructed Ghost to take Rinawen out of there in case something like this happened. Hopefully, she obeyed his commands, and Rinawen was well on her way out.

"You still hope that you, your undeniable skills on display, can somehow sway everyone into thinking you're not as chaotic as those before you?" Nalecht retorted.

"I've proven it to a select few. One has already spoken her mind. And yes, I believe I can convince people I'm not against being civil." Leper gritted.

"Reckon you're an evil person, Nalecht. Does that make all elves evil?" Petrovana seethed.

Nalecht grinned. "Well, when Voldahyl's finished with Leper, he'll eat you next,"

Leper strained against the magic again, trying to break free and reach the shard of Amarook. Its light white glow seemed to call to him to grab it.

Leper's eye caught the movement at the corner of his eye, just beyond Borlden, who was fully engrossed in his malicious scheme. Despite the chaos unfolding around them, Borlden wore a sick, twisted grin, reveling in every moment of destruction. Leper felt a wave of anger and disgust at the man's sadistic pleasure in the suffering he caused. His focus shifted to one of Nalecht's men, whose baggy clothes seemed out of place on the battlefield. The figure moved to the front lines, but with Borlden still blocking his view, Leper strained to discern the details of the situation.

Before any of the soldiers or Borlden could react, the figure sprang from his position with lightning speed. Drawing a dagger from his belt, he vaulted onto Borlden's back, driving the blade mercilessly through his neck.

Borlden gurgled, his life quickly slipping away as the assailant continued to pummel his face with ruthless force. The scene unfolded in a blur of vengeance. As the dust settled, he finally removed his helmet, revealing a face that was not that of a soldier but of a girl he recognized all too well—Leighth. Shock and disbelief washed over him as he stared at her, unable to fathom what he had just witnessed.

"Fuck you! You twisted psycho!" she screamed. "I told you I would kill you!"

"Well, that was certainly unexpected," Nalecht muttered.

Borlden's body withered and seemed to dissipate into black smoke floating off into the distance. Before Leighth could grab the shard of Obidiah that now lay on the ground, Nalecht swiftly tossed Leighth backwards and pocketed the shard for himself. With the magic now unleashed, Leper's heart pounded in his chest as he saw Voldahyl's monstrous maw hurtling towards him. Reacting on pure instinct, he rolled away just in time to avoid being consumed. But the danger was far from over.

A sudden commotion in the sky drew everyone's attention. As a massive bolt flashed and thunder rolled. A chariot came hurtling from the east, shaking and wobbling uncontrollably. Leper's eyes widened as he recognized Madislak and Harmony, their friends, coming to their rescue. It was a relief to see them, but the situation was still dire. As the chariot descended, Harmony hung precariously out of the door. In a swift motion, she sent an ice shard flying towards Nalecht. The ice shard connected with Nalecht's chest, sending him sprawling backward, gasping for breath.

"I grow tired of you and your ice shards, bitch!" he hollered.

In one graceful movement, Madislak leaped from the descending chariot, his sword poised and ready. With a flick of his wrist, he sent a beam of light sailing to the tip of his blade. The light exploded in a blinding burst, engulfing Nalecht, Ace, Voldahyl, and the surrounding soldiers in its radiant glow. Still airborne, Madislak expertly positioned his trajectory, skillfully angling himself towards the head of Voldahyl. Leper held his breath, his heart pounding in anticipation. He had heard about Madislak performing remarkable feats before, but this was on a whole new level of audacity and skill.

Madislak rammed his sword, Skyrunner, straight into Voldahyl's eye. The dragon let out a deafening squeal, thrashing about violently in response to the excruciating pain.

Madislak swiftly withdrew his sword from the beast's eye, climbing with astonishing agility to the crest of Voldahyl's head. With one precise and lightning-fast strike, he buried Skyrunner deep into the dragon's skull. As the blade connected with the massive creature's brain, the thrashing ceased abruptly, and Voldahyl's head crashed heavily to the ground.

Leper couldn't believe what he had just witnessed. Ace hopped off his slain dragon, eyes red and water-filled. The bond riders shared with their dragons was profound. Losing one was devastating to the other. Leper wasted no time racing towards Nalecht.

"Hail the almighty Madislak!" one guard cheered. Followed by many more cheers.

"Fools. You still have an army on your doorstep." Nalecht sneered right before Leper collided with him.

Leper wrestled with him, reaching for the shards, but Nalecht still had the strength and speed lent to him from the shard of Ryollin. But Leper got his fingers on the sword-shaped shard of Amarook just as Nalecht pushed his arm away. Leper felt the magic flow through him, and he sucked in a large breath of air. Fastening the chain of the shard around his finger, he held out his hands, and Maka Kura glided back to his waiting palms.

"That was the dumbest mistake you could've made." Nalecht gritted, his eyes filled with hatred.

Leper sprang into action, whirling and swinging Maka Kura, being guided by the weapon's great battle strategies. Nalecht continued to press back, parrying and deflecting Leper's attacks with strength that sent vibrations through his arms. He wasn't backing down. Leper feigned an attack to the left, then sidestepped twice to the right and caught Nalecht off guard as he thrust his chakram into his stomach. Nalecht winced in pain but shoved the chakram out and began attacking more furiously, landing an elbow to Leper's face and pushing him backwards. His stomach still ached from the boot he took, and his nose felt numb from the elbow. His face was covered in blood.

Leper heard the distant cries of the armies charging through Nalecht's ranks, and it reinvigorated him as he pressed his attack as fast as he could muster. Nalecht remained the quicker and stronger, thanks to the shards. Leper tossed in a quick kick to the back of the knee that threw Nalecht off balance, then plunged another chakram into his gut again.

Nalecht fell to his knees. "No. I don't fucking lose to the likes of you."

Cheers erupted as Nalecht's army backtracked, acknowledging the unexpected turn of events. Leper stood victoriously in front of Nalecht. Blood covered much of Leper as he aimed Maka Kura at Nalecht.

Madislak walked over to Leper, pointing his sword at Nalecht. Nalecht clutched his stomach in pain, hollering for his army to get back here and save him.

"Useless fucking people." Nalecht sneered.

"Restrain him," Madislak commanded, pointing at Nalecht.

Without warning, the clouds parted, and the sun burst through. It was too sudden, too close for comfort, as the light became blindingly bright. Leper squinted, trying to make out what was happening amidst the whooshing of wings. The intense light made it difficult to see. He felt a pull on his hand, and eventually, his vision cleared, revealing another dragon carrying Nalecht and Ace in its claws, flying away from the battle. Riding on the dragon's back, a red-headed woman disappeared into the distance. *Must be Fingin.* The other dragon Ace mentioned. *And could that be? His sister?*

"Damn it! We had him!" Leper roared as he glanced down at the missing shard of Amarook from his hand. He let out a sigh of disgust.

"Shouldn't we go after him?" Petrovana pleaded.

"We have little left. All of us desperately need rest. We've stopped him, for now." Leper added. "We live to fight another day. We still have the shard of Theora, and the shard of Kasherri is still in the rain trials... Whatever that is. As long as we keep those within our grasp, we can rest easy that he won't be back anytime soon. We've just proven we can beat him and an army."

Madislak nodded as he sheathed Skyrunner. "Exactly. He's going to be licking his wounds for a while. We must use this time wisely to rebuild ourselves and be ready for another attack or be aggressive ourselves and go take the shards back from him."

"Guess that means he has access to the shard of Aisha, the goddess of the sun," Harmony muttered. "Who's the girl on the dragon with Ace?" She pointed to the retreating dragon.

Leper shrugged his shoulders, then turned to Madislak. "Thanks for saving my life back there."

"Only repaying a favor once paid to me," Madislak smiled.

"Harmony, I need a healing vial. Lillian is badly injured, and the people in charge of restocking my supply aren't doing a very good job." Leper held out his hand to Harmony.

Leper glanced at the retreating dragon carrying Nalecht away, then back to Harmony. As she reached into her pouch on the side to grab a vial, Nalecht sent one of Ace's axes soaring through the air, lodging into her lower back.

"Unghh," she collapsed to the ground.

Chapter Twenty-One

Madislak's heart pounded in his chest as he caught Harmony in his arms, her limp body a stark contrast to her usual vibrant energy. Panic surged through him, fearing the worst. Memories of Gwen's tragic fate flooding back to haunt him. He gently lowered her to the ground, his hands trembling.

Desperate for a response, he pleaded with her, "Harmony, say something, please!" He searched her face for any sign of consciousness, his mind racing with fear. He couldn't bear the thought of losing another person he cared for, especially not Harmony, who had become such an important part of his life.

"Please!" Madislak wailed.

"I'm still here. It hurts." She faintly called back.

Leper came over, went through her pouch, and pulled out a healing vial. He began dumping it on the wound as they pulled out the axe.

Leper connected eyes with Madislak. "Luckily, she had a healing vial left. She's out of rejuvenation vials."

Madislak had to look away as she screamed. Brebian and his remaining forces chased the rest of Nalecht's army back to the south, where they came from. Madislak then helped Leper dump some more of the vial on it and wrap it with a cloth. Curiosity got the best of him as he licked his finger to taste the liquid and immediately cringed. The taste of the mixture was overwhelmingly unpleasant and off-putting. It was a combination of earthy, muddy flavors from the roots, with a sharp bitterness from the leaves that left a lingering aftertaste.

"It won't heal immediately, but it will quit bleeding quickly and start to heal fast." Leper nodded to her.

Madislak smiled at Leper. "Thank you for saving her life."

"Absolutely." Leper looked at Harmony.

Madislak glanced over his shoulder to Lillian, who had a bandage wrapped around her stomach and was sitting upright, panting. Petrovana was holding on to her.

"Somebody help me!" they heard a scream from inside the walls.

"Rinawen... No!" Leper muttered as he immediately tore off into the city.

"Go. Go with him. I'll be fine. It's already feeling better. I just can't get up yet." Harmony nodded her head towards the city.

Madislak churned his legs as fast as they could go, taking off after Leper. A short, dark-haired girl followed closely behind him.

Madislak's mind raced with questions as he observed Leper's disappearing form. The urgency to find answers gnawed at him. He followed Leper for another minute or two, keeping a safe distance until Leper abruptly came to a stop. As Leper reached the imposing wall that separated the castle from the residence, a heartbreaking sight suddenly drew Madislak's attention. Near the fallen watchtower, he saw Rinawen collapsed on the ground. His heart pounded with concern, and he quickened his pace, praying that she was unharmed despite the perilous circumstances.

Rinawen lay still, a stab wound under her chest. She was reaching for her salve as a skulking, hooded figure loomed over her.

"Do you recognize me now, elf bitch?" he growled.

He pulled his hood back slightly, revealing his face to Rinawen. Madislak, still at a distance, strained to make out any details, but the hood still obscured much of the man's features. Yet, despite the limited visibility, Rinawen's face lit up with recognition, clearly familiar with the man before her. Madislak could only identify him as Blank Face.

"Get away from her, you bastard," Leper bellowed, plowing into Blank Face, knocking him off balance and tumbling to the ground.

"Blank, what are you doing!?" the girl cried.

Madislak's gaze locked onto Blank Face, and he could sense the surprise mirrored in the man's expression. There was an air of uncertainty surrounding Blank Face, and Madislak couldn't help but wonder about the reasons behind his presence here. What intrigued him even more was the shard of Theora that Blank Face held tightly in his right hand.

"What the hell are you doing?" Madislak demanded, aiming Skyrunner towards Blank Face.

"No! Don't kill him. I owe him my life." She argued, getting in front of Madislak.

"And who exactly are you?" Madislak demanded.

"Princess Leighth Or'armwell of Kundry," she asserted.

"Leighth, I suggest you stand down," Madislak warned.

"Stop... Fighting," Rinawen eeked out. "Don't blame him when it's ultimately my fault."

"What are you saying? That this idiot stabbing you is your fault? I think not," Leper retorted, searching frantically for something.

"What are you looking for?" he asked.

"Salve. I'm out. I thought Rin had some." Leper checked her pockets.

The sharp, acidic scent of vinegar mixed with the sweet, floral fragrance of rosemary emitted as Madislak's eyes saw the small round container scattered on the ground and handed it to Leper.

"Damnit. It's contaminated with dirt. This won't work. You're a fucking dead man," Leper seethed.

Blank Face nimbly got to his feet. Leper feared losing his best friend and only lifelong companion. The one who accepted him for who he was. His heart pounded, every beat echoing throughout his body.

"Leper, listen to me," Rinawen broke his concentration on Blank Face. "I know this will be hard to hear, but there's something I've never told you."

"What?" Leper gazed at Rinawen.

Leper's heart pounded, nerves tightening like a vise, as he anxiously waited for Rinawen to reveal her secret. They kept nothing from each other, and the inner turmoil he felt was crushing. Memories of their cherished moments together flooded his mind—their carefree days playing in the woods as children and even witnessing her wedding from afar through a spyglass. She looked right at him, showing off her ring, a gesture that had filled him with both joy and a twinge of jealousy. Their bond was unbreakable, a connection that had weathered countless storms. Yet now, as Rinawen's life hung in the balance, she chose this moment to share her urgent secret. Leper's mind raced with a mix of emotions—fear for her life and a deep longing to know what she had to tell him.

Her breathing was uneven. "When we found you in that boat. You weren't alone."

"What?" his face contorted.

"There was another baby, like you, with horns." She said through labored breaths.

"Yes, I had a brother. I saw it on The Talon. But Ace killed him just to take his power." Leper held her head up.

"That's impossible; he was lying to you," Rinawen furrowed her brow, still panting to catch her breath.

"No, I don't think so, Rin. Ace tried to kill me, too. He's crazy." Leper cupped her cheek with his palm.

"I only say he's lying because your brother is standing right over there." Weakly, she pointed her finger to Blank Face.

"No..." Leper frowned at Blank Face.

Blank Face finally removed the entirety of his hood, revealing a face marred with scars and pain. His ears bore the marks of cruel wounds, cut or torn in two places. But it was the prominent scar that drew Leper's attention, running from the tip of Blank Face's forehead back to the crest and curving down the back, ending at the neck. It cut right between two circular patterns, remnants of where his horns used to be, now gone. The sight left him with a mix of emotions. Leper's jaw almost fell to the ground.

"Why... Why would you do that?" Leper pleaded. "Why would you make me live in solitary when I could've had a brother?"

"It's a decision I regret every day of my life. I traded him to Tamara. In return, she would stay off our shores and never attack." A tear rolled down her eye.

Leper's eyes bore into her. "You mean your parents did?"

"Yes... you both just turned four. Tamara saw him playing on the beaches, but not you. I told my parents what happened. I was only fourteen, but I didn't want them to find out there was another one!" Her eyes welled up.

"Here, take this," Blank Face handed over the shard of Theora. "I got my vengeance. I don't need this shard."

Leper snatched it out of his hand. "You worthless, self-serving, heartless piece of shit."

"I'm sorry, for what it's worth, this woman right here sold me into a life of torture and misery for six years. Do you have any idea what that's like?" Blank Face reasoned.

"You don't know what she was going through," Leper snapped, unsure who to be mad at. "Damn it, Rin. Why... Why wait til now to say anything!"

"Where's my goddamn protection? I was four!" Blank Face retorted sharply. "You have no clue what it feels like to be cut, stabbed, poked, burned, prodded nonstop for six fucking years!?"

"Imagine I don't. But how can you go on a murdering spree, killing whoever you want, and think that makes it okay? How can you kill and blame her for your life when her biggest fault was making a mistake?" A tear rolled down Leper's face.

"I was looking for you!" Blank Face pointed to Leper. "I saw my past at The Talon. I saw I had a brother. I also saw Ace was crazy, and I was using Nalecht to find you! It was mere coincidence that Rinawen had the shard he needed, and you were still with her."

"Why didn't you just seek me out? You obviously found out she handed you over! Why not just come find me instead of becoming Blank Face?" Leper's frustration began to boil over.

"I did," He pointed to Rinawen. "She told me you left years ago. To go to The Talon, at which point I assumed you were Ace or were killed by Ace. But when you came running up here and plowed me over, I knew you were the one I was looking for."

"Why are you looking for me so much? Going to kill me, too?" Leper placed his hand on Maka Kura.

"No, I wanted to talk to you. I wanted to have someone in my life I could trust and figured my own damn brother would be a good place to start." Blank Face hissed.

"So, you kill for money. That probably helped." Leper retorted.

Blank Face let out a dejected sigh. "Hey, I did what I had to survive. Imagine growing up in a castle with the queen you wouldn't understand."

"Leper," Madislak interrupted. "I know this isn't a good time, but look."

Leper followed Madislak's hand, pointing to Rinawen, who at some point lost consciousness.

His heart cracked and felt as if it might stop entirely. Rinawen, his only friend, the only one who protected him, cared for him. Her chest wasn't moving, and there was no pulse. Tears slid down his face like a waterfall. No... No.No.No.

"Harmony... the vial," he muttered, tearing back out through the city. Slipping in the mud that was slowly beginning to dry from the downpour as the sun beamed brightly in the sky.

Arriving at the battlefield just outside the city walls, Lillian was trying to get to her feet. He needed the vial he gave Harmony to save Rinawen, and he needed it fast.

He rushed over, diving onto his knees at Harmony's side. She was lying down, resting. Frantically searching her side pouches, then rifling through her front pockets before rolling her up and checking the back pockets.

"Where is it? Where is it?" he muttered, his hands now shaking, feeling along her belt line.

"Excuse me! What in the name of Obidiah are you doing, Leper," Harmony yelled, anger seething in her voice.

"The vial! I need it now! Please!" He snarled. Harmony's face went from anger to utter panic in seconds. She must have seen the tears in his eyes or their hollowness.

"What's happened? Who's it for?" She asked.

"Just give me the fucking vial!" he shouted.

Harmony swiftly retrieved the vial from around her neck and handed it to Leper, who wasted no time in taking it and bolting towards Rinawen. His heart pounded in his chest as he sprinted with all his might, rounding the wall to find her lying unconscious. Without a second thought, he dropped to his knees beside her and hastily uncorked the vial, pouring a drop of its contents onto her mortal wound. Nothing happened. The medicinal smell filled his nostrils as a single drop leaked out. A sharp, pungent scent of rubbing alcohol mixed with the earthy, herbal aroma of medicinal herbs.

"Work, you bastard, work," he pleaded to the vial as he put another drop on. "Please."

Leper's hands trembled as he poured the vial, but the wound showed no signs of healing.

"PLEASE!"

Panic gripped his heart as he realized that time might have betrayed him. He had seen this miraculous concoction work wonders before, but now, as he looked at Rinawen's lifeless form, none of that magic was taking effect. The dread of losing his closest friend and sister-like figure overwhelmed him, and he couldn't bear to accept the possibility that it was too late, that he had arrived too tardy to save her.

"Please." He whimpered.

The pain of losing Rinawen ripped at Leper's very soul, leaving a void that felt impossible to fill. He choked back tears, feeling a lump forming in his throat as he gently laid the vial on her heart. Tears dripped off his cheeks onto her. Regret surged through him, wishing he had acted sooner, blaming himself for the precious moments wasted in the argument with Blank Face. Not just a sister to him. No, he loved this woman. Loved her and never got an opportunity to share that love. Because of this world, its prejudice, its cruel and utterly ridiculous biases. *I don't need your stupid protection.* The last words he ever said to her.

"I love you, Rin." Leper sobbed as he kissed her mouth.

Loved her and would never get the chance to tell her again. *I don't need your stupid protection.*

A strange sensation overcame him, an overwhelming rage that felt almost primal. It pushed him to his feet, eyes locked onto Blank Face, and with a swift motion, he unsheathed Maka Kura. Hatred and anger surged through his voice as he spoke. "You!" The weight of his emotions made the blade tremble in his hand.

Chapter
Twenty-Two

Madislak's heart ached as he observed Leper's desperate attempt to save Rinawen from the clutches of death. He looked like a shattered soul, and Madislak felt helpless, not knowing how to console him in such a moment of grief. Memories of his own loss resurfaced, recalling the pain he experienced when he lost his mother at the tender age of seven. Though it seemed they may have shared a more profound type of love, one that would've been mocked and likely ended with their execution. It never crossed his mind that, at some point, they may have both loved each other but been unable to share that. Madislak spent years grappling with the profound absence and emptiness, learning that losing someone so dear wasn't something you could simply get over. Instead, it was a wound that would gradually hurt less over time, leaving behind scars of remembrance.

Watching Leper experience this for, presumably, the first time was gut-wrenching. Yet Madislak noticed something change in Leper as he stood up from her dead body, aiming his chakrams at Blank Face.

"I don't want to fight," Blank Face said, holding his hands up. "I didn't know what she meant to you. That's the honest truth."

"I don't really give a shit. I want a fight, and you're going to die right now." Leper's voice was deep and sincere.

"Blank run!" Leighth called out. "Something's not right."

"Damn right, it's not. And I'm going to fix that problem right now," Leper charged at Blank Face.

"Leper! Stop!" Madislak yelled.

Madislak wrestled with conflicting emotions as he observed the tense confrontation between Leper and Blank Face. As a noble and just ruler, Madislak understood Leper's desire to attack the man who caused so much pain and turmoil. However, the journey they shared taught Madislak the importance of giving people a chance to reveal their true selves. Leighth, who had been with Blank Face for a considerable time, believed in him, and her faith held weight. Blank Face's scars bore evidence of his traumatic past, and even if they ultimately had to deal with him, Madislak recognized the potential value of extracting information about Xaneth Harbor's defenses from him. Perhaps there was more to the story than they knew, and gathering any advantage against the enemy was crucial in their fight for the safety and freedom of their world. Despite the anger and pain, Madislak sought a balance between justice and pragmatism, knowing that this battle required him to make tough decisions.

Madislak's heart went out to Leper, knowing that Blank Face was his only true sibling. Allowing Leper to act on impulse and kill him in the heat of the moment would likely lead to profound regret later on. Madislak understood the weight of such decisions, knowing that actions taken in the throes of grief and anger could have lasting consequences. He wanted to spare his friend from carrying the burden of unnecessary guilt.

Blank Face never drew his weapons as Leper approached him. Leper lunged and swung at Blank Face's neck. Leighth closed her eyes, unable to watch. Leper's swing found nothing but air. Blank Face had completely vanished, then immediately reappeared right behind Leper. He wrapped his arms around Leper's, locking his fingers together in the front.

"Stop! I don't want to fight you. We're the only thing each other has." Blank Face pleaded, still no emotion on his face.

"Yeah, now that you've killed Rinawen." Spittle flew from Leper's mouth.

Blank Face's frame was too thin to maintain his hold on Leper as he broke out of it. Leper spun around again. With another blink, Blank Face appeared behind Leper again. This time, Leper anticipated the maneuver, rocked his head back viscously, and head-butted him in the nose. Blank Face cupped his nose. "Ouch. Damnit, now you're pissing me off."

"Blank, watch out!" Leighth screamed.

Madislak's eyes widened as he watched the sudden eruption of tension between Leper and Blank Face. Leper swung Maka Kura with fierce determination, but Leighth swiftly intervened, catching him under the shoulder and using her leg to bring him down to the ground. The clash between them startled him, and he knew he had to step in to prevent things from escalating further.

"When I'm done with him, you're next," Leper snarled at Leighth.

Madislak felt a pang of concern as he observed Leper's uncharacteristic behavior. Leper's calm demeanor, which was usually present, seemed to have disappeared entirely. Threatening someone, especially an innocent bystander like Leighth, was completely out of character for him. As the leader of their group, Madislak understood the pressure and strain that the war placed on each of them.

Madislak rushed over to the scene of the escalating fight, concern etched across his features. Leper, still visibly worked up, feigned another attack on Blank Face. He knew that Leper's actions were born out of the strain of battle and the weight of responsibility they all bore. As Blank Face blinked, Leper adjusted his movements, delivering a powerful kick to his gut, sending Blank Face tumbling backward onto the ground.

Leighth, not one to back down, leaped in Leper's path, attempting to use the same maneuver she employed earlier. However, Leper swiftly countered, bringing his elbow down on her back and tossing her to the ground. Leper's chakram came down after her. Madislak stepped forward, deftly parrying the chakram's attack, then firmly grasped Leper's wrists.

"What the fuck is wrong with you!?" Madislak gritted through his teeth. "You're being a jackass."

"Stay the hell out of it, Madislak, or I'll cut you down, too. This is between me and him." Leper's eyes wandered to Blank Face, picking himself off the ground.

"No, you're being psychotic, like Ace," Madislak felt Leper struggle to break his steel grip, only making Madislak squeeze harder and then jab him in the head with his elbow. *Maybe that'll knock some sense into him.* Blank Face came back over, throwing his arms around him as well to hold him back.

"Get off me," Leper barked.

"Not until you calm yourself down. What's gotten into you? This isn't the Leper I know," Madislak retorted.

"He killed Rin! And you guys are keeping me from getting justice for her!" Leper bellowed.

"Look at her, Leper," Madislak moved his eyes to Rinawen. "She said don't blame him. Don't be mad at him. You're out here telling me you want to prove that all Chernzerk aren't chaotic. You're not doing an outstanding job at convincing me."

Leper's eyes blinked rapidly as if Madislak had just struck a chord. Leper's weapons fell to the ground, and his resistance stopped. Madislak saw a single tear fall down his cheek.

"I'm... I'm so sorry, guys. I don't know what came over me," Leper said, his voice shaking.

"She's the only life you've known," Madislak placed his hand on Leper's shoulder. "I think we can let it slide this time."

"No, I'm unstable. That's unacceptable. I tried to harm a king... Again. I tried to kill Princess Leighth," Leper's eyes went wide, regret soaking his face. "Leighth, I'm so sorry. I can't believe I just did that," he rushed over, helping her off the ground.

"It's okay. She meant a lot to both of us. But never do that again!" Leighth scolded.

Leper shook his head. "I don't know how. I don't know how to control it. But I will find a way."

"I can help you." Blank Face offered. "I can help you learn to control it. It's something we all, as Chernzerk, must face."

"I don't want your fucking help." Leper sneered.

"Okay, I don't want to be ignorant or rude, but we've got some stuff to figure out right now," Madislak interjected.

Madislak's mind raced as he assessed the situation before him. Madislak quelled the immediate threat and pushed back Nalecht's forces, but other pressing matters needed attention. First and foremost, they had to address Blank Face. He was still an enigma, an enemy they weren't sure if they could trust or not. The fight had taken its toll on all of them, and Blank Face's intentions remained unclear. They needed to handle this uncertain situation to ensure the safety of their group while considering all outcomes.

Additionally, the loss of Rinawen weighed heavily on Madislak's heart. They needed to pay their respects and hold a service for their fallen comrade, who had been an integral part of their journey. But he also knew that they had to notify Kordry, the kingdom that lost its queen, and inform them of the tragic news. However, they also needed to delve deeper into this talisman situation and uncover the truth behind it. The sun shining finally brought warmth to the previously chilly downpour.

The weight of these responsibilities tugged at Madislak, leaving him feeling stretched thin. The demands of leadership were taking their toll, and he knew that the road ahead would be challenging. As he looked at Leper, now under control but still visibly shaken, Madislak couldn't help but worry about what might happen if he were to lose his composure again when Madislak wasn't present.

Petrovana, Harmony, Lillian, and Brebian rounded the corner, interrupting his thoughts. He could see the fatigue in their faces, the toll of the battle clear in their movements. Harmony and Lillian were still nursing their injuries, hobbling around as they approached. Taking a deep breath, Madislak steadied himself. He needed to stay focused and lead his team through these difficult times.

Leper felt a pang of guilt as he noticed the rest of the group gathering around the crumbled watchtower. The intensity of the battle still echoed within him, and he couldn't shake the weight of what had just transpired. His actions, attacking Leighth and Madislak, filled him with remorse. He knew he had let his emotions get the better of him, and he felt a deep sense of regret for his outburst. Yet it was something beyond his control. He couldn't stop himself from getting what he wanted. It's something he would have to work on, but there's no way he'd seek Blank Face's help in doing so.

Blank Face's presence now only added to the complexity of the situation. Leper's heart ached at the betrayal that had taken place, losing Rinawen, whom he had cared for deeply. Even though he couldn't ignore the possibility that everything Rinawen had revealed might be true, it didn't excuse her death. The anger and pain inside him were conflicting, but Leper knew that taking revenge on Blank Face wouldn't bring her back.

As the rest of the group approached, Leper took a deep breath, trying to steady himself. He knew they needed to handle the uncertain situation with Blank Face and honor Rinawen's memory without allowing vengeance to consume them. The bond between them all was growing stronger, and Leper hoped they could lean on each other for support during this trying time. He understood decisions needed to be made, and unity was paramount in the face of the challenges that lay ahead.

"So, what are we going to do with him?" Leper pointed at Blank Face.

Lillian picked up her hobbled pace at the sight of a lifeless Rinawen.

"You worthless rat bastard!" she glared at Blank Face. "How could you let this happen?" She looked at Leper.

Leper only looked at Lillian, unable to form words as the tears flowed freely again.

"I'm sorry! I didn't mean it." Lillian immediately offered.

Petrovana quickly wrapped her arms around Leper. "Don't listen to her. She's bein' her typical rude self."

"I should've thought about the vile sooner. I should've been here. It's all my fault... Everything." Leper wiped his face with his bare hands.

"None of this is anyone's fault. Other than Nalecht, Borlden, Ace... they are the enemies here." Madislak took charge.

Keeping everyone calm as he explained the events that had transpired from the moment they left the battlefield until now. The realization of her loss struck them all like a heavy blow, and a solemn silence enveloped the group. Leper's heart ached as he grieved for his dear friend. He couldn't believe she was gone, leaving behind a void that seemed impossible to fill. The shock of her passing weighed heavily on him, and he struggled to come to terms with the sudden absence of the person he cherished so much.

In their sorrow, another revelation left them stunned—Blank Face was another Chernzerk, just like Leper. The connection they shared as brothers added a layer of complexity to the already uncertain situation. Confusion swirled among the group as they grappled with the implications of this discovery. Brebian's actions still stood as controversial even after Nalecht's defeat. His desire to keep the shard himself and willingness to give up in the middle of the battle didn't sit well with Leper.

"I personally vote to put both of them," Brebian pointed to Blank Face and Leper, "into the dungeons until we can figure out what to do with them."

"You're not throwing me into a dungeon. That's not happening again." Blank Face retorted, backing away.

"No. We're all people here. Nobody needs to be thrown into a dungeon," Leighth pleaded.

"Why are you helping him?" Lillian's head snapped to Leighth.

"Because. He's saved my life more than once. He can fight, and it's not his fault that circumstances forced him to do things in a bad way. Rinawen said the same damn thing." Leighth countered, not backing down.

"I do not trust him. Brother or not," Leper pointed to Blank Face.

"I second that," Lillian offered.

The rest of the group all followed suit, agreeing that they didn't trust Blank Face.

"Then I'll just go," Blank Face turned to walk away.

"No. He's a skilled fighter. Just as good as any of you, if not better. Plus, he knows the enemy better than anyone here. He could help us," Leighth argued.

"You make a good point. Having an upper hand against the enemy would aid us a lot in this fight. And having another skilled fighter on our side would definitely be beneficial." Madislak reasoned.

"And he handed the shard of Theora over to Leper. That shows he's willing to cooperate," Leighth continued her defense of Blank Face. "I will hold myself responsible for his actions. If he does anything to go against us, my kingdom will be turned over to Brebian or Madislak."

"Are you certain you're willing to risk your kingdom on the likes of him?" Brebian's scrunched his face. "And why does he get to have the shard of Theora?"

"I'll give it to Zanera when she's old enough," Leper nodded to Brebian. "You have my word."

Brebian scoffed and then pointed at Madislak. "You're alright with all this? Just letting him keep that shard? Don't you remember what we said at the meeting?"

"Brebian, shut your mouth," Madislak demanded. "We need all the allies we can get right now. He's proven himself a warrior. Plus, he's just lost the only person he knows and has ties to Kordry. The shard will be fine, especially if Nalecht doesn't know where it is. He will expect one of us to have it... So, back off right now."

Brebian slinked away.

"They ain't no different from us. Reckon this one here just saved yer entire city...Again." Petrovana put her hand on Leper's shoulder.

Leper nodded in appreciation to Petrovana. He could sense the unease and discomfort that still lingered among the group, aside from Petrovana, Lillian, and Harmony, who had grown more accepting of him. But Brebian held a deep distrust despite Leper's efforts to prove himself. The weight of the past and the shadows of his previous actions seemed to cast a long shadow on the present. Leper understood that gaining the trust of these people wouldn't happen overnight, and he would give them the time and space they needed to come to terms with his presence.

"Fine. He's your responsibility, Leighth. If things go sideways with him, it's on you," Brebian pointed his finger at her.

"So, what's our next move, then?" Madislak poked.

"Well, there are still many secrets left to unlock or explore at The Talon. We need more information on the talisman as well," Petrovana offered.

"We need to rebuild Lantess. We need to maintain the protection of the shards. Nalecht will probably go back to Ambrosia to rebuild his army and try again. Brebian, I need to take all the old texts you have about the shards and anything about a talisman. I'll scour those for more details while Madislak handles the rebuilding process," Harmony offered.

"No. He won't do that. He'll seek out Tamara now and use her army. They're far more ruthless. They enjoy killing," Blank Face offered, drawing a shocked stare from everyone.

"Then we need to form a force quickly to combat that," Harmony said.

Brebian motioned to Harmony, "I'll have my chronicle warden bring those over immediately."

"I think Leighth and I should go back to Kordry. We'll have to break the news about Rin. Then, get Leighth sworn as queen of Kundry. Once that's done, we might use some of their fighters?" Leper offered.

"Blank will come with us, right?" Leighth looked to Blank Face.

Leper rolled his eyes. "Fine. But I'm not riding in the same chariot as him."

Leper's emotions churned as he grappled with the conflicting feelings about his brother, the one he had longed to meet since discovering he had a sibling in The Talon. However, the mere sight of him now was enough to ignite a raging fire of anger within Leper. He resented the fact that his brother survived. The weight of their shared bloodline made the situation even more complex. He couldn't deny the connection they had, but he also couldn't shake the bitterness and regret that swirled within him. A part of him almost wished that Ace eliminated his brother, as painful as that thought was.

"We'll go back to Lantess and start rebuilding and trying to form some kind of army or training, but we could likely use some help," Madislak said grimly.

"I could help train some fighters," Lillian offered.

"That would be appreciated, thank you," Madislak nodded to Lillian.

"Aren't you assholes gonna check the battlefield?" Leper turned to see Theodamar shouting from around the wall.

"Thank the gods you've made it," Madislak called. "Our ranks are running thin, and losing a commander would be detrimental."

"That was the quickest I've had an entire fleet wiped out," Theodamar added.

"I understand we're spread thin, and this battle just concluded, but maybe you and Brebian could seek out Goreldea in Kirilick and petition for help," Madislak suggested.

"I think we can muster something," Theodamar nodded to Madislak.

"Reckon I'll go with Leper, Leighth, and Blank Face. For one to monitor the sketchy one. Also, to help them get things settled," Petrovana offered.

Lillian's eye roll didn't escape Leper's notice, but she refrained from commenting on it. They, Lillian and Petrovana, had come to some un-spoken understanding, putting their differences aside for the greater good. Leper was relieved that they had reached a point of mutual agreement, even if it meant biting their tongues and setting aside their grievances for the moment. With their plans now sorted out, the group eventually parted ways, each member going off on their separate paths. Leper felt a mix of emotions as they departed. He knew that their individual journeys were necessary. Still, he couldn't help but feel a sense of sadness at the temporary separation.

As he retrieved the vial from Rinawen's lifeless body, his heart ached for losing his dear friend. Handing it back to Harmony, he hoped the vial would serve a greater purpose and contribute to their ultimate mission of vanquishing evil from the world. The journey ahead was fraught with challenges and dangers, but Leper was determined to honor Rinawen's memory and forge ahead. He glanced to the blue skies once more, hoping he could get a handle on his mental acuteness before he did something he really regretted.

"I really don't feel this is necessary," Harmony tried to refuse. "Why didn't you use your other one?"

"No. I gave it to you. It's yours. I'm sorry for how I spoke to you earlier," his voice was sincere. "I don't have another one. I lied. I want you and everyone else to trust me. By placing my trust in you, giving you this irreplaceable vial. I only ask that you reciprocate the mutual trust."

"It's okay, but there is nothing to apologize for. I trust you, Leper. I trust you more than a lot of people," Harmony wrapped her arms around him. "I'm sorry... About Rinawen. I know she meant a lot to you."

"Me too...I'm going to miss our adventures together and our conversations about magic." Leper squeezed her tightly.

"Me too! You guys be careful, and if anything goes wrong, you come to Lantess! You'll always be welcome there," her vibrant blue eyes meeting his.

With a nod, Leper moved over to Madislak, who was right beside her.

"Here, I got this for you at The Talon. I don't know what it does, but it looks valuable." He pointed to the shield he picked up from The Talon, which was lying beside Rinawen.

Madislak accepted the shield and put it on his arm, swinging it around and twirling it to get used to its weight and balance. It made a couple of clunks. A piece of paper fluttered from inside the shield somewhere, landing on the ground.

"What is that?" Madislak picked it up and began reading. His eyes went wide.

"What is it?" Leper walked towards him.

"Rinawen must've been saving this for you. It's from... my mom, your mom... We're...brothers." Madislak glanced up at Leper.

"Your mom's name was Ana?" Leper grabbed the note.

"In short, yes. But her full name was Svetlana. Your father, he..." Madislak's voice trailed off. His eyes became glossy.

"Madislak, I'm so sorry, I didn't know...I didn't know she was your mother. I...I don't know what to say." Leper placed a hand on Madislak's shoulder. "But if it's any consolation, my father is dead."

"Can I keep that note? I didn't know my mother very well, and I'd like to have more to remember her by. It's likely one of the last things she ever wrote." Madislak reached his hand out.

"Of course." Leper handed it back. It meant more to Madislak, but at least his mother wanted to protect them. She revealed that much in the letter, along with how they were conceived. Though a heinous crime gave them life, she wanted them to be safe and protected, even giving them their names. Rinawen must've found the note and named them accordingly, but Blank Face's name was not legible. It contained eight letters, and only the fourth letter, a T, and the last letter, an A, were legible.

"Thank you for the shield," Madislak nodded to Leper.

"It's the least I could do, Madi*slap*, the dragon slayer." Everyone chuckled. Madislak offered a slight grin.

Leper reached out to shake Madislak's hand. Madislak grabbed it and pulled him in for a hug before departing. Next, Leper went over to Lillian and pulled her off to the side.

"We make a hell of a team," Leper smiled.

"Reckon we do. So, yer off with... Her again, huh?" Lillian looked at the ground.

"No, we're not at that point yet. She's beautiful, charming, intelligent. I know you told me not to fall for her charms." Leper scratched the back of his neck.

"She ain't so bad. I'd be dead today if not for her." Lillian grinned.

"Look, Lillian. I really enjoyed the time we've spent together, and I don't know what's going to happen. I just hope no matter what, we can continue our friendship." Leper grabbed her wrists.

"The heart wants what the heart wants, Leper. Ain't no denyin' that." She sighed.

"And what does your heart want?" Leper tilted his head to the side.

"Guess you'll have to make some time to find out?" she grinned playfully.

"It's a date then." Leper nodded.

Lillian kissed him on the cheek. "I'm sure I'll be seein' you around."

Leper held Lillian tightly in his arms, feeling a rush of emotions he hadn't yet put into words. Their connection ran deep, and he knew that there was something unspoken between them, something more than just friendship. He cherished these moments when they were close, yet the words to express his feelings remained locked within him.

As they made their way to the landing pad with Rinawen's body, Leper felt a mix of sorrow and determination. He was grateful to have Petrovana by his side, sharing the weight of their loss and their mission. Her unwavering support and understanding meant the world to him, and he couldn't help but wonder if she felt the same way. But he remained resolute in his path to continue to show the world that Chernzerk aren't as bad as the stigma. He would put an end to Nalecht's relentless pursuit of the shards, and once he saved Kalazaar from that, hopefully, their minds would have changed.

Leper glanced up and saw Leighth and Blank Face waiting patiently for them.

"Oh, hell no!" Leper shook his head. "I said I'm not riding with him."

"Well, if Madislak would stop wrecking chariots, we'd have enough to go around, but unfortunately, this is what we got," Leighth pointed to the chariot.

Reluctantly, Leper got inside the chariot, the lavender incense calming him as it always had. He slammed the door. The familiar feel and scent of the chariot brought ease to him as they ascended the skies, heading back to his hometown, Kordry.

The End.

Acknowledgements

This has been such a long journey and there are so many people to thank. It never would've been possible without the many folks I've met and had in my life that have encouraged, critiqued, and pushed me towards publishing.

First, I need to thank my loving wife, Jenn, for supporting and believing in me, even when I didn't believe in myself at times. For offering input on everything from the first page to the last page. Encouraging me to keep going and pushing me to not give up. You are the best! For my three kids, and number one fans, that drive me to continue this journey and constantly support me. Haley, you always know how to keep me motivated and drive me to do better and keep me accountable. Addy, your excitement and enthusiasm about "Dad's book" always makes me smile and keeps me motivated. Peyton, your creativity and astonishing mind have helped me out immensely. Your ideas, wild as they may be, have helped add so many valuable layers of intrigue throughout this process and I can't thank you enough for how much you've influenced and helped me think outside the box on so many levels. Your pure enthusiasm and passion to sit down and just create whatever comes to mind will never cease to amaze me, and I look forward to continuing our bond and brainstorming. I love you all.

To my brother, Dan, who's spent countless hours on the phone or in conversation with me about every tiny little detail I could think of. I couldn't have asked for a better person to plot with. To my sister-in-law,

Miranda, I appreciate you taking the time to listen to me ramble on and offer advice.

To my good friend Jonathan who spent countless hours on the phone going over different ideas, offering incredible advice and helping me discover different avenues for everything related to the entire process and the continued drive to explore different avenues that pushed me out of my comfort zone but were well worth it in the end. Thank you.

My parents, Dan and Lydia, for all their love and support and to all my sisters, Margaret, Jenny, and Faith, for your support and encouragement.

To the team at Miblart for everything you've done to bring this book to life.

To Pam Hines for your incredible job on this manuscript. You did more than just the copy-editing, you taught me more efficient ways to be productive. It was a pleasure to work with you and I look forward to working with you again! Thank you!

To Lucy Cooke. You are one of the most inspiring and smartest people I've ever had the pleasure to work with. I can't thank you and the entire Fictionary team enough.

To Ali Bumbarger. The most creative and efficient person I've had the pleasure of working with. You're an incredible person and this book truly would not be possible without you. Words cannot express how thankful I am for your outstanding efforts, and I am excited to work with you again. You truly went above and beyond all my expectations! THANK YOU.

Lastly, to all who read this book, I hope you enjoyed this first book and are excited to read more of Leper's story.

www.ingramcontent.com/pod-product-compliance
Lightning Source LLC
Chambersburg PA
CBHW030246120726
47903CB00005B/1641